Elizabeth
Just Sixteen

Cecilia Paul

Clink
Street

London | New York

This book is dedicated to all the women with Mayer-Rokitansky-Küster-Hauser (MRKH) syndrome, to salute them for the courage and strength they have shown on their individual journeys to find personal acceptance and an inner peace, and to bring meaning and a sense of normality back into their lives.

having a steady relationship with anyone. Maybe it was her upbringing or maybe it was her parents' indirect influence, because she always admired them and looked up to them.

Her parents met when they were at university. Jan Bingham was studying accountancy whilst Paul Appleton read Commerce and Economics. They hit it off straight away and it was really love at first sight. It was a fairytale romance, and their love for each other never faltered, but grew stronger and continued till today. After they both graduated with first-class honours, Jan landed her first job as an accountant with one of the largest accounting firms in the UK, and Paul got a job in the business management side. After a year, he left to further his studies and to complete his masters. He always knew that he would have his own business one day, and so he did. Soon after, Jan left the company to join Paul, and together they started their own firm in accountancy and business management. They were married a year later and everyone said that they were made for each other, they were a handsome couple. They planned to have a family when their business was more established and when they were financially sound, because they wanted to afford their children with the best of everything. Three years later, Elizabeth was born. They were elated. She was beautiful, and everything they could have wished for. Elizabeth was a 'good baby' and from the start she was never any bother, so Jan and Paul managed to continue with their social life as before. When Elizabeth was a toddler they decided that it would be nice for her to have a sibling to play with, so Emma was conceived. She was beautiful too. Elizabeth doted on her baby sister and immediately took to being the protective older sister from that very early age. The girls inherited their parents' good looks and brains, but Elizabeth also inherited her mother's sensibility and her father's determination and ambition.

Elizabeth always revered her parents' loving relationship and marriage, so she wanted the same for herself. Quite old-fashioned for a sixteen-year-old, she naturally believed in monogamous and long-term relationships. It was another reason why she would not have a steady boyfriend now. It suited her better to have them just as her male friends. She met these senior boys from the private school not too far from hers at the last annual party and other quiz and debate events, organised by her school where the boys were invited guests. She was articulate, and always kind and sensitive, so she never made them feel rejected. Instead they settled for being some of her closest friends. "How ironic" she thought, that so many boys were interested in her before but now, "... now, no one would ever want me. Who would want someone like me now? I'm a freak".

She started to get upset again as she played these thoughts through her mind and wished that she could turn the clock back. She wished she had not seen the doctors, that she had not found out then she would still be the normal Elizabeth whom everyone loved. The more she thought, the more distressed she became. Then her best friend came to mind. She was always there for her, as they were for each other. She had lots of girlfriends at boarding school but her best friend was Sally. They were the same age, although Sally was a month older so she was like an older sister to Elizabeth. They were both enrolled in the same year and ended up in the same class. Sally also came from a similar background – both her parents were lawyers. When Elizabeth and Sally first met, they just clicked right away. Sally planned to study medicine at university and was interested in the field of neurology. She certainly had the brains for it too.

The two of them were inseparable since they met. They shared and told each other everything, and made a pact to never keep any secrets from each other. Only now, it was different. Elizabeth hesitated about calling Sally. It was not because she did not trust Sally, but the truth was, she was too embarrassed. How could she tell Sally about this?! What would she tell her anyway when she, herself, was having difficulty understanding any of it? She felt bad about keeping this from her best friend, but at the same time she was not ready to share it with anyone. In the end, she decided that for the time being, this would be her deeply-seated secret.

Elizabeth was grateful that they had just broken up for the Christmas holidays which would buy her some time away from her friends. She was convinced that not only Sally but her other close friends would be able to sense a change in her mood and she was not prepared to face their questions. It was bad enough having to talk to them on her mobile, and she began to dread taking phone calls because she was finding it increasingly difficult to pretend that everything was normal. She was not normal, and she most certainly did not feel normal. She had been brought up to be respectful and honest, so she did not like having to lie to her friends, especially Sally. It was like living a double life and she did not like it. She wondered how secret agents and spies did it, but of course they were trained for it, whereas she was not even prepared in any way. She also found it hard to be with her family, because she could not stand their sympathy and seeing them struggle to be a normal family. Mostly, she was afraid that she would not be able to control herself and that she might say something disrespectful or hurtful to them, and then regret it afterwards, because right now she was also angry at her parents – especially her mother for her current problem. She knew it was wrong to blame her mother or her parents, because it was a genetic thing. That was what they were told and what she found out when she searched the internet, but she could not help herself, after all it was their genes that caused her condition. Furthermore, why just her, why was she the only unlucky one to inherit their defective gene? How come Emma was not affected, it was not fair. She started to envy her younger sister on whom she doted and had always regarded as her baby sister, even though there was only two years between them, and they were very close before all this happened. Now, she could not bear to be in the same room with any of them, so she chose to shut herself away in her own room, away from them. It was the best for everyone, she felt. She did not know how long she could keep this up and desperately wished for her appointment to be sooner.

Thankfully, it was before Christmas, so at least her nightmare would be over and she would be normal enough to face her family and her grandparents. She was very close to her grandparents too, especially her grandmother, who was like a second mother to her because she was always there throughout Elizabeth's childhood, for as long as Elizabeth could remember. Her grandmother knew everything there was to know about Elizabeth because Elizabeth would tell her things or her mother would, and then her grandfather would also get to know. They were very open with one another. Elizabeth was looking forward to seeing her grandparents of course, but at the same time she felt divided. She was very concerned because the way she was feeling now she was convinced that they would definitely sense something was wrong with her when they saw her this time. She was mortified at the prospect of them finding out – for anyone to find out – so she was desperate to be right again ... to be normal like she was before.

Bargaining And Seeking Forgiveness

Coming from an upper middle class background, Elizabeth attended one of the best boarding schools in the UK. She also had brains, and she was always a straight A student. She had already planned to read medicine at university like Sally, and to become the best paediatrician ever, because she loved children. She herself was going to have at least four. She was always a good organiser, and everything had gone according to plan, till now. Now, everything had changed. She felt completely hollow inside and could not see beyond now. For the first time in her life, she was lost, lost for words and lost for ideas that would make 'this thing' go away. Now, all she could do was to stare at her empty life and cry silently in her room. She tried to sleep but as much as she tried, she could not sleep. If only she could, she would wake up to find that this was all a terrible mistake, just a horrible nightmare. She had not slept properly for days and the sleep deprivation was making her more depressed and blurring her vision, so she could not focus on anything positive.

Suddenly and unusually, she thought of God. Maybe God was punishing her for not going to church, because the only time she was in church was when she was christened, and for her sister's christening, so maybe this was God's way of punishing her. Her family was never the religious type although they were decent honest people, so Elizabeth was not brought up to be religious either. She thought that perhaps she would go to church now, but then she told herself that God would know that she was being hypocritical, going in order to get what she wanted. But even so, she would do just about anything if it would make her whole again. Afterwards, she felt ashamed to be so devious as to even think of it, but she was more surprised at herself for even thinking of God at such a time, which was completely out of character for her. Still she could not help herself, and it was as if she was drawn to Him when she needed help now. Elizabeth even started to self-actualise, to prove that she was a good decent person. She tried to think of past events in her life, where she might have erred, or where she could have offended Him, so that she could tell Him that they were unintentional, and then He would forgive her. She could not think of anything, instead she could only remember the good things she did, like always helping her mother to carry and put away the groceries from her shopping whenever she was home from boarding school. Another time when she was out with her friends, she spotted a blind old lady who seemed lost as she waved her white stick from side to side to gauge what was in front of her, so Elizabeth, without hesitation, left her friends and immediately went to help her. As it happened, the woman did come out shopping with her daughter but somehow got separated from her and did not know where she had gone, or how to contact her. Elizabeth suggested that they went to the customer information counter to ask the staff to make an announcement over their PA system. The blind lady admitted that she was so scared and had not thought of this, but said it was a good idea, so Elizabeth took her all the way there and waited till someone came for her. After about ten minutes, a flushed and concerned woman came hurriedly to the desk. It was the old lady's daughter! She explained that she was trying on some clothes in the women's department and when she came out of the fitting room, her mother had wandered off, and she had been frantically searching for her ever since. They were both very grateful to Elizabeth and could not thank her enough for her help and kindness. "My good deed for the day," Elizabeth thought, but more importantly, she was glad that the old lady was reunited with her daughter. She had been so engrossed with the woman that she did not even hear her mobile ring so when she took her mobile out from her jeans, there were several missed calls and text messages from her friends enquiring about her whereabouts.

Elizabeth continued trying to recount past events where she thought might have contributed to her current plight and became almost insanely frantic trying to remember one where she was bad or horrible. It was not that she was trying to score points with God, but she thought that if she remembered a bad thing that she had done, she could apologise to Him, and He would forgive her and make her right again. She could not think of anything. She became frustrated, and then suddenly she remembered the time when she shouted at her sister. Maybe that was it. Emma had recently turned fourteen and although she had a slightly smaller frame than her older sister, she could wear her sister's clothes. She had taken a new jumper from Elizabeth's room and worn it to the cinema with her friends. Elizabeth was still at boarding school, so when she came back during the half term, she found out. She was very cross with Emma and shouted at her because she had gone into her room, taken the jumper from one of the drawers and worn it without asking her first, although Emma's excuse was that Elizabeth was not there. She could have telephoned or texted her sister if it had even occurred to her, but Emma was not like that. She did not apologise either. Unlike her older sister, she was quite spoilt, being the youngest, and usually took things for granted, so Elizabeth was livid, especially with her blasé attitude. She loved her baby sister very much and would have given her anything she wanted but this time it was different. All Emma had to do was to ask her first, but she did not, so Elizabeth wanted to teach her sister some good manners, because she seemed to have lost them when she became an adolescent. It was important for her to learn, Elizabeth felt, but then she remembered that her sister was only fourteen and like many normal teenagers, behaved like she was fourteen going on thirty and knew everything, so the saying goes, or so she had heard. Elizabeth was never like that though "… is this why I am different?" she asked herself. She felt really bad about it afterwards, and thought that she had overreacted. In the end, the two sisters made up and Emma apologised when she became aware at how cross she had made her older sister, whom she also adored. They never fought again. "It was just that one time God, and I am very sorry I over-reacted. Please forgive me". As she said it aloud, she realised how ridiculous it all sounded.

Elizabeth had given up googling in her room because nothing had changed and she was getting more confused with all the information that she had read on the different sites. Furthermore, she found out that there was another condition that she might have, and she thought that this alternative was even worse. She might not even be a girl. She longed for this 'thing' to go away and everything to go back to normal – so she would be normal – but "I am not normal, I am a freak," she kept torturing herself, over and over. The thought of this terrified her more and more and it also made her ashamed of herself. She really hated this thing and she did not like herself much now either. Then she hoped, "what if and maybe he was wrong, after all he did say that he had never seen anyone like me before. He had no experience in the field and had to look it up on the internet himself". This was her local consultant but he was no expert. Still, deep down, Elizabeth knew that she was only clutching at straws. She and her family had done lots of research, and having surfed the different internet sites, the conclusion was too unanimous to ignore.

Since her appointment with the local consultant, Elizabeth had not felt the same. In fact, everything changed for her. It was all too much for anyone to fathom, let alone a sixteen-year-old, and she was just sixteen. Deep in her heart though, she knew that something was amiss long before, but she did not know what it was, so she tried her best to get on with her life, although this was always at the back of her daughter's condition. She tried hard not to show it, but luckily no one noticed anyway. The specialist continued, and added that Elizabeth, like the majority of the women had normal ovaries, which was why she developed everything else normally during her puberty. He also informed them of her fertility options, and his preferred treatment to create Elizabeth's underdeveloped vagina. After about forty minutes, the Appleton family emerged from the room smiling and for the first time in what seemed like a long time, they were somewhat more relaxed than they had been for weeks. They felt fully informed and had all their queries and concerns addressed, so now they had much to digest and process. Afterwards, the specialist introduced them to two other members of his team, a treatment specialist, Lucy Saunders and a psychologist, Anne Gaston.

Elizabeth and her family were slightly disappointed that the specialist could not make her a womb, but they were informed of some developments in uterine transplants, although these were not available as yet. Still, the Appletons were hopeful that there was a possibility of this in the future, especially given Elizabeth's young age. Elizabeth suddenly felt a huge weight lifted off her shoulders after seeing the team and, although she could not explain it, she suspected that part of it was because she finally got a confirmed diagnosis, even though it was not exactly new information to her by now. Still, somehow it seemed different hearing it from the experts. This time, it was definite and no more 'what ifs'. After all, she had been waiting for this since she was fourteen years old. "Now at last, I know what's wrong with me," she muttered to herself. She had been feeling so abnormal, and even secretly questioned her sexual orientation, but was too embarrassed to ask her GP what was wrong. Her own research informed her that she was female despite her not having a womb, but she was still frightened that this information might be incorrect because "how can any girl not have a womb when women are supposed to bear children.

It's just not possible". She had been struggling to understand, but now she had heard it from the experts. It was true, she was every bit a female and she had ovaries – the team had confirmed this. She did not realise how important this piece of information was to her until now, so she could not hear enough of this, and she made herself repeat the words from the specialist over and over in her head. She felt such a relief that her heart raced and she felt tingly and slightly dizzy with joy because she needed so much to hear this confirmation. Not only that, but he told her that she was not the only one, and quoted the current statistics of one in four to five thousand females being born with this condition. Lucy, the treatment specialist, also asked Elizabeth if she would like to connect with other girls at their Centre, because they had several girls with her condition registered with them. She could not believe it, she could never be in the Guinness Book of Records if she wanted – not that she wanted to because she would never dream of telling anyone or registering herself in any case. "I can't believe there are others like me, I'm not the only one, thank you God!" Elizabeth thought selfishly to herself, holding her breath to stop herself from getting too excited. This was too real. She was not the only one and her condition was not that rare. That's what they said. She nearly pinched herself each time to make sure that she had heard the specialist correctly, but her family, unable to contain their excitement at all this new information, interrupted her thoughts. They were relieved too and could not believe that the afternoon kept getting better, as they were informed of varied help and support available, and of other fertility options like IVF surrogacy and adoption. They had read about IVF surrogacy on the internet, but hearing it from the experts made it more real, especially when they were informed that a few of the women at their Centre had successfully had babies using this method.

They also learned that the treatment for Elizabeth's underdeveloped vagina did not involve surgery, and that she could impeccable taste, something Elizabeth picked up from her, so she bought her a Karen Millen cashmere cardigan, with a scarf to match. Her father too was a handsome man and could easily pass for a male model. He was a six-footer and had a six-pack because he did body building in his younger days and continued to maintain his masculine slim figure. He had a very distinguished demeanour about him too, so together, her parents were the best and the most handsome couple, Elizabeth always thought. She bought her father a tie and cufflink set and a pair of black leather driving gloves. They were expensive gifts but she had saved up her allowance so she could just afford them. Besides, she felt that she owed them, as they had to put up with her mood swings for the last few weeks. For her grandparents, she bought them each woollen jumpers, gloves and socks. For the rest of her girlfriends and boyfriends, she bought books, CDs, iTunes gift cards and a few other gimmicky items, which she thought that they would like. She almost forgot to get her Christmas cards and wrapping paper but was luckily reminded when she saw a gift shop across the street where she happened to be standing.

It was a huge store selling every conceivable gift wrap and stationery that one could want, so she quickly nipped in and bought some glittery wrapping paper with matching bows, ribbons and tags, a few small gift boxes and individual Christmas cards. When she was done, she joined her sister and parents. Emma was trying on some more clothes although she had already bought a couple of jeans, t-shirts and sweatshirts and a pair of ankle boots. She was in her element and on a spending spree. Her parents did not mind though, because they felt slightly guilty that they might have neglected their youngest, as all the attention had been centred round Elizabeth ever since they returned from seeing their local consultant. Elizabeth, however, did not buy a single thing for herself, so her mother asked, "El, would you like to try on something because they have some lovely things here?" Elizabeth replied, "No thanks. I don't feel like it. I don't need anything anyway". Besides, she could not bear to look at herself in the mirror. She did not like her body much now and was ashamed of it. Yet she used to admire her own body every now and again especially after her shower or when she was getting dressed, not that she was particularly vain but she knew she had a great body and breasts, and she loved her body then. She knew that she also looked good in her clothes. Now she could not stand to look at her body and she did not want anyone else looking at her either. She decided that "I'm just going to wear baggy jumpers and pants from now on so that I don't draw any attention to myself". The thing was, it did not matter what she wore, she was a beautiful girl with a fantastic figure, so whatever she wore, it would always look good on her. She could put on a casual t-shirt and an old pair of jeans and still look fantastic and fabulously fashionable. It was a shame that she just could not see it now, because she did not feel that she was normal or whole anymore.

On the train home, Emma was chatting to Elizabeth about putting up the Christmas decorations and decorating the Christmas tree, and the party games they were going to have after their Christmas lunch. Emma was always very artistic and had a flair for the arts, so she wanted to do arts and drama when she was old enough. For the moment, she attended a private school nearby because her parents were more protective over her, as she was the baby of the family and was not as independent as her older sister. The two girls always got on well, not only as sisters but as friends. Jan and Paul looked at their daughters and smiled at each other as if to say that their family was back to normal, without having to say a word. Jan tried to suppress her true feelings because, in a strange way, she wished the specialist had not confirmed that the cause of Elizabeth's condition was genetic, because it made her feel guiltier than she already did. Still, all in all, she felt that this trip had proven to be more useful than they could have hoped for and she knew that this was the break that she and her family desperately needed.

Elizabeth had actually had a great time and managed to enjoy herself so much that she had momentarily forgotten the reason for this trip up to London. When Emma fell asleep on the train, she had time to reflect. She still felt some sadness at the thought of not being able to bear her own children and having to have treatment later, but strangely she did not feel its intensity anymore. This is good, she thought, "I am going to be ok. I am so lucky to have a family who love me". She darted a look at her family. Then she remembered that she still had to get something off her chest, so she went over and sat next to her parents, but she did not know where to begin. After some delibera-tion, she plucked up enough courage to ask, "do we have to tell grandma and granddad about my thing? I mean how do I tell them, and when should I tell them? I don't know what to say to them because I don't want to spoil every-one's Christmas". She was afraid of telling her grandparents in case it ruined Christmas for everyone or even worse, as she told her parents, the unthinkable idea that "my problem becomes the main conversational piece during this whole Christmas break. I can't bear it if everyone keeps talking about it". On the other hand, if she did not tell them, she felt that they would surely sense that something was wrong anyway, because she would not be able to keep up with the pretence all that time, nor did she want to. Moreover, she and her family would also have to be careful at all times, which she thought was not ideal because they had only just recovered from that situation. Her parents said, "we'll do whatever you're comfortable with".

In the end, Elizabeth agreed that her parents should tell them. "But please tell them that I don't want their pity or sympathy and I don't want to have a discussion with them either," Elizabeth added firmly. Besides, there was really nothing else to discuss. All Elizabeth really wanted was to forget and erase everything that had happened since she turned sixteen… if only she could. Jan watched Elizabeth and she knew that this was just the start of a very difficult journey, and it was a long way to go before her precious daughter would feel normal, and for her family to be really normal again. She would readily give up her right arm if only this would make Elizabeth normal. "No words can really describe how I am feeling to watch my own child suffering, and not be able to help her," Jan thought sadly. It broke her heart when she tried to think of what her daughter was going through, and how she must really be feeling. It made her more resolved to help Elizabeth in any way she could, although with no experience in something like this she felt rather inadequate, so all she really could do was to be supportive and to be there for Elizabeth, whatever and however long it would take.

When the train pulled into the station, everyone carried down their own luggage and their added bags of Christmas presents they had purchased over the weekend. Paul instructed them "just wait here for me" so they parked themselves by the side of the station entrance while he went to collect his car from the short-stay parking lot. Luckily, he had brought his BMW 7 series saloon, so they managed to load almost everything into its spacious boot, except for a few small items, which the two girls kept on the back seat between them. It had been a long day and everyone was tired and hungry, and since it was also dinner time by the time they were *en route* home, it made sense to go and have something to eat first. Emma quickly piped up – "I fancy some curry, can we go to our regular Indian, please?" and everyone thought it was a good idea, so they went to their local curry house for a meal. The Appleton family loved a good curry and the aroma of the different curries from the other customers who were already dining there made them even hungrier. They knew what they liked, so no sooner the waiter showed them to their table, they wasted no time in placing their order with him. The service there was fast but it was always impeccable too, which was another reason they liked the restaurant, apart from the delicious food. They were sipping their drinks when the food arrived, and one by one the dishes were placed on the table, which made everyone starving hungry. Elizabeth and Emma were so excited that they almost did a food dance and sang out "yummy, yummy". They shared four different starters before their main course of tandoori chicken, chicken jalfrezi, lamb bhuna gosht, fish curry, some dry cauliflower and potato curry which they ate with their pilau rice, and a couple of naan breads. They thoroughly enjoyed the meal but they had eaten too much and probably too quickly as well that no one had any room left for desserts so they went straight home afterwards.

Home Sweet Home

When the Appleton family reached home, the house was lovely and warm because Jan had deliberately set the timer for the hot water and heating to come on automatically for when they returned. She thought, "Home sweet home". She actually enjoyed the short break away, and it was a successful trip, but there was nothing like home. Of course, this meant that the usual household chores had to be done too but Jan was used to this. There was a lot of washing between them, so she began sorting out all of their clothes for washing whilst the girls sorted out their individual things and shopping. Paul did not have any wine with his meal at the restaurant because he was driving, so he went to the drinks cabinet and poured himself and Jan a glass of red *Châteauneuf Du Pape*. They always appreciated a good bottle. Jan soon joined him on their three-seater leather settee and they comforted each other. Then she asked her husband, "it was a worthwhile trip wasn't it? El seems happier now. She'll be alright now, won't she?" Paul answered, "Yes, I'm sure of that. They seem to know what they're doing up there". They both concluded that the trip to London did all of them some good and all in all, it was a good result. They decided that they would let Elizabeth make her own decision about her treatment, and they would respect and support her all the way. They knew their daughter well, she was always strong and sensible and she would pull through this in her own time. They agreed that they would not influence Elizabeth into doing anything she was uncomfortable with, so they would wait until she was ready to talk to them. Paul also decided that he would tell her this in the morning so that they could all get on with their lives as normally as possible.

It was only fair for everyone. They were thinking of Emma and the impact it would have on her too. Although Jan did not blame herself so much now knowing that it was not something that she had physically done to have caused her daughter's condition, she still could not help feeling guilty. She was also more hopeful after this trip to London. She and her husband liked the London team, and felt confident with their approach, which they found very reassuring. They again comforted themselves that Elizabeth would be alright as they were convinced she was now in good hands. They squeezed each other's hands reassuringly as they retired to their room.

Once in her own room, Elizabeth looked at her Christmas presents and had a new surge of energy. She had forgotten about the past few weeks for the moment, and soon she was back to her usual self. She was excited with what she had bought for everyone so she decided to wrap them straight away. She loved wrapping presents so she put her heart and soul into every individual one. They looked beautiful with the finished ribbons and bows, so she was pleased, as this was how she liked her presents to look. She always had a keen eye for nice things, pretty things – everything had to be just so. She was really a perfectionist, which also explained why she took her problem so hard, and why she could not accept it. She decided to have a soak in the bath although she normally preferred a shower. She poured some chamomile and ylang ylang bath oils into the bath and, as she slid herself in, she thought it was the perfect finish to an almost perfect few days. It was so soothing that she nearly fell asleep. She was so relaxed that she would not have noticed being in the bath for an hour had it not been for the water getting cold. "Gosh it's so cold!" It sent her slightly shivering, so she quickly pulled the plug out to drain the bath and swiftly got out. She creamed herself very quickly with some body lotion, got into her cotton pyjamas and jumped into her bed.

When she was all snuggled up in bed, she suddenly became wide awake. Her mind started to wander, straight back to her problem again. This time though, she was still sad but not melancholy and somehow knowing more about her condition and hearing it from the experts, made her pain more tolerable. She could not bear to relive the nightmare of the past few months with only the feeling of complete desolation. She had felt so lost and so alone that she could not see the light at the end of the tunnel. She was also exhausted, and so emotionally and mentally drained that she could not function properly. Now, with this extra information and support at hand, she did not feel so helpless, and began to feel that she had some control over her life again. She went through everything that had been said to her in her mind. She wished she was brave enough to talk to someone like her though. They told her at the Centre that they would arrange it if she wanted to speak to someone. She thought, "yes, it's a good idea and I won't feel so alone, so isolated but then I'm too frightened and too embarrassed. What would I say anyway? Oh no, I can't!" No she decided, she was not ready to talk to anyone yet, except Sally. She thought about what she would say to her best friend when term reopened, and even this made her feel uncomfortable. Slowly she began to fill up with anxiety and panic. She did not know why she felt like that, because Sally was her best friend and like an older sister to her and she trusted her to understand. Sally was intelligent, a good listener and very sensitive. In the past, she had helped Elizabeth in other situations so she could help her again, especially if she was suddenly to have a panic attack at school. "I must tell Sally. She'll understand. Sally's my best friend and I know she'll help me. I have to tell her". She kept coaxing herself, in case she changed her mind again until, finally, she fell asleep.

After a good night's sleep, Jan felt so refreshed and positive that she decided to embrace the day as the beginning of a new chapter in her life. This was the first good sleep she had for a while because she had not been sleeping well either, spending weeks of restless nights blaming herself, and worrying about Elizabeth. However, she decided that things were going to change. She would start by making today a great day! She had taken time off work till after the New Year so she could spend more quality time with her daughters, and she also had a lot to do before the Christmas break. For a start, Jan decided, "we're all going to have a proper breakfast" so she was going to spoil her family and cook them a full English breakfast, something they used to enjoy at the weekends and which they had missed ever since they found out about Elizabeth's problem, as no one was in the mood, especially Elizabeth who could not wait to excuse herself from the table, and always made a quick retreat to her room after every meal. The atmosphere was awkward to say the least and Jan could feel her family falling apart, yet they used to be such a close-knit family. Jan missed their togetherness and laughter. She had always made sure that mealtime was family time, as this was how she was brought up, and something that she was very accustomed to, so she made sure that this routine continued with her own family. Today, she would get her beloved family back on track, and she was determined that it would be a new start for them.

Jan laid the dining table like a professional with silver cutlery, linen serviettes and cereal bowls, cups and glasses for each of them. She then placed the butter, marmalade, strawberry jam, honey and jars of tomato ketchup and English mustard and a variety of cereals at the centre of the table. She made a pot of English breakfast tea for herself and Emma and switched the Nespresso coffee machine on, which was on their side table in the dining room, so it was ready to go for her husband and Elizabeth, as they preferred their coffee. She then went to the refrigerator to get the fruit juices and a bottle of semi-skimmed milk. The latter she poured into a milk jar, which she placed on the table next to her fine china tea pot. She had already put their plates in the oven to keep warm until they were ready to eat. Back in the kitchen, she placed strips of dry, cured, unsmoked bacon and skinless sausages on the grill whilst she shallow-fried the mushrooms and sweet juicy vine tomatoes in a pan. She also heated up the baked beans in the microwave oven, but she would fry the eggs individually later when everyone was ready. The smell of bacon coming from the kitchen was so tantalising when Paul walked in that it immediately aroused his appetite, but Jan was too busy to notice him, until he gave her a quick peck on her cheeks to wish her a "good morning, babe. I see we're having a proper English breakfast, that's nice". Jan wished her husband a chirpy 'good morning' back and said "yes, it's been a while I know but today's a good start and I think all of us deserve a nice breakfast," then she went to knock on her daughters' rooms to wake them, before she proceeded to make their toast, and fry their eggs as they liked them, sunny-side up whilst Paul went to the dining room to make himself an *Intenso Arpeggio*, a strong flavoured coffee to start his day off. He was anticipating a busy day at the office with meetings and catching up, as he had not been there since the previous Friday. As he picked up his *Financial Times*, Elizabeth walked in followed by Emma. After a quick greeting, Emma sat down and poured herself a cup of tea whilst Elizabeth said, "mmm the smell of bacon is so good," as she walked on to the kitchen to help her mother, which was her norm. When breakfast was ready and everything was laid on the table, Elizabeth poured her mother a cup of tea and then she made herself a caramel coffee, her favourite, because she liked the creamy and caramel flavour of the coffee.

During breakfast, it was established that everyone had slept soundly and they were in better spirits. They chatted casually to each other and about their plans for the day. Jan said that she would take her daughters shopping after they finished breakfast because "we need to get our Christmas tree. It's only a week to go before Christmas and you can help me choose one. I also need some other stuff, so we'll go to the superstore afterwards, because I need to finish my food shopping for the Christmas holidays today". Her daughters said "ok". Jan had already ordered her fresh meats, a fresh 5.8kg turkey, a 4.5kg goose and 1kg beef fillet for her beef Wellington; a leg of lamb and a joint of ham from the local farm a few miles down the road from them, and had also arranged for these to be delivered two days before Christmas Day. As usual, she had placed her order several weeks ago to ensure that she got all the fresh meat that she needed, as this was also a popular practice with the other locals. Jan was always very efficient and organised like that. Of course, it was also a case of having to be, with two young children and working full time, although she had help from an *au pair* when the girls were younger – but now she only had her cleaning lady once a week.

Just before Paul got up to go to work, he broached the subject about Elizabeth's treatment. He said, "El, about your treatment…" Elizabeth froze for a second but then her father, without hedging this time, said, "your mum and I feel that this should be your decision, so we're going to leave you to decide what you're going to do about your treatment, or anything else you need to do. Think carefully what you want, but there's no rush, you can take your time. We just want you to let us know when you've decided what you're doing, so we can talk more then. Ok darling?" He also told her that they would respect her decision, and they would go along with whatever she decided, and that they would not try to influence her or bring up this subject again until she was ready to talk to them. Of course, he also said that they loved her very much and promised to support and help her for as long as she needed them. There was a moment's silence but then Elizabeth managed to recover herself and said, "I've been thinking about the treatment too, dad. To be honest, I'm really frightened about it all and I am not looking forward to it, but like you said, there's really no rush, so I think that I would prefer to concentrate on my studies for now first because I really need to get my grades for my entry into med school". She was not running away from her problem but she knew that she was not ready to do anything about it yet. She would start her treatment during the next summer holidays, preferably before starting university. Her parents were very pleased to hear Elizabeth say that, and they could not have agreed more, so they told her, "that is a very sensible decision, very good El". With that, nothing more was said.

Emma had stayed silent all this time because she did not know what to say to her big sister, but she secretly thought that Elizabeth was the bravest person she knew. She would not have coped herself if their roles were reversed. As soon as she saw the opportunity, she quickly changed the subject and asked if her grandparents were coming down to them on Christmas Eve, as they always did in the past. Jan's parents were approaching their seventies and, Jan being their only child, they always spent the Christmas holidays with her and her family. Paul had an elder brother living in Oxford, and his parents also lived not too far from him, so they usually spent their Christmases together. It was a good arrangement although a couple of years ago, Jan had all of them down for Christmas. It was truly a festive time for them, with lots of laughter and fun. Three of Paul's nieces and nephews were about the same age as Elizabeth and Emma – they got on very well and everyone had a wonderful time. Elizabeth remembered how much she enjoyed that time, but she was normal then. Now she was just grateful that it was not this year. She would not be able to cope this year, not with so many people around, because she was still unsure of herself, and was afraid of having a sudden uncontrollable burst of panic attack whenever her problem slipped into her mind. She was terrified that everyone would find out and she was adamant she was not going to tell anyone about her problem, nor give them any cause to find out. Even now, she thought that she was not sure how she was going to cope this Christmas with her grandparents around. She wished she had more confidence so she would not have to worry so much. Then again, she thought she might be overthinking everything again, and maybe nothing terrible would happen. At least that was what she kept hoping.

Christmas Rush

They bought a six foot Christmas tree and some more baubles, ribbons and garlands to add to last year's, because Emma found these to be her must-haves this year. She made it her job to do the decorations again, as she loved it so much and did it so artistically last Christmas, although she was only supposed to be helping her father then. The tree was too big, so Jan paid for it to be delivered that evening so they could also then carry on with their food shopping. When they got to the supermarket, it was jam-packed with people. They had to wait to get parked, and even had to wait for a trolley to become available. But no sooner was a trolley returned to its parking bay than it was snatched up. Also, some people could not wait and started to give their pound coin to the person returning the trolley before it even got to the trolley park. As they waited patiently in the cold, Jan told her daughters, "thank goodness I have bought most of the stuff already, because there might not be anything left on the shelves at this rate". Emma was too busy playing her games on her mobile to notice anything, but Elizabeth was unusually focused on the number of pregnant women and women with children coming in and out of the store. The more she watched, the more agitated she became. She had never minded them before and, in fact, she had never even noticed them before, but now they seemed to be everywhere she looked. She started to envy and resent the women, because "why should they have children when I can't, it's so unfair". The more she dwelled on such thoughts, the more she thought her head was going to explode. She could feel a massive headache coming on too, so all she wanted to do was to go home, home to hide in her room again. Just then,

and illnesses, and reports of a few fatalities from road traffic accidents so the 'Drink-driving THINK' advertisement came on a few times too. Overall, the news was all rather depressing, especially for this time of the year, which made the advertisements on different products from various stores a welcome interruption, because these at least reminded them of Christmas and gave them a feel good feeling.

After they finished unpacking and putting away the shopping, Elizabeth stayed to help her mother prepare dinner, like she always did whenever she was home. She had not done this for a while, so this was the first time ever since she learnt of her condition, although now she seemed more unusually subdued. Her mother was still quietly hopeful because she felt that this was a good sign to Elizabeth's road to recovery so she said, "It's nice to have your company again, darling," and Elizabeth just said in a quiet voice, "I know". Jan missed her daughter's company and that special closeness and connection they had, and she wondered if they would ever get that back. Elizabeth's condition was a big blow to her as it was for the whole family, so she knew that it would take time before her daughter regained her self-confidence. Still, Elizabeth was very much like her in more ways than one – she was strong and sensible so she would overcome this crisis, given time. Although she was committed to supporting Elizabeth no matter how long it took, it was not easy, because she was not sure how to support her, and it really pained her to see her precious daughter in such anguish, especially when she still felt that she was partly to blame for Elizabeth's predicament. She told herself that she must stay strong and be patient with Elizabeth, so that she could then help her daughter the best as she could, as any mother would.

Emma was still playing games on her mobile in the living room whilst waiting for the delivery of their Christmas tree, as instructed by her mother in case they missed the door bell ringing from the kitchen. Finally, the tree arrived! They placed it in its usual spot, the left hand corner of the living room, because it was the biggest room in the house, and it would be the room most often used over the Christmas period, so everyone would be able to see and smell it. It was also placed away from them so as not to get in their way. The delivery men sat the tree on the stand and skirt which Jan had prepared earlier prior to the delivery. It was a beautifully shaped triangular tree, and Emma became very excited seeing it in the house. She could not wait for her father to return, and she wanted to decorate it straight away. She asked her mother, "Mummy, can I start decorating the tree now and not wait for dad, because I know how to do it? Dad showed me last year so may I please?" Her mother could not resist Emma's plea, so she told her that she could, but she warned her, "Just be careful with the lights because it's electricity, so I don't want you to turn it on until I say so. Call me when you are ready, ok?" Emma said excitedly, "I will, thanks mum". She had all her decorations and baubles out and she also took out last year's Christmas lights, and was pleased that these were the small bulb lights, because she had read somewhere that they tended to look nicer. She started to untangle them before stringing them from the top of the tree to the bottom, carefully hiding the wires in between the branches so they were not visible, like her father had taught her last Christmas. It was amazing how professional she was even at fourteen, but the artist in her made it seem natural. She took her time because it had to look perfect. Then she called her mother and sister in to ask for their opinion on the lights before she continued with her decorations. She hung the red, gold and green baubles that she had from last year and mixed them with her newly acquired metallic gold and bronze ones. She was mindful not to over-decorate the tree because that would make it look garish and tacky but, being a big tree, she felt it was still lacking something. She did not like using tinsel, because she considered them too ordinary and old fashioned. Then she remembered the red garlands and ribbons that she had bought recently, so she hung these in between the baubles. Finally, she stood on the stool and carefully placed her golden blonde angel on top. She wanted a change so she decided on an angel this year instead of the star that they used last year. She was so excited that she had forgotten what her mother had told her not to do, and turned the lights on. Fortunately, nothing terrible happened. She stood away from it for a minute to admire her work of art. The tree looked beautiful, even if she thought so herself. She would ask her mother and Elizabeth to come in to have a look now.

As she was walking towards the kitchen, her father walked in through the door. She was so excited and suddenly, like the child she was, she could not wait for his approval and praise so she said, "Hi dad. You have to come and look at my tree first," and practically dragged him into the living room. Then she swiftly went out to get her mother and sister. The colours of the baubles, the glittery garlands and ribbons complimented each other so well, and they also picked up the reflections in the lights making the tree sparkle and glitter in a most sophisticated way. The expression on her family's faces was sheer magic so Emma felt well chuffed with herself. They too were all very impressed although her mother said, "Naughty girl. Did you forget that I told you not to turn the lights on without me being present?" Emma replied sheepishly, "Sorry mummy. I was so excited that I forgot". In any case, her parents gave her a big hug and Paul gave her a kiss on her head and told her that he was very proud of her and said, "The tree is beautiful darling. I couldn't have done it better myself," and Elizabeth also told her she did a brilliant job. Afterwards, Elizabeth watched her baby sister and thought how talented and artistic she was, and she was so proud of her baby sister. She thought that she was a good kid, too. Then Elizabeth tried to picture Emma in the future. She would have a brilliant career, marry the man of her dreams and have her own family and they would live happily ever after. How lucky she was, and it was all well-deserved, because her sister was a good person. Elizabeth postulated her sister's future with a slight hint of envy, because she would have liked that for herself too. She was almost going to disparage herself again, but then she remembered Emma offering to be her surrogate. She thought her baby sister was so kind and generous and she was grateful to have Emma as her sister. It reminded her how much she loved her too.

Dinner was a roast leg of lamb served with roast potatoes, parsnips, Yorkshire pudding, carrots and broccoli. Jan made her gravy and mint sauce following, Jamie Oliver's recipe, being a fan of his. Paul opened a bottle of his Australian Shiraz Viognier for himself and Jan whilst the two girls had their cokes. The dinner was delicious as usual because Jan was such a good cook. Afterwards they had coffee and finished the remainder of the cheesecake for their dessert. With the dirty dishes in the dishwasher and the kitchen cleaned and tidied up, the family could relax, and they sat in their living room chatting. Jan was telling Paul about their day and how crowded the superstore was with all the Christmas shoppers. She asked her husband about his day but Paul who did not like bringing his work home, just said that he had a busy day at the office too. Just then, Emma's mobile rang and it was one of her school friends, so she excused herself and went to her room. Elizabeth thought that she should maybe ring Sally but she quickly dismissed that idea, because she did not feel like talking to her. In fact, these days, she dreaded talking to Sally because she was afraid that Sally might become suspicious, so instead Elizabeth stayed and watched her parents for a while. She could tell that they loved each other very much. She thought that they were so lucky because they had each other. She, on the other hand had no one, no boyfriend. She wanted a boyfriend just then, if only to prove that she was still desirable, but who would want her now because she was so abnormal. She could not even have sex like normal people unless she had treatment first to make a vagina, her vagina. "This is so not normal," she almost said aloud. She could feel herself starting to get uncomfortable and slightly panicky and suddenly she became aware that she had not been back to her room since the morning, nor had she thought about it, because she had been out all day and afterwards she was busy helping her mother, but now she had time on her hands, she realised, and felt that she had to go to her room. She quickly excused herself. All of a sudden, she felt this urge getting stronger and stronger for her to get away, to go to her room. She swiftly picked up her mobile from the coffee table, and then practically ran to her room.

Screaming Out For Help

Elizabeth did not know why she had to rush back to her room. There was nothing there, but she just felt that she had to get away and be by herself, so she sat on the edge of her bed, staring, and looking around her room. She thought her room suddenly seemed different. It was just not the same anymore. It felt cold, empty and depressing. Of course, her room was not really cold nor empty nor depressing but it was rather a reflection of how she was feeling. She had always loved her room. It was truly a girl's bedroom, taste-fully decorated in a shade of pale pastel pink, which con-trasted well with the white ceiling, her coral-coloured bed with matching pink and coral cotton bed linen and a couple of satin coral scatter pillows with a deep purple tiger-paw design. There was a white-coloured fitted wardrobe on the opposite side of her bed, which stretched right across the whole wall up to the windows. Her room was bright and airy because the light always shone through the big glass windows and the circulating air came through the open top little windows. At the other end of her room, she had a free-standing coat rack in the corner, which she used to hang her different handbags and hats. Next to it, there was an oak and hazel desk with a white chair tucked neatly underneath, where she sat her laptop, her mini hi-fi music system and books. This side of her room led to her own *en suite* bathroom. It had a bath with a power shower attachment, an enclosed toilet and sink basin unit, set into a cupboard, and a set of drawers in a white gloss finish, and a huge fitted mirror above it stretching across its whole length. It was a bright and cosy room, and it was always her private sanctuary. She spent many happy hours in her room, albeit on her laptop, listening to her music, doing her homework or reading, and she'd never minded her own company before. Only now... whenever she was in her room, all she felt was isolation and loneliness... that she was the only one again and she felt so, so lonely. It was a strange feeling and she could not tell her family, they would never understand how she was really feeling anyway because they were normal. "No one can really understand how I'm feeling," she thought, and was saddened again. She did not like being different – a girl but not really a normal girl. It was not right, it was not normal. Just then, it did not matter what the doctors and experts had told her, she thought that they were probably just being kind and sensitive. Her condition was abnormal, so she was abnormal, and no one could change that, or the way she felt about herself. She kept feeling that she was the only one again and no matter how hard she tried, she could not shake off this sense of isolation. Her family had been so supportive and loving yet, ironically, she had never felt more alone and depressed. Tears kept rolling down her cheeks as she delved deeper into her personal misery. She felt the pain in her heart getting more and more intense again, and that her chest was being squeezed so tightly that she could hardly breathe. She did not know why she suddenly felt like this, because she thought she would be ok after seeing the specialists.

After a while, she told herself to stop being so egocentric because she hated feeling this way and it was not like her at all. The only problem was, she was not sure who and what she was anymore. Stop, Stop, Stop! She screamed at herself. She then reminded herself that there were other people worse off than her, remembering the children with life-threatening diseases and with gross physical disabilities that she had seen on television earlier. At least hers was hidden and no one would ever know to look at her, or would they? Suddenly, she was not sure whether they would know or not so she panicked. "Oh no, can they tell?" At that moment, she wanted to rush out to ask her parents, but what was the point, they would be biased and not tell her the truth anyway in case they upset her. Instead she went to the mirror to check for herself but she could not find anything that was telling. "Thank god, it doesn't show," she sighed with relief. She wished that she could stop torturing herself about her abnormality, but how could she, when she just could not accept this very thing she had. "Oh why, why, why do I have to have this horrible condition?!!!" she asked again. She was so happy and perfect before. She had a perfect life in her perfect world so why should she have to have this thing? Why should she have to accept her condition? It was not how she had planned her life. It was so unfair and now she did not know how to deal with it. She kept wishing that everything would go back to the way they were, that she would go back to being the way she was so she would be normal. Oh, how she just wanted to be normal.

After much deliberation, she decided to ring the Centre. She was desperate and needed to talk to someone, someone who would understand and who could help her. She found the telephone number in her handbag, together with her appointment card and information leaflets that she was given, but as she started to dial the number, she realised the time. "Oh no, it's almost ten o'clock, so there won't be any one in the office, which means that I will have to leave a message. Oh no, I'm not doing that, I can't". She became flustered and quickly cancelled the call on her mobile. After a few more minutes, she managed to calm herself down and was rational again. She decided that she would ring them in the morning if she still felt bad. Having made that decision, she was more composed. She decided to have a long soak in the bath because this would relax her and she needed something to unwind. She laid in the hot tub with its soothing and relaxing oils and closed her eyes. Within a few minutes, she was relaxed and started to drift away. She then thought about the day she just had. It was really quite a good day and all in all, it had sailed through without too much angst. There she was, helping her mother in the kitchen with dinner and the dishes, like the norm whenever she was back from boarding school. It was good to feel normal again. Perhaps this was what she should do from now on, to keep herself busy, and avoid thinking too much. This way she could stop her emotional outbursts, along with the pain she felt in her heart. At least this way, she would be like her old self. She would be happy and carefree again. Yes, she must stick to this plan, this was a good plan and the only way she knew to cope, she decided. "I have to keep myself busy all the time, that's right, I must," she reminded herself. This way, she would not have the time to think so much and then she would not feel so sad and angry at herself all the time.

She did not have much time to deliberate further, because just then her mobile rang. She had left it on her bed and forgotten to take it in with her into the bathroom so she dashed out of the bath to pick it up. "Hi Sally". It was her best friend. They exchanged what they had been doing since their school term ended. They had not spoken to each other properly since then, except for that quick phone call last week when Elizabeth was having one of her low moods and made an excuse to end their conversation. Sally was telling Elizabeth that "our Christmas this year will only be a quiet one, just with my parents and my two little brothers". She would prefer a more festive one like last year's but her uncle and his family had made other plans this time. She had just finished helping her mother decorate the Christmas tree and put up a few decorations around the house, but otherwise everything was pretty much low key so she had time on her hands. This instinctively made Elizabeth feel very uncomfortable because she did not want Sally to ring her every day or to drop by. She did not wish to talk to her or to see her every day because she was very astute and intuitive. Elizabeth figured, "Oh no, Sally's going to find out. She's going to suss that there is something wrong with me," and Elizabeth was just not ready to tell her yet. She was very mindful not to give Sally any hint that she was not alright, or about her appointment with the specialists. She deliberately focused their conversation on the coming Christmas holidays and the shopping she had done. She thanked Sally for her Christmas present and apologised for not being more organised with hers this year, but said that she would have to give it to her when they saw each other again. Sally accepted her apologies but remarked that it was very unlike Elizabeth not to be organised. She then told Elizabeth that "oh by the way, Sasha and Joanne were also asking after you. They told me that they'd been ringing you all week but only got your voicemail. Was there something wrong with your phone?" Elizabeth made various excuses that she had been busy with her family, her mobile was playing up, and at other times the battery was flat so she did not get their calls.

In truth, she did speak to one of the boys, a Tom McGuire and it had proved to be very difficult, so after that she had been deleting all their calls, because she did not know what to say to her friends without giving anything away. She was even convinced that Sally was getting suspicious and was afraid that she might probe her for more information so she felt that she had to end their conversation straight away. She also did not care to speak to her about their friends anymore, so she quickly changed the subject and told Sally that her grandparents were coming down next week, and that she on the other hand would be very busy helping her mother prepare for Christmas and would only have time to ring her on Christmas Day. "Anyway, I'd better go and get dressed because I just dashed out of the bath to take your call and I am freezing cold now so I'll talk to you later". She also told Sally that she had a long day and was tired out so she quickly bade her good night and clicked off her mobile. Afterwards, Elizabeth sighed and thought "that was really hard". She should not have rushed to answer her mobile. She even thought of turning her mobile off altogether so she would not have to talk to Sally or any of her friends but that was not a good idea either because this would only arouse their suspicions even more. She did not know what best to do. If only she knew what to do! She felt frustrated at herself again as she got dressed into her pyjamas and climbed into bed. She was mentally and emotionally fatigued and so very weary of everything...

With eyes closed, she blanked her mind, hoping to get a good night's sleep. She would ring the Centre first thing in the morning. She set her alarm on her mobile for 08.00 hours so that she had time to organise her thoughts and compose herself before ringing them at nine. Hour after hour passed and Elizabeth lay in bed, wide awake. She just could not go to sleep. After a while, she gave up trying, so every now and again she would check the time on her mobile. She was not particularly vexed and was quietly calm all night so she should have slept easily, given how shattered she was, but she just could not. In the end she decided not to wait for the alarm to sound so she got out of bed to get herself ready. Surprisingly, she felt very refreshed despite her long tedious night. She thought carefully about the impending phone call that she was about to make and then she was poised to go. "Hello, is this the Centre for MRKH?" The voice on the other line confirmed that Elizabeth was calling the correct number and asked how she could be of help. It sounded very sincere, and she recognised the voice. She immediately felt relieved because she knew that she was actually speaking to the specialist, Lucy whom she met at her appointment. Elizabeth then introduced herself and said, "this is El. I saw you just recently. Do you remember me?"

"Yes, I remember you El. How are you?" came the reply, which immediately set Elizabeth's mind at rest because she could not bear having to explain herself or be put through to various people at the opposite end of the line. After an awkward start and with some encouragement, Elizabeth started to speak, and in a choked and trembling voice, she admitted that she was not coping with her problem. "I don't know what to do. I thought I could cope after I saw you guys but I can't. I'm sorry, I want to believe all of you but I can't. I just don't feel normal. I'm not normal and I can't stop thinking about it. I feel like a freak all the time and I'm so ashamed of myself. I don't want to but I really hate myself now and I just want all this to end. Please help me. I don't know what to do," she pleaded with Lucy for help. She also started to cry whilst she was trying to explain how isolated and empty she felt. She could not adjust from being perfect to being a freak and having everything in her life shattered and tainted. It was all too much! She had another one of her panic attacks as she was speaking. Her voice echoed someone who was in so much pain and emotional distress that she warranted urgent professional help, so Lucy tried to calm her down first. "El, I understand how you are feeling. I'm very pleased that you called me. What you're feeling right now is very normal and I would be more concerned if you didn't have any feelings or reactions after being told that you have MRKH but right now, I need you to do something for me first. You are breathing too fast, so I need you to slow down your breathing, ok? I'm going to help you – I'm going to count and I want you to take a very deep breath, hold for a few seconds then breathe out slowly… ok ready? One, take a deep breath now and hold, keep holding, hold… now breathe out very slowly". After Lucy repeated this exercise a few more times with her, Elizabeth managed to calm down quite considerably, although she was still feeling a little shook-up following her hyperventilation and slight hysteria.

Nevertheless, she felt comforted and reassured, because Lucy had normalised her feelings. Lucy assured her that Anne, the psychologist, whom she had also met at her first appointment, would be able to help her as she had the expertise and the experience in working with women with MRKH. Elizabeth was encouraged to have therapy with Anne but she said that she would not be able to make another trip up to London just now, as it was too close to Christmas. Still, her current psychological status was too alarming to ignore and Lucy was concerned, so she offered her telephone counselling for when Anne was available to which Elizabeth agreed without any hesitation. In fact, she was very impressed and grateful to be offered this service, especially when she now knew how desperately she needed the help to get her through this holiday season.

When the call ended, Elizabeth was happier and calmer and her mental status and equilibrium was similar to that time after she was seen at the Centre. She thought that the staff somehow always managed to have a discerning and reassuring effect on her because they understood her so well and she needed to feel understood. She also needed to understand herself and she needed their support to help her to understand and to make sense of it all, because right now nothing still made sense to her. She wanted to believe so badly that she was a girl despite having this abnormality, but she was still having a difficult time convincing herself that she was. How could she believe and why should she have to accept anything when she thought that nothing even sounded right and since her abnormality was the very thing that was reminding her and making her feel so abnormal every day.

Elizabeth stayed in her room and waited for the call, even though she was not sure how long she would have to wait or when Anne would be available to ring her, since she had been engaged with another patient when Elizabeth rang earlier. However, within the hour, her mobile rang and it was Anne. She said, "Hello Elizabeth. How are you?" This time, Elizabeth was not as guarded as before and she replied, "Hello Anne. I've been waiting for your call. Thanks for calling me back. I'm not feeling too good and I'm not coping very well," so, with some direction, she managed to engage more and talked more openly about her feelings and fears. This was a good start because she needed Anne's professional help to talk about her feelings, and how to cope with situations better than she had done. It was the first positive step that she had taken since her diagnosis, but it was not an easy decision for her to admit that she needed help in dealing with her problem, being the strong character that she was. But at the same time she was riddled with feelings of shame and low self-esteem so, in the end, she knew that she was struggling and that she could not do it alone. She had to admit that she needed their professional help. She recognised that she still had a long way to go, but nevertheless Anne commended her for taking the initial step to ask for help and told her, "You've been very brave. I know it wasn't easy for you to admit that you need help, but I'm glad that you called us because we're here to help you". Elizabeth was both thankful and relieved, and it encouraged her to mention her apprehension about her grandparents finding out, and that she dreaded everyone's reactions including her own. Anne said, "Why don't you talk this over with your parents because they can also help and support you through this so that you don't need to do this on your own," as she felt that Elizabeth had a healthy relationship with her parents and she should not have to deal with her grandparents by herself especially at this early stage on. After an hour of telephone counselling, Elizabeth felt better than she had felt earlier, but both agreed that she needed more therapy so they arranged her next session after Christmas before she went back to school. Elizabeth needed this too because she was getting increasingly concerned about seeing her best friend and she needed some guidance before she confided in Sally. She would go up to London to see Anne the next time.

Elizabeth thought afterwards that she had always been very close to her parents, so she should feel as comfortable talking to them now as she had always done previous to all this happening although she also felt that this was completely different from anything that they had discussed before. Still, as Anne said, it was not as if they did not know about her problem so she wouldn't have to tell them from scratch. They were with her from the very beginning and they loved her unconditionally, so she knew in her heart that they must have been suffering too, because they could not help her since she had closed her door to them. She felt bad about it, but more for blaming them for her condition, irrespective of what she was told or read herself. She accepted now that they were no more to blame than she was, it was just the way it was, she was just born this way, with this horrible thing. Now she resolved that she had to learn to live with it and to get on with her life. It was a strange feeling but this somehow seemed to give her a sense of immense relief and calm and she felt felicitously comfortable with her decision. Besides, she felt that she did not have any energy left to carry on the way she did.

She hurriedly got dressed, because she was excited about telling her parents what she had been doing all morning. When she got to the breakfast table, her father had already left for work but her mother was there on her own, reading the newspaper and having her cup of tea. Emma was still in bed so Elizabeth greeted her mother with a jolly "good morning mummy" and headed towards the Nespresso coffee machine to make her usual coffee. Jan immediately stopped reading as she noticed the striking change in her daughter, but she was weary of stating the obvious in case it altered Elizabeth's cheerful mood, so she just returned the morning greeting. "Good morning darling. What would you like for breakfast? Would you like me to make you some toast or something else?"

"No thanks. I'll just have some cereals and fruits with yoghurt," Elizabeth said, and took a seat next to her mother. She was desperate to tell her mother, and equally her mother wanted to ask, but neither volunteered first. Elizabeth could not understand why she was hesitating telling her mother now when she could not wait to tell her a moment ago, but she was again overcome by nerves, and had difficulty finding the words. Then just when she opened her mouth to say "Mum..." her mother started to say "Darling..." at the same time, so they both laughed. This seemed to clear the air and her mother then asked Elizabeth to speak first. "I rang the Centre this morning..." The words came straight out of her mouth. She did not have time to think about it and she could not believe how easy it was. It gave her the confidence she needed, and afterwards it felt so natural for her to be talking to her mother, that she continued telling her what she had done and she said, "I've made an appointment with Anne, the psychologist, so I have to go up to London again to see her after Christmas". Afterwards, she also said to her mother, "I'm really sorry for blaming you and dad at first, but I know that this is not your fault, so please don't blame yourselves. It's no one's fault but it is what it is so we just have to accept that". She continued to tell her mother, "Another thing, you also need to treat me normally and I know you don't want to upset me but if you keep treating me like you're frightened to upset me all the time, it makes things worse because it just makes me feel more abnormal". So she asserted, "No more kid gloves" if they were to have a sense of normality in their household. Elizabeth said that she could not promise not to have her 'moments' but hopefully she would be able to overcome or deal with them better with their help. Of course, she was comforted by the fact that she was getting the professional help. Her mother was very pleased that her daughter had contacted the Centre because she secretly hoped that Elizabeth would. When she suggested this before, Elizabeth was not receptive so Jan dared not mention it again, especially as she and her husband had agreed that they would not interfere or influence her decisions. She was also wary that it might worsen their relationship and the situation at home. Now Jan was so proud that Elizabeth was so mature all of a sudden – she was just sixteen after all, and yet she was already so grown up in dealing with this very difficult problem. She gave Elizabeth a tight hug and said, "I'm so proud of you. I know that it has not been easy but you've been so brave. I'm just so glad that you rang the Centre, because I feel that they are the people who can help you. You're doing the right thing. You know that I love you very much but this is all new to me too and right now we need these people's help and experience". Elizabeth replied, "I know that too, mum". They started crying together but this time, they were tears of relief and comfort.

When Emma walked in and saw them, she was naturally frightened because she thought that something terrible had happened, but her mother motioned to her to "Come and join us darling. Don't worry, your sister and I were just talking and it's all good". When Emma learnt about what had happened, she too was relieved and also started to cry. Emma had been feeling very sad for Elizabeth since all this started but being a child herself, she did not fully understand, nor did she know what to say or how to comfort her big sister. She also felt that she had lost her big sister because Elizabeth seemed to have changed, and she missed her old sister very much. Now it seemed that all was well and their family was united and whole again. Jan was so emotional that she wanted to share this moment with her husband, so she asked Elizabeth if she could ring her father at the office. When Paul first heard Jan's voice on the telephone, he was slightly anxious too, but once he learnt that it was in fact a positive outcome with Elizabeth, he was so delighted that he said that he would try and finish work early and come home earlier. He was not just a successful businessman but he was a good husband and a wonderful father too, and his family meant the world to him. The news kept him in very good spirits for the entire morning and for the very first time in his working career he was tempted to play truant and to go straight home to be with his family, but it would not be in his character to do something like that, as he had never taken a sick day in his life. Nevertheless, he thought that this was different; it concerned his daughter, so of course this was more important than anything else that was current. Moreover, being the boss of one's own company should have its perks and he could unquestionably leave any time he wanted, especially if he needed to, but then he would have to cancel a couple of meetings and reschedule a client in the afternoon. It was also their busy time of the year with getting their accounts in order and completing clients' tax returns for submission before the deadline – especially with Jan being away too, so he talked himself out of it. He also decided that it was not such a good idea, and certainly not good customer practice to cancel clients at the last minute, unless it was a dire emergency. In the end, he decided that much as he wanted to be home with his family now, he would just have to work a normal day and see his family when he finished that evening.

When Paul came home, the family took a vote and decided to have a Chinese takeaway for dinner as they had not had this for a while. There was a posh Chinese restaurant on the high street which served very good Chinese cuisine, and also did a takeaway service. Elizabeth and her family always ate at the restaurant and enjoyed their meals there, although they had never ordered takeaways from it before. However, the weather was dreadful all day and it was still raining so a takeaway seemed the more attractive option. They ordered their usual BBQ spareribs and prawn crackers for their starters, fillet beef Cantonese style, roast duck, lemon chicken and some stir fried vegetables to go with their Singapore fried noodles and special fried rice. The food tasted just as good as when they ate at the restaurant, and they were all hungry anyway, but they also seemed to enjoy it more, possibly because of their current happier circumstances. The conversation at dinner was casual and relaxed, even when Paul asked Elizabeth about her contact with the Centre. She did not seem to mind repeating what she had told her mother earlier and she was calm and objective throughout, so her father commented, "This is very positive, and I can tell that you're happier about it too". Elizabeth replied, "I am, dad," and she was also more settled and seemed to be confidently coping, because she knew that she could always call the Centre again if she had further difficulties or panic attacks. It seemed to have given her an edge so now all was good. She was actually looking forward to seeing Anne again too, because she was very keen for her help, and with advice about telling her best friend and coping at school. She was also planning to see Lucy, so she would do both if she could. She still had some queries and she also wanted more information about her treatment since she was too overwhelmed to take in or remember everything at her last consultation. She rang the Centre again and was fortunate to get an appointment with Lucy on the same day as her appointment with Anne.

Lying in bed that night, Elizabeth thought of a lot of questions, questions that she wanted answers to, but answers that she might not want to hear, and so she was still afraid to ask them. Still, she needed to know, yet these questions never even crossed her mind before she was diagnosed. But of course, that was the point. Now that she had MRKH, she did not have the luxury of taking anything for granted anymore. She wondered, "do I look normal down below if I don't have a vagina?" and, "would anyone know that I am abnormal if they just looked at my down below?" Then she continued to wonder, if she was to have sexual intercourse, what it would be like for her to do so with the opposite sex, because being a virgin anyway she did not know whether it would feel the same for her as it would for any normal woman. She also wanted to know if it would be painful for her because she did not have a normal vagina. Of course, she would have to have the treatment first before she could try, not that she was ready to do anything yet, especially when she did not even have a boyfriend, but she needed to know this for sure first. Most of all, she was anxious to know if the man would notice the difference. She was mortified at the prospect, because if he did she told herself that she would rather not be sexually active than to risk being humiliated. It was not really the act of sexual intercourse itself that she was thinking of and in fact, this did not even cross her mind, but it was all to do with proving her sense of normality. Just then she thought, "Maybe I can ask mummy, but then what's the point, she probably wouldn't know anyway. How would she know? She's normal and she's not like me. No, she definitely won't know". So she decided reluctantly that "it's probably best to leave it for now and I'll ask Lucy when I next see her," although given the choice, she would have preferred to know the answers right there and then. Even so, Elizabeth actually surprised herself because she remained considerably calm and did not get riled up or have a panic attack this time. In a way, she was slowly beginning to admit that everything was different for her and now she learnt that there was no point getting all agitated again. Of course, she was far from accepting her condition as yet but for now she accepted that the professionals would help her to get there. She turned the lights off, pulled her duvet over her and this time she went out like a light.

Countdown To Christmas

The countdown to Christmas was on as planned, because Jan had organised everything knowing that she would be very busy on Christmas Eve with her parents coming down, and lots of food preparation to do for their Christmas dinner. She told her daughters, "Come on girls, I have a lot to do today. We have to pick up all those cakes and mince pies". She also found that she needed a few other things, so they went to the patisserie and the local woman first, and on the way back they nipped into the local shop to get last minute bits and pieces. Their timing could not be better because when they got back, the farmer arrived to deliver their turkey and the rest of their meat as planned, so Jan stored them in the refrigerator first until she was ready to cook them on the eve and Christmas Day. Then, looking at all the meats, Elizabeth asked her mother, "Mum, there's so much meat, what are we having on Christmas day?" Jan replied, "I know there's a lot of meat but there's a lot of us eating too and we also have to eat on Boxing Day. We're going to have the turkey, goose and beef Wellington on Christmas Day and then we can have the roast lamb and ham on Boxing Day," to which Elizabeth said, "Sounds yummy. You're such a great cook mum. I can't wait".

"Thanks darling. Would you like to watch or help me with the preparation, because I need to prepare the ham first?" Jan asked Elizabeth, so she said, "Yeah sure", as she was not doing anything else anyway. The leg of ham was rather big, and Jan knew that it required more preparation time, so she wanted to do this in advance. "Once prepared and cooked, the ham will keep for a few days," she informed Elizabeth. Elizabeth watched her mother soak the ham in cold water because Jan explained that "we need to soak it for several hours to get rid of the excessive salt, especially as the ham is dry-cured". After several hours of soaking the ham, Jan drained the water from it and boiled it with some leeks, onions and black peppercorns for flavor, before bringing her ham to simmering point. Then she wrapped it in foil, before baking it in her pre-heated oven for another four hours. When the ham was cooked, she took it out of the oven and removed the skin leaving only the fat on the ham, which she scored with a sharp knife, giving it a diamond pattern, and inserted a clove into each of the diamond. Elizabeth was impressed and said, "Wow, it smells so good already, and the pattern is great, mum. You're so artistic, now I can see where Ems gets it from". Her mother smiled and continued to tell her that she would serve it hot first on the day and any leftover ham could be eaten cold afterwards, so she left it to cool on a rack before wrapping it in foil again and refrigerating it. Now, all she had to do on Boxing Day was to spread some mustard and also drizzle some honey over the fat and bake it in the oven again to make the crust golden and glazed, and it would be perfect to eat.

When Jan finished cooking the ham, she asked Elizabeth, "Darling, can I ask you to sort out the guest room for your grandparents because they'll be arriving tomorrow? You'll need to put fresh bed linen on, and make the bed up for them, and put some clean towels in the bathroom for them too". Elizabeth said "Okay, I'll go and do it now," so her mother said "thanks, darling". Whilst she was doing that, Jan asked Emma to help her to lay the table for their Christmas dinner because she felt that they might be pushed for time tomorrow, since she would be too busy cooking and preparing their Christmas dinner. They used a red table cloth and green linen napkins, which Emma folded artistically and then inserted into silver napkin rings for this special occasion. Jan could see that Emma was going to do as good a job as she did with the Christmas tree so, after instructing her on how and where the crockery and cutlery should be placed, she asked, "can I leave you to finish off here, darling?" Emma very excitedly and quickly said "sure thing mum". Jan then left her youngest to it, having entrusted her with the job of laying the table. Emma was only too pleased because she just loved doing things like that, so next she set their white bone china plates for each place setting, and placed the napkins on top of each plate. She continued with the setting of glasses and silver cutlery for everyone, and then placed a Christmas cracker on the side of each place setting to give it that festive effect. For her finishing touch, she placed two red candles at both ends of the table. But the table still looked unfinished. Then she remembered that she had some holly and a few things in her arts and craft bag, so she went back to her room and she found what she felt would complete her setting. She scattered a few white rose petals and holly leaves around the table. The Christmas dinner table looked magnificent! When Jan came in to check on Emma, she was again amazed at how creative her fourteen-year-old daughter was, and was beyond pleased that Emma had transformed an ordinary dinner table into something so spectacular. When Elizabeth saw the table, she was impressed too and said, "Wow, fantastic job, Ems. You are so clever, so artistic," so Emma, who was beaming from ear to ear, said, "thanks El," because she was just so happy to have her big sister's praise as well.

Elizabeth had returned to her room shortly after dinner because she planned to get up early so that she could have a quiet word with her mother on how and when to tell her grandparents about her problem, and she wanted the plan to be fresh in her head. She tried to sleep but she just could not relax, and laid awake thinking about her plan practically all night, and only fell asleep in the early hours of the morning. When she heard the doorbell ring, she said, "Oh no they're here" and shot out of her bed and got dressed quickly. Emma also woke up. Their grandparents had arrived sooner than expected, because they had started their journey early in case the traffic was bad, but instead it was a pleasant drive down and they sailed through. After the usual hugs, kisses and greetings, they settled down for coffee and sandwiches, as it was mid-morning. Jan then told them, "We're going to have lasagne for our lunch because I didn't think that anyone would want a roast, as we'll be having that the next couple of days. I'll make a nice salad to go with it, so I hope it's alright with everyone". Everybody was more than happy with the idea.

The Christmas tree, with all the presents under it, made the room feel really Christmassy! Elizabeth had sneaked into the living room in the middle of the night as she was still awake to put her presents under the tree, only to find that her parents and Emma had beaten her to it. Her grandparents added theirs to the array of presents already there and their grandmother also commented, "Oh my, what a beautiful tree!" Knowing how artistic her second granddaughter was, she asked, "Did you have anything to do with it Emma?" Emma nodded and smiled broadly and her mother told them that it was all Emma's work.

They sat chatting in the living room for a while and they were all excited to be spending Christmas together again because they had not seen each other for a while, although Jan spoke to her parents on the telephone every day. They spent the whole afternoon chit-chatting and catching up with what each other had been doing. Naturally, the grandparents were more interested to know how the girls were doing and what they had been up to, which was what Elizabeth had been anticipating and dreading. Emma started telling her grandparents about her friends and what she did in her school and said, "I love my school and my friends and we do different things everyday but I enjoy doing creative art and drama the most". Her mother stole a glance at Elizabeth and knew that it would be her turn next. She could tell that Elizabeth was starting to get agitated, so she very subtly averted the situation by keeping the vein of the conversation on her youngest daughter, and again praised her artistic talent with the Christmas tree. "You should come and have a look at what Emma's done to our dining table," she said, at which they got up to take a look. Then Jan asked Emma to help her grandparents with their luggage to the guest room whilst she put the lasagne into the oven and told Elizabeth to help her with the Christmas dinner preparation in the kitchen. It was a good excuse, but in truth she really did have quite a lot to do. She had to prepare the turkey, goose and beef Wellington and to make the brandy and rum sauces for the Christmas cake and pudding, and the stuffing for the turkey.

When they were alone in the kitchen, Elizabeth said, "Thanks mummy, for rescuing me back there with grandma and granddad. You were so subtle. I don't think they noticed anything. What should we do now?" As they worked together they agreed on a plan, which made Elizabeth less anxious and uneasy. Afterwards, she also thought her mother was so clever and she was so grateful to her that she was in full admiration, and wished so much to be just like her. She thought that her mother seemed to be able to do everything right, and was always good at everything she did. She was good at her job, she was a good wife and homemaker and a great cook but, above all, she was the best mother in the world. Elizabeth was learning a lot from her mother. Now she was even learning how to cook and to make different types of stuffing, like the traditional breadcrumb and herb stuffing, and her favourite pork, sage and onion stuffing and cranberry, bacon and walnut stuffing. Jan had everything that she needed out because she was organised like that, and made everything look so simple. Elizabeth could see that, in this way, she was very much like her mother. She was very organised too and recognised this trait in herself, at least until of late. Lately, she had been distracted and self-absorbed but she had every cause to be, after all, she just found out that she had this unusual abnormal condition. It was a huge shock for her and it turned her world upside-down. Just as she was going to start re-enacting her experience of the past few months, she quickly stopped herself going down that introspective route, because she did not want to go there again. She was so tired of it, because it had messed her up so much, but she decided that she was better now. "Don't fall back into the slump," she chided herself. Elizabeth had drifted away into her own world for the last fifteen minutes and did not hear her mother asking her to bring the brandy and rum from the drinks cabinet for the sauces that she was making. All she heard her mother say was "a penny for your thoughts, darling," to which she replied, "Sorry mummy," patting her head with her hand as if to bring herself back from her own world.

When she finished making her sauces, Jan took her cake out from the pantry to check it, as she had been doing the past few weeks. The cake was fruity and still moist but she doused it again with more brandy. "One last time for good measure," she thought, smiling to herself as she fed it. Her timing was just perfect because it was lunchtime, and her lasagne was also cooked and ready to eat. She quickly rustled up a big bowl of salad to go with her pasta dish, which consisted of iceberg lettuce, rocket, tomatoes, carrots, peppers, avocados and goats cheese, tossed with a mixture of salad dressings. They ate in the dining room, which was an extension of the kitchen, so as not to disturb Emma's nicely laid Christmas table. During lunch, of course, the inevitable happened. Elizabeth's grandmother insisted, "Elizabeth, come and sit with me and your granddad because we've not had a chance to talk to you yet. You can tell us what you've been doing since you got back from school". Elizabeth was always their favourite if they had to admit, maybe because she was the first born, so she was special. They also loved and adored Emma because she was such a delightful child, but it was just a different relationship they had with her than they had with Elizabeth. Of course, they were always mindful not to make this obvious, so this time, so as not to exclude Emma, their grandmother very delicately pointed out that they had already chatted to her earlier so now they wanted to catch up with Elizabeth.

She started by commenting on how pretty her first granddaughter had turned out and teased her about boyfriends. Elizabeth gave a bashful smile and told her grandmother that "I'm too young to have a boyfriend, grandma," to which her grandmother said, "Of course, that's very sensible, darling. You are still young – only sixteen. You should just enjoy yourself because you'll have plenty of time for that later". She then asked Elizabeth how she was getting on at boarding school, and about her friends. She also asked about her studies, so Elizabeth told her grandmother that she was enjoying school and also a little bit about Sally and her other friends. She was very modest about her grades and said that she did ok for her examinations but Jan, being a proud mother interjected and told them, "She's so modest, she didn't just do ok, she scored all straight As again". Before she knew it, Elizabeth was being kissed and hugged by her grandparents with both of them saying, "Well done darling, we're so proud of you". They also suggested that she deserved a break from her studies and encouraged her to enjoy herself during this holiday season, so they asked her what she had been doing since she returned. Elizabeth and her mother had agreed that they would not mention or discuss her problem unless she was comfortable telling her grandparents herself, which Jan knew her daughter was not. She had seen how worked up Elizabeth had become earlier and she knew that she was not ready to talk about it to anyone else outside of their immediate family, irrespective of how close she was to her grandparents, so she actually advised Elizabeth not to mention anything about her condition for now. She also told her to take her time with this – as long as she needed – because Jan acknowledged that it was only recently that Elizabeth was able to confide in her and Paul. Nevertheless, she also knew how honest and truthful Elizabeth always was, so she tried to convince her that this was different and that it was not like lying. "This is a very private matter concerning a very private part of you so it is yours to keep or to share as you wish, and nothing would be expected of you, darling," Jan explained and she reiterated that not sharing her condition now was not wrong, especially as it was such a delicate and intimate matter. Then Jan could see that Elizabeth was still unsure and needed more convincing so she told her that it was perfectly acceptable for some private matters to remain private, just like the private lives of couples, where no one would expect them to reveal their private activities, out of respect for their privacy. Elizabeth thought that her mother made sense. She repeated, "This is my private concern and it is my prerogative not to say anything if I choose not to, so I shouldn't feel bad about it," and she also tried convincing herself that "It's not as if I am lying to them, I'm not".

In the end, Elizabeth agreed that she would not tell her grandparents, as she felt that it would definitely be worse if it spoilt Christmas for everyone, especially when it served no purpose except to upset everyone at this time of year when it should be a joyous occasion. She always loved Christmas and was looking forward to it, so she was adamant that she and her family would have a lovely and peaceful Christmas together. She really felt that everyone should enjoy this Christmas. They deserved it, especially Emma and her parents, who had been nothing but supportive, putting up with her erratic moods all these weeks. She took a couple of deep breaths like her mother advised and in non-specific terms told her grandparents that "I haven't done much really. I've been out shopping with mummy and Ems and the rest of the time I've just been sorting things out and trying to chill out". This was as close to the truth as she could get without giving anything away, and she immediately gave her mother a quick surreptitious glance. Her mother in turn gave her an approving nod. She could not believe how easy that was. Her grandparents were only too pleased that she was taking a break from her studies and they did not push her for more details. In fact, they just encouraged her to 'chill out' more and to enjoy herself during this holiday.

After lunch, Jan thought that her parents must be tired after their early rise and drive down so she said, "Why don't you and dad have a rest now because you must both be tired. I still have a lot to do in the kitchen so I'll just get on with the food preparation". Her mother offered to help but Jan said, "No mum, you go and rest. Elizabeth will help me because she is interested in cooking anyway and this will be a good learning experience for her". The two girls helped their mother to clear the table, and afterwards Emma went back to arranging the Christmas cards that their friends and relatives had sent them. Elizabeth was with her mother in the kitchen, this time learning how to cook beef Wellington. This was Jan's own recipe which was an adaptation from several different chefs. She wanted to prepare it in advance so all that would be left to do tomorrow would be to bake it in the oven. She cleaned the beef fillet, seasoned it with some sea salt and fresh black pepper and pan-fried it quickly in olive oil. When it was lightly cooked she left it to drain and to cool, and then she spread mustard all over it. She then proceeded to make the mushroom duxelles. She sautéed some chopped red onions, garlic and herbs in butter and then added her mushrooms which she had minced and seasoned lightly with salt, black pepper and red wine earlier, and finally she added fresh cream to the mixture until it became a creamy paste. Then she rolled out a few sheets of Parma ham and spread the mushroom paste over it, before wrapping it around the beef fillet. Finally, she rolled out the puff pastry that she bought and wrapped the beef in it and brushed egg yolk around the edges to seal it. She covered this in foil and kept it in the refrigerator until she was ready to bake it tomorrow. Elizabeth might not have appreciated the amount of work involved in making beef Wellington before but having just watched her mother make it from start to finish she soon appreciated the work that went into making the dish. She told her mother afterwards "I can't believe there's so much work involved. Thanks for doing all these for us, mummy". She was so grateful to her mother for her efforts in planning and cooking special meals for the whole family over this yuletide season and trying to make it an enjoyable Christmas for everyone, that it made her more resolute to not ruin the festive ambience for everyone. She told herself to control her emotions or else she knew full well what the consequences would be. So, just for this short period, she reminded herself to focus on the positives and to stop digressing and dwelling on her private thoughts and to try to enjoy the festive spirit instead.

Paul finished work early and arrived home to the sound of fun and laughter coming from the dining room. His family was enjoying their afternoon tea of mince pies, Yule log cake and cappuccino Pavlova, whilst listening to grand-dad's stories and jokes. Everyone was happy and laughing. It was a wonderful sight to behold, and one that Paul wanted to cherish forever, because it was what he had missed with his family ever since Elizabeth's diagnosis. He had always got on well with his in-laws, and was particularly fond of Jan's father. He respected him not only because he was a formidable businessman but he was also a true gentleman who was always kind and generous. He was a decent human being and a good role model. They also shared the same interests in fine dining, wines and golf, so they had much in common, but right now, Paul was just so grateful that he brought the laughter and joy back into his family. He very much wanted to express his gratitude to his father-in-law, but he had to hold back lest he spilt the beans or aroused any suspicions that there was something going on with his family. He could not do this to Elizabeth, so after the usual exchange of greetings with everyone Paul pulled out a chair and sat down next to him. In the end, it did not matter because his family was whole again and they chatted and laughed all afternoon. They also had a game of charades, which had them all in stitches. They had not had so much fun in a long time and it was wonderful. After dinner, all everyone could do was to laze around in front of the television because they had eaten too much and their sides ached from all that laughter.

Yuletide Jolly

It was Christmas Day! The adults were awake early so Jan gave them a continental breakfast of croissants, homemade bread and rolls that she bought from the patisserie. The two girls joined them later in the morning and when breakfast was finished, it was time to open their presents. Emma was all childlike as she excitedly picked out the presents from under the tree and distributed them respectively. "These are for you, grandma and these are yours granddad and mum, dad, these are for you and El, these are yours and the rest are mine!" When everyone had their presents in front of them, they opened them together. Of course, everyone loved their presents from each other. Elizabeth had an iPad and books from her parents whilst Emma got an iPod and some arts and craft stuff, and their grandparents gave each of them swatch watches and silver bracelets so they were very happy. Emma was thrilled with her presents saying, "Oh I love my presents" and she went round kissing and thanking everyone, but Elizabeth showed less enthusiasm because suddenly her mind was somewhere else again. She wished she was not like this. She so wished that she was less self-absorbed but she could not help it, this thing was always on her mind and she could not focus on anything else, even though she had been trying very hard to not think about it. She knew she only had one wish for a Christmas present and it was "Just to be a normal girl again. That's all I want, all I need. I don't need lots of presents I just need one present, one wish". What a shame, if only it was that simple, she sighed. She was aware that she was turning into a dull person because she seemed to have lost her zest for life and could find no pleasure in anything, but then nothing else seemed to matter to her anymore. It was also depressing her as she felt her life was becoming meaningless and everything in her life was just very tiresome. She wondered when she would return to her old self again and longed for it to be sooner.

Jan went to the kitchen and proceeded to prepare their Christmas dinner. Her mother offered to help again so she followed her daughter into the kitchen. Jan had put the turkey on a slow roast first thing in the morning so she checked it again and basted the skin with more butter, garlic and herbs and left it to slow cook again. When it was cooked, she kept it covered in foil and left it to stand in the oven. She had also started cooking her honey-roast goose in the other oven and it would also be ready in time for their Christmas dinner. Her mother asked, "What can I do to help?" so Jan said, "You can do the roast potatoes and all the vegetables that're to go with our roasts. That'll help me," and put her mother in charge of these so that she could continue with finishing roasting her beef Wellington and making the Yorkshire pudding and gravy. She felt very relaxed and enjoyed her mother's company and help, and it reminded her of her childhood days when she used to help her mother in the kitchen, except now their roles were reversed. As she started to reminisce, she was suddenly saddened when she thought about "My poor Elizabeth. It's so sad. She'll never be able to have this experience because she can't have any children". Her eyes started to well up with tears which caught her mother's attention, so she asked Jan if anything was wrong. Jan was tempted to tell her mother but she had promised Elizabeth she wouldn't say anything so she quickly responded that "I was just remembering our happy memories when I used to help you in the kitchen and the laughs we had". Her mother praised her for the way she had turned out, and told her how much she loved her and that she was the best daughter she could ever have. She told Jan, "I'm so proud of you. Just look at you,

you're a successful career woman, a good wife and you're such a wonderful mother to your two girls. They're such lovely girls and so well turned out. They are a credit to you so you should be proud of that. You've done a brilliant job with them". Jan wished her mother had not said that and that she was a wonderful mother because it made her feel even more guilty and ashamed. She felt that if her mother knew about Elizabeth, she would not have thought that of her so Jan did not respond and just managed to give her mother a sheepish smile.

Christmas dinner was well worth waiting for. There was a lot of food, all nicely laid out on the table, and everything looked and smelt so wonderfully appetising. Paul did the honours of carving the birds, and said to the family, "Okay, everyone just dig in and help yourselves," so all of them helped themselves to the turkey and the goose and afterwards they had the beef. They took their time to savour all the food. They thoroughly enjoyed their Christmas dinner and Paul said to Jan, "You've excelled yourself again, babe" because everything tasted exquisitely delicious. Paul also kept the champagne flowing, so their glasses were never empty and even his two young daughters had some, although Emma had Buck's Fizz. They did take a short break to pull open their Christmas crackers and everyone donned their different coloured paper crowns and read the silly jokes and puzzles provided inside each cracker. They finished dinner with their traditional Christmas pudding, topped with brandy and rum sauces, but the festive spirit did not end there. The adults progressed onto drinking their fine wines and brandy with an accompaniment of a variety of snacks. Elizabeth on the other hand slumped herself into their comfortable couch. She had eaten too much and on a full stomach, the thought of taking a nap was very tempting but instead she decided to play with her new iPad. Emma was also busy downloading songs on her new iPod, so it seemed fitting then that everyone had some space to themselves to do their own thing for a change, because the family had spent most of their time together since their grandparents arrived.

Then at some point, Emma finally got bored so she asked, "Can we play our party games now please?" The family always enjoyed quizzes and board games so they played Trivial Pursuit and Who Wants to be a Millionaire. Just when they had finished playing, the telephone rang. It was Paul's brother ringing to wish them a happy Christmas. Elizabeth suddenly remembered that she had not phoned Sally as she said she would so she excused herself and went to her room to ring her friend. She kept the call short and sweet and she also let Sally do most of the talking. Elizabeth's grandparents had also eaten and drunk too much, so all they wanted to do for now was to take a nap, so they too went to their room for a rest. Emma however, was too excited with her presents so she stayed on her mobile to her best friend to tell her what presents she got and vice versa, while her parents relaxed and watched an old movie on the television. It was not until late evening when everyone gathered together again. As there was still plenty of food left over, Jan made turkey sandwiches and a fresh salad to go with their sandwiches, and afterwards they had her Christmas cake and mince pies for dessert.

Boxing Day was another day of pure indulgence. Jan cooked her roast leg of lamb and the ham she prepared earlier. She roasted more potatoes and vegetables and made fresh gravy to go with their roasts, which everyone again relished. Jan's roast was exceptionally delicious so they leisurely took their time to appreciate their meal, finishing off with the scrumptious desserts from the patisserie and more mince pies. It was wonderful, but everyone had eaten far too much again so the adults were quite happy to have a lazy-do-nothing day afterwards. Elizabeth and Emma however had more energy, being years younger, and Emma asked her mother, "Can we go shopping now, because it is the first day of the sales today?" Elizabeth said that she would go with Emma but Jan, who had been working and cooking for the last few days, was grateful for a quiet rest so the thought of joining the hordes of shoppers was definitely not appealing at all. She dropped her daughters off at their local shopping mall and arranged to pick them up later when they were done. On the way back, she stopped by the local shop to pick up some more fresh produce before heading home. The weather had been kind and it was a brisk but a dry sunny day. When she got home, she felt really refreshed so she suggested to Paul and her parents that they take a nice country walk. They must have walked for a good two hours and they thoroughly enjoyed the fresh air and exercise, but once they were back home in the warmth, some hot mulled wine and cakes was a much appreciated welcome. Paul started a log fire and played some Christmas carols on his CD player, and the four of them cosied up around the fireplace, drinking their mulled wine and eating Christmas cake and mince pies. It was all so fitting, so Christmassy and peaceful.

Elizabeth and Emma returned from the sales, excited and happy because they managed to pick up some really good bargains. "The mall was so crowded, mummy," Emma told her mother, to which Jan responded, "That's why I'm glad I didn't go, but you're both young so you'd enjoy it". Elizabeth also told her mother that in some of the shops, clothes and shoes were strewn all over the place. Despite the shop employees' continued attempts to tidy up after the shoppers, their efforts were in vain. Yet somehow the crowds did not seem to bother either Elizabeth or Emma in the slightest. Perhaps it was because they too were busy looking for bargains themselves, just like everyone else, to mind the people or the mess. On the contrary, Elizabeth had a good day out, and she enjoyed going shopping with Emma because her sister was so enthusiastic about everything, that she even forgot about her own troubles and worries. Emma was certainly a good tonic for her. This was how Elizabeth was before, just a normal teenager enjoying life. Now more than ever, she wanted to be that girl again, to be normal again just like Emma and all the girls. She never imagined that her life would change so dramatically when she turned sixteen and the thought of having to carry this heavy burden with her for the rest of her life was just unbearable. She felt it was all terribly cruel and wrong but, sad as it was, she reminded herself that it was what it was. Somehow she would have to try to forget and carry on as if nothing had happened, and just get on with her life. She really felt that she had no other choice if she was to have a chance of a normal life, whatever that was now.

Still, this holiday season had not been too bad, Elizabeth thought, trying hard to convince herself. She managed to stay composed throughout this time, with her mother's support of course. She also avoided having to air her problem quite effortlessly, so her secret was still safe. Although she knew that, realistically it was only a short-term escapism. But, it was all she could master for now. She would deal with her problem later. She only wished that she could get it out of her system, because whatever she was doing or wherever she was, it always came back to her problem and it was always there even when she was not deliberately thinking about it. She did not know why, but she knew that she needed help again, except this time she was not as desperate. In fact, she had remained rather calm throughout, probably because she knew that she had an appointment with the psychologist after this holiday break. She had come to trust the staff at the Centre. They were always kind and reassuring and she liked their honest approach, it always seemed to give her more confidence too. Now, she would wait till her grandparents went home and then she would go up to London with her mother, as arranged.

Elizabeth's grandparents left the day after Boxing Day. Jan got up early with them to give them breakfast because they wanted to leave as early as possible to try and avoid the traffic rush, in case a lot of people like them had the same idea of going home that same day. Elizabeth and Emma kissed their grandparents and said, "Bye grandma, granddad, safe journey home," and then they went straight back to bed, as they had only arisen early to say goodbye. As it so happened, the traffic was not bad at all and it only took the grandparents a couple of hours to reach home, so they rang their daughter to let her know that. Jan stayed with Paul until he went to work. She herself was only due back to work the following week. She could have gone to play tennis and afterwards socialise with her friends as she normally did at least once a week, but this time she did not want to leave her daughters at home by themselves, especially when she had already decided that she was going to spend more time with them. Family always came first with her too. After all, she could play tennis at any time but should Elizabeth need her and she was not there, she would never be able to forgive herself. Besides, she wanted to speak to Elizabeth about the last few days and she also needed to arrange and book their train tickets to London.

Jan sat reading her newspaper and when she finished, she busied herself doing the usual household chores, washing, cleaning and tidying up the guest room. It was amazing how much stuff there was to put away and rubbish to throw out after just a few days she thought, but then again they did not do much except sitting around eating, drinking, chatting and making merriment. Jan did not mind because this was what Christmas was all about every year, their family reunion with all the fuss and the hype that went with it, so theirs was really no different to any other families who celebrated Christmas. She always enjoyed their Christmases at home and having her parents around, but it was different this year. This year, she had mixed feelings. She loved having her parents around and it was good to see them again. All in all, they had a lovely family reunion, but at the same time she was feeling sad and very weary, not surprising considering what she and her family had been through. Jan had always been very close to her parents, being their only child, and she would have liked to be able to tell her mother about Elizabeth, because she needed her mother to comfort her and to tell her that it was not her fault, even though she was now a grown woman with her own family. She kept feeling terrible and sorry for Elizabeth and mimed to herself, "If only I don't feel so bad for Elizabeth," then maybe she would not blame herself this much. She wished that she did not feel so helpless and lost herself, but Elizabeth's condition was so hard to accept because she felt that it only reflected badly on her as her mother. This was increasingly getting her down so she tried her best to ignore it, because somehow she still had to keep her family together.

Just when Jan had finished her household chores and sat down to relax with a nice cup of tea, her daughters woke up, so sure enough, she got up and started again. "I'll make brunch for us, some toasts, sausages, scrambled eggs and baked beans," she told her daughters and Emma said, "Yes please, that sounds great, suddenly I'm very hungry". Whilst they were eating, Jan asked them what they would like to do for the day. But, first and foremost, she wanted to confirm the date of Elizabeth's appointment so that she could book their train tickets to London. This time, it would just be the two of them, as Paul was too busy to take more time off work, and Emma would have gone back to school after the New Year. It did not seem daunting though because they had already been to the Centre and met the staff, so they were more relaxed about going by themselves. She went ahead and booked their train tickets. When it was done, Jan asked Emma again what she would like to do and Emma asked, "Can we go ice skating? We haven't done that for a while and I'd like to go. What do you think, El?" Elizabeth replied, "Sure, why not. It'll be fun," and so they went to their local skating rink. They thoroughly enjoyed themselves. Both girls were very good at ice skating, because they had been doing it since they were little. They stopped by a McDonalds afterwards, and walked around the shopping mall for a little while too, popping into a few shops that took their fancy. Emma bought some earrings and bangles but Elizabeth was not in the mood for shopping, and besides she did not need anything. Her mind was on her appointment. She was going to ask her mother about their travel arrangements anyway, but of course her mother had asked her about it first. It was like a reminder – as if she would forget, since she had been thinking about it all over Christmas. Only now she had a strange feeling, thinking about her appointment, and started to become apprehensive and nervous. She could not explain it, since she could hardly wait for it, but now she could not wait for it to be over with. She admitted that she had changed almost overnight since she found out that she had MRKH and, much as she considered herself to be independent and capable of handling her own affairs, she was struggling with this. She was just sixteen, so maybe she was not adult enough, but nevertheless she felt compelled to grow up quicker. It was just too hard though, and she was not coping very well with it. It was also worse because her pride would not let her admit it, which then made it more difficult for her to accept. For Elizabeth, that would be regressing, so she did not like any hint of that suggestion, but at the same time she did not like to be going nowhere with her problem, so she was forced to admit that she needed professional help. Deep inside though she was doubtful about the appointment and felt that all the talking in the world was not going to change anything. It would not give her what she wanted. It would not make her whole again, which was all she wanted. She just needed to feel normal and be a normal girl.

Elizabeth was just at the beginning of her journey and she had yet to appreciate the benefits of professional counselling. Still, she had arranged her appointment, so she would try it out, because she had nothing left to lose. Besides, she did not seem to have any confidence left in her, so she was having difficulty coping with anything, especially when not only was she changed but she felt that everything around her had changed too. Now she had a different perspective on everything. Even the slightest thing seemed to affect her in the most unlikely way, innocently relating to, and bringing her back to, her problem, and she was at a loss to stop it no matter how hard she tried. Then it came to her, she knew that Anne would not be able to make her normal after all, she was no magician, but she acknowledged that she needed Anne's help to cope with all her negative and conflicting thoughts and feelings, so that she would not feel so bad about herself, and then she would at least be able to function better. She looked at her mother and sister and thought, "You've no idea how lucky you are. How I wish I was like you... if only..." then she tried to be more positive. She remembered that she was seeing Anne soon and Anne would surely help her feel less sad and bad all the time, so she started to look forward to seeing her again.

Jan rang her husband and said to join them at the restaurant after work because they decided to go for a Chinese meal since everyone had enough of English roasts. They had their usual order at their regular local restaurant and went straight home afterwards. Paul poured himself and Jan a glass of wine as he updated her on the work at the office, although they had agreed to never bring their work home with them. He made an exception this time because she had not been to the office for the past couple of weeks. Whilst he was talking to Jan, Elizabeth made herself a coffee and got Emma a can of coke from the fridge. The family sat around together for a while chatting, like they normally did. Then Jan mentioned to Paul again, in case he had forgotten because he had been so busy at work, "Elizabeth's appointment at the Centre is this Thursday," and Paul replied, "Yes, I know," because he too had been thinking about it. They had already agreed that Jan would accompany Elizabeth, so she told him that she had booked their train tickets to London. Nevertheless, Paul still needed to ensure that Elizabeth was ok with that, because he was mindful not to add any further stress to her already presumably anxious state. He asked, "El, how do you feel about going with just your mother? If you want me to go with you as well, it won't be a problem because I can always arrange to take the day off," but knowing how busy her father was, Elizabeth said, "No, it'll be fine. I can go with just mummy because we've been there before so now we should know how to get there". Jan was equally prepared in this respect and booked an earlier train to give themselves plenty of time to get to the Centre, in case there were any unexpected delays with the train service or should they get lost. In any case, Paul went through the directions and also wrote them down for them to make sure that they would not.

Learning Coping Strategies

Paul drove Emma to school first before he dropped Jan and Elizabeth off at the train station. Emma gave her big sister a hug and wished her "good luck El," so Elizabeth whispered, "Thanks Ems" in return. She did not know why she was feeling all anxious and nervous now, but she knew that she would relax once she got to the Centre. She was so looking forward to her appointment with Anne, and had built herself up for it, but now that the time had arrived, all she wanted more than ever was to get the appointment over and done with as quickly as possible. She even almost wished that she was not going. It was strange, and she could not understand why she felt so anguished and torn about this appointment again. She remained quiet throughout the journey, engrossed in her own thoughts. Jan instinctively sensed her daughter's predicament but she was mindful not to sound too prying, so she just asked Elizabeth, "Are you alright, darling?" hoping that Elizabeth would tell her what was troubling her. Instead, Elizabeth just nodded that she was, even though she clearly was not, because she did not wish to have to talk about her real feelings, at least not to her mother anyway. Her mother reluctantly accepted the fact, and continued to read the book that she had brought along with her, although she was not really concentrating because she was really worried and thinking about Elizabeth. She tried making some small talk about this and that every now and again to break the uncomfortable silence between them – not that the silence mattered to Elizabeth in the slightest, as she was oblivious to everything other than her own inner thoughts.

The train pulled into Euston station on time and all the

passengers disembarked, as this was its final destination. Since it was close to lunchtime and they still had plenty of time before her appointment, Jan said, "We're still early so we should go for a bite to eat first". Elizabeth was not hungry but she felt slightly overcome by her nervous nausea so she agreed, as she thought that this might help to relieve her sickly symptoms, so she said "Okay". They stopped by a little Italian cafe not far from the station and ordered a pasta dish and a salad each. They did not bother with dessert and finished off with a coffee and tea. Afterwards, they headed straight towards the underground station to catch the tube to the Centre. It was not a straightforward journey because there was no direct tube that would take them there, so they had to change lines a couple of times, but Jan had already made provision for this and allowed them ample time. It was not in Jan's nature to be late for anything and, especially in this case, she knew too well that it would be preferable to be extra early than late, so as not to add to her daughter's stress. As it happened, they arrived at the Centre an hour early, but it was worth it because Jan could see that Elizabeth had immediately relaxed as she went to check herself in at the clinic reception. She herself felt more relaxed too. She went to get a cup of tea at the little coffee shop in the foyer and told Elizabeth, when she was called in by Anne, "I'll wait here for you so come and find me here when you've finished".

Elizabeth spent an hour with Anne and when she came out, she looked a lot happier and more relaxed than when she went in, because at least now she felt that she had learnt some tips to help her cope with the issues she mentioned in her session with Anne. It made a lot of difference just learning these coping strategies as it gave her more confidence and control over certain situations. She went to look for her mother afterwards and told her, "Sorry mummy, but I'm not quite done yet because I have to see Lucy next and I think that I'll be another hour," so her mother said, "That's alright darling. You do what you have to. I'll just wait here until you're done. Don't worry about me. I have my book so you go on ahead with Lucy". When Anne finished, she contacted Lucy, but Lucy was still busy with another patient just then and was running slightly late. Anne informed Elizabeth about it, so Elizabeth said, "That's ok. I'm here now so I'm happy to wait for her because I don't think that I can make another trip up again". She went out to the foyer and told her mother about the delay, so Jan decided to wait with Elizabeth until Lucy was ready to see her. Whilst waiting, Elizabeth became more talkative and voluntarily told her mother why she wanted to see Lucy. She told her mother, "I just need to get some more details about the treatment because I can't remember everything they told me the last time," which was understandable since she'd had information overload, and was also overwhelmed by some of the information, and did not absorb everything she was told. She added, "I think that I also want to confirm a date for my treatment". She did not have to wait long before she saw the familiar face of Lucy as she walked into the clinic. "Hello, El, Mrs. Appleton. I'm really sorry you've had to wait. I was a bit busy just now". Lucy apologised to them and Elizabeth said, "That's ok". After that, Elizabeth went with Lucy into another room and Jan took her cue to get herself another drink from the coffee shop.

Elizabeth asked Lucy all the questions she needed to ask about the treatment, and after half an hour of explanation and discussion, it was agreed that she would start her treatment during the coming summer holidays as it would otherwise be difficult for her to make several trips up to London whilst in school as this would interfere with her studies. Elizabeth was keen to not let anything disrupt her studies, not if she was to get the grades she needed for entry into medical school. It was always her goal and what she had been working towards all along – of this she was still firm especially having been informed that the treatment required a lot of commitment and time. Elizabeth then asked, "How long does it take for the women you've treated to complete their treatment?" Lucy said, "It varies. The treatment usually takes a few months to complete but on average I'd say, anything from three to six months". Elizabeth asked, "But why does it vary so much?"

"Well, it depends on how frequently they did their treatments because ideally these should be done three times a day," said Lucy. "Some women found it difficult to continue with this regime and often they could only manage their treatments twice daily, so this obviously slowed down their progress and therefore their completion, and that is why we have some women finishing quicker than others. Of course, it is not just this because it also depends on how stretchy your vaginal skin is, so the more elastic your skin, the faster your progress and your completion and for the women whose skin is tighter, they tend to take slightly longer to achieve their vaginal length. Whatever the case may be, I assure that this treatment works but as I've told you, it does take a lot of time and commitment so you need to be ready to do the treatment".

"Oh I'm ready. I've been waiting for this for a long time, so I really want to do the treatment and I want to complete it too. I have to, I want to be normal," Elizabeth said with conviction. Lucy was rather impressed with Elizabeth's determination but she also wanted to explain her slightly distorted sense of normality so she said, "El, you are normal. I acknowledge that you have a genetic malformation but that does not make you an abnormal person".

"I am abnormal! How can I be a girl, a female when I don't have a womb and I don't have a vagina? That's why I need this treatment so that I can make myself normal otherwise I'm just a freak," Elizabeth retorted. "El, I think you are being very harsh on yourself. You are already a female because you have 46XX chromosomes, which means you are a female, do you remember us telling you this?" Lucy tried to explain to her. Then Elizabeth said rather tearfully,

"But I don't feel normal".

"I do understand what you are saying El," said Lucy, "because we associate the womb and vagina as being part of a woman, a female, and they are, but you have ovaries and they produce your female hormones and that's why you are a girl, a female. You have breasts, and your female body shape and your external genitalia or 'down below', these are all characteristics of a female too. I understand that it is a big deal to you not having a womb or a vagina but that doesn't make you a freak or turn you into a man. You were born slightly different but I want you to remember too that apart from not having these that you are every bit a female, you are still a girl so I don't want you to call yourself a freak. You are not, you are a girl and a beautiful one at that too," Lucy assured her. Elizabeth stopped crying and said, "Thank you for being so nice to me. I'll try, but I still want to have a vagina". Lucy told her, "You will, and I'm here to help you to create it".

Elizabeth thanked her again and afterwards, she happily set a date for her treatment. Then Lucy told her as she handed her the paperwork, "Here's all the written instructions about your admission, and the unit where you are going to be admitted. Now I understand that it is not till the summer so should you need to speak to me again about anything, please don't hesitate to call me. You have my number so you can call any time and if I am not in my office, please leave me a message and I will get back to you when I can". Elizabeth replied, "Thank you. That's nice to know and I will ring you if I think of anything else".

"Yes, please do" Lucy told her again. Elizabeth was grateful for it as it also reassured her more. When she finished her appointment, Elizabeth went out to look for her mother at the coffee shop.

Now Elizabeth felt that she was back on track and she also felt that she could cope. Everything seemed clearer and she was in control again. She was pleased that she had a long talk with Lucy because she was so kind and sincere that she felt less like a fr... Elizabeth stopped herself in time as she remembered what Lucy just told her. Then she thought about her session with Anne and it seemed that talking with Anne had also helped her to mentally organise herself, so now she felt even more confident that she would be able to cope. She did not even find the prospect of telling Sally daunting now as she had rehearsed in her head how she would tell her best friend. It also helped her to cope knowing that she had the support of the staff, especially when they never made her feel uncomfortable or abnormal. They always treated her like a normal person, which boosted her morale and self-confidence so she would feel better about herself after talking to them. She appreciated that these people had a special way of helping her and they were exceptionally professional and empathetic, but not condescending nor judgemental, and although she did not wish to be selfish, she secretly wished she could take them home with her, because then she would know what to do whenever she felt angst and she would always have their help ready at hand. Elizabeth also felt that they managed to help her to overcome her distorted perception of herself and to accept her condition for what it was. Most of all, she still could not believe how they genuinely treated her as a normal person and told her that she was a beautiful girl. She really wished she had their mindset because they were so sincere that everytime after she talked to Anne or Lucy, she could accept her condition better. Now having seen the both of them, Elizabeth could feel that the heavy burden she was still carrying had been slightly lifted. She also did not feel so isolated and alone or abnormal anymore, just different from everyone else. Somehow, this was more acceptable, especially when she started to compare herself again with other people with conditions that were worse than her own. It was sad that she had to make this comparison just to make her feel better about herself but it was also her way of coping. She tried to convince herself that she was not a fr..., and that her condition was not a taboo. As she understood it, she was simply born different. It sounded better, so she kept repeating it to herself and as she did, it did make her feel slightly less ashamed of herself too. After all, she knew she could not do anything to change her genetics so it was something that she would have to live with. She was trying to learn to come to terms with it and to get on with her life because she could not bear living in limbo all the time, not knowing what would trigger her off or when her next outburst would be. She could see now that acceptance was the key to her wellbeing again, but it was easier said than done.

Still, she would try harder because she was getting very tired of feeling lonely, depressed and becoming an introvert. She missed her old self, that confident and happy outgoing person. She thought about her friends and the great times they had and about her school, she loved being at boarding school. "School", the word resounded in her head. She was back in school next week. Suddenly, she had a mad rush of urgency to feel normal, to be normal. She needed to be normal when she went back to school so that no one would notice any change in her. She must not give her friends any cause to suspect that there was anything wrong with her. This was her greatest fear, for her friends to find out and for her to have to tell them about her problem. She could never look them in the eye again if they found out, and she was convinced that they would also not treat her the same way if they knew. Their friendship and everything would be ruined and she was not going to let that happen. It made her more resolute and focused on being her normal self. In any case, she had just about accepted that although different, she was normal and told herself that she was already feeling better about herself. Furthermore, she was reassured that she was not going to turn into a man, something she was afraid of. The staff at the Centre had confirmed that she was indeed a girl because her blood chromosomes test proved that she was a female. The specialist and Lucy also told her that she had functional ovaries that produced her female hormones so she developed her breasts, her vulva and body hair normally when she reached puberty so "Yes, I am definitely a girl," Elizabeth repeated to herself. She kept repeating everything that she was told, to try to make herself believe it more, and she tried to ingrain into her mind that Lucy had also reassured her that her gender would not change just because she did not have a womb. She was smart enough to understand this so she wished that she would stop doubting herself and carry on with her life as she did before, with confidence. "Come on El… you can do this" she tried to spur herself to be positive and to look forward from then on. Besides, she knew that she just had to, she was due back at school and she would be seeing all her friends and her schoolmates, so of course she would have to behave normally. She told herself that she was normal. After a while, she felt quite good and having just convinced herself, she felt that she would be alright and that she could cope.

Elizabeth did not know how long her feel good feeling would last this time and was aware she might still have her 'moments', having been informed that this was normal and part of her healing and recovery process, so she wanted to make the best of her enlightened state. She said to her mother, "I fancy doing some shopping. Do you think that we have time to go shopping or just walk around London before we go home?"

"Of course we can. We have plenty of time, because our train is not till later this evening anyway," her mother informed her. Jan was only too pleased that Elizabeth had suggested shopping and seeing her daughter so happy she had to hold back her tears, because she would have given anything to see Elizabeth happy and back to her old self. In truth, she too was desperate for things to change and to improve for Elizabeth because she could not bear to see her daughter go on suffering. It also reflected her own mental state and the guilt she was carrying and despite what the experts or anyone had said, she still could not stop feeling guilty for making Elizabeth the way she was. She was only thankful that there was someone out there who could help them and more importantly, whom Elizabeth liked and trusted. She was so grateful to the staff at the Centre for helping Elizabeth that she must have secretly thanked them a hundred times.

They made their way to Oxford Circus and when they got there, Elizabeth immersed herself in some serious shopping. She was enjoying herself and because of the mood she was in, she managed to buy something from every shop that they went into. She bought a couple of jumpers and a pair of jeans from Top Shop and a jacket from GAP. Later, she saw a stunning Donna Karan black dress, which she thought she could wear at her next end of term party, but deliberated because "It's too pricey". Her mother also liked the dress and thought that it was the perfect dress for Elizabeth, so she said, "Nonsense, I think it'll look really good on you. You should try it on anyway and don't worry about the price. It'll be my treat," and so she encouraged Elizabeth to try it on. Elizabeth came out of the fitting room looking sensational as if the dress was made especially for her, so of course Jan could not resist buying it for her because she looked so beautiful in it. She also bought her daughter a pair of black leather stiletto shoes to go with her dress. Jan was only too happy to do something that made Elizabeth smile for a change and what was more she felt that Elizabeth deserved this after what she had been through. Elizabeth was just ecstatic and started kissing her mother and kept thanking her – "Thank you, thank you so much, mummy. I'm so happy!" Afterwards they proceeded to another one of her usual trendy shops but this time, she bought t-shirts and leggings for Emma and Sally. Soon it was time for them to head back to the train station and having spent most of her allowance by now, Elizabeth was more than ready to go home. They had to take the underground tube to the train station again. This time it was jammed packed with people as it was the rush hour, so luckily they only had a few stops in between before they reached their destination. When they arrived at Euston station, they stopped at a cafe situated inside the station and bought some sandwiches and coffee to go.

The train was already sitting in wait on the platform so they boarded it straight away. It was also fully packed being that time of the day and it was fortunate that Jan had booked them seats. They were both exhausted, it had been a long day as they were up since very early that morning, so Elizabeth slept all the way home whilst Jan read her book and dozed off periodically. Jan had pre-arranged with Paul to pick them up from the station so when they arrived, he and Emma were already there waiting for them. In the car, Elizabeth updated her father on her appointment with Anne and Lucy without any hesitation or difficulty, and she ended with, "You know dad, I'm so happy I saw Anne and Lucy. I had a really nice talk with them" which, demonstrated a significant improvement in her mental state. It was so obvious that her parents noticed immediately and, for that brief second, they smiled and gently nodded to one another in deep appreciation. Elizabeth then asked Emma "how was your first day back at school Ems?" Emma started to tell her sister and soon they were chatting happily together. Elizabeth also told Emma about her shopping spree and gave her the t-shirt and leggings that she bought for her, so Emma was delighted and thanked her big sister. On the way home, they passed a Thai restaurant that had newly opened on the high street so they decided to try it, as it would be a change from their usual Chinese. They had never eaten Thai food before so it was different. The dishes were well presented and they were very tasty although they were spicier but everyone still enjoyed the meal.

Disclosure To Best Friends

Elizabeth spent a quiet weekend at home, doing her final packing and getting herself organised ready for school. She was looking forward to going back to boarding school and seeing her friends again. She was initially going to take the coach to school by herself but with an extra bag of presents and her own belongings, her parents decided that they would take her instead. They could not bear to see her lugging three pieces of luggage all by herself and they also wanted to ensure she was properly settled in. They saw her to her room and then left but not before reminding her, "Don't forget to phone home and let us know how you are getting on or if you need anything, darling," so Elizabeth said "I will and thanks for bringing me here". Her father also gave her some pocket money in case she needed ready cash to buy odds and ends from the school shop whilst settling in although he had already paid in her usual fees and allowance directly into her bank account.

Elizabeth was in the middle of unpacking when there was a gentle knock on her door. It was Sally. She popped her head inside as the door was ajar and said, "Hi there". When Elizabeth saw Sally, she motioned her to enter and promptly dropped what she was doing to go over to give her a big hug. Then, uncontrollably, she was overcome by her emotions and the tears started to roll down her cheeks. She fought hard but she just could not hold them back, which surprised Sally because although they had not seen one another for a while, Elizabeth had never done this before, so her display of emotions was totally unexpected and over the top, to say the least. Sally immediately sensed that there must be more to this unusual behaviour of Elizabeth's and became very concerned, but she was mindful not to further upset her friend, so she just asked, "Are you alright El? What's wrong?" There was no response from Elizabeth, and instead she seemed to be hesitating. She could not really explain her hesitation and what she was waiting for. After all, she had been planning and rehearsing this scenario for so long. This was her best opportunity to tell her best friend but now that the moment had arrived, she had forgotten everything. She began to admit that perhaps she was not really as well as she thought she was, because she noticed that this was a regular occurrence, this uncertainty and the lack of self-confidence each time she had to talk about her problem. She also started to question if she would ever recover and be herself again because she seemed to have lost all her self-confidence and self-belief all over again. She would have continued to drift further into her private thoughts had Sally not interrupted her by calling out her name "El, what's wrong? Talk to me please, you're really scaring me now".

Elizabeth very quickly shrugged off her introspection and tried to focus but she could not find the words to say to Sally. Instead she just shook her head and went to sit down on her bed. Sally followed suit but by now she was truly worried about Elizabeth because she had never seen her friend this distressed before. She refused to think the worst and prayed that it was something simple that she could help to rectify. She sat down on the bed next to Elizabeth and kept asking her what was wrong and urging her to "Tell me what's the matter El. This is not like you". After a few more minutes of repeated probing by her best friend, it suddenly dawned on Elizabeth that of course she did not need a plan. This was her best friend and confidante. Face to face now, Elizabeth soon realised and everything became clear and her fears vanished. It seemed only natural to be talking to her best friend so she relaxed and told Sally "I have terrible news to tell you about myself. I have this thing called MRKH..." Soon she told Sally everything. Initially, Sally was so shocked that she was speechless. She had never even heard or come across anyone with this condition before. "Oh you poor thing, you must have been so scared and so alone. Why didn't you tell me sooner?" Sally felt devastated for her friend and she could only imagine what the enormity of its impact, this would have had on her friend. She also thought that everything started to make sense now and no wonder Elizabeth did not want to really talk to her on the phone and was making up all kinds of excuses. It also made her realise how difficult it must have been for Elizabeth to even tell her now. She was therefore mindful not to worsen the situation by saying something inappropriate as she knew that Elizabeth was really waiting for her reaction. Sally also thought that the last thing Elizabeth would want was her pity because she would have hated it herself and in any case, her condition was not the end of the world although admittedly, it was very unusual. Sally knew that Elizabeth was very much like her, so she knew that if she was to help and support Elizabeth, she had to be frank and honest with her and behave as normally as they always had done with each other. She was intent on helping her best friend through this ordeal by being there for her and making sure that she had the right focus. They hugged each other for a good few seconds and they had a cry together but no words were needed just then.

After a few minutes, Sally was the first to speak, "El, it will be ok. I'm just sorry that you couldn't tell me earlier. I understand though. You must have been so frightened and confused but you don't have to do this on your own, I'm here for you. That's what best friends are for right?" Elizabeth nodded and replied, "Thank you, Sal. I knew you would understand and I'm really sorry I didn't tell you before but I was so embarrassed and so confused".

"Don't be sorry, I understand. Anyway, I'm glad I know now so we'll do this together ok?" Sally said, as she tried to further support her friend so Elizabeth thanked her again.

The disclosure of Elizabeth's deeply guarded secret soon left Sally with an appetite to learn more about her friend's medical condition, once she recovered from the initial shock. She wanted to know everything about it so she asked Elizabeth, "Have you got anything that I can read?" Elizabeth told her "Just these, but there's more on google," as she handed Sally all the information leaflets that she was given by the specialists. It was some reading and it left Sally flabbergasted. Afterwards, she admitted that she was as shocked as Elizabeth probably was when she found out, but nevertheless she tried to pick out the positive aspects. Sally always had a discerning quality, but even so she knew that she had to cautiously choose her words this time, so as to not trivialise Elizabeth's feelings, because she was made very aware that her friend was now more unusually sensitive to things that they usually took for granted before this happened, and especially after Elizabeth told her how she currently felt about pregnant women and children. Sally herself would happily not have periods because she suffered from abdominal pains and cramps every month and had to take regular painkillers. Her periods were also heavy and her mother had taken her to see her doctor. She also googled and found out that she might run a risk of getting a condition called endometriosis, which have caused cysts on the ovaries and infertility in some women. She also found out that some of them had to take the oral contraceptive pill to control their symptoms by stopping their monthly periods altogether and some even had to have operations including hysterectomies. She wanted to share this information with Elizabeth and to say "who wants periods anyway" but was afraid of sounding insincere and insensitive because despite her problem with her periods, she still had a choice whilst her best friend did not. She knew that Elizabeth was aware of her unpleasant experiences with her monthly cramps and period pain, as they had also spoken about her periods pre-viously. Back then, she had told Elizabeth how lucky she was that she was a late starter, as previously informed by her GP. They also joked about the money Elizabeth was saving every month so she could spend it on nice things like clothes and shoes whilst she was just flushing hers down the toilet. Now, she would not even contemplate using the word 'lucky' to describe Elizabeth. In fact, if she was really honest, she thought that what was happening with Elizabeth was terrible and her monthly suffering was nothing in comparison because, despite it all, she had a womb and would always have the choice of having her own children but her best friend's hope was just taken away from her. Sally also knew how much this meant to Elizabeth because she loved children and had always wanted a family of her own, so she really felt terrible for Elizabeth. She vowed never to complain about her period pain again but more importantly now, she felt that she had to find something that would encourage and help Elizabeth more.

Sally continued to look earnestly for the positives so that she could convince Elizabeth that her condition was not so bad but the more she tried, the harder it proved. Elizabeth had become hypersensitive and her perception of everything had changed, so Sally was afraid that Elizabeth might take whatever she said in the wrong context and the fact that they knew each other so well did not help. For the first time, Sally found it very difficult to say anything to her best friend. She could not find the right words or say the right things without the risk of offending her or coming across as being callous or indifferent. Yet, this was her best friend sitting next to her, facing her and looking to her for comfort and help. Sally desperately wanted to comfort Elizabeth but right now she did not know how to. This thing was too profound and so different from anything she had experienced and, besides, she had only learnt about it a few minutes ago, so her head was still spinning and she herself was also just sixteen. Then without saying anything, Sally reached out and held Elizabeth's hands and as she did that, it came to her. She knew that if she said nothing, it would make Elizabeth feel worse because she would perceive it as confirmation that her best friend also thought the worse of her problem. In the end, she decided best to tell Elizabeth how she really felt. "El, I'm not going to pretend to know what to say that will make you feel better. It sounds like an awful condition, what with the treatment and all especially the children part of it but you are still the same El that I know. You are still my best friend and that will never change and no one will ever know anything different. The treatment sounds horrible and scary but it will make you ok and I promise that I will go with you when you start your treatment so we can be frightened together. The children part, I'll definitely carry your child for you. This way, we will be related, like real sisters. That's so cool! Don't you think, El?" Sally surprised herself because she did not know where all that spiel came from but nonetheless she was pleased that she got it out of her chest. It also lifted the brief tension and atmosphere between them, and Elizabeth replied, "Yeah I think it'd be cool too. Thanks, Sal. You're the best. At least you were honest and you didn't pity me as if I was a freak or a lost cause. You always know how to make things better. I'm so lucky to have you as my best friend. Best friends forever, yeah?" Sally nodded as she fervently echoed Elizabeth's words, "Best friends forever" and then, simultaneously, they high-fived each other.

They were so engrossed all morning that they did not realise the time and missed their lunch. The school cafeteria had closed by the time they noticed, but fortunately they managed to buy a couple of sandwiches from the little tuck shop and brought them back to eat in Elizabeth's room. Then Sally helped Elizabeth to unpack the rest of her things and they came across her belated Christmas present so Elizabeth gave it to her with her apologies again for it being late. Sally was very pleased with her unusual silver twisted bracelet and earring set so she said, "Thanks, I love them especially the bracelet," which Elizabeth had known she would appreciate. When they finished unpacking her things, Sally asked her if she had decided when to do her treatment so Elizabeth told her that she had arranged to start during the summer holidays. She admitted, "I'm not looking forward to it though because I'm really frightened that it will be painful but most of all, the thought of having to stick something inside myself is just so repulsive. I feel sick just thinking about it. Ugh, it's so gross!" Then she tried to explain to Sally what the dilators looked like and described them as huge long rods, which were so huge that it made her hair stand on end simply thinking about them. She also told Sally that they came in different sizes and the largest was so big that she nearly died when she was first shown it because she could not imagine any man having such a big penis. Sally was equally as horrified as her friend and she was wide-eyed and her mouth gaped wide open too so she quickly put her hand over her mouth to cover it. It would have been endearing to have such innocence and childlike qualities, but right now these did not help them. They were both as inexperienced as each other with regards to sexual activity, being virgins themselves, so Sally, very childlike, said, "El, you know what you have to do, you'll just have to choose a boyfriend with the smallest dick" and "We'll have to ogle our boyfriends' private parts the next time we meet up with them so we can check this out". It sounded so funny that they could not stop giggling afterwards. When they stopped laughing, it got Sally thinking more. She was getting equally curious to know so she asked rhetorically, "I wonder what sex is like?" although up until now, she had no reason to think anything of it, but now she was very keen to know. She said that she would ask her mother what it was like and whether it was painful so that they would at least have something to gauge it by. Then she soon talked herself out of it because she was afraid that her mother might get the wrong idea and think that she was going to engage in sex, so they decided it was best for Elizabeth to ask Lucy instead.

They spent the whole afternoon talking about Elizabeth's problem. Most of the time they were serious but at times they also managed to laugh at some things. It was because they both felt very comfortable and natural with each other and Sally was always very easy to talk to. This was exactly what Elizabeth needed. It also made her realise how much she actually needed to have Sally's understanding and acceptance because she felt that if she did not, then no one else would understand or accept her. Elizabeth thought that Sally was amazing because she did not make a big issue of it, nor did she belittle her emotions and instead managed to bring a little humour into her world of desolation, something which she never thought was possible again. Now and in what seemed like a very long time, Elizabeth felt a little more like her old self again. She was actually talking about her condition to Sally without any inhibitions and for the first time, she did not feel ashamed or embarrassed anymore. She could not believe that she was even laughing about it instead of just crying alone, because Sally made it possible. She was also able to share her feelings and innermost thoughts with her best friend instead of keeping it to herself until sometimes she thought that her head was going to explode. If only she had known that this was the outcome and had not been so frightened to tell Sally, she would have done it sooner. In any case, she was both relieved and glad that she did because she felt this huge weight being lifted off her chest again, because now that Sally knew everything about her she did not have to keep up this uncomfortable pretence with her anymore. She could be normal around Sally again and furthermore knowing that her best friend was around to help her now if she needed support, made Elizabeth feel less isolated and lonely too.

When they became aware of the time again, Elizabeth felt

guilty and said most apologetically, "Gosh, look at the time! I'm so sorry we've done nothing except talk about me all day. I never even asked about you. How are you, Sal?"

"No worries, I'm fine. I don't have a problem or at least nothing in comparison, so yours was more important and we needed to talk about it. Anyway, what concerns you, concerns me too. I'm so glad that you're ok now," Sally replied. "Yes, thanks to you. You're really the best, Sal," said Elizabeth most appreciatively. "It's cool. El, I keep telling you, that's what best friends are for and you know what they say about a problem shared. But enough already, I'm starving! Shall we go and eat now?"

"Yup, let's go. My treat ok, I owe you big time," replied Elizabeth as she quickly stood up and walked over to get her purse. Sally did not want Elizabeth to feel indebted to her because she was only doing what any good friend would do. She was only too glad to be able to help her best friend, but she was too hungry to argue so she just said, "You don't have to but ok, whatever. Let's just go and e..a..t".

On the way down to the cafeteria, Sally pointed out her room to Elizabeth. It was at the end of the same corridor on the second floor. They also met a few of their friends who were going to the cafeteria too so all of them went off together. After dinner, Elizabeth invited a few of them back to her room because she wanted to give them the Christmas presents she had bought for them. When everyone left, Elizabeth rang her parents to tell them about the day she had with Sally and added that they need not worry about her because she was now doing ok. Needless to say, her parents were relieved beyond words because their little girl sounded like she was back to her normal self again, thanks to Sally no doubt, so they felt more reassured that Sally would always be there to help and support Elizabeth. They also felt very gratified that Elizabeth had such a good friend in Sally.

School reopened on Monday and everyone received their sixth form curriculum and the class roster. Sally was the head girl – not surprising because she was not only brainy and sensible but she also had a kind and pleasant personality, so she was very popular with the other students and the teachers. When she was elected as the head girl, the headmistress and teachers were convinced that Sally was the right choice since to them, Sally was their ideal model student. Elizabeth was one of the prefects so, as usual, they had their extra responsibilities towards the school and fellow students, but they did not mind. In fact, they took their roles seriously but in their stride because they had been doing it for a while so nothing seemed to faze them. It was also part of their character building and they rather enjoyed it, and accepted this added responsibility as part of their extra curriculum, although sometimes it was quite hard work. Still none of that seemed to have affected their studies, as these two girls had both proven.

Elizabeth managed to get through the whole term without having to disclose her problem to anyone else and she had been so busy with her studies and school work that she just carried on with her school life as usual. There was nothing happening at school either to trigger off her panic attacks, so she soon forgot her problem. When she spoke to her parents on the phone, the subject never cropped up either and even when she was alone with Sally, they never spoke of it again. Sally also did not want to be the one to initiate it because she knew that if Elizabeth wanted to talk about it then she would. Besides, she saw Elizabeth every day and she knew her so well that she would recognise the signs if her friend was not feeling well again. Moreover, being the head girl, she was also very busy herself preparing speeches, organising different school events and attending meetings with the school board and school committee. Meanwhile, Elizabeth along with some of the other prefects were helping Sally to organise their end of term quiz event with the neighbouring schools, so they were both too busy to delve into each other's individual zones. Elizabeth was also in the quiz team and, as such, she barely had time to herself, what with her studies and lots of meetings and revising for the quiz with her teammates, so there was not much time left to think about herself and, even in bed, she was too shattered for anything else other than to sleep the minute her head hit the pillow, except for the night before the quiz. That night, she just could not sleep because she was worried. She had forgotten about her problem since school started until now.

Suddenly, she felt this sense of urgency, this anxiety building inside her because she would no doubt have to see Tom at the quiz tomorrow. She also knew that she could get emotional again very easily, and she was not very good at pretending either. She started to get worried because she was sure that Tom would start asking her questions, questions that she could not and did not want to answer and then he would definitely get suspicious. "Oh no, what should I do?" she asked herself. She did not know what best to do and almost started to panic again. Then she decided, "I'll ring the Centre first thing in the morning," because she felt sure that they would know what to do. She thought "They deal with girls like me all the time so they can tell me what to do best". She seemed to calm down once she made this decision so she set her alarm on her mobile before she fell asleep.

When she rang the Centre, she managed to speak to Lucy. She told her about Tom, this boy that she liked and whom she felt also fancied her. She asked for advice as to whether she should tell him and what to tell him. She was expecting Lucy to tell her what to do but instead she was disappointed because she was told that it had to be her own decision because only she would know her situation and relationship as to whether she felt right about telling him. Nevertheless, Lucy did give her some pointers to think about before she made her decision. In truth, Elizabeth knew that no one could tell her what to do best in this situation but she was just hoping that Lucy would make that decision for her anyway. Still, she was glad that she called the Centre because now she could focus on the advice she was given instead of getting into her usual panic and anxiety attack. She remained positively calm as she thought about the advice she was given and began to conscientiously run these thoughts through her mind. Lucy had advised her to think about her reason for wanting to tell him and to also weigh her reasons for telling Tom or not to tell him very carefully. She thought that she need not tell Tom anything at all, but because she was not the same Elizabeth anymore, she just knew that she would feel awkward around him if she kept it from him and, in the end, she would feel worse for it. It was bad enough when she had to speak to him on the phone. She also thought about why it was so important for her to tell Tom and then she remembered Sally telling her, "It might actually help you to cope better if he knew otherwise you'll always be wondering and I know what you are like and I know you won't be able to cope. You'll always be feeling awkward or even worse what if you were to have a panic attack when we're out with our group then everyone will want to know what's wrong with you".

Elizabeth was already panicking to think of that possibility and she knew that Sally was right. She should tell Tom if he was that important to her. She was forced to think deeper about her relationship with him. She knew that it was platonic but she knew that she liked him very much, and had also secretly hoped that he might wait for her until she was ready to commit. The trouble was, even though she thought he quite fancied her, she was not sure how much he really liked her so she was terrified in case she had imagined his feelings for her and, even if his feelings were mutual, she was not sure if she could trust him enough to stand by her and accept her for what she was after she revealed her secret to him. After all, she was not a normal girl anymore and, from earlier conversations with him, she knew that he wanted children of his own, as he was an only child and missed not having siblings and a big family. She thought that he would probably walk away and think of it as a lucky escape because they had not committed to a steady relationship yet. She reassured herself that she would be ok if he did that, as long as he promised to keep her secret. She felt that although it would be painful, the latter was more important to her because she would be mortified not only if her secret was out but she always prided herself as a good judge of character, so she needed to believe that she was right to trust Tom in the first place. Then again as Lucy and Sally had told her that if he meant that much to her for her to want to tell him, at least she would be sure he liked her for the right reasons. Elizabeth was really in a quandary as to what to do best so she told herself "I wish I knew what to do, if only I knew the answer". There were so many questions running through her head, so many questions with no concrete answers because there was no right or wrong. She wished it was as simple as the quiz later on, where the answers were either right or wrong.

Quiz And More...

It was the day of the quiz! There were three schools participating including Elizabeth's school so the teams took their places as instructed. After the usual formalities, the quiz started and continued until the team with the lowest score was eliminated then the two remaining teams competed for the coveted trophy, which had been previously won and kept by Elizabeth's school, so it was important for her team to retain the trophy and title again this year. After a close fight with the team from the neighbouring boys' school, Elizabeth and her team won again. Afterwards, all the quiz participants, their supporters and teachers were invited to stay for tea, cakes and sandwiches. This was the opportunity for everyone to mingle and to socialise, and where Elizabeth and Sally first met some of their closest boyfriends. They met again at Elizabeth's annual summer dance and when term finished, a group of them arranged to meet up for coffee. They found that they had gotten on so well that afterwards, they met up regularly at the shopping mall and sometimes to the cinema or to go bowling whenever they could.

One of the seniors, Tom, was a tall, handsome and charismatic boy and he also had a fresh look about him. He was very attracted to Elizabeth because she was attractive as she was clever and witty and she could also be a real tease when she wanted to be. He sensed that Elizabeth liked him as well from their innocent flirtations whenever they were out with the group, but she told him that she only wanted a platonic relationship so he respected her decision although secretly, he still yearned for her to be his girlfriend and felt that she was his ideal soulmate. He decided that he would be patient and wait for her – after all she was still young, just sixteen.

He was christened Thomas McGuire although his friends called him Tom. He was from a very affluent background and he was a true gentleman quite like his father, who was the quintessential Englishman. Mr James McGuire was a successful banker, who, like his own father worked himself up the ladder and eventually inherited his family's business. Later he also expanded into the property development business and now practically owned most of the properties in town, so it was unsurprising that Tom would also follow in his father's footsteps and planned to read economics and finance at university. Sally was not left out because she too had admirers, in particular, a John Barnes who was also Tom's best friend. John was always in awe of Sally because she was a tall slim beautiful blonde with brains, contrary to what people said of blondes. She was always as articulate as she was funny, so she was fun to be with and he liked her a lot! Sally was also drawn to him but like Elizabeth, she was not ready for a steady relationship because she felt that she was too young for any emotional attachment. She wanted to enjoy her freedom and adolescence first. There was always time for all of that later, she told herself. Besides, there was no more room in her life as she was far too busy with her studies and school responsibilities and activities. To add anything else into her life now would be insanely silly and far too complicated. It would be too stressful and she would have none of that, so she told John that she liked him too but was not ready to be in a relationship with anyone and was happy just hanging out with the group as good friends. John understood because although he was attracted to Sally, he was not entirely sure that he was ready to commit himself to having a steady girlfriend either, but the idea of it just sounded great. He was going to do law at university and maybe the fact that Sally's parents were both lawyers also added to his interest, but he was not sure. The group which consisted of two more girls and two other senior boys remained the best of friends ever since and they would meet whenever there was an opportunity but they texted and emailed each other very often and continued to stay in close contact with each other.

During afternoon tea, Tom could not wait to talk to Elizabeth. He had been so looking forward to this event so that he would get to see her again. He had been thinking about her because he missed her terribly, especially when she had not been taking his phone calls when he tried ringing her. He kept looking out for her and tried to catch her on her own. Then at one point, he spotted her when she was by herself, so he swiftly walked towards her before anyone else moved in. He gave her a broad smile and was so excited at seeing her that he almost hugged her spontaneously and only stopped in time when he realised where they were, and instead settled for a handshake. Just then, Elizabeth had a strange feeling and she quickly pulled her hand away, which surprised Tom too because he really thought that she would be just as happy to see him as he was. She suddenly felt awkward, and realised what she had done so she quickly apologised and said that it was because she did not want to give anyone the wrong impression about them. It was a feeble excuse and she knew it, but she was embarrassed and felt guilty at the same time. In reality, she knew that in that split second he reminded her of her problem, so despite her earlier anticipation and preparation, she panicked. She thought that she could handle it but seeing Tom in person now made it real and she felt vulnerable because, in a strange way, he made her feel inadequate and reminded her of the one thing that she most wanted to forget. She longed to get her old life back. Then she asked herself, "What am I thinking? I already have my life back and I have been doing ok. Why am I having doubts again now?" She could not explain it. She just felt that it was too weird because as far as she was concerned, she really thought that she had been her old self and had been getting on so well with her life since she came back to school, so now she decided that no one, not even Tom was going to change that. "Who does he think he is? Why is he doing this to me?" She asked herself, getting increasing annoyed until, "I'm sorry, I can't do this" – the words spurted out as she felt her panic escalating.

She knew that she had to get away from him before he had the chance to question her more. She hastily scoured the room to see if she could see Sally because she needed her best friend now. "Do what, El?" Tom asked, clueless as to what was going on in Elizabeth's mind. He had never seen her like this before so he was troubled and confused at her unusual behaviour. Elizabeth did not stay to answer his question and uttered again "I'm sorry, Tom," as she walked briskly away, because by now she had started shaking uncontrollably. "El, stop and tell me what's wrong?" Tom said in a voice now raised in a slightly higher octave out of sheer concern, as he followed close behind her. She quickened her pace instead and did not see Sally coming towards her. She ran right smack into her, but Sally had just time to anticipate the collision so she managed to catch Elizabeth before she did any damage. Still, this caused a slight disturbance in the room, so Sally quickly added "It's ok, everyone, she just felt faint, I'm taking her outside for some fresh air but please carry on as you were". She looked up at Tom and whispered reassuringly, "Don't worry, I've got this, you go ahead in and enjoy yourself". Then looking at Tom's face, she knew that he was not going to budge so she quickly added, "She'll be fine in a few minutes. It's a girl's thing". She did not like lying either but that was the first thing that came to her mind and she hoped that this would ward off further questions from him, although as soon as she said it, she realised how ironic her lie was, especially when Elizabeth did not have periods. Tom knew that he would not be able to enjoy himself now because all he wanted was to be with Elizabeth, and he did not want to leave her in the state that she was in, especially when he now suspected that it had something to do with him, but there was nothing he could do to help anyway, Sally was with her best friend so he reluctantly gave in. "Ok, I'll leave her in your capable hands".

"Just slow down the breathing, El, you're breathing too fast. Just take some deep breaths and breathe out... slowly". She then dashed off but returned within a few seconds and said to Elizabeth, "here, breathe into this" as she handed her friend a small paper bag she obtained from the school shop by the side of the school main entrance. When Elizabeth started to calm down, Sally said, "Ok, he's gone. Tell me what happened, El?" Elizabeth just shook her head and said miserably, "I don't know. I guess I just panicked".

"Good job I found you first. You know for someone who didn't want to cause a stir, you very nearly did in there," Sally commented lightly. "I know and I am really sorry. Thanks again Sal. What would I do without you?!" was Elizabeth's rhetorical response, because she meant every word of it. They sat side by side in silence for a few minutes. Then Sally said, "Poor boy, he was really scared. He likes you a lot, you know and I know that you like him too. You saw that he wasn't going to leave you so I had to lie to get him to leave us alone, but I still think that he's going to want to know what happened. He's not stupid. Will you tell him the truth?"

"I can't. I don't know what to tell him. I do like him but I'm afraid that if I tell him everything, he would not like me anymore and worst, what if he told other people. I can't take that chance..." Before Elizabeth could finish, Sally interjected, "I don't think that he's that sort of guy. He genuinely cares about you. I don't want to force you, El but I am just saying that maybe, you need to take a chance with him. At least, this way you will know for sure if he really likes you, otherwise it's only going to get worse every time you see him, you know that, don't you?" Elizabeth did not respond because she knew that Sally was right. Just this morning, she had played the scenario in her head and was in control, so she could not understand her own her behaviour now. Deep down, she was desperate to tell Tom because he meant a lot more to her than she cared to admit, which made the embarrassment and humiliation and her fear of his rejection more frightening and it was overriding her logic and reasoning. "Come on then if you're ok now, we'd better go in or else they would be wondering where we got to. I'll just have to glue you to my side," said Sally jokingly. "You go in first, Sal. I'll be ok," said Elizabeth as she ushered Sally to go inside, but seeing the concerned look on her friend's face, she forced a smile and repeated, "I'm ok now, don't worry. I just need a few more minutes out here by myself. I'll go in when I'm ready, I promise".

"Ok, I'll see you in a bit but don't be too long or else one of the teachers might come out for you," Sally said as she made her way back to the hall.

When Sally entered the room, some of the teachers noticed her and came over to ask her what did happen with Elizabeth, so Sally told them that Elizabeth just felt faint because of "her period pain" and reassured them that she was alright now. She thought that it was best to continue with the same lie despite the fact that like her friend, she did not like lying. The teachers seemed to accept her explanation and did not probe any further. The minute they left her side, Tom did not hesitate to head towards Sally. He had been waiting anxiously for the two girls to come back in, because he could not help wondering if he really had something to do with Elizabeth's earlier outburst and if he had, he did not understand what he could have done, since she would not talk to him, and practically ran away from him, so he was very keen to find out. He had no choice but to wait patiently for them to rejoin everyone in the room. When he did not see Elizabeth, he asked Sally where she was, and if she was ok. Sally told him that Elizabeth was feeling better and would be rejoining them very shortly, deliberately avoiding volunteering any details. Tom was also trying not to appear too pushy or presumptuous so he awkwardly asked if he could see her and if there was anything that he should do, although what he really wanted to ask, which was uppermost on his mind, was if he had anything to do with Elizabeth's reaction towards him earlier. Sally sensed his attempt to be diplomatic and felt sorry for him but more importantly, she felt that he should know the truth because she truly believed that it would help Elizabeth to cope better. Still, it was not her call, because it was not her news to tell. Furthermore, she could also appreciate Elizabeth's reluctance and respected her decision and wondered what she herself would do if she was in the same predicament. She told herself that she would probably react exactly the same as her best friend since they were both practically cut from the same cloth, so there was no point giving hypothetical suggestions or advice. In the end, Sally decided that Elizabeth just needed more time to adjust and to get her confidence back. She excused herself and told Tom that she had better get back to the others.

Tom did not know what else to do, since Sally gave nothing away, but he was determined to find out so he immediately went outside to look for Elizabeth and found her sitting alone on a bench off the side of the entrance to the school. She was enjoying the fresh air and was drifting off with the tranquility of the place. At first, Tom could not see her because she was camouflaged by the various luscious landscaped plants on both sides of the entrance. He called out to her and Elizabeth nearly fell off the bench as she was unexpectedly awakened and turned too quickly to get up, but Tom was there in a flash to catch her. Just then, he wanted to hold her in his arms forever, but Elizabeth just as quickly pulled herself away before she succumbed to his comforting embrace. "Thanks, I'm fine now," she said very coyly and felt herself blushing. "What is it, El?" asked Tom. "Why are you pulling away from me, I don't understand. Have I done something to upset you or do I repulse you or something?" There was no response from Elizabeth so Tom continued with more pleading and searching questions, "El, please talk to me. I'm not sure what's going on here. You know how I feel about you and I know you have feelings for me too. I know you wanted us to be just friends so that's fine but please don't shut me out. If I have upset you, then I am sorry. Aren't we still friends? Please El, talk to me. Tell me what's wrong". Elizabeth was desperate to tell him then, but she was numb with fear and the words she rehearsed in her head just would not leave her mouth, so Tom continued, "Sally said you had period problem but I don't believe her. I think it's me because you're acting all strange with me, and you won't talk to me or take my calls. Did I upset you the last time I called you? El, I can't fix it if you won't tell me what it is I've done. Please, just tell me what's going on, El. I need to know what's happening with us".

"What us?" said Elizabeth. "We are nothing. I told you Tom, I don't want a boyfriend, I can't, so stop forcing me". The words came out so spontaneously that even she surprised herself and she felt guilty for blaming Tom for her problem just because he reminded her of it. She knew that he did not do anything wrong and he was only trying to help but the more he tried, the worse it got, because she felt worse about herself, that she was not good enough. She then went into a self-punitive stage until her mental torture became physically manifested and she was nauseous and shaking violently. Tom automatically reached out and held her tightly, "It's ok, everything will be ok, just try and calm down El. Whatever it is, we'll work it out, ok?" Tom did not have any experience dealing with anything like this before yet right then, it seemed so natural for him to be holding her and stroking her hair until she finally stopped shaking. "That's very good". Then he could not help himself as he whispered in her ear, "I love you, El". At first, Elizabeth did not react, she was feeling slightly drowsy and exhausted after her anxiety attack and felt comfortable and relaxed, leaning close against his strong shoulders and body, so Tom repeated, "Did you hear me, El? I said I love you. I love you so much..." She quickly tore away from him as the words resounded in her head, and she said "No you don't. You think you do but you don't," but Tom interrupted and said "Of course, I do. I've loved you from the moment I met you. You're so beautiful! I can't stop thinking about you and I want to be with you all the time". Elizabeth kept shaking her head, adamant that she was anything but beautiful, and that he could not possibly love her and she was no longer that same person. Tom was equally defiant that he loved her, so he asked her "What do you mean you've changed. Do you love me, El, or is there someone else?" She denied that there was anyone else and told him that she liked him a lot and that she was the problem and not him. She tried very hard to avoid his probing questions and avoided telling him about her condition, but eventually she just screamed out "I'm a freak, ok?!" It took Tom by complete surprise because he never expected this and it was another few seconds before his brain registered what he had just heard and he asked, "What do you mean El? Why would you say something so horrible like that? I don't understand". It was all too late for Elizabeth to retract her sudden outburst, so she told him that she would only tell him if he promised to keep it to himself and to not breathe a word to their friends, not even to a single soul.

It all sounded so mysteriously ominous. Judging by the intensity and seriousness in Elizabeth's voice, Tom suddenly felt a real sense of dread and he began to appreciate the enormity of what she was about to tell him. He tried not to show it though, because he could see that she was petrified, so instead he tried his best to appear calm. Then in a quiet reassuring manner, he said, "Okay, I promise". Even so, Elizabeth made him promise several times before she mastered the courage to tell him, "I have MRKH". She stopped, which prompted Tom to enquire more —"English please, El". Then, rather amazingly, her nerves left her and she continued, "I have this thing. It's a genetic condition. I am not a real girl". Tom immediately asked, "What do you mean you're not a real girl?" Elizabeth said, "I'm not normal. I don't have a womb so I can't have children. I know you love children but I can't give you any so you see, you say you love me but you can't love someone like me". Shock! Horror! Silence! What do you say to something like that, Tom was indeed momentarily shocked. Still, he quickly forced himself to say something, because he felt for her and thought that it must have taken her a lot of courage for her to tell him. "Phew! That's a real shocker, El. I didn't expect that". Elizabeth tried her best to put on a brave face as she told him "I know and I don't blame you if you walk away now but please you can't tell anyone, you promised…" Tom stopped her short as he grabbed and held her tight and told her that he loved her even more. "You don't get rid of me that easily, El. I'm not going anywhere. This doesn't change a thing. You are still the same person that I love. I am glad that you trusted me enough to tell me, because at least now I understand why you were trying to avoid me. I know that you have feelings for me too otherwise you wouldn't be acting this way. Don't you see, it makes me love you even more".

"Really?" she asked in surprise because she felt so terrible about herself that she dared not expect anything from him, other than for him to keep her secret, but now he was professing his love for her even more. She had never been in love before so she was not sure if her feelings for him were love or gratitude, but she knew that she was attracted to him and had always liked him very much and it was different from what she felt for the other boys in their group. She thought that he was right, maybe she did love him too otherwise why would it be so important for her to have his acceptance. Then all of a sudden, she felt guilty and pulled away from him. "It's not fair on you. You want kids and being the only son, you've always wanted a family of your own. You said so yourself". But Tom was unwavering. "I don't care. If I can't have you, then I don't want any kids with someone else. Besides, we're both young and when the time comes, we can always adopt. It's not a big deal. Stop being so selfless, you're always putting other people first. What do you want, El?"

"I want... I want to be normal! I just want everything back to normal. I want to be normal like everyone else..." Her voice trailed off as she started to get emotional again. Ever since her diagnosis, she dared not wish for anything other than to be back to being normal, although she knew that it was just futile to wish for something that was never going to happen. She had MRKH and that was that. The trouble was that she still could not accept it and she could not stop wishing...

Of course, she also wanted children, the same as Tom, but she could not tell him that because what was the point. She could never have what she wanted now. It was useless wishing for the impossible. She could not envisage a future with Tom or with anyone since she had nothing to offer. She was convinced that if he knew everything about her, he would certainly turn tail and run this time. She had not told him everything and if not for his relentless questioning, she would not have said anything at all but she did so she decided that she might as well tell him everything now. She said, "There's more. I haven't finished telling you everything". Then she hesitated momentarily because she did not know how to tell him what she was about to say, but a voice in her head told her to just say it as it was. She knew she had to tell him now so eventually she said "I really am not a normal person. I told you I don't have a womb, but I don't have a vagina either. I have nothing! I can't have sex, and I can't have children. There, you see, you don't want someone like me, Tom. I told you I'm a freak!" This was another shocker! Tom did not think that it was conceivable for a girl to not have a vagina and especially Elizabeth because she looked so normal, so beautiful, you just could not make this up. He was so flabbergasted that this time it took him a few more minutes to recover. This made Elizabeth feel so ashamed that she buried her face in her hands and regretted telling him. If only she did not feel so much, she would not have been so stupid as to be misguided by her emotions. How could she be so stupid as to secretly hope that he was different, that he would still like her and accept her when she could not accept herself or what her condition had made her become. She felt so ashamed and embarrassed that she wished she could dig a big hole there and then and bury herself in it, because she would never be able to look at him again. She had destroyed whatever friendship they had. She even thought of running away. She did not care where to, just somewhere, anywhere, where no one would know her or knew anything about her but she could not bear causing more pain to her parents and Emma. That would be so selfish and unfair. She knew that it would break their hearts and destroy them such that they might never recover and after all they had done for her, she could never do this to them. Then she wished again that this was all a horrible nightmare and that she would wake up soon to find everything back to normal.

Alas, everything was real. After a while, Elizabeth chided herself to pull herself together because she had gotten herself into this mess and now she had to get herself out of it. So, with a brave face, she said to Tom, "I told you I'm a freak so you can go away now. I won't blame you, but you promised so please, you have to keep your promise. You can't tell anyone". She was begging him to keep her secret. Then she saw how upset he really was so she said, "I'm sorry, Tom, I'm so sorry". She started to cry, but more for him because she actually felt his pain and his disappointment. "No don't even apologise, El, I'm the one who should be sorry. It was difficult for you to tell me because you were afraid of how I'd react and look at what I did. I'm so sorry but it was just a shock you know. I'm fine now and nothing's changed. To me, you're still the same El that I love, only now you are special and you are so brave and so beautiful. I will always love you. I'll never give up on you. I'll never give up on us". Elizabeth could not believe what she just heard. He was too good to be true, he must be a saint. Her heart skipped a beat, so she asked, "How can you still love someone like me? I've just told you that I have nothing," but Tom replied "I just do. I've always loved you and I always will". This gave Elizabeth the courage to tell him more, so she told him, "I can have treatment to make me normal. I'm going to have the treatment to make my own vagina". She continued to tell him a bit more about the treatment and that she was not looking forward to it, but it would make her normal again so she was prepared to do it. Tom listened intently, because all this was so foreign to him that he had to make sure he heard every word. In the end, Elizabeth told him everything. She was relieved that she did because now that he knew everything about her she could relax around him instead of trying to pull away or avoid him, or having to go on with the agonising pretence anymore, especially when he still accepted her for what she was. She knew she could not go on wishing and pretending with him because she already saw how badly it had turned out earlier.

Sally was right and she was also right about him, she was right to trust him. Elizabeth was now crying and laughing at the same time and then without a second thought, she hugged Tom and kissed him. Of course, she felt all embarrassed afterwards, although Tom rather liked it. She quickly looked around her in case anyone saw them because she was reminded of where she was and how long she had been outside. She quickly changed the subject and told him that they had better go inside before they sent a search party for them. Tom took her hand and noticed that she was wearing the bracelet he had given her. They had been out with their usual gang at the shopping mall one day and Elizabeth mentioned how much she liked the bracelet but that she would have to save up to buy it so Tom secretly went back to the shop afterwards to get it and gave it to her for her sixteenth birthday. He smiled and asked, "Are we fine now?" so she nodded and replied decisively, "Yes, we are more than fine, Tom. Thank you, thank you. I'll call you tonight and we'll talk more then, ok?"

"Sure thing, I can't wait," Tom said, and he meant every word because he would have preferred to not let her go and wished that they did not have to go inside at all. Elizabeth said that she would go in by herself first because she did not want any rumours to start circulating, especially when the headmistress and the teachers were also in the vicinity.

Sally had been mingling with the guests and teachers and doing her job as the head girl, making sure that everyone was enjoying themselves. She was chatting to some of the student guests as Elizabeth walked in so she waved to her. She excused herself and walked over to her friend. "Are you ok? You were out there for ages. I was getting worried about you".

"I'm great Sal. You were right. I told Tom and he's fine with it. I can't believe it!" she replied excitedly so Sally said, "That's fantastic. He's a great guy, hang on to him El". Before they could say anything more, one of the teachers came over to check on Elizabeth. She told her that she had fully recovered. Within the next few minutes, her other friends spotted her too and also came over to see if she was alright. Apparently, she had given everyone such a scare but Sally reassured them that everything was under control and they were encouraged to continue normally. The afternoon soon drew to a close and at the end of the event, Sally made her usual speech, thanking all the guests, students and teachers for coming and making it an enjoyable and successful day and she also thanked her fellow organisers and helpers for their contribution and their hard work.

Elizabeth felt exceptionally energised throughout the rest of the afternoon that she could go on forever. There was a lot of tidying and clearing up to do but she did not mind and volunteered to stay back to help some of the other organisers, since she felt a little guilty for not being around earlier. All afternoon, she could not stop smiling quietly to herself while she worked, because she felt so exhilarated. She was in a world of her own again, although this time it was all good, all positive. She replayed everything that had happened between Tom and her earlier. She thought that he was amazing. He had renewed her faith in trusting other people and in their good decent human values. She could not believe how easily Tom had accepted her for who she was and to think that he even told her that she was special. She had never thought of it that way before and always felt that her condition was more of a curse because it made her feel so abnormal and different from other girls. She still could not quite fathom how he would still find her desirable after knowing what he knew about her when she was convinced that no man would ever want her once they found out about her 'thing', but he did. This improved her self-esteem and boosted her self-confidence. She felt free for the first time and she was feeling on top of the world. Tom was definitely a star. In fact, he was 'the special one', she concluded.

Tom also had time to reflect on his earlier engagement with Elizabeth. He knew that his feelings for Elizabeth were real and nothing had altered but now he admired and loved her even more. He was pleased they managed to be open with each other and the experience, though painful, was what they needed, because he found out that his love for her was not just one-sided so he was more optimistic about their relationship. He thought more about the treatment that Elizabeth mentioned and decided he would tell her not to bother if it was too horrendous, because he cared too much for her to see her go through further pain, especially when he felt that she was doing it for his benefit. It did not bother him if they could not have sex or could not have children but he cared that they would be together. That was how much he loved her.

Later that evening, when they spoke on the phone, they were more relaxed with each other. Tom told her how he felt about the treatment, and Eizabeth was moved because it proved that he really loved her. Still she had to tell him that she needed to do the treatment not for him but for herself. She desperately wanted to feel normal and to be normal at least in this respect. She needed to do the treatment, otherwise she knew that she could not move on with her life. For Elizabeth, it was never really about having sex, even though she and Sally had joked about it, but it was rather the ability to have sex like a normal female because this would then make her feel normal. She could almost accept that she was a female like the specialists had told her but she needed more. She needed to be a normal female and this was what she had been struggling with ever since she was diagnosed. She felt that if she could only make her vagina normal then she would be able to feel like one. Besides, she was now in a different situation. She was with Tom and although their relationship was still new, Elizabeth was conscious that he was young and despite his altruistic gesture, she could not deny him the very fundamental act of nature when the time came. Of course, Tom told her that he would respect and support whatever decision she made and if she still decided to go ahead with the treatment that he would accompany her if she wanted him to, so Elizabeth told him that it was all arranged. She was not going to change her mind. It was something that she had to do. She told Tom that she had already confirmed her date to start the treatment in the coming summer holidays and that her mother and Sally were going with her.

The Road To Self-Acceptance

It was the school half-term again, so Elizabeth came home for a much deserved break. She had been through a lot mentally and psychologically since she went back to school and she was forced to grow up faster than she could ever have imagined. She was exhausted, but still she survived all the pressures and stresses that she had gone through, and felt stronger for it. She was a different person again now and having somewhat accepted herself for who she was, she was more relaxed and less ashamed of herself. Of course, Tom had much to do with this. His support and acceptance of her, irrespective of her condition, meant a lot to her, but despite the ways he tried to make her feel special, what she still really needed was to just feel like a normal girl. It had nothing to do with vanity but more of the intrinsic essence of being a female, so no matter how many assurances she received from the experts that she was a female, she was still troubled by her gender identity if she had to admit it. Elizabeth always needed more credible proof because this was how she was and how she perceived herself to be. Fortunately, she had Tom because he believed in her and she could feel that her perception had changed slightly especially when he told her how beautiful she was and how much he still loved her. It was like the evidence she needed, evidence that she was indeed a female irrespective and that she was still attractive and desirable to the opposite sex, and good enough to get her man. It still did not make her feel normal, but it gave her back her self-confidence and self-worth. She also began to believe that it was not altogether bad to be different after all, especially when she was special in Tom's eyes. Elizabeth tried to look for the positives of being different for a change and thought of Sally and what she had to go through every month with her heavy periods and pain. She counted herself lucky and thought, "Poor Sally, who wants periods anyway?" She did not really want to have periods, if not for the need to feel normal, nor did she want to have children now because she had her career mapped out, and especially given she was not into the teen-age-mother fad. Besides, what did she know about mother-hood when it was hard enough being an adolescent?!

Nevertheless, it pained her, because she would still have liked to have the choice to have her own children. Still she was only sixteen and she was secretly hoping that when the time came, she might be able to have a uterine transplant and carry her own child. For the time being, she settled for the options available to her, which were either adoption or IVF surrogacy. With the latter, both Emma and Sally had already offered to be her surrogate, so she was not too concerned about having to find a surrogate when the time was right. She also remembered Sally joking about being slightly envious of her because "You will get to retain your lovely figure without any stretch marks, whereas mine will look horrible and wrinkled," which surprised her, since she never thought that anyone could ever be envious of her or her condition. Now thinking about it, she could not agree more, and actually thought that it was quite cool, and was again impressed that Sally always had a way with words to make her feel better. She reminded herself that she was so lucky to have Sally as her friend too, as her best friend.

Elizabeth had changed. She had become this young lady, stronger in all ways, more mature, more secure and she was at peace with herself, at last. She had fought the demons that held her captive in her own world and she managed to win in the end. She was not afraid of her own image anymore and she no longer needed to hide away in her room. When she recalled the events of the past few months, she appre-ciated that she could not have done what she did without the love and support of her family and her closest friends and she felt very blessed that she was truly loved. The change in her was quite dramatic and it was obvious to her parents too, because her whole demeanour was different, it was definitely more positive. They also thought that their little girl appeared so grown up now and they could not be more pleased with what they were witnessing. Most of all, they were relieved that Elizabeth managed to overcome her problem beyond their expectations, and they could not be more proud of her. As her father commented, "It's amazing how she's improved by leaps and bounds". Jan added, "Yes and she's no longer a child but a beautiful, confident young lady". They were right to allow her the time and space to find herself. They believed in her, and knew that she would always come through, given time. It was lovely when she was home this time. The whole family was able to relax and be a normal family again without having to worry about Elizabeth, or try to avoid upsetting her. This time, Elizabeth was behaving like a normal adolescent, although she was probably now more mature than most of her peers, having gone through what she had. Indeed, she was very adult about everything too and did not get easily embarrassed or vexed anymore, and she even dared to ask her mother about some of the intimate adult questions which she had been too afraid or embarrassed to ask. One day, she asked her mother, "Mum, do you and dad still have sex?" although what she really wanted to know was what sex was like and whether sex would be painful, but she did not ask her mother because she always felt that her mother would not know since she was normal and not like her, and that only Lucy would be able to tell her that.

Elizabeth spent most of her short break at home with her family, although she spoke to Tom every day. She also met up with Sally and her group of friends at the shopping mall a couple of times and attended one of the senior boys' eighteenth birthday, and was looking forward to Tom's in the summer. He was just over a year and a half older than her and was in his final year at his school. He had already secured a place at a university in London pending his final results so they would not be able to see each other except during the breaks and holidays, but of course they would continue to ring and text each other every day. Elizabeth found herself in a steady relationship, albeit unplanned, but she was comfortable with the idea because it was clear that both she and Tom had strong feelings for one another, so what happened between them might have been inevitable anyway. She was also probably ready to have a partner now and rather liked the idea of having him as her boyfriend. Tom on the other hand, had always wanted her as his girlfriend and was prepared to wait for her, so although the progress of their relationship was unexpectedly escalated and happened a lot sooner then he could have hoped for, he was very happy with the outcome. However, he would still have preferred that it was not under such circumstances, because he felt that it was slightly unfair to Elizabeth, since she was forced into a situation where she had to admit her real feelings for him, but then again if this had not happened, it might have taken her a much longer time to admit that she did love him as well. Furthermore, having gone through the experience of the past week, their true feelings were revealed and their relationship was well tested, so he was confident that they were meant to be together and that their relationship would now last forever.

The next few months passed quickly because Elizabeth was busy with her examinations and school activities, and then it was the summer holidays again. She had forgotten about her problem ever since the day of the quiz but she was soon reminded when she had to go up to London to see Anne again. Sally went with her this time, because Jan had her own doctor's appointment which she was unable to cancel. Elizabeth assured her mother that she knew how to get there anyway, and besides she had her best friend with her. Elizabeth had agreed that it was a good idea to see Anne before her treatment to discuss her progress and any issues she might still have. At first, Elizabeth found it hard to open up, especially when she had to talk about herself again. She always had difficulty at the start of each session and it was strange because she trusted Anne and felt safe with her, and always felt better after their session, but sadly Elizabeth felt that "it was *déjà vu* all over again". In reality, she knew that it had nothing to do with Anne, but the mere fact that she had to keep going to the Centre repeatedly, which meant that she was constantly reminded of her abnormality, when she would sooner just forget about it and just get on with her life. It was a vicious circle because, sadly, she could not just get on with her life like everyone else, not without help anyway so she had to make the trips up to London. They were important and Elizabeth knew this. Besides, she had to agree to counselling and it was also her decision to have counselling, because she admitted that she still needed Anne's help so she did not really resent having therapy. But, she just wished that she did not have these feelings whenever she had to go up to London to see her. It was the same every time when she made the trip up, she would feel nauseous and she could not stop the flutters in her stomach. Of course, Anne being an expert psychologist, understood Elizabeth's psychological state perfectly so in each session she managed to relax Elizabeth before she got her to open up, but she had yet to enable Elizabeth to admit and overcome her fears and denial, because whenever she tried to help Elizabeth address this particular issue of hers they would reach an impasse, every time. You see, it did not matter that it was very evident to Anne why Elizabeth was still having difficulty and going round in circles, because until Elizabeth herself could see and accept it too, she would still have this same problem. This was why she was unable to really move on. In fact, this was the very essence of her ongoing therapy and it was Anne's role to help Elizabeth to get past this phase.

Acceptance is often a painful process and it is also something that cannot be rushed or forced, especially with a disorder like Elizabeth's, and when she was not ready to do so. She was finding it very difficult to have to admit that she had such an imperfection because it was against everything that she believed in, and especially when her MRKH had such complex inferences regarding her femininity and womanhood. So very understandably, she could not and would not accept her abnormality. She was just not ready to accept it yet, and she was still fighting and struggling with herself and her concept of the person she now was because of her MRKH. This is why the role of an experienced psychologist is especially vital in the management of women with MRKH. Elizabeth appreciated that too, and she resigned herself to the fact that until she accepted it she would still need Anne's help. She was also optimistic that her therapy would help her to get there, because at least now she knew that she had to face up to the challenge. Anne also thought that this was a positive step forward because Elizabeth was slowly starting to appreciate the importance of her acceptance. At one point, Anne challenged and asked her, "Why do you think you still need to see me if you say that you are doing well?" Perhaps it was just denial but Elizabeth told Anne, "I really thought that I had already accepted my condition because I felt good and I was coping so well at home and in school," but in truth, "I know that I was only managing because I blocked it out of my mind, so that I don't have to think or talk about my condition, and that's how I've coped so far, so that I could function normally". Deep down, she knew that it was just superficial and she told Anne that, "I'm still so angry and I'm also embarrassed and ashamed of what I have and I really hate it". Anne reassured her that, "These are all very normal reactions," but she also asked her, "why do you think you want to block them out?" Elizabeth answered, "Because it's easier this way, otherwise I have to keep admitting that I'm no longer normal, no longer perfect and it's not who I was. I hate my MRKH and I hate myself for having it. It's so unfair and I just want everything back to what it was, to how I was". It was not until she spoke aloud about the difficulties she had in accepting all the mixed, het up emotions she still had that she was able to admit she was not there yet. She was an intelligent girl and by now she understood her condition very well but acceptance had nothing to do with her intelligence. It had more to do with her intrinsic values and feelings about who she was, and her ability and readiness to admit and to accept that she had MRKH, that it was a part of her, so that she would no longer be frightened or be resentful and angry or be ashamed of it. She also knew that only when she could accept her MRKH for what it was and who she was, could she then learn to cope, and to live with it. She also knew that this was the way forward but she told Anne, "I'm so desperate to move forward only it's just so hard".

"I understand it's not easy but I'll help you if you are willing to try and face it," said Anne. Elizabeth said, "I'll try because I really want to get better". She realised now that she could not recover, not yet, not until she comfortably achieved her self-acceptance with all her imperfections.

Elizabeth might have improved, but now she admitted that she was only at the beginning, because she had to admit that a part of her was still very much in denial which was why she was having such difficulties moving on. Somehow, it was easier to deny the hard facts because the truth went against everything she believed about herself. All this time, she had been bargaining and even wishing that she did not have this MRKH, and that if she could go back in time she would stop this from happening to her, even though she knew that no amount of wishing would change her genetic makeup, nor make it go away but at least now, she was actually doing something about it. Her therapy also made her realise that she could not do it by herself, she tried, but she was not making any progress. She had to admit that she needed professional help, so now she was prepared to work out her issues with the help of Anne, no matter how painful or long the process. She admitted too that this angst and nervousness she still had whenever she went up to London, only further highlighted her need for ongoing therapy and support.

During her therapy when she relaxed more, Elizabeth was in full flow, and managed to speak more openly about a lot of things to Anne. She also updated Anne on what had been happening in her life since they last met, about Sally and Tom. Afterwards, it was no wonder that Elizabeth felt mentally drained. It was such a release for her and she obviously needed to let it out. All in all, it was very helpful therapy and she appreciated its benefits and thought, "No brainer, much better talking to a professional," although to be fair she was also in a better place now, so she was able to open up and engage more. Talking to Anne also enabled her to actualise that telling Sally and Tom was the best thing she had done, because it freed her from the clutches of her own demon in her head, torturing her day in and day out. She now felt free to be her natural self around them without having to plan her every word and every move lest they should find out that she was this abnormal freak. She was also relieved of all that pain and shame she suffered all those lonely months, because her friends just accepted her for who she was, regardless of what she had. Their acceptance and support was a tremendous help. After all, at sixteen, it was important for her to be accepted by her peers and to have peer support and she was grateful she did with her two closest friends. She told Anne, "I can't believe how they just accepted me for who I was. I just wish that I could do the same and accept myself that easily". They did make it slightly easier for her to accept herself, so she felt more encouraged towards her road to self-acceptance and recovery. Elizabeth felt that she did very well this time, because for the first time since she was diagnosed it felt different from the other times when she thought she felt normal again. This time, it was definitely different. This time, she was not afraid to admit that she had this abnormality and that it was not going to go away. She was urged to accept that it was a real part of her, so now she was ready to learn to cope and to live with it. She was surprised that she also did not hate herself that much anymore and she also started to forgive herself for being the way she was, and this somehow made her feel more positive about herself.

When Elizabeth finished her session with Anne, she felt so good that she treated Sally to a burger meal at TGI Friday's. Besides, she felt she owed her best friend a lot. Sally was always there for her and if not for her, Elizabeth felt that she might not have come this far. She was so glad that Sally accompanied her this time. They were hoping to do some shopping and girly things together, but they did not have time for anything else, so they decided to just stay where they were and enjoy their burgers and cokes in a leisurely fashion until it was time for them to catch their train home. Elizabeth told Sally about her therapy with Anne and how it helped her, but that she still needed more help. Sally herself had never required any counselling so all this was new to her too, but she was learning. She could see that Elizabeth needed it and, what was more, it was evident that it was helping her. She was pleased that her friend was getting the right support, although she was surprised that Elizabeth had agreed to this type of therapy, because until now she, like a lot of people, had associated counselling and psychology with psychiatry and mental illness. Sally told Elizabeth, "You know El, I've always considered counselling or therapy to be a stigma and pooh-poohed it, because I thought it would be the height of embarrassment to have something like that, but seeing you today and how it's helping you, I've changed my opinion, so thank you". Elizabeth responded, "I know. I was the same too but it really works and I feel better for it. To be honest I never thought that I'd say that but then everything's different now, everything's changed for me now, so I have no choice. I have to do it if I want to get better". Sally held her hands and said, "It's ok. I understand that now too". Sally was really pleased that she came up with Elizabeth because she was definitely beginning to have a better understanding of Elizabeth's condition, and she also appreciated that this experience had given her an insight into the hospital workings and environment too, which would benefit her when she was to start medical school.

The two best friends had been chatting and laughing non-stop, so when they boarded the train, it was rather nice to have a rest and some peace and quiet. Sally suddenly felt exhausted as she sat down on her seat by the window and rested her head against it. She remembered that she had been up since 7.30 am, which was the time she would normally get up for school anyway, but because she was not doing anything except sitting around, she was unusually more tired, so she said, "El, I'm so tired, I'm going to crash". Elizabeth nodded and replied "Okay". With Sally asleep, Elizabeth had more time to reflect on her own. She smiled when she thought how far she had come and right now, she felt very comfortable with herself and, as long as she did not start torturing herself with negative introspection again, she knew that she was heading in the right direction. At least now she was able to refer to it as 'MRKH' instead of calling it 'this thing' and she no longer hated herself too much for it. Nevertheless, she reminded herself that this was just the start of where she needed to be. Furthermore, she had yet to start her dilator treatment. This was another big issue and she was very concerned and nervous about it. She was dreading it, to be honest, but she knew that she still had to go through with it because she needed to do the treatment. She wanted, no, *needed*, to be normal so she must do this treatment. She knew that this was the only way for her to be normal, to feel normal. She wished that she could be more accepting of herself, just as her friends had been, but at least now she was trying, and she was no longer struggling on her own because she now had Anne to help her. She also realised that every time she managed to express her true feelings aloud with Anne or Lucy, it would make her feel better afterwards so she felt that it would help her to talk about her treatment with them next time because she was getting increasingly nervous about it. She decided very sensibly that she would arrange another appointment with the both of them prior to her starting her treatment.

Weekend Break In Paris

Elizabeth was back in school and the months flew by and soon it was the summer holidays again. She was determined to carry on as normally as was possible and tried not to think too much about her treatment although it was always at the back of her mind. She felt she needed a break just to chill out before doing anything else. Normally, she and her family would have gone away on holidays at this time of the year, like they did every summer, but because of her various appointments, her parents did not book anything this year. They thought it would be better to wait till Elizabeth's situation was more settled. Then Sally rang and said, "El, my dad's taking my family and me to Paris for a short weekend break next week. Would you like to join us? My parents are ok with this so if you want to come, I'd love it". Elizabeth practically jumped at the chance and agreed to go with them, but she obviously had to ask her parents first. Afterwards, Elizabeth thought that it was as if Sally could always read her mind and she felt it would do her good just to chill out with her best friend. She was very excited about Paris, not having been there before, but it was a city that she always wanted to visit. She had been on holidays overseas before, but she had only been to Europe once with her family and that was to Rome, soon after her sixteenth. It was part of her birthday present from her parents and she thoroughly enjoyed it. Jan and Paul were happy for Elizabeth to go with Sally and her family although Elizabeth had never been anywhere without them before. Still, they felt that Elizabeth deserved a break since she had worked very hard at her studies and were only too pleased that she was going to enjoy herself first before she embarked on the biggest challenge of her life. They were aware that her imminent treatment would again be life changing and were just as nervous about it as she was, although they did not dare to share this with her. They hoped that the treatment would not be too traumatic or painful for her, knowing how innocent she was in this respect. Jan was especially keen for Elizabeth to complete her treatment successfully, not just for Elizabeth's sake but for her own too. If she was honest, she was being selfish too because she secretly hoped that this would lessen the guilt she was carrying, which was why she dared not think too much about it. Of course, she wanted more than anything for Elizabeth to complete her treatment so that she would feel normal and be able to have a normal relationship, but she knew that it would also make her feel less guilty for the way Elizabeth was. In a way, Jan was suffering like her daughter because no matter how many times the doctors and the staff at the Centre had told her that it was not her fault, Jan could not help it – she was her mother and she still blamed herself for Elizabeth's condition.

Elizabeth had a fantastic time in Paris. It was as she had imagined it, simply magical. There, they were with no cares in the world, walking leisurely down the avenue of the Champs-Élysées right up to the famous Arc de Triomphe, stopping at the many various stores, gift shops and cafés on the way, whenever they fancied. They wanted to take in as much of the city sights as possible, so they went on a city bus tour, which took them to the tourist sites like the Notre Dame Cathedral and the Louvre Museum and afterwards, they proceeded to a riverboat cruise down the Seine, to get a panoramic view of the city. It was wonderful and they thoroughly enjoyed it. The next day, they made their way to the Eiffel Tower. It was a beautiful sunny day with blue skies above so Elizabeth and Sally were adamant that they would climb to the top of the tower. They managed to climb to the second platform, which was a pleasant climb but they had to take the lift to the top of the tower. When they reached the top, it was well worth it. Elizabeth had always wanted to do this, so standing at the summit platform of the Eiffel Tower with the magnificent view all around her, she felt on top of the world. The panoramic view of the city of Paris, with the Seine running through it, was just breathtaking. She felt at peace with herself and the world. It was surreal, and Elizabeth wanted to stay up there forever because there, nothing could touch her, she was free and she could leave all her troubles behind. She suddenly thought, "If only I can stay here and not return home then I won't need to face reality. I won't need to have my treatment. If only I could, it would be so good". She was really nervous and frightened of the treatment and was beginning to dread it more each day so the thought of it was starting to terrify her. Just then, Sally grabbed her hand and said, "Come on El, we'd better go down now or else my mum would start to worry about us". Elizabeth immediately shrugged off any negative thoughts. Sally's parents and brothers were waiting for them on the second floor because they had to wait for the lifts to take them there, and there was a very long queue then. By the time they reached the second platform, the lifts going to the top were full with another long queue so they decided to have some snacks at the cafe instead and afterwards they browsed through the gift shops whilst waiting for the two girls to come down. On their final night in Paris, Sally's parents treated all of them to a dinner and dance at Le Moulin Rouge which included their transfers to the cabaret and back to their hotel so they could relax and enjoy the evening. The show was fun, vibrant and entertaining and the can-can dancers were perfectly synchronised, so everyone enjoyed it very much. The whole evening was an experience that Elizabeth would never forget.

Paris was an amazing city and Elizabeth loved it. She had such a wonderful time as did Sally and her family. She could not believe that they had done and seen so much in those four days, and there was a lot more to see and do.

She promised herself that she would return some day and that she would take it at a more leisurely pace the next time. Besides, she read that it was a city of love and romance so she thought that maybe she would come back here with Tom one day.

Sally's father had left their car at the short stay car park at the airport as this was the most convenient arrangement. On the way back, he dropped Elizabeth home first before driving his family home. Elizabeth had a great holiday and she also enjoyed being with them so she could not thank them enough for including her in their family holiday. She thought that they were such kind and generous people, very much like her own family and possibly the reason she connected with Sally from the outset and always regarded her not just as her best friend but as a sister too.

Jan, Paul and Emma were waiting for Elizabeth to return, so when they heard the car in the driveway they quickly came out to welcome her home. Jan also thanked Sally's parents for taking Elizabeth with them and asked them, "Would you like to come in for a coffee or tea?" but Sally's mum said, "Thank you for the offer but I think we'll just head on home, maybe another time," and they said their goodbyes. Emma was so excited to hear about her big sister's holiday but being a child, she could not wait to see what Elizabeth had bought her. In fact, Elizabeth bought gifts for everyone. She bought Emma a t-shirt with Paris written on the front, some Parisian jewellery and a little souvenir of the Eiffel Tower. She bought a beautiful Louis Vuitton handbag for her mother and a Ralph Lauren polo shirt for her father. She also bought a bottle of red wine and a bottle of champagne for her parents from the duty free. She bought presents for everyone and she did not forget Tom. She bought him a couple of t-shirts, which she thought he would like and she'd bought herself a dress, a pair of shoes and a pair of jeans when she was browsing at the Galleries Lafayette. It was only a short holiday but Elizabeth had spent well over her budget because of the expensive presents she had bought, especially for her parents, so she was glad that she had her mother's credit card with her. Jan had insisted on giving Elizabeth her credit card because she wanted her to enjoy herself and not have to worry about money or be penny-pinching whilst she was in Paris. She also asked Elizabeth to treat Sally and her family to a nice gourmet restaurant as a thank you gesture from her and Paul, which Elizabeth did. When she was in Paris, she googled the best restaurants to go to eat and she managed to find a Michelin-starred gourmet restaurant. It was near the Champs-Élysées so it was easy to get to, but it was a 'classy' venue and everyone had to be suitably attired. Elizabeth thought that it would be nice to dress up for the occasion so she tried to make a dinner reservation on their second day in Paris, but it was fully booked, so instead she booked them a table for lunch. It was an experience! The restaurant was impeccably laid out and decorated and it was boasted as having some of the best food and service in Paris. It also had a history of having catered for stately functions in the past, and name-dropped a few famous people who regularly dined there like Audrey Hepburn and Salvador Dali. The restaurant lived up to its reputation. The food and service were outstanding but, of course, so was the bill! Still, Elizabeth thought that it was well worth the experience, although she did think that it was lucky that they only had lunch and not dinner, as she thought about how much more it would have cost them. Jan and Paul did not mind at all. They could well afford it and besides they would have done the same for Sally and her family had they been there themselves. It was after all a small price to pay for taking Elizabeth with them on their family holiday and they were also only delighted that Elizabeth had a wonderful holiday.

After telling her family all about it, Elizabeth went straight to her room. She did not bother to unpack anything but instead rang Tom straight away "Hi Tom, I'm back. Did you miss me?"

"Of course I did, more than you, I bet. How was Paris?" Tom asked her. "It was brilliant! I had a blast. You'll love it too. We'll have to go there some day. Oops, my battery's going," Elizabeth told him. Tom was as excited to hear her voice as she was his but unfortunately she only had a few minutes because her battery went flat, so she quickly charged her mobile. Tom was glad to hear that Elizabeth had a fantastic holiday and he could not wait to hear more about it, but it was more of an excuse to see her. He missed her and could not wait to see her and he also had news of his own to tell her. It was his eighteenth birthday coming up and he was having a big celebration do. He was also planning a short trip to Barcelona and was hoping that Elizabeth and their usual gang would accompany him, but he was aware she was going to the Centre for her treatment, so he wanted to ensure that their dates did not clash. Elizabeth decided to unpack her luggage whilst she was waiting for her battery to charge and afterwards, she went straight to have a shower. Tom rang her again just as she had got out of the shower. They made a date to meet up for lunch before the end of the week at the pizza place in the city centre.

Paul left for work early as he had an important meeting at the office but Jan took the morning off. She dropped Emma off first at her best friend, who lived only a few roads away from them, and then she dropped Elizabeth off at the shopping mall in town before driving herself to work. Her office was also in the city centre and not too far away from the mall. She arranged with her daughters that she would pick them up where she had dropped them respectively when she finished work later that evening.

When Elizabeth walked into the pizza restaurant, Tom was already waiting for her there. He smiled and waved to her and said, "Hi beautiful" as he stood up, and gave her a kiss on the lips before pulling out a chair for her. She gave him his present from Paris and he thanked her with another kiss on her lips. Initially she felt quite strange and bashful because this was the first time they were meeting without their usual gang, but the awkwardness soon left her once he started talking and asking her about her wellbeing and "How was Paris? Was it as fascinating and romantic as you thought?"

"Oh it was and it was elegant and sophisticated too. I can also see why they say it's a romantic city, although it wasn't like that because I was with Sally and her family, but you and I must go there by ourselves sometime, Tom," said Elizabeth and he replied, "And we will, I promise". Afterwards, Elizabeth felt very relaxed to be alone with him. Tom was always very astute and good at starting conversations so he could always read situations, no matter how difficult or uncomfortable they were. He was very witty, funny and smart but was also always a gentleman. Soon they were chatting away very naturally as if they were the only people in the restaurant, and then it occurred to Elizabeth that they did not need anyone else there because they were oblivious to everything and everyone around them anyway. It also felt right that they were alone together so now she did not mind that their other friends were not there, and she told Tom, "This is nice, isn't it? I mean just the two of us without our usual gang". In fact, she rather liked it, as did Tom, who said, "Yeah. This is great. I've always wanted to be alone with you, so now we are and we're on our first date". It had not occurred to Elizabeth before that this was a date so she thought that this must be what it was like to be all grown up, because she was no longer that easygoing, carefree teenager anymore. She was a young lady now and she happily thought "I'm on my first date!" She also could not be happier that her date was Tom because she only had eyes and feelings for this young man sitting across from her. She thought he was so handsome and strong, yet gentle and a truly genuine person. She thought herself very lucky because he chose her to be his girlfriend knowing that she could not give him what any normal woman could give him and when he could have any girl he wanted. Yes, he was definitely one of the good guys. She also remembered Sally telling her to hang on to him because she said that he was a rare gem and, after all they had been through, she knew she was right and she could trust him implicitly.

Elizabeth was happy and behaving normally as any girl would on a date with someone she loved. Then suddenly she remembered her impending treatment and she could not block out her fear of it. In fact, it was all she had thought of the last few days since her return from Paris, whenever she was by herself. She decided to talk to Tom about it, and told him how much she was dreading the whole thing. Tom could see how affected she was so he told her, "El, you have my support whatever you decide to do but I don't want you to do the treatment because of me, especially if it is going to be painful. I can't bear for you to be in pain so you don't need to do it for me. It doesn't matter to me I love you just the way you are". Elizabeth thought it was very sweet of him to say that again, but she was also disappointed because she thought that he of all people should have understood the reason she had to do the treatment, especially when she had already told him before that she was not doing it for him so she reminded him, "I know, but like I said before, this is something that I have to do for myself. I need to do it otherwise I am not normal and I want to be normal". Just when she said that, she felt that no one really understood how she was feeling, not even Tom, and it made her feel sad and isolated again. It was crucial for her to have the treatment because she truly believed that this would normalise her and it was the only way that she would ever be able to feel normal, so not going ahead with the treatment was not an option for her. Before any more was said, a waiter brought the pizzas and drinks to their table and asked if they needed anything else, so when they did not, he said *"Bon appétit"* before leaving them to it. The pizzas looked and smelt so yummy that Elizabeth and Tom stopped talking and delved straight into them. They were both hungry too. She ordered her favourite Quattro Formaggi because she loved her cheeses, and he had a meat pizza topped with minced beef, Italian sausages, pepperoni, mozzarella and peppers, all held together with another generous topping of cheese. They tried a slice of each other's pizza and slowly they finished everything on their plates. "That was great, I really enjoyed it," Elizabeth said with a gratified smile on her face, and proceeded to finishing her Coke.

Afterwards, Elizabeth was glad that they did not talk about her treatment again. She thought that there was nothing left to discuss, she was going ahead with the treatment and that was that. Tom seemed to get the message too because he knew how headstrong Elizabeth was, especially when she had already made up her mind. In reality, it was not that Tom did not understand because he understood her rationale all too well, but he was being protective over her too. In any case, he decided not to broach the subject again so instead he told her, "you know my birthday's coming up soon. My parents are arranging a party for me and no doubt, there'll be lots of people they'll invite, but of course, I'm inviting our usual gang. Anyway, how would you like going to Barcelona after that? I'm going to ask our group so there'll be the eight of us. Wouldn't it be great El, our own holiday, without any adults". Elizabeth listened and although she was excited for him, she was not sure about going to Barcelona. She did know how the treatment would affect her once she started it and she also could not help thinking of the cost involved, especially as she had already spent a fortune in Paris. She was torn because on the one hand, she did not like taking advantage of her parents' generosity although she thought that they probably would not mind, but on the other hand she did not want to put a damper on Tom's spirits by telling him that she would not go to Barcelona when he was so enthusiastic. She really felt bad about it but in the end she felt that it was only fair to tell him her predicament, so she told him, "I'm excited about your party, Tom but I'm not sure about Barcelona, especially when I've only just come back from a holiday in Paris and spent a fortune. I'm not so sure if my parents would be happy about it and also I'll be in the midst of my treatment and I don't even know how that's going to go". Tom was disappointed of course but he also understood. Still, he was not discouraged and would not give up on the idea. He wanted her to be there with him so much that he even offered to pay for her but, of course, Elizabeth would not have it. Tom would not give up easily either. He was aware that it was the height of the holiday season but he was still confident that he would find an affordable deal on the last minute booking or special deal offers. "I'll google when I get home. I'll let you and the rest of the guys know when I find something ok". Elizabeth smiled and just nodded. Tom also suggested that, "in the meantime, you should ask your parents' permission and tell them that I really want you to come". Elizabeth thought that it was not just them she had to ask, because she would need to speak to Lucy first too. Elizabeth was not sure if Lucy would agree because she would be in the midst of her treatment, and she herself, was worried as she did not know how she would continue with the treatment if she went abroad. She was adamant that she would not let anything interfere with her very important treatment, so if it meant not going then she would rather not go and Tom would just have to accept it, although she did not tell him as such yet. She thought that she would wait till she knew for sure.

Tom was only glad that the date of his party did not coincide with Elizabeth's treatment appointment, and he would ensure that the Barcelona trip would not either. He was slightly puzzled at Elizabeth's response though, because he expected her to be more enthusiastic, but she did not seem too bothered about going. He had actually thought that the trip would cheer her up if she was doing this unpleasant treatment but instead she seemed to be distracted, so he thought, "she must really be so worried and scared, poor thing". He was not wrong in thinking that because Elizabeth was getting increasingly petrified as the time drew nearer. She was going for this life-changing treatment in a fort-night's time and she was not sure if it would be successful or not. She was mortified at the prospect that it might not work. "What if it was so painful and I can't do it? What then?" she asked herself. "I'll be a freak forever," she answered her own question, sadly. Stop! Stop! Stop! She took a few deep breaths like her mother had taught her and then she forced herself to change her negative tune, "Of course the treatment will work. They said the success rate is very high. I need to focus here. I have Lucy to guide me, I will complete the treatment and I will be normal. Failure is not an option! I can do it!" She had drifted off for the last fifteen minutes, so she did not even hear Tom calling her name several times or feel him holding her hand. "El, where were you?" Elizabeth eventu-ally heard him ask, so she replied apologetically, "sorry, I was just thinking about my treatment," to which Tom said, "I guessed that much. I know you're scared but you'll be ok, El. You are the strongest and the most determined person I know. Are you sure you don't want me to go with you?"

"No, my mum and Sally are coming with me. It's all arranged. It's ok, I'm fine now," she asserted in a sudden calm manner, as she attempted to compose herself. "Well, if you change your mind, you know that I'm always here for you," Tom told her.

After lunch, they decided to take in a movie at one of the cinemas on the top floor of the shopping mall because they had a few hours to kill before Jan was to pick Elizabeth up as arranged. Elizabeth did not really care which movie they saw, but she was glad that Tom had suggested it because she was not in the mood for talking anymore and welcomed the escape. They saw an action-comedy film, which she quite enjoyed because it took her mind off her own problem, at least for a couple of hours. It was nearly time for her pick up but Tom insisted, "Let's go for a coffee while we wait for your mother to come. There's a Starbucks just by the entrance of the mall". Elizabeth thought it was a not quite the first date she expected but Tom seemed unperturbed and told her that he had a great time. He just enjoyed spending time with her so it did not bother him how they spent it, as long as they were together. He could not wait to see her again. He thought she was so beautiful and smart, strong yet fragile, with a touch of innocence, which made her all the more alluring to him. He had never felt like this about anyone before, but there was something about her and he knew he loved her the first time he saw her, if only she knew how much. Jan arrived as they were finishing their coffee so he asked for the bill and paid it. They said their goodbyes. "I'll call tonight," he told her so Elizabeth said "Okay, later. Bye now," then he made his way to the car park where he had parked his car. Tom got his driving licence the year before and his father bought him his car when he passed. He had not driven much except locally but he was already a competent confident driver. He also did not have to drive too far because he lived in the suburbs, not too far from the city centre.

When they were in the car, Jan asked her daughter about her day so Elizabeth said it was 'fine', which was her typical answer if she did not feel like talking so Jan did not pry any further. She could see that Elizabeth was attracted to Tom and she also liked Tom because he was always polite and a gentleman. Jan had met all of Elizabeth's friends and she was grateful that she had some very close ones. She thought they were a good bunch so at least she never had to worry about them getting into trouble. At dinner that evening, Elizabeth mentioned the Barcelona trip to her parents but she also very quickly added, "I don't really mind if you think that I shouldn't go because I've only just come back from Paris so I've already had a holiday". Then to her surprise, both her parents could not be more pleased and were very agreeable with the idea that she should go. Her mother said, "That's a wonderful idea. We know and trust all the girls and boys in your group. They're a nice bunch. You should go with them and enjoy yourself. Barcelona is an interesting and exciting city, great for young people and you haven't been there before. It's different from Paris but we think you'll like it so if you want to go, your dad and I would be more than happy for you to go with your friends". Her parents were also conscious that Elizabeth would have started her treatment and felt that the trip might also help her to de-stress and take her mind off it for a bit, so they encouraged her to go but only if she was happy to go, because they were also being mindful to respect her decision. Elizabeth was rather surprised that her parents were so willing for her to go, especially as she had only just returned from her short holiday and spent a bomb – although she knew how generous they were. In a strange way, she had hoped that they would have objected because this would have made it easier for her to tell Tom that she could not go. In any case, Elizabeth said that she would have to check with Lucy first, so they decided to leave it at that. Then Jan mentioned that Emma was also going away. They had already planned to send Emma to her grandparents when Elizabeth went in for her treatment, and the grandparents were taking her to Disneyland for a couple of weeks so she would also have her holiday. Jan and Paul were very fair and good parents so they made sure that their youngest would not miss out in the midst of all the focus on Elizabeth. When Elizabeth heard that, she felt a little guilty, as she had actually forgotten all about her little sister because she had been so engrossed with only herself, so she could not be happier for her. She also felt a lot of respect for her parents then and thought that they were so good to not forget about Emma, so she told her parents, "Aw, that's really nice, you're the best," then turning to her sister, she said, "Ems, you lucky thing. I'm sure you'll going to love it and grandma and granddad will spoil you rotten. I'm so happy for you. I bet you're really excited". She was not wrong, because Emma was so excited and could not wait to go that she said, "Yeah, you bet! I've already looked up all the rides and I know exactly which ones I want to go on. I can't wait to go!"

Treatment, At Last

Elizabeth was sick with worry and could not settle all weekend. She did not sleep a wink that night because she could not wait to get the treatment started so she would know for sure how it would feel, rather than imagining what it would be like. At the same time, she was terrified. At breakfast, she was very quiet, deep in her own thoughts. Her parents were equally anxious but they tried not to show it. They were pleased that they had sent Emma to her grand-parents yesterday so they could just concentrate on support-ing Elizabeth. Her father gave her a hug and told her he loved her very much, as he wished her luck. He also told her that he would support her no matter the outcome, then realising how negative that sounded he very quickly added, "I'm sure you'll do just fine, darling. I have full confidence in you," so Elizabeth forced herself to whisper, "Thanks, dad". Jan rang Sally to inform her that they were on their way to her. Paul picked Sally up before dropping all of them off at the station. Elizabeth remained silent throughout and even her best friend could not distract her despite her every effort. As the train approached London, Elizabeth started shaking vigorously so her mother quickly hugged her very tightly and Sally held and stroked her hands. Sally also reminded her to breathe slowly and her mother said something similar, but Elizabeth was having such a violent panic attack that she did not hear or feel a thing. Sally quickly grabbed the little scrunched up paper bag in which she had wrapped her sandwich earlier, and put the empty bag over Elizabeth's face and told her, "El, breathe slowly into the bag". After a few moments, Elizabeth started to calm down and her tremor also became less intense, but Sally continued to encourage her to breathe slowly and kept talking to her. Jan was so thankful that Sally was there to help because she was brilliant. Until now, she had no idea how frightened Elizabeth was. She knew that Elizabeth was worried but she had not realised that she was this terrified because she had kept her fear to herself all this time. Jan blamed herself again and felt that she had failed her daughter, because, as her mother, she should have known, but Elizabeth seemed so grown up about it when she was at home this time that she missed the signs. "This is my fault again. Why didn't I see it coming? I should have known. I should have talked to her more. I'm a bad mother," Jan cursed herself, although in all fairness it was difficult for her to do much as Elizabeth was not telling her anything these days.

When they got to the Centre, they took the lift straight up to the unit. On arrival, they were greeted by a receptionist, who showed them to her room and told her that the specialist would be up shortly. Elizabeth sat on the bed and fixed her eyes on the floor the whole time. She just sat very silent and still. In fact, she had barely uttered two words since she got up this morning. Sally on the other hand, orientated herself with the bedside gadget and turned on the little television, which was hung high up on the wall facing the bed. She had a good look around the room and found the *en suite* bathroom and toilet, and was rather impressed that Elizabeth was given a room to herself. Sally then tried to relax and distract her best friend from her almost catatonic state but her efforts were still in vain because Elizabeth remained impregnable. Jan went to sit next to her daughter and started stroking her hair with one hand whilst also holding her hand with her other. "You'll be ok, darling. You've waited so long for this but you are here now. Sally and I are also here with you. I love you so much," she whispered as she kissed her daughter on her forehead.

There was a gentle knock on the door and then Lucy walked in. She smiled and greeted them with a "good morning everyone". Jan stood up to move out of the way as Lucy walked over to Elizabeth. "Hi, how are you, El?" Elizabeth looked up. It was the first time she had reacted to anyone and she said, "I'm really scared," and she started to cry. She told Lucy that she was terrified of the pain, terrified of the whole treatment but most of all she was terrified of the outcome, lest she should fail. This was also the first time she had openly voiced and displayed her emotions about her treatment in front of her mother, although she had enacted all sorts in her head a thousand times, but of course she had kept everything to herself. Then slowly she could feel her panic attack and tremor coming on again, which was also evident to Lucy, so she instinctively held Elizabeth's trembling hands with hers and advised her on her breathing, because Elizabeth was starting to hyperventilate now. Lucy also tried to reassure her that "The treatment will not be as painful as you think or imagine," and confirmed this by telling Elizabeth that, "The other women, who were just as frightened as you, all said that the treatment was not as bad afterwards". It seemed to allay Elizabeth's anxiety slightly so Lucy continued to share the experiences of the other women with her, to reassure her even more. This somehow helped to further assuage Elizabeth's fear and after a few more minutes of Lucy's calming transference, Elizabeth began to relax and her stance also changed completely. She then asked, "Were they really scared like me? And they said it was not as bad?"

"Yes, all of them said that it wasn't as bad as they had expected so I'm sure you will be the same too so don't worry too much. I won't lie to you because it will be painful but it's nothing that you can't bear. I'll explain every step to you so there will be no surprises and I'll be with you the whole time, ok?" Lucy reassured her. Elizabeth nodded and said, "Ok". Then she relaxed and became more confident and positive about her treatment, but most of all she felt safe because she trusted this person whom she believed was going to change her life. Her mother could not believe this almost immediate transformation, this sudden improvement in Elizabeth and she hoped that it was going to be permanent. She could not explain it, but it was surreal, because she thought that she could actually feel what Elizabeth felt just then. There was also an air of fresh tranquility and as it filled the room, it brought with it a fresh air of optimism and positivity. Jan looked over to Sally and they smiled quietly at each other because they too appreciated the reassurance and calm especially, after having been overwhelmed by Elizabeth's display of mental anguish earlier on.

Elizabeth said she wanted her mother and Sally to stay for a while, which Lucy agreed and said, "That's fine as long as you're happy then I don't mind. In fact, I'll explain everything to all of you while you're here, and if you don't understand or if you have any questions then please ask me and I'll try and answer them so everyone is happy before I start the treatment". Lucy also felt that they could support Elizabeth better if they knew more, so she went through the procedure in detail with Elizabeth with her mother and Sally present. She was keen to ensure that they, and especially Elizabeth, understood, so she again encouraged questions from all of them and once everyone was happy and fully informed, she told them that she would start the treatment. Elizabeth was quite composed by now and she could not wait to start so she quickly made arrangements with her mother and Sally to meet up afterwards before they left. Jan had booked accommodation for Sally and her at a hotel nearby so they left Elizabeth to have her treatment whilst they went ahead to sort themselves out.

Elizabeth was first asked to take her jeans and panties off prior to her treatment. She did so reluctantly and was instantly engulfed in embarrassment. She also felt terribly awkward lying on the bed naked from the waist down so she put her hands over her private part to cover herself. Lucy offered her a sheet to cover herself up and also assured her complete privacy, confirming that the door was locked so that no one would walk in during her treatment. She reassured Elizabeth that she had seen and treated numerous women so she understood how she was feeling. She acknowledged and normalised Elizabeth's feelings of embarrassment as she told her, "El, I have treated a lot of women before and they all feel the same as you so I fully understand that you feel really embarrassed right now and that's normal, but I want you to try and focus on the treatment ahead and not think too much about your nakedness. I promise you that we'll just be focusing on your treatment and nothing else. I'll also let you know what I'm going to do first before I do it so we'll take it a step at a time". Elizabeth nodded nervously. Lucy then explained the need for an examination before starting the treatment and she also encouraged Elizabeth to examine herself afterwards. Elizabeth was horrified and almost froze when she heard that and then she quickly said "No thanks, I don't want to, you do it," but with further encouragement, she agreed that she would do it after Lucy if she guided her.

Lucy knew full well how important it was to relax Elizabeth first before they started anything because she wanted to try to make the experience as comfortable as possible for Elizabeth, which might then encourage her more, especially when this was going to be her first treatment. First, she taught Elizabeth some breathing and relaxation exercises and when she was more relaxed, Lucy examined her. Elizabeth hardly felt a thing. She could not believe it. If she had to admit it, she thought that it really was not so bad. For the first time, she was not crying or screaming in pain and not only that, it felt different, because when she was examined previously, she would always still continue to feel the pain, hours afterwards. This was somehow different, she felt. This was definitely her best experience. She began to think that maybe the treatment would not be as painful as she had anticipated. It also gave her the confidence to embark on her treatment with a more positive attitude. Of course, it helped because she trusted and had full faith in Lucy, who exuded a natural sense of confidence and expertise. It was also something about Lucy's calm and genuine personality and her whole approach and attitude that Elizabeth liked very much. Then Elizabeth did something that she never thought she would ever do. With some guidance, she put one of her fingers into her little dimple but quickly pulled away because it was the strangest sensation she ever felt. "Ugh! I don't know what I'm supposed to feel but it feels all weird and squidgy". Lucy was more encouraging and confirmed that it was her vaginal dimple and it was good that her skin was soft and 'squidgy', as this would be easier to stretch. Lucy then continued the treatment, this time using a dilator, which was a cylindrically shaped rod. She applied some lubricating gel on the dilator so that Elizabeth's skin would be lubricated thus making it easier to stretch. She used the smallest dilator first, which was the size of a finger and inserted it into Elizabeth's little dimple at an angle avoiding her 'wee hole' and then she told Elizabeth that she was going to press it in very hard so as to stretch the skin, and warned her of the pain beforehand. She also advised Elizabeth to take a few deep breaths. Then she pushed the dilator in hard and Elizabeth felt the pain instantly, which brought tears to her eyes despite her efforts to be brave. "El, I know it's painful but try and concentrate on your breathing as I've taught you. It'll only be for a few minutes and I promise you that the pain will ease so just continue to breathe deeply and slowly," Lucy advised her whilst still applying very firm pressure on the dilator, to strech her vagina. Elizabeth tried her best to concentrate on her breathing as she was taught but it was so difficult because the pain was excruciating and she felt as if her inside had been split open. She desperately wanted to scream "Stop" but she trusted Lucy that the pain would ease after a few more minutes so she closed her eyes and tried to focus on something else – but it was just too painful. It was only for a few minutes but still Elizabeth felt that this was the longest few minutes she had ever had to endure. Lucy kept talking to her throughout the procedure, asking her different questions so Elizabeth tried to concentrate and answered them, even though she knew that this was only to distract her from the pain that she was experiencing. Still, she did as she was told and then true enough, after a few more minutes, it eased and turned into a numbing pain. Elizabeth could not quite believe it but she was grateful because she did not know how much longer she could have tolerated the pain. "Are you ok?" Lucy asked Elizabeth so she nodded. "Good girl, you did very well. That's the worst bit over with," Elizabeth was told and she automatically assumed that she had finished her first treatment. Then she heard, "We'll do the next size now and you are going to do it this time".

Elizabeth looked horrified again but Lucy said, "Don't look so worried, you'll do fine. I'm going to guide and teach you how to do it and I'll be here with you the whole time, ok?" Elizabeth nodded nervously because she really did not know what she was doing but she remembered Lucy highlighting the importance of the angle of insertion so she was even more terrified at the thought of doing it wrong. Lucy calmly took her hand and, before Elizabeth knew it, she was being taught to hold and position the dilator, and afterwards, she was guided into the dimple. Even so, she could not stop her hands from shaking because of the intense nerves she was feeling within, which was unsurprising given that this was her first attempt. Lucy subtly advised her to focus on her breathing once more because she saw that Elizabeth was holding in her breath so hard – she had forgotten to breathe. When Elizabeth was more focused, she pressed the dilator hard into the vaginal dimple to stretch the skin again. She instantly felt that tearing pain as her skin was being stretched, but thankfully it was not as bad as the first time but maybe it was also because she now knew what to expect and was therefore not as tensed this second time round. Still, she had to keep pressing the dilator in for a few more minutes until her pain changed to a vague numbness again. Afterwards, she was instructed to remove the dilator and once it came out, the pain went. Elizabeth could not quite believe how this intense pain could suddenly go away once the dilator was out but she was just grateful that it did. Lucy then examined her again and smiled as she told Elizabeth, who was watching her with intense anticipation, "This is a really good start, El. I think you will be pleased when you examine yourself this time".

"What do you mean I have to examine myself again? Have I finished?" Elizabeth asked, so Lucy confirmed that she had completed her first treatment. Wow! That was it, done? Elizabeth could not believe that she had actually done the treatment. At last! She felt stunned and could not get over the fact that she had been agonising over this treatment for months and it was over in a few minutes. She had imagined that the treatment would be far worse than this and had been so worried that it would be so painful that she would not be able to do it, but it was not even half as bad as she had thought. "I can't believe it. I did it! I really did it and it wasn't so bad," Elizabeth admitted to herself and started to drift away into her inner thoughts again because now she felt sure that she would be able to finish the treatment. She told herself that she would be good from now on. She would listen to whatever Lucy advised even if she would prefer not to, especially having to put her finger into her vaginal dimple again. She was miles away by herself again so Lucy had to bring her back as she asked her, "El, are you ready?" By now, Elizabeth was getting quite accustomed to touching her vulva so she was less squeamish this time but all the same she still felt repulsed and did not like touching herself there. Sensing this, Lucy explained its importance to her and hinted again that she would be pleasantly surprised, so Elizabeth did as she was told like a good girl. As she did, she could not hold back her surprise and she screeched out, "Oh wow! I can't believe it. I can feel something there now". Lucy confirmed, "Yes, that's your vagina".

"I have a vagina! Oh my god, I have a vagina! You have no idea what this means to me. Thank you," she said in an almost tear-jerking voice as she became all emotional and choked up. Then she looked up at Lucy and immediately corrected herself. "Sorry, I didn't mean it like that. Of course, you understand. You know everything. It's just that this is so awesome! I wish I had met you sooner".

"It's not too late, you're here now. In fact, this is the right time to start your treatment because you are motivated and you are ready to do it, and your skin is also more elastic now. This is crucial because it takes a lot of time and commitment to successfully complete the treatment. It is also important for you to know how you are progressing to help you achieve your goal so that's why I want you to examine yourself after each treatment". Lucy stopped briefly to allow Elizabeth to ask her questions but Elizabeth was still too stunned to say anything, so Lucy continued, "this is just the beginning but I am confident that you will succeed and I will be here to help you all the way". Elizabeth nodded and answered in a more positive, "Okay". Lucy then said, "Anyway, tell me. Was the treatment as bad as you had thought?"

"No, it wasn't. The first one was very painful but like you said, the pain didn't last long and although it was still painful, I could bear it. Honestly, it really wasn't too bad. I really thought that it would be horrendous, that's why I was so scared," Elizabeth answered with great relief. Then she asked Lucy, "I had to go through this to know what it was like but how come you know so much?" Lucy smiled and replied, "I have been doing this for a very long time". Even so, Elizabeth thought, as she continued "but you must like your job very much because you're very good at it. I'm just so grateful that there is someone like you to help girls like me". Lucy nodded and said, "You're right. I do love my job and it makes me very happy that I am able to help".

Whilst she was putting her jeans back on, Elizabeth remembered something she had googled previously so she thought she would ask Lucy because she knew that Lucy would know the answer. "May I ask you another question because it's been bothering me? Do you think that I will still need to have an operation?" She was initially informed by her local consultant that she would need surgery and had also read that for some girls, the dilators did not work, so Lucy informed her that the majority of women did not require surgery and had successfully created their vaginas using the dilators. This was reassuring to know but Elizabeth was more interested to know on a personal level so she interjected asking again, "but can you tell now if I will need the operation or not?"

"It's hard to say for sure at this stage but from examining you now, I honestly don't believe that you will need surgery since your skin is soft and stretchy, which is a real plus, because your skin will stretch and continue to stretch," Lucy explained but she went on to stress that "The crucial part of your treatment is that you must do your treatments regularly and correctly to be successful. I understand that this might be a challenge for you to fit all your treatments in with your busy school schedule, so I will let you fit them in accordingly. The treatments don't have to be done strictly to time but they must be done at least twice but preferably three times a day. You may organise when you do them so hopefully this gives you a bit more control. Can you manage this?" Elizabeth nodded and then answered very convincingly, "Yes. I can, I'll make sure of it. I don't want the operation".

"Ok. I'm sure you won't need it and I'm here to guide and support you. We'll also need to assess you regularly until you finish so you will need to come back regularly for your assessment and your progress," Lucy informed her. "That won't be a problem. I'll come back and I'll do what you say. I just want this treatment to work," Elizabeth answered with conviction. Lucy smiled and assured her, "Then I'm sure it will, as long as you continue to do your treatments properly".

Elizabeth was indeed very relieved to have this reassurance, but she realised that she had only just started her treatment and she still had a long way to go. She was also aware now that it was ultimately her responsibility to ensure that she did her treatments properly if she was to succeed. Then the realisation suddenly hit her. She had been waiting for something like this to happen for so long and now at last, she was really here. This was really happening. This was real. Now, her life would change, she would be changed. She would have a vagina like any normal girl. She would be a normal girl. She would be normal again! She became all excited and could hardly breathe just thinking about it so she remembered to take a few deep breaths, like her mother and Lucy had taught her, as she tried to compose herself and to not let her excitement run away with her. After a few more minutes, Elizabeth again remembered the women who had to have surgery because they did not get on with their dilator treatment and when she thought more about them, it made her more resolved that she was not going to be the same. However, she was also now very aware that the treatment would demand a lot of her time and commitment so it was down to her to make sure she did her treatments if she was to succeed, so she became slightly worried. She tried to fight off the conflicting thoughts going through her mind because, "What if I can't complete the treatment… no way, I'm not having the operation. It's too painful and horrible. I would rather just use the dilators". She had to force herself to stay focused, "El, stop being negative, you can do this," remembering the reassurance she was given and trying to psyche herself on. Lucy perceptively noticed Elizabeth's uncomfortable stance again, so she enquired, "Is there something else that's bothering you El?" She then told Lucy that she wanted to be normal more than anything in the world, and, as such, she was driven to complete the treatment at all costs, but she was still worried in case she needed surgery. By now, she had become almost obsessive about the idea so Lucy advised her, "I know you are concerned but let's take things a step at a time, ok? There's no reason to concern yourself about surgery if you continue using your dilators as I have taught you, so let's just concentrate on doing your treatments for now". Then looking at Elizabeth's face, Lucy could tell that she was still not quite convinced so she continued, "Everyone is different, El. You are very motivated and you want to succeed. Your vagina also feels elastic so it will stretch well with the dilators. The women you've read about are different from you. Some of them became fed up so they gave up before they completed their treatment. That's not to say that they failed either but maybe they weren't ready for such a big commitment at the time of their lives so when the time was right for them, they returned to recommence their treatment and they succeeded. This is why I told you earlier that the timing to do the treatment is very important. You have to be ready and want to do it so that you can successfully complete it".

"I'm ready and I've never been more sure that I want to do it" Elizabeth replied so Lucy said "I know you are and that's very good". After a few more minutes, Elizabeth enquired "so why did the other girls need surgery when they can do it with dilators?" Lucy explained that "a few girls just didn't like using dilators and thought that surgery was a quick fix. Unfortunately, for them, they still needed to use the dilators afterwards. In fact, for them it was vital that they did otherwise their vaginas would shorten or even close up". Elizabeth did not know this before so it made her more determined and she said "I didn't know that. Now I definitely don't want to have an operation. I don't mind how long it's going to take because I'd still rather use the dilators but as long as I know they will work for me".

"Yes, they will but you must stay focused and motivated. El, I have confidence in you and I honestly believe you can do it too and I'm also here to help you," Lucy reaffirmed. "Thank you so much for helping me" Elizabeth said sincerely. Lucy replied "You're very welcome".

Then Elizabeth continued, "I don't know where I'd be now without your help. You guys have done so much for me and I really appreciate it, thank you". In response, Lucy told her, "That's what we're here for. It's what we do. That's why we have Centres such as ours to help all of you because we know that it's hard for you to manage on your own, and why we provide help and counselling throughout your treatment until you finish. We also understand that you need further help along the way too, so we will support you in every way possible to enable you to cope with different challenges until you succeed, so that you don't have to keep looking back all the time but instead move forward. El, we're not just here to help all of you complete your treatments, which of course this is very important but we want to help you succeed in life too. We want to enable you all to have a real chance of leading normal lives because it will give us no greater pleasure than to see all of you happy and getting on with your lives normally".

"Thank you. It means a lot because it shows that you guys really care for us girls," Elizabeth said gratefully. Then she thought about some of the women that Lucy mentioned earlier. "You said that some women stop and defer their treatment, but I don't want to stop until I've finished, because I know that I won't come back if I was to stop. That's just me".

"Good, that's exactly what we'd like for you too. We don't want you to stop either and it's only a few women who sometimes have a break for good reasons. Anyway, I'm sure it won't happen with you, so let's just focus on your goal here," Lucy reassured her with a smile.

Afterwards, Elizabeth rang her mother to let her know

that she had completed her first treatment. She also told them that they need not rush back to the Centre because she was also seeing Anne and would be at least another hour. Nevertheless, Jan and Sally swiftly left their hotel and made their way to the Centre. They could not relax anyway because they could not stop worrying about Elizabeth and wondering how she had got on with her treatment. Elizabeth might have seemed calmer when they left her, but they were still concerned about her as it was evident how much her condition was really affecting her, especially after her overwhelming manifestation earlier on. They felt that Elizabeth's circumstances had escalated way out of control with her emotional paroxysms becoming more intense and exploding so unexpectedly that they were just hopelessly out of their depths to help her. It was all too frightening and upsetting – especially for Jan to have seen her own daughter in so much anguish earlier, and even worse to not be able to comfort her or to stop her suffering. She felt very inept and ashamed and blamed herself again for letting things get this far. She should have been more aware of the signs and the enormity of Elizabeth's feelings sooner, although everything seemed to be going so well with Elizabeth recently and there was not a hint that she was even suffering.

Jan had always respected her daughter's decisions and she and her husband had also agreed to respect her privacy. Furthermore, Jan was determined not to be one of those mothers who was always meddling or even smothering their daughters so much so that they could not breathe. Besides, she felt that her Elizabeth was strong like her and she always managed. It did not occur to her that Elizabeth would have hidden her true feelings from her all this time. They had always been very close and Jan could always read her daughter, even when they had drifted apart slightly of late, so she could not accept how she could have missed the telltale signs so badly. Of course, in all honesty, she was waiting for Elizabeth to make the first move and truly believed that Elizabeth would talk to her when she was ready as they had agreed. They always had this understanding too – that Elizabeth would come to her if she came unstuck with anything, although she rationalised that this thing was just so different from anything they had to deal with before. Even so, she should have known better. After all, she was an intelligent and perceptive woman and most of all, she was her mother. Jan felt worse than ever about herself. She had never felt so helpless in her life and it pained her more because she again felt that she had failed Elizabeth for not being there for her as she should have done and that she did not help her more. She could not bear to see her Elizabeth suffer a second longer, yet she did not know how best to help her and she was really at her wit's end. She kept wishing that she had seen through her daughter's act and had been a little more proactive and intervened sooner. After all, Elizabeth was only sixteen. "I must be the worst mother on earth. I couldn't even help my poor baby. I didn't make her pain go away. Oh my darling Elizabeth, mummy's so sorry that you are suffering so. This is my fault!" Jan blamed herself. Then she remembered that fortunately, there were professionals like Lucy and Anne to help. Now the only thing she kept hoping was for Elizabeth to continue to get better, because she would never forgive herself otherwise.

Jan's self-reproach was abruptly interrupted by an announcement over the intercom system on the train. Apparently, there was a signal failure on the line so passengers were warned of a delay and also advised to change to alternative lines when it reached the next destination, as it would be terminating there. Jan shook her head in disbelief and thought that it was just as well that they had started out early. Their hotel was actually within walking distance to the Centre but Jan thought that they would take the tube instead as the station was literally next door to their hotel and it was only two stops away. However, no sooner the tube pulled out, it stopped almost immediately and sat on the underground platform somewhere in between stations. It was so near and yet so far. Jan smiled and shrugged her shoulders as she looked over to Sally because there was nothing they could do except to wait patiently until the train moved again. In a strange way, although it was unexpected, it was probably the break that Jan needed because it stopped her going further down her guilt trip. Well, at least for the next half an hour or so, otherwise she could feel herself verging on hysteria, which was so unlike her because she was usually very calm, confident and composed. Now that she had time to reflect sensibly, she was truly grateful to the professionals who were providing her daughter with the appropriate help and support that she so desperately needed and which was beyond her own capability. She trusted that Elizabeth was in the right place now and yes, like Elizabeth, she too placed all her hopes on this treatment and on the staff at the Centre to make her well again.

Elizabeth waited eagerly in her room for her mother and best friend to arrive because she was so excited and could not wait to tell them about her treatment. She had also had a very therapeutic session with Anne so right now, all was good. The immense fear and the sense of dread she had been feeling all those months had vanished once again and she hoped that it would be for good this time. Now, her heart felt so much lighter that she could almost lift off with its every beat of excitement. This thing that she referred to had taken so much out of her that she never thought she could be happy again, but now she was smiling all over and why not, she felt that she had finally arrived. All that confusion about her sexuality and her agony over the loss of control of her life and her negativity over her future had finally ended. She wanted to be normal and now she was really beginning to feel normal again. Ever since she found out she had MRKH, she had been waiting for this treatment, the one thing that would change her life, and bring normality back into her life. Now at last, she got to start her treatment. For Elizabeth, it was this very one thing that would make her feel normal. You see, it did not matter what the experts told her about her being a definite female. In Elizabeth's mind, she was not the same person anymore – she certainly did not feel normal. In truth, there was only ever one belief Elizabeth held. She knew in her heart that she could only feel normal if she had the treatment to correct her abnormality, because she just could not accept that she was a girl or a female when she did not have a vagina because that was just so not normal. Having just started her treatment, it did not matter that she had a long way to go before she completed, she still had this opportunity to change the way she felt about herself, and to turn her life around, and she was already feeling more optimistic about the treatment. It was also a bonus that it was not as bad as she had initially dreaded so it gave her the confidence that she could really do it. It was such a relief and she could not help feeling jubilant about it.

When Jan and Sally walked into the room, Elizabeth was so excited that she burst out, "I've done it mummy. I've done it at last!" It was an unforgettable moment, the moment everyone had hoped would happen. Both Jan and Sally's faces lit up instantly and simultaneously, the room seemed to brighten up too, emitting the most positive feel. In that treasured moment, Jan automatically burst into tears and very soon they were all crying, crying and laughing and hugging each other. No one uttered a word, none was needed. It was understood. Besides, Jan was too choked up with emotions of joy and relief. All she ever wanted for Elizabeth was for her to be happy and to be a normal teenager and to enjoy her adolescence without any of this adult angst, at least not at this stage anyway. She had been feeling so sorry for Elizabeth because she felt that it was not right that she was forced to grow up this quickly when she was still very childlike at sixteen. Then again, she reconciled herself that sometimes life was unfair and although this whole experience was very painful and cruel, it probably made her daughter a stronger person. She was always proud of her daughters, but right now she could not be prouder of Elizabeth. Shame, she could not say the same for herself. Instead she felt so ashamed that she made up her mind right there and then that she was not going to stay in the background anymore. She was going to be a better mother and really support Elizabeth. She would be more involved in Elizabeth's decisions from now on. She would let her head and not her heart rule, and not be so afraid of making mistakes or upsetting her daughter. She appreciated that it would not be easy as she had no experience being a mother of a daughter with MRKH so it was all new territory for her. Still she reminded herself that she was her mother and Elizabeth was the child here. She was also very much like Elizabeth, so she felt that if Elizabeth could do it, so could she. She realised her mistake now so now she would be mindful not to be too interfering but at the same time, not leaving Elizabeth to make all the decisions by herself without having discussed them with her, as she used to before even though this whole affair was out of her comfort zone. She would behave as her mother and the adult and be there for Elizabeth, irrespective.

When Jan thought it through, she realised that she had a few unresolved issues of her own and these were stopping her from functioning as she normally would. The normal Jan was confident and sensible and would never have allowed Elizabeth to shut her out like that but ever since Elizabeth was diagnosed she was riddled with self-guilt so she could not be her normal rational self. If she had to be really honest, she was being selfish and vain too because she thought she had perfection. She had a perfect life and a perfect family. Only now, nothing was perfect anymore and like Elizabeth, she too was having difficulty accepting this. She was no longer perfect and blamed herself because she believed that she must have passed her defective gene to Elizabeth, causing her to be born without a womb and a vagina, even though there was no conclusive research evidence to support this. She felt gutted and terribly embarrassed and could not talk to anyone about her true feelings, not even to Paul. It also pained her to look at Elizabeth sometimes, because it reminded her of her own imperfection and her guilt, which made it harder for her to talk to Elizabeth. She became self-obsessed, and it suited her to let Elizabeth get on with her problem with the professionals whilst she waited and hoped for a good outcome, because it would invariably absolve her from her own blame and guilt. She admitted that she failed as a mother in this respect, and promised to do better from now on, but to do so she needed help herself first otherwise she would not be able to help or support Elizabeth. She had done a lot of research on MRKH but she was still no expert and since she had no help in dealing with it or how to support Elizabeth, she decided "I can't go on like this anymore. I'll have to speak to Lucy or Anne about this maybe they can recommend me to see someone who can help me". This was her chance to make things right so she was determined to be more involved this time. She felt that it was up to her now to re-establish the close relationship she always had with Elizabeth before all this happened and maybe then she would have her perfect family back – well her almost perfect family. In reality, this was no longer important to her anymore. She only wanted her daughter back. She wanted to be able to talk openly with Elizabeth about anything as they always did before but most of all, she just wanted Elizabeth to be happy and for her to enjoy her life again. She wanted her daughter to be able to have a normal future.

"Mummy, are you alright?" Elizabeth asked her mother. "Sorry, what darling?" replied Jan, trying her best to re-orientate herself, which made the two girls laugh because it was so obvious that she was a million miles away just then. Elizabeth repeated that she had a few hours before her next treatment so she asked, "What should we do for now?" Jan thought that she would take the two girls to the West End and show them what London was like as the two of them had never really been to London before. They took the tube to Leicester Square and after walking around for a short while they decided to have their lunch, and afterwards Jan said that they would see about booking a theatre show for the next evening. She treated them to a nice steak and chips at one of the steakhouses in town. During lunch, both her mother and Sally were curious to know how Elizabeth had got on with her treatment, so her mother asked her. Elizabeth shared her experience with them saying, "It was weird at first but Lucy was very good and she stayed and guided me the whole time. She made me put my finger inside me which was gross then I had to use two dilators and the first one was very painful but the second one was still painful but not as bad". Sally then asked her, "What was the pain like El?" Elizabeth said "To be honest, it felt like my inside was being ripped apart. It was quite horrible but luckily it did not last long. I don't think that I could have done it otherwise but once I finished my treatment, the pain went, so, like now, I have no pain". It all sounded painful enough but because Elizabeth was so positive about it, both Jan and Sally could feel and share her sentiment and were drawn in by her enthusiasm.

Afterwards, they went to the West End and walked along London's theatre land to book a show. They all agreed that they wanted to see *The Phantom of the Opera* and they were thrilled that they managed to get tickets for the following evening. Soon it was time for them to get back for Elizabeth's next treatment, so they casually made their way to the underground station. This time there was no drama as Elizabeth was rather nonchalant and treated her treatment as a matter of fact because she knew what to expect now. The transformation in her was quite amazing because of the person she was. She was always organised and liked to have control of her life, so the unknown was just too frightening, especially when everything she believed in and her whole being had been violently shaken. Now, having experienced her first treatment, she felt the most settled since her diagnosis. She did not even mind the pain anymore because she truly believed that it was well worth it if this corrective treatment would make her normal. It renewed her self-confidence and gave her fresh hope of having a normal life. She was even able to think ahead objectively about her future for the first time. She recalled Emma and Sally offering to be her surrogate and Tom mentioning adoption. It was very generous of them, not that she wanted to go there just yet but at the same time, it was reassuring to have those options. Of course, given the choice, she would rather have preferred to be able to have her own like other women when she was ready to start her family. This was always something that was at the back of her mind and it was also one of her main issues, because she really resented not having the choice like normal girls. She felt cheated too and also considered her condition to be most unfair and a curse because she was always having to prove to herself that she was a normal girl, so that she had to do this and that, and to go through this and that, to be a normal girl. It was all too much of a hard ask for Elizabeth, but slowly she was beginning to accept that this was who she was and that she was really different. She felt different alright, but at least now she was also starting to feel normal again but she had yet to feel special like Tom had told her. She accepted that until then, she would have to soldier on with her life the best she could and she would try not to step back but instead she would move forward, taking one step at a time, like Lucy had advised.

When Elizabeth stripped off her jeans for her treatment, she felt the same embarrassment all over again. She thought that she would have got used to this by now, but she could not shake this feeling. It was just that she did not like undressing in front of a total stranger although Lucy was not really a stranger anymore but again, this was not what normal people do and it was not through choice, because she felt that it was an encroachment on her privacy. Then she had to remind herself that she was only doing this to achieve her goal and she needed to focus on the treatment as Lucy had advised, instead of letting her mind wander off again. It was always easier said than done with Elizabeth, because it was still bothering her, which was the point. She decided that she must talk to Anne about this later on. In any case, she did what she had to do. She did her treatment again and, fortunately, this went without a hitch. It still hurt but she managed to shrug it off because she was expecting the pain anyway but more than ever, she could not wait to find out what further progress she had made. She was not disappointed and was again wowed when she put her finger into her vagina to find that it had grown even more this time. This was the concrete evidence she needed and oddly, she found herself wanting to do the treatment more times because she felt sure that she could finish it in no time if she kept doing it, but Lucy advised her against this, as she warned that, "It could make you too sore to do it properly and if you cannot then continue to do the treatment correctly, it will defeat the purpose. Besides, I don't think that you will have time to do the treatment more than three times every day". Elizabeth however was not fully convinced because she thought that she was tougher than that and she was certain that she would be able to handle the pain, especially now that she knew what it felt like. Still, she also trusted that Lucy must know what she was talking about so she did not pursue it.

Elizabeth went back to the hotel with her mother and Sally afterwards. They spent the rest of afternoon lazing around in their hotel room and even managed to have a nap because they were overcome by tiredness. Besides, they decided that it was not worth going into town again as Elizabeth still had one last treatment to do. After a short rest and a quick freshen up, they walked around the shops in the area and had something to eat too before escorting

Elizabeth back to the Centre. They were early so Jan and Sally stayed with her until it was time for her treatment but before they left, they made arrangements for the next day as Elizabeth would be staying overnight in the unit at the Centre. Elizabeth repeated her last treatment of the day and continued to be encouraged by her progress. She had a quick shower afterwards before settling down for the night. She thought that she would have an early night because she was feeling rather tired and there was not much else to do in her room anyway. She did turn on the little television but there was nothing interesting on to watch so she switched it off again. She decided to ring Tom to tell him about her treatment and they chatted for a while. Tom told her that he wished that he was there with her but was relieved to hear that her treatment was going well and that it had turned out better than she had expected. They said goodnight to each other and she promised to call him again the next day. She turned the lights off and then she fell fast asleep.

Elizabeth was already stirring in her bed when there was a knock on her door. It was the ladies serving breakfast. She thought to herself, "Breakfast in bed, not bad!" All in all, she was impressed with the service she was receiving. It inspired her to want to be a doctor more. She thought that it must be so rewarding to have the knowledge and be in a position to help someone in need and to make a difference in his or her life. She really liked the idea, and promised to care for her patients in the manner that she herself was being treated when she became a doctor. Elizabeth felt exhilarated and started to look forward to the day. She remembered that "Mummy always said that breakfast is an important start of the day so I'll have to make an effort," although she was not hungry but still she thought that she ought to have something to keep her strength up, so she had some cornflakes and coffee. Afterwards, she had a quick wash and got herself dressed because she wanted to be ready for her treatment. As she sat down on the big armchair in her room to wait for Lucy, she noticed that she was quite sore in her nether regions. In fact, she thought she felt the soreness when she was showering last night but she shrugged it off. Lucy was so right, she thought because she did warn her of the soreness yesterday.

Lucy came to do her treatment with her but this time, Elizabeth was so sore that she could not do it properly. It almost brought tears to her eyes so she said, "I don't understand it. Why can't I do it today? Why am I so sore today? I was doing so well yesterday". Lucy explained to her that this was the norm. "Don't worry about it. It's normal to be sore because we did stretch your skin very hard all of yesterday so it's expected and I'm not worried, because I also know that this soreness will subside after a day or two, but what's more important is that we have to continue stretching as we have done in spite of the soreness. This is also why we have kept you in because we know how hard it is for you to do this by yourself and we know you will need help over these few days".

"Thank you because I wouldn't have been able to do this myself, not with this pain and the soreness," Elizabeth replied because she had never experienced this soreness before. It was a different kind of pain. She told Lucy "I actually think that this soreness is worse than the pain because at least with the pain, it went when I finished my treatment but this soreness is still there. It's so strange but it feels like I'm bruised inside. Do you think that I'm bruised inside?" Elizabeth had always considered herself to have a high pain threshold but this sheer tenderness, this soreness made it very difficult for her to push the dilator into her vagina. It was as if the pain had doubled because of the soreness and she still felt like she was badly bruised inside, so naturally she was also worried that something was wrong. Of course, Lucy had to reassure her again that "no, there's no bruising and you are not bruised even if you feel like you are. The soreness is because we have really stretched your skin very hard and to the maximum that it would give so I'm not surprised that you feel very sore".

Then Elizabeth said, "It's funny that the pain goes soon as I take out the dilator but now, I have this soreness," so Lucy explained "At the moment, every time we stretch your vagina very hard, the skin will ping back just like if you were pulling a rubber band and when you let go, it pings back to its original size. The same thing is happening here so when we finish each treatment and remove the dilator, your vaginal skin pings back to what it was and therefore the pain settles. That's why you said that the pain goes when you take the dilator out". She then asked Elizabeth, "Am I making any sense so far?" Elizabeth said "Yes, but I don't understand why I am having this soreness now". Lucy explained further "Your skin has already stretched a little and your vagina has grown in size and you already know this from examining yourself. Even so, at this early stage, your skin is still slightly taut especially at the top end but as we keep stretching it, that skin will become tender because it is not ready to give fully yet so this together with your skin at the entrance that has already stretched so far, will obviously feel quite sore. This is the soreness that you are feeling right now so when we continue to stretch it very hard again each time, it will become even sorer still. As I said before, I am not concerned because I expect that you will feel very sore after a few treatments anyway". Lucy then stopped to ask Elizabeth again, "Does this make sense to you?" Elizabeth said, "I think so".

Lucy continued explaining the process of stretching to her. "Our skin will always stretch if we continue to stretch it. I know you probably don't have this problem because you are very slim but if you can imagine some people who put on too much weight and when they lose their weight again, their skin will have loosened and stretched so it simply hangs or they end up with stretch marks. It is the same with your vaginal skin, so if we continue stretching it regularly, at some point the skin will give fully and then it will stay stretched. Of course, we're only going to stretch your skin until it is the normal size and length but unfortunately, we can't rush it. We can only keep stretching the skin very hard regularly and gradually. Once the skin is used to the stretching and it loosens more, the pain and soreness usually goes and that's why most women don't have any more pain when they start using the bigger sized dilators, and it will be the same for you when you go on to the bigger sizes. Then when your skin is fully stretched, you would have completed your treatment and you will have a normal vagina". After listening intently, Elizabeth said, "Thank you for explaining to me. Now I understand". Lucy said, "Good so we can continue".

They continued with her treatment using her next-sized dilator and when it was inserted, Elizabeth tried her best to tolerate the pain, but she just could not push the dilator in herself so Lucy had to help her with it again. When she finished her treatment, she was pleased that the terrible pain went although she was still left with that soreness and tenderness afterwards as explained, so she was not too worried this time. She now understood what Lucy meant when she told her that it would be too painful for her to do her treatments several times a day and would therefore not be beneficial if she could not do them properly. "Lucy was right. She's so clever, how does she know all these things?" Elizabeth wondered.

Elizabeth got herself dressed again and then she washed her dilators, dried them and put them into a toiletry bag that she had bought specially for them. Afterwards, she thought that she would sit down on the chair and wait for her mother and Sally but as she did so, "Ouch!" She really felt this terrible sting and had scrunched up her face, when there was another knock on the door and then her mother and Sally walked in. When they entered the room and saw Elizabeth's face, their smiling faces soon changed to a more concerned look so they asked "what's wrong, are you alright?" Elizabeth told them that "Yes, I'm alright thanks. It's just that I'm feeling a lot sorer today than I did yesterday". They were both relieved. Still the soreness did not prevent her from doing anything else so Elizabeth went out with her mother and Sally as her next treatment was not until later in the afternoon.

They took the underground to South Kensington tube station and walked towards the Science Museum, because Elizabeth and her family did not go there the last time, but it was somewhere that both she and Sally were naturally interested in. They spent a few hours in the museum and were fascinated by the displays and exhibits there, and they also went into the IMAX theatre to see a show on the human body. They were very enthralled by the experience and wished they had more time to spend as they did not manage to see everything but they had to go back for Elizabeth's treatment. They stopped by a noodle place near the station for lunch before heading back. When they arrived, Lucy was already waiting for them, so Jan and Sally decided to have a coffee at the cafeteria whilst they waited for Elizabeth. Jan thanked Sally for being a good friend to Elizabeth and for coming to support her. She was also impressed with Sally's help during Elizabeth's panic attacks and told her, "I can see that you really have the makings of a good doctor because you are such a natural". Sally appreciated the compliment but said that she was only glad to be able to help her best friend.

Elizabeth repeated her treatment in much the same way as before. She still required some help from Lucy due to the soreness but the pain eased again when she finished the treatment. This time though, she thought that the soreness was getting better so she immediately felt that her skin must have loosened more like Lucy had explained, so she was confident that she would be able to do it on her own later on.

When she finished with her treatment, she rejoined her mother and Sally and spent the next few hours at a mega-mall not far from their hotel. They took their time browsing through some of the shops because they did not have anything in particular in mind, although Sally suddenly said, "Oh, I just remembered. I need a new pair of trainers". In the end, the two girls bought some causal tops and a pair of trainers each. Jan bought some Belgian chocolates for all the Centre staff because she was very appreciative of their help and Elizabeth bought thank-you cards for both Lucy and Anne. She spent quite some time at the card section trying to select something appropriate which would express her feelings and what she wanted to say to them, but there was only a couple of cards that came close. She decided to get them anyway and she would add her own words later. She had so much to say to the two of them but most of all, she wanted to thank them from the bottom of her heart for understanding what she was going through and for helping and supporting her. With their help, she was changing her attitude and the way she felt about herself. They taught her coping strategies and gave her hope, optimism and the strength to face new challenges and steered her back on track. Elizabeth felt she had control of her life once again which was very important to her since she always needed to know where she was heading and what her endgame was, so that she would strive to get there. This was how she had always lived her life and who she was, always an achiever and quite the perfectionist. She felt the most confident when she was in charge of her life and when she was responsible for the choices she made, otherwise nothing in her life would make sense. Sadly, her condition robbed her of her choices so she had to learn to accept and to cope without the choices everyone else took for granted, but it made her more appreciative of the ones she had to earn. She felt she would never have succeeded in getting this far without the help from Anne and Lucy. She therefore felt a deep sense of gratitude towards them although they told her that they were just doing their jobs, but Elizabeth felt that they did more than just that. In Elizabeth's eyes, they far surpassed their roles and they managed to transform a frightened young girl to a more confident and happier one. They were always friendly and they made her feel comfortable, so much so that she regarded them not just as professionals but as her new best friends. She had got on very well with the both of them right from the beginning because they did not pity her, nor did they treat her with prejudice or derision. They were always professional yet they were very easy to talk to and she felt as if she had known them all her life. She knew it was absurd because she only met them fairly recently but still this was how she felt.

One thing for sure though, she knew that if not for them she would not be here today, doing well and feeling well. Of course, her friends' and family's support also played a big part but this was different. To Elizabeth, Lucy and Anne were the ones who made the biggest difference to her life. She thought that they gave her a second chance, a second life where she would be normal. They opened up avenues for her and guided her towards her goal and when she felt drowned by her own emotions, Anne always managed to make her feel better so she really appreciated that. Then Lucy, the person who actually made it happen for her. Elizabeth had been waiting for someone like Lucy, who would change her physically, to change her from an abnormal person to a normal girl so she felt she owed her the most. Lucy was the one who was helping her to create her vagina, which would then make her normal. This was all she wished for ever since she was diagnosed so it meant the world to her, to be normal like all her girlfriends. She did not mind being different now, but she hated being a freak so she knew that she had to change this aspect of her, because only then could she consider herself to be a normal girl. So now at last, she was normal again because now, she had a vagina. She was so overwhelmed by her own emotions that she was nearly in tears as she stood holding the two cards in her hand and staring at them. She was soon reminded that she was in this big and slightly crowded card shop when another customer rudely shoved into her and stretched across her to reach for a card. She was too stunned to say anything so she briskly walked away and headed towards the cashier counter. When she paid up, she looked around the shop to see if she could see either her mother or Sally, but they had already left the shop. Then Elizabeth spotted them waiting for her outside. She apologised to them, "I'm so sorry I didn't even realise that you'd come outside. I hope that you weren't waiting here for a long time. I was stuck with a couple of the cards and I guess I lost track of the time. Was I really in there for a long time?" Sally said, "You were in there for ages. My toes are frozen from just standing here waiting for you". Elizabeth felt terrible but then her friend laughed and told her, "I'm only joking but you were in there a while though". Elizabeth gave her friend a hug and rubbed her all over with her hands as if to try to warm her up, so Sally said, "It's ok. I'm not that cold". Jan could only laugh at the two girls because she thought they were such good friends and so lovely to watch.

They stopped for coffee and cakes before returning to their hotel. After a rest and freshen up, they caught the tube to Leicester Square before they went to the theatre. As they were still too early for the show, they walked to Covent Garden and watched a fire and dance performance in the central square. Afterwards, they walked around the market place. It was buzzing with people and they appeared to be mostly tourists, much like themselves. There was also a choice of restaurants there with lots of people dining in all of them. Jan and the girls were not hungry yet, having just had their afternoon tea, so she suggested that they looked for a nice restaurant instead so that they could come back to it after the show. They could not make up their mind so they decided to make their way to the theatre instead and they would find something somewhere in Leicester

Square or Piccadilly Circus afterwards. *The Phantom of the Opera* was an entertaining success! It was brilliant and the vocals were to perfection and all three of them thoroughly enjoyed themselves. Sally could not help singing the theme song afterwards and even Elizabeth joined in and at one point, they were swinging and swaying to their own synchronised singing, "In sleep he sang to me, in dreams he came, that voice which calls to me and speaks my name... the Phantom of the Opera is there, inside my mind... pum pum pum pum pum, da da". Jan just adored watching them because they were fun and for once, she felt that Elizabeth was like a normal adolescent again. She really loved them and thought that Sally was such a good positive influence on her daughter, and was again grateful that she came up to London with them.

They walked towards Leicester Square and Soho and again there were a selection of restaurants for them to choose from but all serving much the same type of food like the pizzas, burgers and steaks. In the end, they decided on a Chinese meal in Chinatown because Sally said that she liked Chinese very much and had not had it for a while. The meal was beyond their expectations. In fact, they thought that the quality and the variety was so exceptional and far superior to their local, so Elizabeth said, "I can't believe that we'd always thought that our local was very good, mum. We obviously don't know what we've been missing. This is the real deal!" They had eaten so much because in their excitement they had ordered too much, as they were very hungry at the time. The food was too delicious to waste so they took their time eating it because they felt guilty about wasting food, and it was not as if they could ask for a doggy-bag either as there was no facility in the hotel for heating up food. So there they were the three of them eating and eating and eating and then Sally said jokingly, "I think we should have ordered more because I don't think there's enough food here". They could hardly move afterwards but they decided to walk around the West End anyway to try to burn off some of their calories. London's West End was still very much alive and teeming with people and activity. Very soon, they were swept in by with the hustle and bustle going on around them and began to feel they belonged with the city's megalopolis of people. They could not help noticing a lot of other people walking very briskly though, and a man even brushed harshly against them without apologising as he walked past, rushing off somewhere oblivious to everyone and everything around him and only bent on his own agenda. Jan then said "I like London because it is such an amazing and exciting city but I'm so glad I don't live here," and the two girls agreed. They were just not used to the pace, so much so that Sally asked, "Don't you feel that London just makes us feel like we're simple country bumpkins?" to which both Jan and Elizabeth agreed, yet they lived in a big city too, only theirs seemed to be a little more civilised and definitely quieter and calmer by comparison.

When they reached their hotel, it was close to midnight. The hotel was situated in one of the busiest boroughs of inner London yet the whole area seemed quieter compared to London's West End. The hotel itself was still quite busy because there was a coach party of people who had just arrived and were being checked in at the hotel reception. There were also groups of different people drinking by the bar and by the pool. Jan and the girls took the lift straight to the ninth floor. They had been out the whole day and enjoyed themselves very much but they were ready for bed, so Sally said, "Good night. See you in the morning," and went to her room. Poor Elizabeth though did not have that luxury and much as she too was tired and ready for bed, she still had to do her treatment. After a quick shower, she organised herself to do it whilst her mother was having her shower. She suddenly became nervous because she had not done the treatment on her own without Lucy before, so this was the first time, although she told herself, "I should still know what to do by now. I have only been doing this same treatment for the last couple of days. Come on El, you know how to do it". Still she had to rehearse the procedure step by step in her head prior to starting, so that she knew exactly what to do. It also helped her to ignore her palpitations and her slightly trembling hands, so with sheer focus and determination, Elizabeth told herself "Just get on with it, El. You have to do this before mum comes out. Come on, quickly!" She wanted to be all done before her mother came out of the bathroom. She could not explain this new-found embarrassment but ever since she found out she had MRKH, she could not bear letting her mother see her naked, let alone see her sticking something inside her vagina. It was not as if she was trying to hide anything from her mother but this just felt different. She wondered if it could be that she was ashamed that she was no longer perfect in her mother's eyes. Indeed, to Jan and Paul, she was their perfect child and they were extremely proud of her but now, because of her abnormality, she felt she had embarrassed them. Maybe she was being oversensitive or maybe it was her paranoia but Elizabeth felt her parents had lost the sparkle in their eyes whenever they looked at her, or when they spoke of her to her grandparents and friends. She felt sad that she had let them down and although she desperately longed for their relationship to return to what it was, she could not get back what was lost. How could she, when the thing that perversely changed everything remained as a constant reminder of her imperfection every day. Now, everything was different and she was different. She had no choice but to accept things for what they were. Nevertheless, she could not disembarrass herself when it related to her private parts and especially in the presence of her mother. She felt that this was her private affair and just as her mother had told her previously, some things were best kept private. "Enough of this already, better get a move on". Elizabeth reminded herself to stop introspecting further and to do her treatment instead.

To her surprise, the treatment could not have been easier. No fuss, just straight in. It was done within a few minutes. "Oh, that was easy". She had surprised herself. She did not know why but she anticipated more pain but there was no pain at all, just that little tenderness despite her pushing really hard, but most importantly she had done it all on her own! Elizabeth felt really chuffed with herself. Then she thought, "Lucy would be proud of me," even though she knew that she was only doing it for herself and not for anyone else. Still, the first person that came to her mind was Lucy. It was not that Elizabeth was trying to impress her but it was important to her to know what Lucy thought of her, especially as she was the one who taught her. Elizabeth had this unusual and yet a natural closeness to her, because she felt that Lucy was like a teacher, a mother and a friend, all rolled into one and in the short space of time they had known each other, Elizabeth had managed to establish a good rapport with her, because she always thought that Lucy was not like the other professionals she had seen. She had such respect for her because she knew that Lucy was very experienced in her field, and yet she had no airs about her. Instead Elizabeth found her to be always kind and down to earth so she felt at ease talking to her, and she also liked that Lucy was personable and brought the human touch to her profession. In fact, she liked that a lot. But most of all it was the fact that she felt normal around her, because Lucy was very natural about her abnormality and she had this way of then transferring and making Elizabeth believe and feel she was normal. It must be an art, Elizabeth thought, to enable someone like me to feel normal in spite of an abnormality such as mine and, not derogating it. Yes, Lucy made her feel good and positive about herself, every time. Furthermore, Elizabeth also had no doubt that she was helping a lot of other women, but whenever she was with her, Lucy always made her feel as though she was the only one she was treating, so Elizabeth felt that she really cared about her and was genuine about helping her. This was important since they had to spend a lot of time together doing the most intimate things, something Elizabeth could never have imagined. Still, here she was, doing the unimaginable. Just then she thought she must be the luckiest person because she had Tom, who was a saint because he was so altruistic that he accepted her and offered her a future with him, and now she had Lucy, who was her guardian angel guiding and helping her to change her abnormality, so she felt truly blessed and was immensely grateful.

Elizabeth was feeling very optimistic thinking about her experience thus far and she also felt that her confidence had returned. Now that she was at a slightly better place, she could see how much her MRKH had affected and crushed her and she appreciated how much the professionals had helped her. In fact, since seeing the whole team, she felt that the course of her life had changed and she could feel her quality of life slowly improving, so she felt forever indebted to them but she was not quite there yet, and it made her realise that she still needed their help and support to see her through to where she needed to be.

As she sat and waited for her mother to come out of the bathroom, Elizabeth had a sudden rush of panic. When she thought about the treatment she had just done by herself, she could not believe that it went so swimmingly, so she started to doubt herself, thinking that perhaps she did not do it correctly. Lucy had stressed to her that she had to do it right if she was to have a positive outcome. She needed Lucy to check her technique there and then but she was on her own this time. She could not wait to get back to the Centre so that she could find out for sure and wished she could put the clock forward in that instant. When Jan finished, she did not just come out of the bathroom because she was mindful not to interrupt Elizabeth's treatment as she was also too aware of her daughter's sense of embarrassment, so instead she asked first, "Darling, are you done? May I come out now or do you need more time?" so Elizabeth told her, "Yes, it's ok mum. You may come out, I'm done". Elizabeth told her mother very briefly that she had done her treatment and that it was ok because she did not want to have a discussion about it, and besides she could not help her anyway, so instead she just said, "Goodnight mummy". Jan intuitively understood and although she was tempted to probe further, she could tell that Elizabeth was not in the mood to talk and it was already late anyway so she just said, "Goodnight darling, sleep well". Besides, they were both very tired and needed their sleep and since Elizabeth was seeing Lucy in the morning. Jan felt assured that whatever it was that was bothering her daughter, Lucy would sort it out for sure.

Elizabeth was the first to rise because she must have been subconsciously worrying about her treatment although she did sleep. In fact, she fell into a deep sleep straight away, and when she awoke, she felt quite refreshed. Jan said she also felt well rested after a good night's sleep. It was checkout day for them so they took their luggage with them and when they were ready to leave, they called in on Sally and the three of them made their way towards the lift. They took the lift down to the hotel restaurant on the ground floor for breakfast, as this was included in their hotel package. It was a very big restaurant and already it was nearly full with diners, so Jan commented, "And we're not even that late. It's only gone eight. They must be early-risers here". After giving their room numbers, they were shown to the last but one remaining table. It was indeed very busy in there as most of the hotel guests must have decided to have their breakfast around the same time. Still there was plenty of food to go round. They could see at least three or four chefs continuously coming in and out of the kitchen to replenish the food at the hot food servery counter. They were spoilt for choice because breakfast was a sumptuous spread of continental and cooked English breakfast, a huge fruit basket of local and exotic fruits and a generous selection of different cakes and pastries. They were all hungry and the smell of bacon and eggs that was circulating in the restaurant was just too good to resist, so they decided to have everything on offer. After their juices, fruits and yoghurt, they had their hearty cooked breakfast of bacon, sausages, fried and scrambled eggs, mushrooms, tomatoes and hash browns to go with their toasts and pancakes. When they finished with their breakfast, they walked over to the cake section and Sally said excitedly, "Oh I think I've died and gone to heaven. Look El, everything's to die for, they all look so yummy!"

"I know it just makes you want to have everything," Elizabeth added. They were very tempted to have a plate each but because they were already quite full and they did not want to appear too greedy, they shared a small plate of cake slices and a selection of choux, puff and flaky pastries. The waiters and waitresses were also very attentive and kept topping up coffees and teas for everyone. They were well contented with their breakfast because the food and service was excellent. Elizabeth even managed to enjoy breakfast without a second thought given to her earlier concern. Afterwards, they went to the reception in the hotel lobby to check out before they made their way to the Centre again.

On the train going to the Centre, Elizabeth then started to think about the treatment she did last night. She kept hoping that Lucy would confirm that she had done it correctly because she was getting increasing concerned that, if not, she would have to stay an extra day for more guidance, or even worse face the possibility of not progressing with her treatment and not achieving the outcome she wanted. She had become such a worrier these days. She was never like this before but her condition had completely knocked her for six and she seemed to have difficulty maintaining her self-confidence. She was also aware that she was getting rather attached to and dependent on Lucy, but she could not stop herself. She had a high regard for her expertise so her advice and reassurance mattered a great deal. Besides, it was still early days and what was more, Lucy had told her that she could ask for her help whenever she needed it. Elizabeth was also convinced that Lucy would make her vagina normal so she could not wait to be normal again soon. She could already see the difference and improvement so she trusted Lucy fully. It was a shame she did not trust herself as much but she was trying to slowly but surely. It just seemed like a long journey but despite her wavering self-confidence, she was still happy now because she was making progress and she could see that her efforts had already produced some results.

Jan and Sally tried talking to Elizabeth a couple of times when they were on the train but they hardly got a response so they knew that she was again in a world of her own. Jan suspected that it had something to do with her treatment last night and wished she had asked her a bit more about it then. She felt that now was definitely not the time or place for her to bring it up, especially in a fairly crowded train. Just before the train reached their destination, Jan placed her hand on Elizabeth's to tell her, "We're getting off at the next stop darling, so we need to get to the front". The three of them took their own roll-on luggage, excused themselves and wriggled to the front of the doors so that they could get off the train easily when it stopped. It was only a short walk to the Centre and when they reached it, Elizabeth asked her mother and Sally, "Will you have your coffee or tea and wait here for me, so I will come and find you when I have finished my treatment?" Sally told her, "Sure, no worries. See you later," and with that, Elizabeth took out her bag of dilators from her luggage and went straight up to the unit. When she arrived on the unit, she saw that Lucy was busy doing something for another young girl so she greeted her with a "Good morning" before going straight into her room. Lucy acknowledged her return and told her that she would be with her in a few minutes. Elizabeth went to the toilet first and laid on the bed to wait for Lucy. By now, she knew the routine well and she just wanted to get on with her treatment. She did not have to wait long. Lucy came into her room within the next few minutes and asked, "How are you?" so Elizabeth replied, "Fine thank you". Then Lucy asked her "How did you get on last night?"

"Ok I think but I'm not sure," Elizabeth answered and then she hesitated for a second before she continued, "I mean, I don't know. I did what you taught me to do but there was no pain, just a little soreness and I pushed really hard too. I think I did it wrong. Do you think I could have dilated my urethra?" Then in a reassuring voice, Lucy said, "No, I'm sure you didn't, the dilators are too big and they would cause you a lot of pain or bleeding if you did".

"Thank goodness, I was so worried" Elizabeth said, with a huge sigh of relief. Then Lucy thought it would be helpful to remind her of the simple pictorial diagram of the female genitalia she had drawn for Elizabeth initially, which demonstrated where the urethra or "wee-pipe" and vagina was. Of course, Elizabeth had forgotten all about that because she was just so frightened then, and only remembered Lucy reiterating the importance of inserting the dilator at an angle to avoid dilating her urethra. Lucy continued to reassure Elizabeth that she was quite sure that she had been using her dilators correctly so "don't worry. I'm sure you did just fine. Anyway, shall we do your treatment now and I will examine you afterwards".

"Ok," Elizabeth said as a matter of fact, now that she was reassured, and got herself ready on the bed. Her doubts and fears went just like that, and it was as if in the presence of Lucy nothing could go wrong. Then she recalled Lucy telling her that the pain usually eased after a few days of stretching anyway and that after a while, most of the women did not have any pain at all. She knew from examining herself that she was progressing well so she thought she should have had more faith in herself, but she just could not maintain her self-confidence. She thought again, no matter, she would address this lack of her self-confidence with Anne when she saw her next.

During her treatment, Lucy and Elizabeth were having a general conversation about their preference in music and artists. This was always a good distraction and it also made the treatment seem less tedious. Elizabeth took this opportunity to mention Tom's eighteenth and their intended short trip to Barcelona. She voiced her concerns because she would still be in the middle of her treatment but to her surprise, Lucy told her that she should go and enjoy herself. "What about my treatment? I don't want to take the dilators with me because I would die if they searched my luggage!" Elizabeth cried out. "I understand. I can give you a medical note and it won't be a problem or..." Before Lucy could finish what she was saying Elizabeth said, "It's not that, I would be so embarrassed if they found the dilators in my luggage and asked me about them. I would die! I'd rather not go". Elizabeth was quite dramatic so Lucy said, "As I was going to say, don't bring them. If you don't do the treatment for a few days, it's not going to hurt. You'll just have to restart your treatment when you return. As long as you don't make a habit of it, it shouldn't delay your completion". Elizabeth was shocked, but at the same time, she was pleased to hear this so she asked "Oh, you mean I don't have to do my treatment? But I don't want to delay my completion".

"I know and you won't as long as this is a one-off short break. It's not a problem," Lucy reassured her. Elizabeth was almost speechless so she just said, "Hmmm, ok. Thank you, thank you," and without a second thought, she lunged forward to give Lucy a hug. Afterwards, they had a laugh because she had splattered Lucy with the gel on her hands so she was most apologetic afterwards, "I'm so sorry about that". Elizabeth's confidence was also boosted when it was confirmed that her stretching technique was correct, and when she examined herself after Lucy, her vagina had stretched even further. Lucy informed her that "Your vagina is soft and feels rather normal, apart from being slightly short and tight at the very top but it's still a good five centimetres in length. That's why you did not have any pain last night, so well done you". Elizabeth was so thrilled and over the moon that words failed her. It was surreal. She became emotional and felt choked again. Everyone in her family had told her that being sixteen was special because she would become a young woman. Never would she have dreamt that she would have to be doing this at sixteen, especially when she was still quite naive and innocent in this respect. No wonder she was so obsessive about it and no wonder she became an emotional roller coaster. She had done the unthinkable, and although she was not there yet she was already impressed. A few days ago, her future was hanging in the balance, but now it was becoming more real and she could actually visualise a future.

She felt so charged that she asked Lucy again, "Do you think that I can do my treatments more often because I really want to hasten my completion? Is that possible do you think?" Elizabeth was so enthusiastic that Lucy was mindful not to dampen her spirit so she told her, "El, you know what I think but if you still really want to try then go ahead and try" although in reality, Lucy felt that Elizabeth probably would not. In any case, she would not advocate it because, as she had explained, she knew all too well from experience that this would make her too sore to stretch properly again, which would defeat the purpose in the long run. Furthermore, the treatments were time consuming and, having discussed her school activities with Elizabeth, it did not seem feasible, and because Lucy knew what she was like, she was concerned that Elizabeth would only get too stressed trying to fit more treatments into her day which might then compromise her overall wellbeing.

Lucy watched her and understood Elizabeth's current state of mind, because she recognised that familiar look.

She had seen that same expression before and shared many similar experiences with the other women she treated in the past and although Elizabeth might well be different, Lucy was more prudent, knowing what she knew, so she decided to reserve her judgement on this matter for now. From her experience, the treatment usually followed similar if not the same pattern, where the women would be so impressed with their initial achievement that they would run away with the notion they could complete the treatment in a few days, but when the progress slowed down their enthusiasm often dwindled along with it. Some became disinterested when their progress was less obvious, and they began to resent their treatment, so they needed constant encouragement and support to continue. A few had to stop and only recommenced their treatments when they were ready to try again, so it was not always easy. It was just that the treatment itself sounded simple enough but the commitment and a positive mindset at all times made it difficult for some women. Then Elizabeth asked Lucy again, "You don't think that I will still need surgery now, do you Lucy?" so Lucy reassured her with, "No, I am pretty certain that you won't. You have done so well and I know that you will continue to stretch with the dilators, as long as you carry on doing your treatments as you have been doing. You don't need any operation and I am positive that you will achieve a normal length vagina with the dilators soon, so don't keep worrying about surgery – just stay focused on doing your treatments properly. To tell you the truth, we haven't done surgery on any woman here for a very long time so we've only been treating all the women who come to us with just the dilator treatment and the vast majority of them have all completed their treatment successfully".

"Wow, that's pretty impressive," Elizabeth said. Then Lucy went on to explain another benefit of the dilator treatment to her, which was that it was also the least intrusive treatment on offer, and why she and the team at the Centre still believed that this was the best treatment for creating vaginas for the women with MRKH, especially when their outcomes were excellent. In addition, it was also very important that this treatment did not physically scar or de-normalise their external genitalia, which was again a plus, since the women already felt abnormal in the first place. Not adding to their sense of abnormality made it easier for them to be normal and to carry on to live a normal life so Elizabeth was again filled with gratitude and said "I can't thank you guys enough because you think of everything for us".

After listening to Lucy and having another short discussion, Elizabeth was slightly disappointed that Lucy did not advise more frequent dilator usage, nor did she agree that it would hasten her completion, but she was not too disheartened because she was always informed that it normally took a few months before she would achieve her goal anyway. In reality, she also realised that it was going to be difficult enough to do her expected treatments without having to do more. Lucy had also grown to know Elizabeth quite well by now and knew that her emotional status and confidence was easily shaken, especially at this stage, so she was keen to support Elizabeth the best she could in order to ensure that she continued and completed her treatment. She actually believed that Elizabeth might well finish sooner rather than later if she was diligent, so she was especially keen to make it more feasible for Elizabeth to do so. She again advised Elizabeth to try to not make a big issue of her treatment in case she came to resent it, but instead advised her to blend it into her life so that she could still carry on normally. She told Elizabeth again, "I don't want to specify when you should do your treatments because I don't know your daily routine so I will leave it up to you. You can do them when it's convenient to you, whether it be morning, day or night, ok?" Elizabeth seemed more compliant with this arrangement and pledged that, "I will try very hard because this is the most important thing in my life right now and it's something that I want very badly, so I have to complete my treatment. I can't ever think otherwise and I cannot see myself not ever completing my treatment because all I've ever wanted is to be normal again and this is my chance to make me normal so I'm not going to throw it away. I can't and I won't". Elizabeth was so determined and so very convincing but then this was always her goal, her chance of being normal as she believed all along, and she would succeed or die trying. This was how strongly she felt on this matter. Lucy had never seen such determination in a sixteen-year-old and it was very admirable so she was equally determined to help her succeed.

During the course of the conversation, Lucy decided to ask Elizabeth about her relationship with Tom. Initially, Elizabeth felt quite shy acknowledging Tom as her boyfriend but once she started, she was a natural. She told Lucy all that had happened between them. She still could not get over the fact that he was so mature about her not being able to have children, knowing that he always wanted children of his own. It was obvious that she adored him because he sounded like he was a special guy and that he truly loved her. After all, according to Elizabeth, he could have any girl he wanted but he chose her knowing that she had MRKH, so it was obvious that he really loved her and that he was not just after her for sex, which was a commendable trait in a young man of his age, because most would be guided by their testosterone. Elizabeth then asked Lucy the questions she had been waiting to ask her because she felt sure that Lucy would definitely know the answers. She asked her if it would feel the same for her if she was to have sex but more importantly, if Tom would know that she was different from other women. She was very relieved to learn that he would not notice anything different when her treatment was completed, but that he probably would if she tried intercourse at this stage because her vagina would not be adequate enough. "That's ok because I'm not going to do anything until I finish," replied Elizabeth but then Lucy said, "I understand but since Tom already knows about your MRKH, you could try with him if you wanted to or if you felt ready. It shouldn't be too uncomfortable, as long as you both know that he probably won't be able to enter fully if you tried now. Still it is long enough if you decided to try and you could even count it as a treatment because he would be stretching you too, albeit more naturally". Elizabeth opened her mouth in disbelief as if to say something but no words ensued so Lucy continued, "Some women preferred this than just using the dilators at this stage because it obviously felt more natural for them. Some combined the dilators with having sex and they succeeded, so you can too if you wish. I'm not saying it's easy but with perseverance all the women we treated so far have succeeded". She also told Elizabeth that a few women who tried sex first also came for treatment because their vaginas were still too short. Some of them bled initially when they had sex, which was quite frightening for them but with treatment, they managed to stretch their vaginas fully and were able to enjoy sex afterwards. She added, "You're going to be fine too El and it sounds like you have found your Mister Right".

"I have, Tom's really great".

Lucy was very discerning in sharing the information about other women with Elizabeth because she felt it would widen Elizabeth's perspective of her condition and the treatment. She knew that Elizabeth was a highly intelligent girl but at the same time, her confidence and self-esteem were easily shaken, especially if things did not go to plan. She could sense Elizabeth's brain ticking away so she paused to allow her to take in the information. "I'm glad I didn't bleed because I would have been terrified". Lucy reassured her that despite the bleeding, the vagina would heal up just like if she had a cut on the finger or any part of the body. Elizabeth was still worried so she asked again, "Are there a lot of girls who bleed?"

"No but some do. You didn't because your skin is very stretchy and we also stretched you gradually using the smaller dilators first," replied Lucy but Elizabeth was still thinking about the other girls. "Are there a lot of girls who try sex first?" she asked, because she thought that they must be very brave, so Lucy told her that sometimes this was how some of the women found out about their MRKH. "It must have been so embarrassing for them. If that was me, I would die! Were they very scared too? I can't imagine what that must have felt like for them. Did their boyfriends stay with them afterwards, I mean?" she enquired with concern, so Lucy informed her that "To be honest, there are not that many girls who tried sex first. I know of a few women who were married and they tried with their husbands and yes, most of their husbands were very supportive, like your Tom, but of course there were a few partners who probably did not understand".

"That's terrible. It must have been so awful for them, poor things. I'm so glad that Tom stood by me," Elizabeth said empathetically.

"You know when you first showed me the dilators, I nearly fainted. They looked huge, and I didn't believe you when you said that they were only the small ones. I never thought that I could put anything inside me but now compared to the ones I am using, I can say that the small ones look tiny. I still can't believe that I am using these big dilators and they don't even look so scary anymore. I showed them to Sally and she thought they looked horrendously huge. She said I'd have to measure Tom first and we had a laugh about it," she told Lucy. "That's lovely to hear. I'm glad that you have a good friend too. It's important to have someone you can trust and who can support you and have a laugh with you," Lucy said encouragingly. Then, looking at Elizabeth's face, she could tell that Elizabeth was again beginning to become unrealistic about the completion of her treatment, so she continued "You see El, I want you to know that sometimes the whole process can be arduous and although you have made great progress in these few days, you might reach a stage where your progress slows down, and this is normal, so I don't want you to get angst if it does. It can get difficult sometimes, so you need to stay focused and if you persevere and continue with the treatments, I know that you will complete in good time". Elizabeth had just been thinking about that before Lucy spoke – that maybe she would be able to finish her treatment soon since she had accomplished so much in three days – so she could not believe that Lucy knew what she was thinking, and she asked herself, "How could she have read my mind?" Then she relented and said, "I know, I got carried away. It's just that I want to finish quickly. I know that I will complete too and I won't let you down". Lucy reminded her that she should do it for herself and not for anyone, which Elizabeth understood very well but she still could not help wanting to please Lucy too. She was like a child and, being very competitive too, she wanted to be Lucy's best student. She also felt that she could not disappoint Lucy after everything she had done for her, and even though Lucy said that she was only doing her job, Elizabeth always felt that she did more than that, and she would not have a vagina now if not for her. She was so grateful to her that it made her more determined to succeed and to make Lucy proud.

Lucy discharged Elizabeth that day but before doing so, she asked her if she had any further queries so Elizabeth asked, "When will I know that I have completed my treatment?"

"We will let you know but usually it's when your vagina measures around a stretchy six to six-and-a-half centimeters or more, or when you can have sex comfortably" Lucy informed her. "Is that the normal length for normal women, I mean?" asked Elizabeth. Lucy confirmed that, "It is slightly longer for other women," but she reassured her that "your vagina will continue to stretch with dilators or sexual intercourse as the skin becomes more elastic so don't worry, yours will stretch to the normal length too". Elizabeth also asked Lucy the size of a man's penis, so Lucy informed her that the average penile size was anything from fourteen to sixteen centimetres on erection. Elizabeth's jaw dropped when she heard that because, "I only have five centimetres," so Lucy reminded her, "Yes I know, but do you remember me telling you that if you were to have sex with Tom at this stage, he would not be able to have full penetration because your vagina will still be slightly too short?" Elizabeth was gob-smacked so Lucy continued, "But it's ok, because your vagina is very stretchy so if you continue using the dilators or to have sex with Tom, it will also continue to stretch further". Then Elizabeth asked, "What if Tom is very big? Will I bleed then?" Lucy told her that she might, as do some women who would bleed if the man was very well endowed, even if the women did not have MRKH. She also reassured Elizabeth that if she was to bleed, her vagina would heal but that since she had not bled with the dilators, it would be unlikely that she would bleed with sexual intercourse. She again reiterated that Elizabeth's vagina would continue to stretch with time if sexual activity continued. She could still see the look of concern in Elizabeth's face so she said, "Don't look so worried, El. I'm not suggesting that you should have sex with Tom right now, I'm just letting you know that when you are ready and you feel like you want to try with Tom, you can, as long as you both know that he won't be able to enter fully at this stage, so just do it gradually". Elizabeth listened intently so Lucy continued, "This will also help you to determine the length you both need to be comfortable and to enjoy sex. If you are comfortable with Tom, he could help you with the dilators. He could also try using them as sex toys, like foreplay".

By now, Elizabeth's face was getting so red with embarrassment that she wanted to laugh out aloud, but then she noticed how open and frank Lucy was, talking about such intimate matters, and was amazed at her professionalism that it gave her the courage to ask rather bashfully, "I feel really stupid but I have one more question. You're the only person I can ask and I know you will tell me the truth. Do I look normal to you, down below I mean?" Lucy told her affirmatively, "Yes, your external genitalia or down below looks absolutely normal. The folds of skin on each side are the vulval lips. I know you want to study medicine, so the medical term is labia and they cover and protect your vagina and urethra. You also have a clitoris, so you will be able to have orgasms like any woman". Elizabeth was grateful for the information because she did not know whether she should ask Lucy about it so she said, "Thank you for telling me. I was not sure if I should ask you about that too. You don't mind me asking you all these questions do you? I know you are very busy".

"I'm never too busy for you and I don't want you to hesitate asking me anything. I will try my best to help and if I can't, I can always ask my colleagues. That's what we're here for" added Lucy. "Thank you, you guys are so nice to me and I won't disappoint you," Elizabeth said sincerely. "You could never disappoint me, El. In fact, it is me who is privileged to have known you and all the other women. I know it's not easy for you but you still try so hard and it makes me very humble every time I work with you," Lucy told her. "Aww, that's so nice. Can I give you a hug?" Elizabeth asked, quickly looking at her hands to ensure there was no gel left on them and then answered her own question "My hands are clean, I've just washed them". They laughed as she said that, and it was evident that they had got to know each other very well by now and they had a very special relationship indeed.

They said their goodbyes and Lucy gave Elizabeth her next appointment to review her treatment. Anne also came to see Elizabeth and to arrange her next therapy session.

When she left, Elizabeth handed Lucy the card she had got for her. Inside the card, Elizabeth had written a separate letter, pouring out all her inner feelings and her heartfelt appreciation of the help she received and how her life had changed because of it so she was now more positive of her future, a future she did not think was possible when she first found out she had MRKH. When Lucy read her letter, it nearly brought tears to her eyes, because it was very poignant yet very positive at the same time. She had received several similar letters and cards from other women before but this was slightly different. Elizabeth was different, she was just sixteen but she was very articulate and Lucy was especially pleased that she was able to express all her fears, thoughts and true feelings into words. She managed to release all that anger, and her different and often negative emotions that she had kept to herself all this time, and it showed how far she had come. It was a very healthy start and showed promising progress, and Lucy was only too pleased to have a role in it but she always believed in Elizabeth and thought that she was a special girl. For Lucy personally – she loved her job and every girl, every woman she had treated had a special place in her heart. She herself had a decent upbringing so good manners, respect, honesty and humility were ingrained in her. She was also used to giving and helping people, but she never expected anything back in return and she never took anything for granted. She came from a modest working background so it was not always an easy ride and she had to work very hard to get to where she was, so she understood only too well what it was like to have to work and strive hard to get there. She was in teaching for a short period of time. Then she did some counselling and nursing before she entered this very specialised world of medicine and psychology. With all her life experiences, she found this job to be the most gratifying and challenging, especially as she always gave it her all to try and help each and every individual woman she had the pleasure to meet. Yes, she loved her job, because through it she was fortunate to have met so many genuine and decent people, who reminded her of her own principles, virtues and values. She liked that and was always humbled. It also made her feel worthwhile to be able to make a difference and to improve the quality of life for these women, and she felt that she had the most rewarding and interesting job in her whole career. Of course, it helped that she got on very well with all her colleagues and that they had a very special working relationship too and she also felt that she worked with the best team in the field. This was also evident to Elizabeth and her family, who felt that not only was all the staff so knowledgeable and experienced in their own areas of expertise, but more striking was how well the staff worked together as a team, and they were so aware that there was such a good communication and liaison between them, which they not only found reassuring but also terribly important, since they felt that Elizabeth's welfare and future was in their hands.

The next few weeks passed by quickly and Elizabeth had a good routine going with her treatments. She took Lucy's advice and fitted them in according to what she was doing everyday but mostly, when she was not out with Tom or her friends, she would do them in the mornings, afternoons and before she went to bed. Her family remained supportive and respected her privacy but every now and again, Jan would ask her about her progress and on a couple of occasions, when Elizabeth tried to let slip because she was tired, Jan was not going to make the same mistake of shying away again so she encouraged and gently reminded her daughter of her goal. Elizabeth did not mind and, in fact, appreciated her mother's input because it somehow reminded her of the way Lucy used to encourage and urge her on when she was at the Centre so she would say, "Thanks mummy. I'll go and do it now". She needed that because although she never complained, she was starting to get slightly bored with her treatments after a while, especially when she felt that she had not made much progress, just as Lucy had warned her, and she was again amazed that Lucy could know even such details. It made her more appreciative that there was a Centre for girls with her condition to go to, and she felt for the other girls who have not had such support, because she thought that it must be very difficult for them, of this she knew all too well. She shuddered to think where she would still be had she not had the appropriate help and support from this team, but she knew that she would not have come this far today without them. She was even thankful to her local consultant for admitting that he did not have the experience to help her, and then referring her to this Centre. She thought that this referral system really worked because otherwise how else would anyone with unusual conditions such as hers get the right treatment? She thought that she must bear this in mind for when she became a doctor. When she reflected on all the help she received, it also made her more appreciative of her parents, especially her mother. She realised how difficult it must have been for her when she had been shutting her out so she could not quite believe how her mother could still keep trying to help and never gave up on her. In any case, she felt very fortunate and found it rather comforting to know that she had the backing from everyone.

Tom's Eighteenth

Elizabeth wore the long black gown her mother had bought her when they were last in London. It was supposed to be for her end of term ball but on the day, she changed her mind because she felt it was too formal and inappropriate, since everyone else was wearing short summer party frocks and she did not want to stand out amongst her friends. Instead she bought herself a simple stylish A-line knee length cocktail dress. It had a navy blue see-through lace at the top with cap sleeves, wide neck at the front and a V-tapered neck at the back, and the lace was continued and sewn over a navy blue satin material for the fitted bodice and the flowing, flared knee-length skirt. She then wore a pair of silver double cubic zirconium ear rings and a matching bracelet to enhance her dress and to match her pair of silver ankle strapped peep-toe high heel sandal shoes. Elizabeth was not one to use a lot of face makeup. After all she was just sixteen and still at boarding school. Besides, the school did not allow the girls to wear makeup so she only used a light gentle face mois-turiser every day but for the occasion, she put on a light foundation cream and applied a coat of black ruby mascara to her naturally long eyelashes, which further enhanced her deep set blue green eyes. To complete, she wore an orange red lipstick for her lips. She looked fabulous but it was her best friend Sally, who stole the limelight at the ball because she was so beautiful. She wore her natural baby blonde hair down with its spiral curled ends, which was a change from it being tied up in a ponytail at school. Like Elizabeth, her makeup was minimalistic but then being such an attractive girl too, she did not need much either. Her gown was red with a single jeweled shoulder strap and a moderate straight cut back and sweetheart neckline. The top of her dress had a curvy design, which was sewn over with the same rhinestone jewels from the strap down and across to the waistline where it was joined at a V by another strip of jewels from the other side of her waistline. Her dress then continued into a knee length skirt, which was a two layered netted lace skirt and it showed off her fabulous figure even more. She wore dangle earrings with matching bangles and a pair of high-heeled stiletto sandal shoes. She was gorgeous and looked like a million dollars. Elizabeth could not be happier for her friend and was actually grateful that she was overshadowed by Sally in this instance. Of course, Tom told Elizabeth that she was the most beautiful girl there and he meant it but then he was biased and only had eyes for her.

Tom's eighteen birthday celebration was a big hit. His father, being a local businessman, had done enough entertaining to know most if not all the venues for such special occasions and private functions, so it was not difficult for him to choose the appropriate one for his son's eighteenth birthday party. He decided on this exclusive private venue to host the party, so that Tom and his friends could enjoy themselves without any restrictions on the time or loud music. It was a big exhibition hall in the best hotel in the city, which catered for such big functions. He also happened to own the hotel. The place was big but with all the decorations and fixtures, it had a great party atmosphere. Tom invited all his friends and some of his closest friends' parents. His parents also invited a few of his father's business associates and their wives and partners, some relatives and a few of their neighbours, and there must have been just over a hundred people altogether. The celebration started in the early part of the evening with a substantial serving of food, courtesy of the well-known hotel chef. This was mostly for the adults with the understanding that they would then leave to let Tom and his young friends enjoy themselves in the evening, although this did not quite go as planned because only a handful of the adults left and everyone else stayed because they were having such a great time. Fortunately, as it happened, it did not matter because the grown-ups who stayed were all up for a party. They were very sporting and joined in the fun so Tom and his friends did not feel restricted, and managed to enjoy themselves irrespective. Besides, Tom and his friends including Elizabeth, Sally and the other girls seemed very grown up and mingled well with the adults although for the most part, they were naturally engaging and socialising with their own age group of friends.

There was a second round of food served later that evening. This time, it was more the party finger foods, which were exquisitely made by the same chef and his staff. Mrs. McGuire made sure that there was plenty of food to go round because she was aware of the appetites of young people, so she again catered for a hundred people. It took three long tables to hold all the food so there was more than enough. Still, most of the food went as people kept going up to pick at the food all night long. The dancing commenced in the later part of the evening. Tom's parents had organised a disco for their dance and they hired a local DJ, whom they knew. He was very good. He played a mixture of retro dance and pop music from the 80s and 90s and some classic party and slow dance music, and also songs requested by various people. The dancefloor was never empty from the time the disco started till it finished at one in the morning. The dance area itself was adequate enough and although it was crowded at one point when everyone was on the floor dancing, it just added to the fun and everyone was laughing and enjoying themselves.

Tom felt on top of the world because he felt that he had the most beautiful girl by his side. It was his best eighteenth birthday present ever. He was right about Elizabeth because he always felt that she was his soulmate and he could not think of being with any other woman. He counted himself very lucky to have Elizabeth as his girlfriend and was grateful for the past events because they brought the two of them together, otherwise the thought of losing her to another would be unbearable. All evening, Tom could not keep his eyes off her because her beauty was so mesmerising, and he kept smilingly to himself. When they were dancing together, he told her, "You look so beautiful tonight El. I love you so much". Everyone else in the room also thought that Tom and Elizabeth were made for each other because they made such a handsome couple. It was strange that it did not cross anyone's mind that Elizabeth was maybe too young because she was just sixteen, but they looked so good together and perhaps no one could deny their young love. Meanwhile, Elizabeth who was unaware of what everyone was thinking, was enjoying herself and having a great time with her friends and, of course, she just loved being with Tom. She appreciated that he made all the difference to her and could not be happier that he came into her life because through him, she was finally getting on with her life too. She thought that he was the most understanding, compassionate and loving man she had ever met and she had been counting herself lucky every day to have his unreserved love, especially in spite of her MRKH.

Elizabeth was happy and enjoying herself again. She used to be like this and she loved being in the company of people and all her friends, which for a while had become a rather rare occasion so it was good to see that she was back in form. She was excited and was looking forward to Tom's party. She so wanted to look her best for him that she was less self-conscious about being the centre of attention. No, this time she just wanted to look beautiful for Tom and was more engrossed about what she would wear to his party, so she did not have time to think of anything else. She chose to wear the long black maxi gown with a thigh split and a scoop back, which revealed more than what she had been trying to hide the past few months because she was ashamed of her body, ashamed of herself back then. Not anymore, now she no longer obsessed about her MRKH and was less aware of herself and her body image. In fact, not once did she think or dwell on her condition. This time, she was just a normal sixteen-year-old girl again, although she could now pass for an eighteen-year-old, but all the same she was very excited about going to her boyfriend's birthday party. Her confidence had returned and her attitude had changed. She no longer felt like an innocent adolescent anymore but more like a young lady. Indeed, she was very much a young woman now and she also had a boyfriend. She was with Tom now. She also came to realise how much she actually loved him and she was sure that it was not gratitude anymore. She thought he was so handsome and she only wanted to make him proud that he had an equally attractive girlfriend. She did not disappoint because she was as elegant as she was sexy and desirable on the night.

When she was getting herself ready for the party, Elizabeth suddenly became aware at how normal she was again. She thought that Tom really was her knight in shining armour, not only because he saved her from her world of desolation and solitude but he gave her a hope for a future. Now she no longer felt doomed as she could envisage this future, a promising one with the man she loved, albeit maybe a different future to the one she had originally planned. Her plan had always been that she would not enter into a relationship until she finished medical school, but after she was diagnosed with MRKH, it became irrelevant and seemed impossible. After that, she no longer knew what to expect and she dared not allow herself to dream of anything good to happen to her, so she never expected to be in a relationship with Tom, especially now when she was just sixteen. Still, it did happen, and normally this would all go against the grain. The old Elizabeth was too sensible but when her only plan was shot into pieces, she had no plan B so then she found herself thrown into a labyrinth of chaos and confusion for a brief period in her life and naturally she was very frightened and confused. It deflated her and she lost control for a while. "Damn MRKH! Why did I have to have it!" she would curse herself frequently out of sheer frustration, but that was then. She had such a hard time accepting it then that it made her feel more lost and isolated than ever because she became distanced from everyone and everything around her. Her perfect life had vanished together with her plan of having her own family in the future and she suddenly found herself grieving, grieving for her sudden loss of independence and her freedom of choice and she was struggling with her self-image, her own identity and her place in society, but most of all her womanhood.

When she was first diagnosed, she struggled with her sense of normality because of her absent vagina but as she progressed through her journey, her absent uterus became her biggest issue. Whilst other women might grieve for the loss of their children, Elizabeth was now grieving for the loss of her choice to have children. She now believed that this was by far the most painful and cruel, because she loved children and wanted a family of her own one day. Of course, this was all a part of the healing process, a process she had to go through in order to get better. Still, now that she was with Tom, she was already feeling better and was beginning to live her life normally again.

Elizabeth had always been academic anyway and was not particularly vain so she never paid too much attention to her looks. She did not think herself as being particularly beautiful but she knew she was not ugly either. When she found out she had MRKH, she was forced to look further into this, except this was worse because she felt like a lesser woman, a woman without a womb or a vagina. It was no wonder that she lost her self-worth and confidence but with the love and support of her family and Tom and the help from the likes of Lucy and Anne, she eventually harmonised with her new situation. She realised that first, she had to recognise and accept herself as a worthy young woman, which was the most important. Then she had to have acceptance from the people around her, and, finally, she had to have acceptance from the opposite sex. Once she had these, she was able to prove herself so she felt better and she was able to cope. She had gone through and overcame all the physical, mental and emotional challenges, so now she felt the strongest she had ever been. She also had to accept the changes in her life, which meant she too had to change. Nowadays, she was less rigid and exacting with herself and with her life and she learnt to take each day as it came. It was not easy and her mood would still fluctuate but at least now she was trying to be more positive. She accepted Tom as the best thing that happened to her and she acknowledged that she actually had a choice, a choice to have a future with him and to leave all that doom and gloom behind her. It was her shot to make things work. She would still be able to realise her dream to finish medical school and become a paediatrician so at least this facet of her life had not changed or faltered and would go ahead as planned. It was a long and painful journey and at one point, she thought she would never recover but she did, she got there in the end. Elizabeth finally accepted herself with her unusual imperfection and she learnt to live with her MRKH so now she dared to look at herself in the mirror again. When she was getting dressed in front of the mirror earlier on, she saw her mirror image, but there was also a different person within and she began to like the person she saw again and thought, "Not bad. I look pretty good tonight". Elizabeth really felt very comfortable and at peace with her current circumstances right now. This was real progress. Her parents watched her and they could also see that she was positively different. Paul told his wife, "She looks gorgeous tonight and so do you, babe". They could hardly believe that their sixteen-year-old girl had transformed into this confident beautiful young lady. It was all true, although Jan would have liked to be completely convinced. In honesty, she was still slightly erring on the side of caution because she knew how good Elizabeth was at keeping a brave face, and much as Jan tried, she still could not forget Elizabeth's emotional outbursts in the past. She desperately wanted to believe with all her heart that Elizabeth was truly well, but no matter, she felt that as a mother she would always worry about her daughter anyway so at least for now Elizabeth looked really good, she looked happy and everything seemed to be going well.

Testing Out In Barcelona

Elizabeth had another appointment to see Lucy, but this time, she was happy for Tom to accompany her and even agreed to let him go in with her to see Lucy. She trusted him fully now and she was also excited about introducing him to her, to get her approval, as if she was bringing a boyfriend home to meet her parents. Tom was equally looking forward to meeting Lucy too, having heard so much about her from Elizabeth, but all of this was still a new experience to him. He watched the interaction between the two of them with amazement because it was evident that they had a very special relationship. They were like old friends yet he could sense that there was a professional boundary that they both understood. Elizabeth was so at ease with her the whole time and Tom could not believe that it could be so casual yet so professional. It relaxed him too and soon he found himself engaging in their discussion on Elizabeth's assessment and progress. He asked Lucy a few questions about MRKH and his role, so that he could be of more help and support to Elizabeth. During their conversation, the discussion on sex cropped up although it was unclear who initiated it first, and it embarrassed Elizabeth a little but all the same, she was glad of it. She felt that at least this way, Tom was fully aware and she would not have to explain any of it to him because, to be honest, she still felt embarrassed talking about the sexual side of things. For her, the main reason she was doing the treatment was so that she would have a normal vagina like any woman, so that it would then make her feel normal. She was so hell-bent on proving that she was a normal girl and had not really thought about anything else, so sex was the last thing on her mind, especially when she had decided not to be sexually active until much later on, but of course now her circumstances had changed and everything was different. She was not that same sixteen-year old-girl anymore. She was a young woman and she was also with Tom now, but she had been so engrossed with her treatment and had not really given much thought about the actual act of having sex with Tom, even when she and Lucy had talked about it previously. Then she thought selfishly, "How else would I know that my vagina is normal, that I am normal?" She thought that maybe sex would not be a bad thing because this would prove that her vagina was normal, as Lucy had mentioned before. She would definitely find out if she was really normal too, so she decided that this was what she should do. If it happened, then she would try to have sex with Tom. Elizabeth kept trying to convince herself, so now she resigned herself to the fact that she needed the evidence to believe that she was normal, despite Lucy and everyone else telling her that she was, so this way she felt that it would conclusively confirm what she needed to know. She also never expected to do this well with her treatment, so it gave her more confidence to move on to the next step, especially when it would provide her with the evidence and the answer she needed. It was all credit to her that she had progressed very well with her treatment though, because she was so diligent and determined to finish within the said period that she never grumbled or missed any of her treatments.

The whole appointment went smoothly and Tom was glad that Elizabeth had agreed to let him go with her this time. He himself had never had to go into hospital for anything before so he was quite inspired by the whole experience. He liked Lucy a lot and he could see why Elizabeth did too because he observed that not only was she helping Elizabeth with her treatment but she had a positive effect on Elizabeth. She was very knowledgeable and experienced and Tom did not doubt her expertise for a second as she exuded confidence and trust but more striking was that she managed to positively normalise some of Elizabeth's negative and irrational thoughts and beliefs, and her positive transference to Elizabeth was so remarkable that Tom was well impressed and encouraged. Most of all, he was pleased that Elizabeth had found someone whom she trusted and in turn, who genuinely cared about her.

Elizabeth carried on with her treatments as usual and by now she was only using the big dilators. She already had a good routine going, so now she did not mind or begrudge doing her treatments or feel them interfering with her life because she could see a result, as she kept improving each time and it proved that the treatment was working, which made her more intent on completing it, so she just continued as if this was merely a part of her life. In fact, she was so religious with them that she did not want to miss any of them and decided to bring the dilators with her to Barcelona. The day before they were to leave, she developed cold feet. She only had a small cabin bag and a shoulder duffer bag, as they were only going for a short weekend break but she remembered Lucy advising her to put her dilators in the check-in luggage or else these would show up on the X-ray screen at security. In any case, Lucy also gave Elizabeth a letter and a leaflet proving the dilators as medical instruments in case there were any queries about them if she was to pack them into her carry-on luggage. She kept her two dilators in her toiletry bag as usual but when she was packing them in, she suddenly panicked and did not feel as brave bringing them along. She thought of asking Sally for her help but soon decided against it because she remembered Sally's reaction when she first showed her the two big dilators that she was using. Sally almost fainted at the sight of them so she knew that Sally would probably be equally if not more embarrassed, should there be any query about them at the airport security. In the end, she decided to ask Tom instead so she rang him to ask if he would take them for her. Of course, Tom readily agreed so they arranged to meet earlier at the airport and she would then pass the dilators on to him. Tom also had only his cabin and duffer bags so he packed them into one duffer bag. He did not anticipate that there would be any problem, but in any case he was not in any way perturbed about taking them. They met up at the airport as arranged and as they were early, they went for a coffee whilst they waited for the rest of their friends to arrive and when everyone was there, they all checked in together.

Tom was the first in line because Elizabeth had suggested that Tom should go before her in case there should be any query. As Elizabeth expected, the dilators showed up on the security X-ray screen so the officer took them out to examine them. Tom very calmly produced the letter that Lucy had given Elizabeth so when the officer read it he put the dilators back into his bag without any further fuss. Elizabeth who was standing right behind Tom, however she was not as nonchalant as her boyfriend and instantly went bright red in the face as she stood frozen on the spot holding her breath and clenching her fists. Tom could sense that Elizabeth would be very embarrassed so he turned around to her and when he saw her still holding her breath, he whispered to her, "Breathe El". Elizabeth gave out such a big sigh of breath that she started to feel her whole body shake and her ensuing breaths were also trembly, so Tom casually put his arms around her and held her tightly to calm her down. The officer asked if anything was wrong so Tom just told him that Elizabeth felt faint but that she would be alright and ushered Sally and the other friends to go on ahead. Thankfully, within the next few seconds, Elizabeth recovered sufficiently enough to check herself and her luggage through, apologising to the officer as she went through security. She could not be more embarrassed and of course by now, the rest of her friends with the exception of Sally wanted to know what just happened with her because they were really concerned. Sally knew full well because she had been down this similar path with her best friend before, but it was Tom this time who was her protector. He told them the same story, that Elizabeth felt faint just now and Elizabeth also told them, "I'm fine now, thanks". They seemed to accept it as she appeared to be well again, but Sally came over to her and squeezed her hand to indicate that she understood and that she was safe now. Elizabeth squeezed her hand back and said, "Thanks, Sal". She did feel safe, safe in the knowledge that both Tom and Sally knew about her MRKH so they would somehow take care of her and anything untoward that might happen with her as discreetly as possible and still keeping her secret between them. This was very reassuring to Elizabeth and she was able to relax more afterwards.

On the plane over, Tom sat next to Elizabeth and guarded her with his dear life. He was still thinking about her reaction earlier on and was surprised that she had reacted that way, because she seemed to have coped with her MRKH very well these last few weeks. He had not realised that she still had some issues with it, so this was a reminder of her insecurity and lack of confidence, the common psychological aspects of her condition that Lucy mentioned at their previous meeting. He began to understand and appreciate the psychological impact it had on Elizabeth more. He also recalled Lucy telling him that no matter how well women with MRKH coped, especially in the early stages of their diagnosis, the psychological inferences indicated that it would not be unusual for little everyday occurrences to trigger and offset their psychological state because of their wavering self-confidence, their unstable perception of their self and body image, and thus their real fear of anyone knowing they had MRKH. Then, he also remembered Elizabeth referring to herself as a 'freak' when she first told him about her condition, so everything started to make more sense to him. He made a mental note of this so that he could anticipate situations better in the future.

The flight to Barcelona was a short one. It took just over

two hours and before they knew it, they had arrived at El Prat International airport. They went straight to the airport information desk to get directions to their hotel and were advised to take the metro as this was the quickest way, although they had to take two lines to get there. Still, it was easy enough and they were at the hotel within the hour, so they checked in at reception straight away as the hotel did not seem busy then and there was only one other couple checking in at the time. Elizabeth shared a room with Sally and the others also paired up, as the package included two sharing a room. It was a good package that Tom got them and it worked out to be quite a cheap weekend break with their flights, hotel and breakfast included. The hotel was aptly situated for them, as well as being in the city centre with the train station and shopping centre all within ten minutes reach. The rooms had twin beds as requested by Tom and they were fortunate to have all their rooms on the same twenty-second floor. The rooms were clean and well kitted up with the usual facilities but most important for them, because they were of that age, it also offered free wifi. The view from their rooms was exquisitely stunning and pleasing too so everyone was well impressed and they thanked Tom for organising this whole trip. "Thanks, man. This is really cool," his best friend told him.

They did not waste any time and wanted to make the most of their four days in Barcelona so they dumped their luggage in their respective rooms and met up in the hotel foyer. They spoke to the concierge to get information and guidance on all the city's sights, transportation, entertainment and recreational facilities and were also given some brochures and the local map, and afterwards they headed straight off to the city centre. It was a bright sunny day with the temperature hovering around 30 degrees centigrade but there was also a consistent light breeze blowing, so it was a very pleasant walk downtown. They stopped at different shops that took their fancy and had a late lunch at one of the restaurants in the city square. Most of the restaurants opened out onto the forecourts so they sat outside to have their tapas and to enjoy their cold served local brew. Elizabeth and her friends were aware of Europeans taking their siesta but were pleasantly surprised so John asked, "Not that I'm complaining but aren't the Europeans supposed to have their siesta?" because there was no sign of any siesta in the city centre as every shop and every restaurant was open. The city square was packed with people because it was also their school and summer holidays over there, evident from the scores of families out for the day with their children of varying school ages. There were also hundreds of tourists from all over the world, as far as Asia. The whole place was very picturesque, where the new and old city merged bringing together a blend of the richness of its new and old Gothic architecture alongside one another, which somehow worked very well. Tall stately buildings surrounded the square and within the square itself, there were lots of tall statues and fountains and different avenues off shooting from the square leading to more restaurants and quaint little shops selling all kinds of gifts and souvenirs tempting tourists and customers. In the city square itself, there were flocks of pigeons feeding on the food left by local children and visitors. "It's so very reminiscent of Trafalgar Square in London don't you think?" Elizabeth asked Sally, who said "Yeah it is, but just without the iconic Nelson's Column". Afterwards, they took a train to Barcelona's most famous Boqueria market in Las Ramblas. It was as amazing, as they had been informed by the concierge. The market was huge and it was also densely visited by locals and tourists. Elizabeth, who loved her fruits, was overwhelmed by the display and choice of the different varieties of fruit and vegetables that looked so lusciously inviting and she was very nearly tempted and told her best friend, "Oh, I want to buy everything. They're so nicely displayed as well". There were also numerous stalls selling different kinds of food produce from seafood, meat, cheeses, to nuts and chocolates. Dotted inside the market were also little restaurants and tapas stalls all packed with people eating and drinking at all times. It was buzzing in there but they managed to find a table at one of the stalls situated at the far end of the market so they stayed there till the evening, leisurely enjoying a selection of tapas and cold beers and watching everyone else buying and selling, as if they were one of the locals.

They loved Barcelona. It was such a vibrant city that it filled everyone with excitement and vitality and the group felt they could just go on and on. Afterwards, they went back to their hotel for a shower and a change of clothes and they were ready for the nightlife. "Shall we have a meal first because I really fancy a nice proper local cuisine instead of tapas," said Joanne, one of the girls in the group, and everyone agreed because no one fancied any more tapas. They felt that they had eaten enough tapas for the day! Sally suggested, "Maybe we could try their local Catalan cuisine," but there was so many restaurants offering their famous Catalan dishes that they were hard pressed to choose. In the end, they decided to walk towards the harbour because they had read good reviews on some of the restaurants there. As it happened, they could not be more impressed. They thought they had the best meal in town and everyone enjoyed what they ordered. Of course, by the time they got there, everyone was probably hungry for some real food anyway. Afterwards, they did a bit of pub crawling for a while and then ended up in a club on the harbour. They drank and partied the whole night long and they were on the dance floor practically all night because the music was so good, and they did not leave till six in the morning the next day. It was a great night and Elizabeth thought that she had never partied like that before nor any of her friends for that matter because, being sixteen, most of the parties she attended finished around midnight or one at the latest. She felt all grown up all of a sudden.

When they got back to their hotel, there was no time to sleep, so instead they freshened up and went down to the hotel restaurant to have their breakfast. The hotel provided a very wide selection of continental breakfasts ranging from a variety of cereals, rolls and bread, cakes, cheeses, ham, fruits and yoghurt to fried or scrambled eggs on request. It was more than adequate. During breakfast, one of the boys in the group, Sean, who was very interested in the architecture of the buildings and cathedrals in Barcelona suggested, "Shall we do some sightseeing today if no one has any objections?"

"Not at all, we're free and easy so you carry on and tell us where to go," John replied, as he looked over at his other friends since he had taken it upon himself to speak on their behalf, so they all said, "Sure, good idea". Sean was very excited of course. He had been accepted to study architecture at Oxford University so naturally, he wanted to see the artworks of Gaudi, which was not difficult since Barcelona was filled with his rich works of art but there were so many, and they did not have the time to see them all so Sean hand-picked a few must see buildings. They rest of the group were quite happy to go along and were grateful that Sean was taking charge of their sightseeing.

They started out with a visit to Gaudi's main residence, La Pedrera, then Palau Güell, the palace of the Güell family, then Casa Calvet, home to one of his rich industrialist clients, and last but not least, of course, La Sagrada Familia, Gaudi's most famous architectural work. This was a Roman Catholic basilica that he had started to build, with eight of its towers completed to date, although the rest was unfinished. Irrespective of that, uncompleted and with scaffolding around parts of the church, the facade of this basilica looked magnificent. Sean had done his research so he told his friends that Gaudi was trying to symbolise the relationship between man, nature and religion with his architectural expression and sculptures here. He also explained that when completed, "The building will have eighteen towers, the tallest symbolising Jesus Christ, then there was one for the Virgin Mary, four were for the evangelists and the rest, for the twelve apostles". Sean was so excited and inspired by Gaudi's genius that he could not wait to get inside to have a closer look, because he had also read that the stained glass windows were beautiful and that the view from the bridge from one of the towers was equally breathtaking. He was so in awe that he quickly joined the queue to buy his ticket and forgot to consult with his friends. The group laughed and Sasha, the last girl in the group, said, "Look at him. He's like a child with his new toy". Then Sasha, who was acrophobic said that she would not go up to the towers and would wait for them in the grounds, because she was aware that although they could take the lift to the top, the walk down was not easy so she did not fancy any of that. She said, "I'm going to stay on the ground. The thought of going up there is already making my legs start to tremble". Joanne also said that she would not go up and would keep her friend company so instead they got tickets to see the inside of the church. Elizabeth and Sally however said, "We'll join you, Sean. We want to go up to the top of the towers. The view from the top must be magnificent". They had both walked up to the Eiffel Tower before and Elizabeth remembered that the view of Paris from the top was breathtaking so she did not hesitate with her decision. Tom and his two other friends, John and Adam also decided to go up to the towers, although Tom was surprised that Elizabeth was so brave all of a sudden as to even want to go up to the top. When they reached the top, they were well charmed. They edged themselves around the crypts and walked out to the little balconies and crossed the bridge which connected the two towers. The aerial view of Barcelona from there was a sheer delight, it was indeed breathtaking!

Unfortunately, the way down was not as pleasurable. In fact, it was rather nerve-wrecking because they had to walk some four hundred steps down its very narrow and spiralling stairs in almost pitch dark conditions, apart from the little blinding light coming from the small nooks they passed every now and again. They had to walk in a single file too because it was that narrow, and everyone had to concentrate because there was no room for errors or else it would cause an avalanche of cascading bodies downhill. Eventually, they made it safely down, relieved, although no one would admit it. Afterwards, Tom looked at Elizabeth with amazement because he still could not believe and wondered, "How can someone be so courageous like this and yet be so affected and vulnerable when it related to her MRKH. I just don't get it". He tried to understand but he still could not quite marry the two sides of Elizabeth, so he again accepted that this was part of the psychological effects of her condition and he was learning a lot about her. Meanwhile, Sean was in his element, so he bought tickets for them to see the inside of the church. There were conducted tours available but they decided to do it by themselves. It was even more spectacular inside. The stained glass windows were truly magnificent but Sean was more in awe of the architectural structures and precision of every stone and pillar inside the church, that he kept muttering "Awesome!" to himself. He was even more impressed that Gaudi had managed his calculations and the precise creation of such a monster project without the help of modern technology. They had viewed his other works earlier on, but the genius of his icon still did not cease to amaze Sean. Elizabeth too was blown away by the prowess of this man because everything was indeed awe-inspiring. After an hour and a half, everyone came out except Sean. He had wandered off by himself so the group left him because they knew that he would want more time inside. Elizabeth texted Sasha and soon all the friends met up again and regrouped. They spotted an ice-cream parlour nearby and as they were parched and needed something to quench their thirst, they decided to go in for some ice-cream and refreshments whilst they waited for Sean.

Over the next few days, they went to a flea market and did shopping at the mega-mall but for the rest of the time, they did not have any agenda and did things spontaneously. They walked down to the marina and the port one evening. The harbour was another lively place with lots of restaurants and shops and all types of ships and yachts, from sail to power to super yachts, neatly berthed alongside each other. They had dinner at one the restaurants there and after a short stroll along the pier, they decided on an early night because they had not slept since they arrived in the city and they were all tired by then. When they reached their hotel room, Elizabeth suddenly remembered that she had not done her treatment for the last couple of days but she was not too angsty about it because of Lucy's reassurances. Nevertheless, she thought that she should do it when she had the chance now especially when she had brought the dilators along on this trip, so she told Sally that she would do her treatment whilst she was in the shower. She was pleased to find that her treatment went easily despite not having done them for two days and when she examined herself, everything remained at status quo. Still, she was slightly troubled because she wanted to know if she was really normal, normal enough to have sex and whether or not it would feel the same for her and for Tom so she was quite keen to try. She had to experience it for herself and the only way to find out would be to try it out with Tom. She was confident in the fact that her vagina was almost normal so she convinced herself that she was ready to have sex with Tom, but she wondered when she would get the opportunity. It seemed impossible on this trip because the group was always together and she and Tom were never alone by themselves. She also did not like to appear calculating so in the end, she reluctantly shrugged off the idea. She felt a little embarrassed afterwards to think that she would even be so calculating about it and it made her feel cheap. Sally came out of the shower and caught Elizabeth muttering to herself so she asked, "What's cheap El?" Elizabeth was so embarrassed that Sally might have overheard her that she ended up telling her best friend what she was concerned about. "That's not cheap, El. You need to know what you need to know. After all, you've been doing the treatment for a couple of months now and it's only natural to want to know whether it has worked. If I was in your position, I would too," Sally reassured her. "Really, you think I'm right to think this way?" she asked. Sally said emphatically, "Of course, if this was me, I'd be trying to shag anybody I can find".

"No you wouldn't Sal, you're like me. You're only saying that to make me feel better," Elizabeth told her best friend, so Sally nodded and replied convincingly, "Yeah, you know I wouldn't but I'd still try with my boyfriend if I had one". This made Elizabeth feel less of a loose woman and she thought that it was so typical of Sally to say something like this just to make her feel better. She was truly a sensitive and thoughtful friend.

On their last two days, the group did what they fancied at the time. As they had no other fixed agenda, Sean was keen to see more of Gaudi's work so they visited Casa Batllo, another one of his masterpieces. It was a wavy-shaped building, which was as colourful exteriorly as it was fascinating interiorly. Sean was so exhilarated that he could not stop saying "Genius and awesome!" They then walked towards Parc Guell, situated within a nice walking distance. When they reached it, the girls thought they were in fairytale land. They were met by this gigantic multi-coloured mosaic salamander at the entrance and as they walked along the whole park through to the museum, Elizabeth at some point wandered off from them. It was as if the magic of the place had invoked something in her, and for a brief second she had engaged in wishful thinking that her problem was just imaginary too, and that she was normal – "I wish I didn't have this thing. How wonderful my life would be," she drifted off with the thought. Suddenly, she felt a strong hand around her shoulders and alas everything was back to what it was. "Hi. Where are you going by yourself, El?" It was Tom. He was keeping a watchful eye on her and saw her wander off by herself. By now, he was getting very good at reading her signs, so without saying anything he kissed her and held her tight towards him. His love and kindness seemed to make her want to cry even more and she tried to explain what just happened. There was so many things that she wanted to tell him, so many things going on in her head that she wished she could share with him, but she found that she could not, nor could she explain why she would feel emotionally insecure all of a sudden again. She could not even try to control her emotions because they seemed to have come out from nowhere. She was getting frustrated with herself because she felt that she was becoming a bore and was also concerned because she felt that Tom must feel it too. She knew that it was not fair on the poor guy, and she felt that eventually this would drive him away and she only had herself to blame. She was terrified of this happening because she was convinced that no one else could ever want her if Tom was to leave her. Then, as if by telepathy, Tom read her mind and said, "It's ok El. I told you I'm not going anywhere. I still…" She did not wait for him to finish as she interrupted saying, "But I don't understand. I was doing so well. I don't know why I still keep feeling so hopeless sometimes? I just can't help wishing for everything to be back to normal, for me to be normal".

"You are normal El…" Tom tried to reassure her, but Elizabeth would not have it and retorted, "But I am not normal, am I? Look at me, Tom. I have no womb, no vagina, I have nothing. I don't think I could ever be normal!" Tom tried hard to conceal his surprise and discomfort at Elizabeth's remark, and he wondered how anyone could respond to such a harsh and personal criticism. He had always had the maturity of someone older than his eighteen years which was why his friends and fellow schoolmates looked up to him, and why he was elected the head boy, but this time he felt out of his depths. Nevertheless, this was not just anybody, it was his girlfriend, so he concealed his ineptness and tried to focus on how he could best help her to deal with her situation. He could now see that Elizabeth had not really accepted her condition, which was why she was still having a hard time reconciling her abnormality with her own beliefs and self-concept, so he knew that he had to be honest with her if he was to really help. It was also quite apparent to him now that she was still in denial, and this was stopping her from moving on with her life, so he implored her to accept her condition for what it was and that he would help her. He could tell that this thing was eating her up inside so he continued to reassure her that it did not bother him in the slightest that she had MRKH and it was what made her special, different and special, and that he loved everything about her. Elizabeth would not hear of it and kept on repeating that she had already accepted her condition and she could not understand why she was still having these thoughts and doubts about herself, so in the end Tom pointed out to her that he could see that she was in denial and said, "Look El, I'm no expert here but the fact that you are still wishing that you don't have MRKH and that you wish you are normal tells me that you haven't accepted it, and now you are even denying that you are in denial. You can't change anything, El. It is what it is and you know that, so please just accept it. It doesn't bother me at all. You are still my beautiful girlfriend, still the same El that I love so no MRKH will ever change the way I feel about you".

He reassured her again that he would be around for a very long time and that he did not mind that she had to get a lot of things out of her system. It was all positive, all part of the process, as he understood, but he suggested that she should just try to be less harsh and less self-punitive so that she could see what a beautiful person she really was and to him, she was just perfect. He was so sincere that Elizabeth did not argue this time and settled into his arms. His warmth and compassion seemed to relax and reassure her too. It felt nice. This was the first time on this trip that they were intimate and that they were actually apart from the group. It did not last long though because they heard Sally's voice as she walked towards them "El, where did you go? I was worried. I thought we'd lost you". Sally too had noticed that Elizabeth was missing from the group and came back to look for her. "I'm fine, I was just looking at something but Tom found me anyway," replied Elizabeth but when Sally looked at Tom, she just knew. She did not ask anymore but she just smiled because she was just relieved that Tom was there for her friend. They rejoined the group and when everyone was finished with the park, they were ready for some refreshment, so they found a tapas bar nearby and just chilled out for a while. Afterwards, they walked every side street there was in the city centre, picking up various gifts and souvenirs and then they did some serious shopping at the mega-mall. They had bought so many things each that they decided to return to their hotel and to do their packing as they were also leaving the following day.

On their last evening in Barcelona, they walked back to the pier. The weather had been superb and they had plenty of sunshine every day since they arrived, with temperatures soaring above 30 degrees Celsius. It was also very humid on a couple of days but no one complained because they were only too grateful that the weather had been kind to them and allowed them to get out and about to sightsee and to do so many things. By evening, the temperature would plummet down to a comfortable low twenty degrees and below, like on this night. There was also a refreshing gentle sea-breeze blowing, which made it feel much cooler, so their light cardigans and sweaters were much appreciated. This was the typical summer weather in Barcelona and Elizabeth and her friends loved it and they made the most of it. As they walked along the beach, they could see that the whole length of the seafront was well lit, and it had such a lively atmosphere because there were people just about everywhere they looked. They made sure that they stayed close together because it would pose a real challenge should anyone of them got separated from their group, so Tom and Sally instinctively grabbed Elizabeth's hands simultaneously. They had to laugh – it was so obvious that they were both thinking along the same lines because they knew full well what Elizabeth was like at wandering off by herself. As they continued along this sandy beach, they saw rows of restaurants, bars, clubs and discotheques all in plain sight, one after the other, so they were spoilt for choice. The cacophony of people chatting, eating and drinking and enjoying themselves and some loud music blaring in the background made it impossible for them to hear themselves talk so they held each other's hands as if they were young children on a school outing, until Tom gestured to them and he pointed to a restaurant that had an available table to accommodate all eight of them. They loved the city and the people there and, although the Spanish people seemed loud and sometimes crass, it did not bother any of them in the slightest. They were young and free and they were out to have a good time, so naturally they tried to blend in with the locals, because they saw how they were enjoying themselves. They especially loved the Spaniards' zest for life and enjoyment. When the waiter came to their table, they ordered their meals, cold beers and Cokes, chatted to themselves for a bit, then sat back, relaxed and watched the world go by. Elizabeth sat in between her two best friends and apart from when they were eating, Tom had his arm around Elizabeth the whole time and then looking at her, he thought, "I'm the luckiest man on earth.

This is my best birthday present ever, thanks mum and dad".

The group had thoroughly enjoyed themselves and had got on so well together that before long, they found themselves planning their next trip together. Afterwards, they went into a club that played the best disco music and they danced their feet off. Elizabeth suddenly remembered her treatment and thought that she had better get back to the hotel to do it because she only managed to do it once since they came over, even though she knew nothing had changed but that was it, she did not want things to stay as they were. She wanted more progress, so of course, the more she thought about it, the more she felt guilty for neglecting her treatments. But at the same time, she did not want to be selfish and spoil the fun for her friends so she discreetly whispered to Sally. Naturally, Sally said that she would walk back with her and made an excuse that she had to finish her packing anyway. Tom overheard the gist of their conversation and he could tell that Sally was not really ready to leave as she was enjoying herself and it was still early so he told her to stay and that he would go back with Elizabeth. Sally did not argue because it suddenly dawned on her that this was a good opportunity for them to be together by themselves and she hoped that Elizabeth might try to have sex with Tom. They had talked and joked enough about it but now there was this real opportunity. Still, she did not want to sound too scheming but she wanted to help her best friend. She was fully aware that Elizabeth was desperate to be normal, to prove that she was normal, so she thought what better evidence than for her to try to have sex with Tom now whilst they had this opportunity. Then she felt that she was being manipulative, and she did not like that, but she soon rationalised it as her intention was good, and this was something that would help her best friend, and it was what couples do anyway. After all, Elizabeth and Tom were both of the age of consent, and furthermore she knew that they loved each other. She convinced herself into thinking that she was right, so before they left, Sally tried to steer them in this direction and suggested that it would be the most natural progression in their relationship.

Elizabeth felt a little embarrassed at Sally's candour, although it was really no surprise because only last night they were talking about this. If she had to admit, the thought did cross her mind when Tom offered to walk her back to the hotel, but she was too shy to say anything then so in a way, she was relieved that it was Sally who spelt it out for them. Tom was also quite taken aback at Sally's frankness and he could sense Elizabeth's embarrassment and discomfort from her silence so he responded, "Thanks Sal, you're a great friend and I know you mean well, but El and I will decide when the time is right, and it won't be until El is ready". Then turning to face Elizabeth, he continued "El, you don't need to decide now. We don't have to do anything. I will never hurt you or force you to do anything you're not comfortable with. You know I love you too much for that".

"I know, but Sally is right otherwise I will never know". Then she became more assertive and said "I am ready. I want to try, that is if you want to as well". The words came out so naturally from Elizabeth's mouth as they were prompted by the openness and maturity of their conversation, which really surprised Tom, so he very quickly and rather clumsily replied, "Yeah sure, of course I want to but only if you're really sure". Elizabeth nodded and said that she could not be surer of her decision so Tom just said, "Ok". They made a quick exit and headed back to the hotel, leaving Sally to say good night to their friends when she finally found and rejoined them on the dance floor.

On the way back to the hotel, Elizabeth and Tom stopped by at a pharmacy to buy some condoms because, of course, neither of them carried these on them, but it was something that was consciously on Elizabeth's mind. She remembered Lucy advising her on their use as protection against sexually transmitted diseases and infections, which might then cause scarring or close up her vagina too, so she was keen to follow her advice. It was not that she did not trust Tom but he was not a virgin like her so she was not taking any chances, not even with him, especially when she had painstakingly created her vagina. After they bought the condoms, they headed towards the hotel and went straight up to Elizabeth's room.

When they were alone in the room together, Elizabeth suddenly felt awkward because she thought that this whole thing was so contrived, when she had always felt that sex should be more natural and spontaneous between lovers. She became less confident the more she thought about it too, because not only was she still a virgin but she also started to worry that her vagina was not adequate so it would be painful. Tom was also not very experienced having only lost his virginity to a one-night stand when he was just seventeen, before he met Elizabeth. He also started to feel less confident, especially when he remembered Lucy telling him that he might not be able to fully penetrate Elizabeth so he was worried that he might hurt her. Needless to say, there were a few awkward minutes between them so Tom reassured Elizabeth that he understood if she had changed her mind because, by now he had also somewhat started to talk himself out of it, especially when he had always said that he would not pressurise her into anything, and was prepared to wait for her anyway. He could not bear to cause her more pain or distress.

Elizabeth apologised and tried to explain her slight hesitation saying, "I'm sorry Tom. I really felt that I was ready and I really wanted to try sex with you a moment ago, but now I'm not so sure because I'm so frightened that it would be painful since my vagina is not normal yet. I'm really sorry". She was also very concerned in case Tom would not be able to even enter her and this would be the height of her embarrassment, and she was afraid that this might then ruin any chances of their future together, although she dared not tell him that. She felt totally useless and inadequate because here was an opportunity where she and Tom were alone together, yet she could not even do anything. She began to feel very abnormal again, because she felt that she would never be able to have sex like normal girls and therefore she would never ever be normal. She told him, "I'm not trying to mess with you but I feel abnormal all over again and I feel that nothing is going to change". She started to get upset, so Tom told her, "Hey, it's ok to change your mind. It's your first time so I understand besides sometimes girls do that anyway". Then seeing how upset she still was, he continued, "To tell you the truth El, I wasn't too sure myself because I'm also frightened that I might hurt you. You know what, I think we should just leave sex out for the time being and just carry on as we did before". Elizabeth felt slightly better after he said that but she still had to ask, "Are you sure you don't mind, Tom?"

"I'm very sure. We have plenty of time so I think we should wait and not rush into it until we are both ready, until you are ready," Tom told her very convincingly.

They sat on her bed chatting for a while then Tom told her, "You are so beautiful, you know that". He kissed her and then they started kissing and before they knew it, they were making out, they were having sexual intercourse. It was spontaneous but by the time Tom put on the condom, Elizabeth had tensed up because she was so nervous. Then it was all over within a few minutes. Elizabeth was not sure if she should be feeling more because she could only feel Tom pushing inside her, which felt slightly uncomfortable but that was it. She did not feel anything else but then she did not know what to expect anyway so naturally she wondered, "Was that it? What's the big deal?" Elizabeth was trying to understand why anyone would rave about sex when she was not even impressed, because she just had sex and she did not think much of it. She was only pleased that it was not painful. Still, she was very keen to know how it was for Tom and she also wondered whether he felt that she was the same as his first experience so she asked him. She had to know if only to prove her sense of normality, so she said, "Tell me the truth. What was that like for you?" Tom was honest with her so he told her that, "It felt normal except that I could not fully penetrate but then I did not expect to anyway because I know that your vagina is still slightly short". He then asked Elizabeth, "What was it like for you El? I didn't hurt you did I?" So Elizabeth very innocently told him that, "It wasn't painful although I could just feel you pushing into me but that was it really". Tom immediately felt disappointed for her and asked, "What you felt nothing at all?" because he expected her to say that she enjoyed it a little especially when it was not painful, but Elizabeth felt nothing. He thought that even with his one-night stand, the girl came. Then again, she was eighteen and older than him so maybe she was the one who made his first sexual encounter pleasurable, or maybe she was just faking it because he had heard that sometimes women can do that. He started to blame himself for his own inexperience. Elizabeth suddenly saw that Tom was actually more upset about it than she was and she could not quite understand it. She started to feel really bad for him especially after what he had done for her so she quickly took the blame and said, "Don't feel bad please. It's my fault not yours. I told you I'm not normal so now we both know". As she tried to convince him, she began believing it more. It reinforced her feeling of abnormality all over again and then she started to feel very cross and disappointed that all that time she had spent tirelessly doing her treatments had come to nothing. The more she thought about it, the more disillusioned she became.

She began to wonder if it was really just wishful thinking that she could ever be normal. She desperately needed to be normal, so when she thought that there was a real possibility with this treatment of course, she put her all into it. She was expecting a positive outcome as she was led to believe all along so she was not prepared for anything different. She was so ready for the truth that when it was not as she had presumed, she could not handle it. It was too painful for her to accept. She became confused and insecure once more and started to get cross with herself for letting herself believe that she had a chance to be a normal girl. She truly hoped that when her vagina was normal, she would be normal, but now she did not even know what normal was anymore. It was hopeless! She felt that everything she had done was useless, she was useless and even chastised herself as a 'loser'. By now, Elizabeth was beside herself. She really did not want to cry but the tears welled up in her eyes anyway and she could not then stop them flowing down her face, as she resigned herself to the fact that she would always be abnormal no matter what she did or how hard she tried... she would never be rid of her genetic aberration.

Elizabeth's emotional anguish became so intense that her self-esteem and self-worth continued to plummet downhill and now she was at her lowest since she started her treatment. She began to feel worse when she reflected more about the people who were helping her. She actually trusted the experts and most of all, she trusted Lucy because if anything, she could always trust her. Only now this made her feel worse than ever because she felt so betrayed. She started to believe that everyone had lied to her to make her feel better. She even became annoyed with Tom because, "Why did he have to tell me that I was to feel something?!!" She would have been none the wiser and she would not feel this bad had he not told her that. Now, she felt all alone again and more abnormal than ever. She tried to fight back her tears of frustration and anger but they just kept rolling down her cheeks. Tom hugged her to comfort her but she pulled away from him and told him that, "This is all one great big mistake," and that "I should never have listened to them! They all lied to me Tom. I'll always be abnormal".

Then she went limp as she let her body slump against him, and, almost whimpering, she said, "I give up. I don't care anymore. I'm just so tired, so tired of everything". Her voice and the words sounded so eerily final and hollow that in that instant, it scared Tom. He did not care that she meant giving up her treatment because he was not very keen on anything that was going to bring her pain anyway, but he cared that she should give up on life. That would be a real waste, because besides being intelligent and beautiful, she had such a bubbly and wonderful personality and she had so much to give and so much to live for. He blamed himself for the way Elizabeth was feeling now because he should have been more considerate and made the experience enjoyable for her, but he had failed to do so due to his lack of experience. He also thought that, better still, he should have had more self-control and waited until she was really ready as they had decided earlier. He should not have encouraged her and he should not have kissed her like that although she responded and the feeling was mutual. She seemed so sure at the time, so it was consensual, and everything happened spontaneously. Now he was not sure what he could say or do to make her feel better so he just told her, "I know you're tired, El, but you can't just give up. This is all, my fault. I should have taken better care of you. Trust me it's got nothing to do with your MRKH. It's not your fault, El".

"Please Tom, stop! Don't you start lying to me too! I'm fed up of everyone saying things just to make me feel better because it doesn't help," she pleaded but Tom was equally quick to respond, "I'm not lying to you El. Nobody's lied to you. You are normal, just because you have this abnormal thing doesn't mean that you are not normal. Besides, you know that Lucy would never lie to you. Anyway, the enjoyment bit has nothing to do with your MRKH. It's my fault not yours, ok? It was your first time so I should have relaxed you more first. I was not experienced enough but in hindsight, I should have done some foreplay". When

Elizabeth heard that word, something immediately clicked in her head as she remembered Lucy also mentioning foreplay and suggested that Tom could use his fingers or use her dilators as sex toys only at the time, Elizabeth did not pay much attention because she was too embarrassed and could not think of anything grosser. Now, as she pondered over it for a bit longer, it all did not seem so risqué or disgusting. When she stopped crying, she told Tom that Lucy had also advised her to use her dilators first because these would stretch and open up her vagina before they had sex, and to use the lubricating gel so as to make it less uncomfortable for the both of them. It actually made her feel better after she reflected on Lucy's advice because she felt that Lucy genuinely cared about helping her, and it also reaffirmed that her trust in Lucy was well invested. Tom was only too relieved that Elizabeth was rational again because he did not know what else he could have done or how he could have coped otherwise, especially when he felt that he was to blame for the situation he had created. If he had to admit, he was actually quite frightened and he also started to hate what Elizabeth's condition was doing to her, because he did not like to see her in so much pain and anguish. He had only known Elizabeth to be a strong and level-minded girl before, although he accepted that she was more vulnerable now, but he still had no idea that her confidence and self-esteem had been knocked for six because of her condition, especially when he did not think it to be such a big deal. He still loved her anyway but after what just happened, he felt very ignorant and appreciated that this MRKH was more complex than he could have imagined.

Elizabeth was keen to try to have sex with Tom again because she felt that if she did what Lucy had advised that it would be better this time. She just needed to know that she would be normal this time but also, in a strange way, she also wanted to prove that Lucy was right because she felt bad about not trusting her earlier. Tom was more cautious this time because he could not bear to repeat that experience, and he was also certain that he would not be able to help her if things did not work out again this time, and he would then lose her forever. This was his greatest fear. He could not bear losing her. He tried to dissuade her and suggested that they should wait as agreed but Elizabeth became playful and kept teasing and kissing him so in the end, he could not resist her anymore. This time though she used her dilators first and then Tom helped her with those too, and he also used them as foreplay. He stimulated her clitoris which suddenly made Elizabeth climax. She did not know what that feeling was but she liked it, in fact she liked it a lot. Tom told her that she just had an orgasm. Elizabeth could not believe it. She had obviously heard of women having orgasms but she never knew what it meant. Now she, Elizabeth, had an orgasm, which meant that she was normal like them. She felt so good to be normal that she totally relaxed so sex this second time round was much better and Tom felt that he even managed full penetration. It was great and they both enjoyed it! Elizabeth was thrilled because she had experienced sex and now knew what other people meant when they said that sex was great. Still she was terrified that she had dreamt it all up because she could not believe that she could ever have sex let alone enjoy it so she kept asking Tom to reassure her that it was real. She was screaming so excitedly all over and inside her head that she thought that it was going to explode into fireworks and crackers. She kept repeating to herself and to Tom that, "I'm normal now Tom! I'm really normal". Tom nodded and reiterated, "You've always been normal El, and you are so beautiful. You just needed to believe in yourself". Tom was now happier and relieved that they did try again, not only because he thought their sex was great but it made Elizabeth so happy and restored her self-belief and confidence. He was also pleased that Elizabeth was the one who initiated it, even though he knew her reason for wanting to do it, but he did not mind especially if he could help her to get better. Afterwards, they laid in bed, close in each other's arms for a while. It felt so comfortable and they felt so right. They must have fallen asleep for about an hour. Afterwards, Elizabeth said that she was going to have her shower and Tom said he still had his last-minute packing to do so he kissed her goodnight and went back to his room.

Elizabeth felt exhausted and she was half asleep when she went into the shower but once that lovely warm water fell on her skin, she soon woke up. She was still holding the dilators in her hands because she had taken them in with her so she could wash them at the same time. Then it came to her. She remembered what just happened between her and Tom. She had sex with him! She was actually able to have sex and it was wonderful as she recalled. It also meant that she was normal. She was delirious with excitement and she could not wait to tell her best friend. She hurriedly washed herself and got out of the shower. She left the dilators in the bathroom to dry on one of the hotel hand towels and got herself into her pyjamas, then quickly grabbed her mobile. She started to text Sally to ask her to come back to the hotel because she had this wonderful news to tell her. Then she stopped herself in time when she realised how selfish she was. She thought that Sally was probably enjoying herself and she could not spoil her fun so she decided that she would just have to wait patiently for her best friend to return in good time. As it so happened, she could well have texted Sally because although Sally was having fun with their other friends, she was also deliberately staying out as late as possible because she wanted to give Elizabeth and Tom some space and their alone times together. Sally was always very considerate like that.

Alone in the room, Elizabeth sat on her bed, refreshed from her shower. She still felt exhilarated and could not contain her emotions. She just needed to talk to someone. She thought of Lucy. Yes, she could ring her. Lucy would want to know that her treatment worked and that her vagina was now normal. She proved it because she'd had sex and Tom said it was normal. Lucy would be happy for her and she would be so proud of her. Elizabeth wanted to be Lucy's success story because she felt that Lucy had done more than her job's worth, helping and supporting her all this time, and she felt somewhat indebted to her. Then without a second thought, she picked up her mobile to call Lucy. She was so emotionally engrossed that she had forgotten that she was not in the UK and she also did not realise the time until she saw it on her mobile. It was too late to ring Lucy anyway but she still wanted to share this important piece of good news with her. Then she felt ashamed that she even doubted Lucy in her earlier moment of despair. She should have known better because like Tom said, Lucy would never lie to her, but she was not thinking straight then so it made her feel even more desperate to talk to her now if only to get everything off her chest. It was just not feasible though so after a while, Elizabeth thought of ringing her mother to tell her that she was normal now but thought afterwards that she too would probably be asleep by now. It was hopeless, she had this important news to share yet there was just no one around she could talk to, not at this hour anyway.

Elizabeth used to be quite childlike and was easily embarrassed by any talk of her intimate or private life, but not anymore, not after what just happened between her and Tom. Now, she definitely felt all grown up. After the uncertainty over her normality and her womanhood, which so psychologically crushed her a moment ago, all her negative feelings about herself vanished just like that because she managed to prove to herself that she was indeed a normal female. It felt so good to be a real girl at last that she wanted to tell the world. She knew it was ridiculous of course, because no normal girl or woman would do that, nor would they need to either, but this was the point, for Elizabeth, she was not born normal and she had to struggle to prove that she was normal, so it was a big deal to her.

Given the choice, she would rather that she did not have to prove anything to herself or to anyone. If only she did not need to do that, she wished. Everyone including Tom kept telling her that she was a beautiful girl but she could not visualise herself as one, not until she could feel that she was a real female so finally she started to believe, and she wanted everyone to know too. In the end, she just reminded herself again that Tom was the best thing that happened to her since she found out that she had MRKH. Thanks to Tom whom she felt helped her to regain her sense of normality by proving that she was normal, she also began to believe that she could have a normal life after all. Now, even the fact that she could not have children was not as painful but of course it still hurt and vexed her when she thought about it, because she would have liked to have had a choice in the matter. Still, she seemed to have accepted it for the present time. Besides, she resigned that she could always adopt like Tom said so they would still be able to have their own family in the future.

It was a while before Sally came back and Elizabeth had nodded off by then but when she heard the door open, she quickly propped herself up in bed and switched on her bedside light. She saw Sally creeping in because Sally was not sure what she would be walking into and was afraid of disturbing them. She did not know that Tom had already left but when the lights came on, she saw that Elizabeth was by herself, so she immediately asked, "Are you ok, El?" Elizabeth was fully woken up by now, so she got herself all excited again and said, "Yes, I'm fine. I've been waiting for you to come back so I could tell you but I must have drifted off. What time is it?"

"Just past two o'clock. Anyway, go on, tell me what happened," urged Sally, so Elizabeth, who was equally as eager to tell her friend, very promptly said, "We did it Sal and Tom said it was normal. Can you believe it, it means that I'm normal, Sal". Sally ran towards her best friend to give her a tight hug and said, "Oh El, I'm so happy for you. I would've come back sooner but I didn't in case I interrupted you guys". Then Sally, curious to know more, although she suddenly felt slightly bashful and started blushing, asked Elizabeth, "El, what was sex like?" Without hesitation, Elizabeth said, "It was great! I never knew that it could be like that". Then discerning that Sally being still a virgin, really wanted to know more details, Elizabeth shared everything with her best friend in their usual girly-girl talk manner, except there was not much to tell other than that she was able to have sex with Tom, which made her feel normal. This was Elizabeth's biggest issue, so Sally fully appreciated how much this really meant to her best friend. She had been through everything with Elizabeth from the beginning so this was indeed an achievement for Elizabeth to finally be able to feel normal again. She was also pleased that everything turned out alright because she was slightly nervous, in case the outcome was disappointing, especially when she was the one who initiated and encouraged the pair of them, and when she had no experience herself.

Then for a brief second, Sally thought that she could not believe that she was even having this conversation with Elizabeth because it was so different from what they would normally talk about, yet it also felt quite natural. She thought that maybe this was also a part of growing up, although she was sure that if not for Elizabeth's MRKH they would not be talking so casually about Elizabeth losing her virginity and being so happy for her, especially at sixteen, and when they had always said that they would not do anything until much later on. Still it was important to Elizabeth so she appreciated that this was something that her friend had to do to prove that she was a normal female, which was always the point and she was only too pleased that she managed to do so. Nevertheless, Sally could not help feeling slightly sad for her friend too, because she felt that even though Elizabeth might have enjoyed the experience and it was a result, she had no other choice and was therefore compelled to do what she did. In any case, she found that through supporting her friend, she was also now more mature, and was growing up as quickly as Elizabeth. The two girls sat up talking till almost dawn. It was amazing that they had so much to talk about but then they always did. It was like old times again where they would share and confide in each other on everything. Eventually, their tiredness caught up with them. Sally climbed back into her own bed. They said goodnight to each other and no sooner their heads touched their pillows, they fell asleep straight away.

The telephone in their room rang a few times before either of them stirred. It was their early morning wake-up call from the hotel reception. Elizabeth made a quick dash to the bathroom but Sally remained semi-comatose and could hardly open her eyes. Elizabeth had three hours sleep although it felt as if she had only just fallen asleep, but she did not feel too bad for it. When Elizabeth finished with the bathroom, she tried waking Sally again with a chirpy, "Rise and shine, sleepy head. We have to go down for breakfast," to which Sally muttered, "I don't want breakfast. I just want to sleep". Elizabeth said ok because she felt slightly guilty that she had kept Sally up talking till the early hours of the morning, so she told her that she would bring some breakfast up for her from the restaurant when she finished hers. It was amazing that Elizabeth was so energetic and sprightly despite having had so little sleep but then she was feeling the happiest she had felt for a very long time. She proceeded to get her dilators because she would do her treatment once now and the next one when she got home later. She was determined to complete her treatment, although she was tempted to think that she might have actually completed it because she had sex last night and it was pain free and normal. Still, she wondered if this meant that her vagina was now normal. Of course, being the person she was, she needed confirmation that it was, so she decided that she would continue her treatment anyway until she spoke to Lucy. "Yes, I'll ring Lucy when I get in," she resolved because she also had so much that she wanted to tell her. She could not wait to get home now so that she could ring and talk to Lucy properly.

By now, Elizabeth was an expert at doing her treatment discreetly so she did it under the bedclothes in case Sally decided to get up. It was effortless and she thought that the dilators went in a lot easier. "Nah," she muttered to herself, thinking that she was just imagining things. She was done in ten minutes. Whilst she was washing her dilators, her mind flashed to Tom. She remembered his warmth and gentleness and the way he made her feel and she smiled to herself. She wondered whether he was thinking of her and their night of passion together right now. Suddenly, she could not wait to see him but she did not want her other friends to know that they had sex last night, in case it made them feel awkward. In truth, she was the one who would feel awkward and embarrassed because she was funny like that. She was such a private and conservative sixteen-year-old, not just because of her MRKH but she was never that touchy, showy in public type of person. She did not mind seeing couples holding hands in public. She thought that was quite sweet but she always found couples who were too lovey-dovey with their affections when they were out with friends or in a group rather nauseating and she sometimes felt sorry for their friends. No, Elizabeth thought, she could not embarrass her friends that way. She would have better self-restraint, even though by now all her friends already knew that she and Tom were together as an item, but she still preferred and felt that they did not need to know the details. Deep inside though, Elizabeth could not wait to be affectionate with Tom again but she would have to restrain herself from being too obvious, lest she became one of those nauseating couples that she detested.

There was a knock on the door. Elizabeth knew that it was Tom so just before she opened it she quickly dashed into the bathroom to straighten her hair and to make sure that she looked alright, even though she already looked her usual gorgeous self – but she wanted to look good for him. She felt all tingly inside and even slightly flirtatious at the thought of seeing him, and, in fact, she was just acting like a normal young girl in love who could not wait to see her boyfriend again. When she opened the door, she saw Tom first, but he was not on his own. The rest of their friends were with him, so she very quickly changed her stance to one that was almost civil, which puzzled Tom and he raised one of his eyebrows and gave her a teasing cheeky smile. He bent down to kiss her but she casually turned her face away as if to ignore him because he looked so handsome and irresistible that she was afraid she would succumb to his charms. She was determined not to do so in front of their friends, so instead she made out that she did not want to wake Sally up and told them that they should just hurry to the restaurant. Tom still put his hand around her shoulders as they walked towards the elevator and when they got in, he manoeuvred her to the back of the elevator and then he whispered in her ear, "I miss you already". Elizabeth thought that if only he knew how much she missed him too and she so wanted to tell him, except not in public. She forced herself to have a bit more discipline and self-restraint but it was hard because she wanted him as much as he did her.

Then she began to wonder when they would get another opportunity to be together again, because they were both in boarding school and still living at home, so even during their school holidays it would be impossible for them to be together like this again. She yearned to be close to him once more and started blushing at the thought so she could barely look at him. Tom found Elizabeth's coyness rather alluring so he waited for the elevator doors to close and when everyone stood facing the front, he whispered "I love you, El," and then he kissed her. Elizabeth could not hold back her feelings any further so she mimed, "I love you too" and she kissed him back. When the elevator doors opened, they were still kissing so their friends teased them, "Hey, we're here, lovebirds". Elizabeth was so embarrassed that she felt the rush of blood to her face and her face went the colour of beetroot in seconds because everyone in the lift was now staring at them and a few people even clapped. She could not believe it. She had let herself become one of these overly affectionate in public couples whom she had been repulsed by in the past. Tom on the other hand, seemed unabashed by it all. In fact, he rather enjoyed the acclamation, so he proudly gave them a nod and a broad smile. If he was honest, unlike Elizabeth, he could not be happier to let everyone know that he was in love with this beautiful girl standing beside him.

All through breakfast, Elizabeth was unusually quiet because she was still feeling the embarrassment of her earlier public display, but Tom was in a playful mood and he kept teasing her, which made her feel even more uncomfortable in front of their friends. Unfortunately for her, Tom seemed to find her bashfulness rather delightful and adorable that he continued to flirt with her and kept telling her how beautiful she was and that he loved her very much. He also tried to kiss her a few times and when it was not reciprocated and instead she mouthed, "Stop it," he reassured her that it was cool to be affectionate and encouraged her to chill and to be herself. What Tom failed to realise was that Elizabeth was being herself. She wished that she could be as relaxed and open as he was but she had set herself some very strict morals and principles, which were unusual for someone so young, someone who was just sixteen. It was hard then for her to simply dismiss them. She also kept her private thoughts to herself and would only share them with her best friend because Sally was like the other half of herself. It was difficult to know if her MRKH had made her become more emotionally introverted, because now she just wanted to keep all her private affairs private, including her relationship with Tom. Tom also wondered when she became so reserved because he had only known her to be brave and sometimes even audacious in the past. He suspected that her MRKH had much to do with it and it reminded him again of her vulnerability and he was more determined to try to protect and help her. He could not help worrying about her, although he did not want to show it. He knew that he might have exaggerated his outward behaviour towards her, perhaps just a titch, but then he was so much in love with her. He loved her so much and he only wanted to make her happy. Elizabeth loved him too but he was getting too embarrassing with his touchy-feely in public that she wanted to get away from him so she ate her breakfast as quickly as possible.

When she finished, she told her friends that she was getting some breakfast for Sally. One of the chefs at the food servery-counter was very helpful so when she told him that she was taking some breakfast up for her friend in her room, he asked if she would like coffee or tea and then organised a small pot of coffee, milk and sugar on a tray for her. Elizabeth then helped herself to a roll, a croissant, some slices of cheeses and ham and a bowl of fresh fruits and yoghurt for Sally. The tray was quite heavy so as she excused herself and walked away from her friends, Tom being the gentleman and wanting any excuse to be alone with her, very quickly took the tray and offered to go up with her. Elizabeth had not anticipated this because the last thing she needed was for her friends to think that she and Tom had planned it so that they could be alone together, so she wanted to go up by herself, but there was no time to argue since Tom had already walked away with the tray. She was left with no choice so she quietly followed suit.

When they were alone in the lift, Tom remarked that Elizabeth was very quiet and asked if she was alright so she told him that she was still feeling embarrassed at what happened in the lift earlier. "We're in love El. I don't care if the whole world knows. In fact, I want the world to know because I'm proud of us," he told her so she said, "and that's the problem, you're enjoying it and making it worse..." Tom interjected, "How so? We didn't do anything wrong, we just kissed. Are you ashamed of us, because I'm not! I love you and I'm not ashamed of loving you," but she asserted, "I know and I love you too, but I don't like to be on show, not in pubic. I don't need the world to know, I just need us to know. I'm sorry Tom but I'm just funny like that. I'm a very private person especially when it concerns matters of the heart and my..." Of course, she was going to say her "MRKH" but she suddenly stopped herself. She could not explain why she could not even bear to say that word but she knew that she just did not want to, because she was getting very tired of letting her condition rule her life. She also felt that she was finally getting on with her life now and she did not wish to be reminded of it anymore. Tom astutely chose to ignore it too. Besides, he was more interested in the present, and although he did not agree with Elizabeth's views altogether, he respected that she had a point so as long as they loved each other and stayed together, that was all that mattered and it was no one else's business. He admitted that he might have slightly over-displayed his affections earlier but he could not help himself, he just wanted to touch her and to feel her close to him all the time. It was after all young love. It was also new love for Elizabeth but for Tom it was not new because he had already loved her for a very long time.

Elizabeth entered the room by herself in case Sally was still asleep but she was already awake and getting dressed in the bathroom. Their timing could not be better so she called out to Sally and told her that she had left her breakfast tray for her on the side table and then she went to Tom's room. The minute they walked into his room, he grabbed her and kissed her lustfully because he could not control his testosterone anymore. He was also aware that this was going to be the last time that they would be together on their own again for a while so they had to make the most of it. Elizabeth made sure that he locked the door first and then she was a different person once she felt secure in the privacy of their four walls. They stripped off each other's clothes excitedly and embraced each other's bodies and made passionate love. It was extemporaneous because they were so much in love and they were both very sexually aroused by one another, and it was even better than the last time. Elizabeth did not think that it was even possible because she thought the last time was great. In fact, when she thought about it, they did not even have to use her dilators or any lubricant but then they did not have time nor did they need any help this time. They had sex like a normal couple and it was wonderful! She could not believe it, 'normal' she uttered. She was so elated that she kept kissing Tom. They stayed in each other's arms for a while again. Then she said, "I don't know when we could be together like this again. I don't want this to end," so he said, "I feel the same. I can't bear to think about it. Maybe we should run away together and live on an island all by ourselves".

"It sounds nice but it is all wishful thinking, and besides we'll miss our families and friends too much," she told him and with that she said, "come on, lover boy dreamer, we've got to get going". She got herself dressed, kissed him again and then she went back to her room to have her shower. When she walked into the room, she had such a broad smile on her face that Sally said rhetorically, "you just had sex, didn't you?" but Elizabeth was so excited that she shrieked out, "Yes and it was the best" and she hugged her friend before going into the bathroom. When she was in the shower, she decided to examine herself and she was beyond astonished. Her vagina had stretched so much that she could hardly feel the top of it. "It's normal, I have a normal vagina. I'm really normal now," she said to herself. Elizabeth was jumping for joy and she wanted this feeling to last forever because at last, she managed to change her abnormality to normality and it felt really good. She did not wish to be cocky but right now she was very proud of herself and felt that there was nothing that she could not handle after this. She was so happy then, but she soon brought herself back to reality and felt that no matter what she thought and how much she wanted to believe, she still needed expert confirmation. She could not wait to see Lucy and to hear Lucy tell her that it was normal, that she was normal, but for now she would speak to her best friend. Sally was just as happy for Elizabeth and she told her how pleased and proud she was of her but most of all, she was just so happy to have her best friend back.

When they arrived at London Stansted airport, all their respective families were there waiting so they said their goodbyes and parted company. Sally had a lift from Elizabeth's parents as it was the sensible thing to do, since she did not live far from them, so Paul dropped her off on the way home. All the time, Elizabeth remained in an excitable mood and she told her parents that she had the best holiday ever, and to even think that she was in two minds about going in the first place! She was so pleased that she went and that Tom had been so persistent and insistent that she went, because this trip had made such a dramatic difference to her. Of course, she did not know at the time but this trip was the opportunity she needed and she could not thank Tom enough for arranging it but, most of all, for all his input in making her feel normal at last and for making her life better now. Then she thought that it was not just Tom. She also owed this to her parents not just for paying for this trip and encouraging her to go but for their continuous support in everything.

Of course, there was Sally, her best friend, always helpful and considerate and who never gave up on her either. In fact, when Elizabeth reflected more, she knew that it was actually Sally who was the one who believed in Tom and encouraged Elizabeth's relationship with him in the first place and she was also the one who created opportunities for them to be together. She could never repay her best friend for all the things she had done for her. In that moment, she felt truly blessed and elated to be surrounded by so many people who really cared about and loved her, although she always knew that all along, except that she had been so pre-occupied with herself and her problem that she did not have time to tell them how much she appreciated their support and how much she loved them too.

When they entered their house, she went straight to her parents and said, "Thanks for everything, mum, dad. I love you so much," and hugged them at the same time, so her father told her, "We just want you to be happy, darling because we love you so much too," and then they kept hugging each other dearly. Just then, her mobile rang. It was Tom to say that he had reached home and that he was missing her already. She felt herself blushing in front of her parents so she quickly excused herself and went to her room. They spoke for a long time and afterwards she felt worse because she missed him so much it was unbearable. She decided to ring her best friend, because talking to Sally always made her feel good, and besides she wanted to let her know how much she really appreciated her help and her friendship and how very much she loved her too. She was right, she felt a lot better after talking to Sally.

Treatment Finale And
The Road To Recovery

Elizabeth had a pre-arranged appointment with Lucy and
Anne a week before she was due back at school, but of course
she could not wait till then as she needed to speak with Lucy,
so she rang and left a message on her voicemail for a call
back because Lucy was not in her office, and it was also
the weekend. Elizabeth pottered around her room sorting
out her clothes and the gifts she had bought for everyone.
Since her trip to Barcelona, Elizabeth had remained in
good spirits. She was chatty and when she was not out with
Sally, she would help her mother in the kitchen like she used
to before. One evening when she was helping her mother
to prepare their dinner, Jan asked Elizabeth how she was
getting on with her treatments. Elizabeth told her mother
that she felt she had nearly completed but that she would
rather wait for Lucy's confirmation. She very nearly told her
mother that she had already had sexual intercourse with
Tom but for whatever reason, she suddenly found that she
could not bring herself to tell her. Elizabeth could hear a
little voice inside her head telling her to tell her mother about
everything that had happened, but just then she felt like a
naughty child who had done something that she should not
have done and she became overwhelmed by this strange
feeling of embarrassment and guilt that she chose not to
say anything in the end. She wished she could confide in
her mother like she used to, although admittedly they never
really talked about such intimate matters before. Elizabeth
was back to her usual self, except she was not quite the same
girl anymore. In fact, she was just this different new person
in the same mould. She was all grown up and felt better for
it and she did not need not to confide in her mother so much

now. Maybe this was it, maybe she was just not that sweet innocent sixteen anymore, she concluded.

Elizabeth was very comfortable and confident with the person she now was and she no longer needed to search for answers nor did she need to hide herself away in her room. Nowadays, she only went to her room when she was on the phone to Tom and when she had to do her treatments. She kept on with her treatments like a good girl because she thought she ought to until she was told otherwise. She also never really minded doing her treatments anyway, if she could achieve her goal, so to her it was no different from her studying hard for her examinations to get the good grades she wanted. The only difference was that this treatment was not always easy because it kept reminding her of her abnormality, which she would rather forget. Still it had to be done so she did it and she felt that it was definitely worth every bit of her angst and tears. She thought that of all the outcomes she had achieved, this was by far her greatest achievement. After all, it was not every day she could say that she had created her own vagina from nothing. Just then, her mobile rang so she rushed to answer it. As expected, she recognised Lucy's voice on the other end of the line so she immediately became very excited. After the usual civilities, Elizabeth updated Lucy on her trip to Barcelona, or rather what she did in Barcelona. Of course, Lucy was equally pleased for her that her treatment was successful and from what she just learnt, she thought that Elizabeth might have completed her treatment. Still they agreed that she should attend her appointment as arranged, which Elizabeth preferred as well because she could also then keep her appointment with Anne.

Jan had initially planned on going with Elizabeth for her appointment but Elizabeth was aware that her parents were rather busy at the office so she convinced her mother that she was capable of going up to London with Sally. Sally had also gone up with her before and besides Elizabeth had made this same trip up to London so many times already, so by now she felt very confident going without her mother. Jan trusted that they were both very sensible and intelligent girls but she also felt that it was her role as her mother to accompany Elizabeth, and not her friend's. She also wanted to be a part of her daughter's life again as she felt that Elizabeth was hardly telling her anything these days and she could not afford to make the same mistake as she did in the past of not being involved in her decisions again. She loved her daughter too much and also hoped that she would come to trust and confide in her like the old times again although she noted how grown up Elizabeth had become. Still she did not want her daughter to think that she did not care enough. She had telephoned Lucy when Elizabeth was in Barcelona to ask for help for herself so Lucy gave her a couple of parent support groups to contact. Jan later also found an online support group for parents and had been corresponding with a few of them, which she found very helpful. She received good sound advice from other mothers, who had similar experiences with their daughters and they reassured her that this was a common phase their daughters went through so she should not feel too excluded or useless.

They also advised her against being too pushy with her approach to compensate for her own inadequacy and instead she was advised to gently remind Elizabeth that she would always be there for her if and when she needed her motherly advice or guidance. Since finding her own online support group, Jan felt more secure and relaxed around Elizabeth, so although their closeness was not as it was, their mother–daughter relationship was still good. She also thought that maybe this had nothing to do with her MRKH but rather the fact that Elizabeth was no longer a child. She accepted that her daughter was now a young lady and that this was probably her normal progression into adulthood, so she was happy to step back and to let her grow up instead. Besides, there was no cause for her to be meddling into Elizabeth's affair now because she could see that she had already grown into this very fine confident and beautiful young lady anyway, and she could not be prouder of her. She felt that this was good enough for any mother to wish for and this was also comforting enough for Jan, for now anyway.

Elizabeth invited Sally to stay the night because they had gone out with their friends for the day so Jan picked them up afterwards and took them straight home. It made more sense for her to stay over instead of Jan having to drop her home and then picking her up again in the morning, when she was going up to London with Elizabeth the next day. Emma was also staying over at her best friend's down the road because Jan was originally going to take Elizabeth to London so she had made this prior arrangement with the other parents. That evening, Jan decided not to cook and they ordered a takeaway instead, as there was only going to be the three of them eating because Paul was also working late at the office, so they would just keep some food aside for him. After dinner, they sat around chatting and watching television until Paul returned and then the two girls went into Elizabeth's room. Jan knew what they were like so she advised them, "Now girls, don't stay up too late. You don't want to get up too late tomorrow because you have to go up to London," but they did anyway. Elizabeth was in a hyper mood so she could not sleep and the two best friends chatted till the early hours of the morning again. Fortunately, it was not bad this time because they did not have to wake up at the crack of dawn since Elizabeth's appointments were not till mid-afternoon and Jan had booked them a later train. Paul went into the office early because he was meeting with a new client, a company that recently opened a branch in town. Jan hung out the clothes in her laundry room and then she rang her parents as she usually did every morning. She also rang to check on Emma and afterwards, she read the papers whilst she waited for the girls to wake up. When the girls finally got up, she made them breakfast.

During breakfast, Jan could not help herself, because as a mother she still worried about her girls even though she trusted both of them. She had to make sure that they remembered how to get to the Centre so she went through the route with the two of them again, and she also asked Elizabeth to ring or text her when they arrived. When it was time, she dropped them off at the train station before going in to work herself.

Elizabeth tried her best to relax so she was much better this time although she still could not help feeling anxious. It had started again. She could not explain her feelings but she still felt uncomfortable and nervous having to go to the Centre, yet she knew the place and the staff so well by now, and besides she could hardly wait to see Lucy and Anne, especially when she was anticipating a good outcome this time. Sally held her hand and suggested that, "Hey, this might well be your last appointment, El" but Elizabeth just said, "I'm not so sure. I don't really want to get too ahead of myself and jinx it". Furthermore, she knew that this would not be her last because, although she might have completed her treatment, she had not quite finished her therapy with Anne. She felt that she was nearly there but she wanted to be absolutely confident that she was really ok with who she was. If she had to put her hand on her heart now, she would have to admit that she could not say that she was totally comfortable with her MRKH nor could she get on with her life normally without help just yet, because she knew she still had unresolved issues. She knew she had come a long way having managed to find her way back from a state of being lost and alone and utter confusion but she could not say that she was fully well just yet not until she could be normal like other women or at least to come to terms. No doubt, she now had a functional vagina and she proved that she could have sex like other women so in this respect she felt normal, but she did not have a womb, not like other normal women. She still kept feeling cheated and it still pained her when she saw women with their children. She would get especially angry when she heard of the parents who abused their children because she felt they did not deserve to have children. She, on the other hand, loved children and she wanted children of her own, yet she could not, at least not naturally anyway. She just felt that it was so unfair. It was maddening and this was something she still found very hard to accept, so she was still struggling to come to terms with it. Not only that, but she also did not know how she would feel or react if Sally or any of her friends should fall pregnant and she was concerned that she might feel envious and resentful towards them. Elizabeth was such an intelligent girl and she had thought of everything, so she knew that she still had big issues to resolve before she could safely say that she was back to her normal self and back in control of her life. Until then, she accepted that she would need the continuous support of the experts even if it meant that she would continue to feel uncomfortable every time she went up to London to see them. This alone was progress, because at least now she was more rational and she was able to acknowledge her difficulties and was up for the challenge.

Elizabeth and Sally found their way to the Centre without any difficulty and, as usual, they were early for her appointment, so they had a drink at the little coffee shop before checking in. Elizabeth remembered to text her mother so she quickly sent her a message to let her know that they had arrived. When she walked into the clinic, Elizabeth saw Lucy talking to another specialist so she said hello and proceeded to check herself in at the reception. Sally found a couple of seats at the far end of the clinic so they went to sit there. Then Elizabeth recognised a young girl whom she had seen before on her last visit to the clinic. She looked about her age too so Elizabeth wondered if this girl also had MRKH. She was by herself just like the last time she saw her and Elizabeth thought that she was so brave to come alone. In that moment, she was even tempted to go over to talk to her, but instead she held back and just smiled when the girl happened to look up at her. She thought, "I must ask Lucy about the girl later," but before she could think of anything else, "El", she heard her name being called, so she got up and walked over towards Lucy and they went into the room. Elizabeth was so happy to see Lucy that she gave her a hug and a kiss on the side of her cheek as if she were a friend. Then again, she had come to regard Lucy as a friend as well as her specialist. She always felt comfortable with her so they chatted first and Lucy then said, "so you did go to Barcelona in the end then and from what you said on the phone, you enjoyed it and you also had a result". Elizabeth got really excited and said, "Yes. Barcelona was great. I'm really glad that I went. The city is amazing, so much culture and history and we did lots of sightseeing and shopping. There were lots of different places to eat and to chill out. It was the best holiday ever! I really enjoyed it even though it was only four days but it seemed longer because my friends and I had so much fun together". Lucy then asked her, "So what happened between you and Tom?" She had already spoken briefly to Lucy on the telephone about her experience with Tom but she still became very excitable at the mention of him. Then suddenly, she also became slightly embarrassed talking about the sexual side of things so she just told Lucy that she had sex twice with Tom and that it was normal but she seemed keener to mention that she had examined herself afterwards and was amazed at how different her vagina felt. She said, "I still continued with my treatments, though, because I wasn't sure that I should stop until I saw you," so Lucy said, "Let's take a look now, shall we?" She could not wait so she promptly got up and went behind the curtains to get undressed, laid herself on the couch and said, "I'm ready".

When Lucy examined her, she too was very pleased, because her vagina was indeed normal. It had stretched to beyond a good seven centimetres and the skin felt so stretchy that there was still room to continue stretching. This was better than Lucy had anticipated. She always believed that the dilator treatment worked, especially when the skin was elastic at the outset, but it usually took longer for the majority of women to achieve this outcome, so she wondered if they were as diligent with their treatments as Elizabeth obviously had been. "Well done, El. You've done it. Your vagina is normal," she informed Elizabeth. "Thank you, thank you. I'm so glad I came up to London to see you guys," replied Elizabeth who was so happy that she did not know whether to laugh or to cry and although it was not exactly a surprise, it sounded so good hearing it from Lucy. Then the consultant came in to review her too and also confirmed the outcome. This was the moment Elizabeth had been waiting for and what she so desperately needed to hear. She was right to believe in this treatment and not opt for surgery just as the other experts had advised on her internet searches. She was so grateful that she came up to London because the team here knew exactly what she needed. She could not thank them enough because at last, she did it, she got there in the end and it was all worth every bit of her sweat and tears. Now, she knew for sure that she was normal because she managed to normalise this aspect of her abnormality with their help and support. It made her feel really good and she also felt rather proud of herself because of her amazing accomplishment. It made her more positive and sensible about her other issues and she became more certain that she could overcome any thing now and she was prepared to face up to the challenge so with a calm determination, "I will do it. I'm going to finish my therapy too, my next hurdle", she reassured herself.

Lucy confirmed Elizabeth's completion of her treatment with gold stars, and she also advised her to stop using the dilators. Elizabeth had guessed as much since these were just slipping in and out of her vagina with such ease. Even so, Elizabeth needed reassurance that her vagina would not shrink if she stopped using them. She was aware that some girls had to continue using their dilators, even when they had completed their treatment, to maintain vaginal patency, so she told Lucy, "I am still slightly worried though that if I stop using the dilators altogether then my vagina will shrink, so I want to be absolutely sure that I really don't need to use them before I stop, because I know that some girls still have to use them when they have completed their treatment. Another thing, I won't be seeing Tom for a while now because he's starting university in London in the autumn, so it won't be till the Christmas break that I'd get to see him again, and even if we do see each other then, I'm not sure if we'll have the opportunity to be alone together like that again". Lucy explained, "I understand your concern El but whilst some girls need to continue using their dilators, you don't need to because your vagina has not only stretched but it is fully stretched and the skin is still very elastic, so I assure you that your vagina will not shrink back down at this stage, even if you did nothing. Do you remember me telling you about the people with their excessive loose-hanging skin or stretch marks left from their skin being overstretched whilst they were overweight, that their skin cannot shrink back to what it was again, because once the skin has been overstretched, it remains stretched?"

"Yes, I remember. I'm sorry Lucy, it's not that I don't believe you, but I'm just frightened and I felt that I should tell you because I just had to be sure. I hope you don't mind," Elizabeth said, so Lucy reassured her that, "it's not a problem. I don't mind at all. I want you to be sure of every-thing so it's good that you talk about your fears and concerns rather than to keep wondering and having inaccurate information. Is there anything else? Have you any further concerns or questions that you'd like to ask me?" Elizabeth said, "No thank you. That was really my main worry and you have put my mind at rest so I'm happy". After a few minutes, she told Lucy, "I have been doing my treatments religiously every day for over two months so it would feel very strange now for me to not have to do any more treatments. I'm not saying that I want to or that I'll miss them or anything but it just feels really strange all of a sudden. Don't you think it's funny? I'm really happy though, because now I can get on with my life and not even think about them". She also added, "Do you know why I cannot be happier to stop using the dilators? I don't hate them because I knew I had to use them to make me normal, but the worst thing was that they were always a constant reminder of my abnormality and that I was abnormal. Have any of the women you treated ever told you that, or am I the only one?"

"No, you are not the only one. A few of them have said exactly what you've just said and I totally understand how hard it must have been for you to have to do something like this, yet all of you did. This shows courage, strength and determination. The good thing is that it's usually only for a short period of time, so once you have finished with your treatment and get the outcome you require, you won't need the dilators anymore and you don't have to look at them again" Lucy said empathetically. Elizabeth said "Yes I know. I was only saying that but we couldn't have done it without you and I'm still glad I did them rather than to have surgery. I guess I was also lucky that my skin was stretchy so I didn't have to use them for too long either. I am very happy because now I am normal, well in this respect anyway. You know what I mean". Afterwards, she gave Lucy a hug and she thanked her again. As she did that, she remembered the young girl in the clinic, so she asked Lucy if she had MRKH too. Lucy could not confirm straight away due to confidentiality reasons, which Elizabeth understood, but she was feeling so happy with her own progress and achievement that she told Lucy she wanted to help that young girl if she could. Elizabeth told Lucy, "The girl looked like how I was a few months ago. I want to help her if I can because you guys have helped me so much. She looks really scared and I feel that if I can talk to her maybe I can encourage or help her". It was so typical of Elizabeth because she was always kind and helpful this way. Lucy also thought that it made perfect sense as this was exactly how their patient to patient contacts support worked. She was especially pleased that Elizabeth was the one who offered this time because previously at the beginning when she herself was offered a contact, she had turned it down, but of course back then Elizabeth was not ready to talk to anyone but now Lucy believed that she was ready and in a strong position to help others too. She thanked Elizabeth for offering to help but of course, she would have to speak to the girl first which, Elizabeth understood, so she said, "No worries, I understand because I couldn't talk to anyone before too. I have to see Anne now but after that I'll wait around to see if you need me".

Elizabeth went back to join Sally in the little cafe and when Sally saw her face, she knew that it was all good. Elizabeth gave Sally the good news but told her that she still had to see Anne and then she went back to wait in the clinic. As she walked in, Anne was just about to call for her but when she saw Elizabeth, she said "hello" and took her to her room. Elizabeth remained in high spirits throughout her therapy session, so the hour with Anne seemed to go very quickly and this time, it was more helpful and productive because she was more receptive and was able to open up more. Elizabeth was ready and determined to get to the bottom of her issues this time, but agreed that she still needed a few more sessions to get there so she made another appointment. When she came out of Anne's room, she noticed that the young girl was not in the waiting area so she gathered that she must be seeing Lucy. She decided to wait as she had told Lucy that she would. Whilst she waited, she quickly texted Tom to let him know the outcome and that they would talk more when she got home later that night.

Not long after, Lucy came out from her room with the

young girl and she introduced her to Elizabeth. She then took them both to a vacant room so that they could talk in private. At first, there was an awkward silence between them and the girl seemed more timid than Elizabeth, so Elizabeth introduced herself, "Hi, I'm El. What's your name?" The girl gave her name as Melanie Smith but that was all she volunteered. Elizabeth identified herself with her straight away, because, until recently, she too could not talk to anyone either so she reckoned that Melanie was probably at that same stage she was at back then and assumed that she must have just been diagnosed. Elizabeth tried to break the ice between them so she asked Melanie for her age and how she found out about her problem. This really helped because once Melanie started to talk then there was no stopping her. She told Elizabeth that she was eighteen years old although Elizabeth thought that she looked a lot younger, but maybe it was because she was a slight girl. She said that she was diagnosed when she was sixteen. Like Elizabeth, her mother had taken her to see her GP when her periods did not start at fourteen but they too were told that she was a late starter so she waited but still nothing happened. She went back every year until she was sixteen. Then her GP decided to refer her to their local gynaecologist. Elizabeth could not believe what she was hearing. It was déjà vu as Melanie's story resonated so strongly with hers, and in that moment she thought she was reliving her own life story all over again. It was surreal and she was beyond shocked so all she could do was to echo what Melanie told her. "You're exactly like me. My GP told me the same thing". The only difference was that Elizabeth felt luckier than Melanie because at least she had lots of support and she did not have her same experience with her local doctors. She could not help feeling really sad and upset for Melanie when she heard about the horrific experience Melanie had with her local doctors. Melanie told Elizabeth that the consultant she saw admitted that he had never seen anyone like her before, so she felt instantly scared but he did not explain and instead he brought in a group of doctors to come and look at her. They were all none the wiser so they gawked and spoke about her as if she was not there. Then she said that each of them took turns to "prod me like I was just a piece of meat". Melanie became slightly tearful as she started to recall that terrible experience so Elizabeth reached out and held her hands.

After a few more minutes, she was more composed and was able to continue her story. She said, "It was so painful and embarrassing. I tried very hard to be brave and not to cry. I didn't want them to think that I was a cry-baby because I was afraid that they would get angry with me but after the fourth doctor prodded me it was too painful and he was very rough so I started to cry". She said that it was only then that they stopped but no one apologised and instead they looked at her as if they could not understand why she was crying and as if she had no right to cry either. She also told Elizabeth, "I have never felt so humiliated, so I just had to get out of there. I quickly put my jeans back on and ran out of that clinic as fast as I could. My mother didn't know what had happened so she came out after me. She told me off for running off like that because she said that now we wouldn't know what was wrong with me". Then afterwards, she told her mother what they did to her and that "they didn't know what was wrong with me anyway and I said that I never want to go back there again".

"No, course not and I don't blame you. I wouldn't either. That's really awful Melanie!" Elizabeth exclaimed. The hospital also never tried to contact her and she was eventually lost in their system. Melanie felt so terrible after that experience and she still did not know exactly what was wrong with her, but she said that she only remembered overhearing those doctors when they were talking amongst themselves, one said something like "this is really freakish, is she a girl?" and another said "this is weird, there's nothing there" then all four of them agreed and said that "I can't feel anything.

I can't find her vagina". She explained to Elizabeth that she did not understand what they were talking about so naturally she became very frightened and confused, especially as this was her first experience in hospital and she did not know what they were doing or what they were trying to find. Of course, she was also only a sixteen-year-old at the time and quite an innocent one at that, and, being quite fit and healthy, she had never had to see any doctor before and she had only gone to see her GP because her periods did not start at fourteen years of age. She said, "You know El I wish I didn't have MRKH. I wish I never saw those doctors. I will never forget what they did to me and even now I still find it hard to trust anyone. I daren't have any friends so I'm always alone". Elizabeth felt so empathetic towards Melanie and enraged at those doctors at the same time, because she thought that it was bad enough to have MRKH but to have to also experience what Melanie did was just too heart-wrenching. She told Melanie "I feel so upset for you because you didn't deserve to be treated like that. I just hope that now you're here that maybe you can learn to trust again, because they are so different here. They are kind and understanding and they know everything about us and they know how to help us. They have helped me so much and I'm sure that they will be able to help you too". Melanie was very soulful as she answered, "I hope so too. I'm really messed up, El," so Elizabeth reassured her. "It's ok because they are very good and clever here. Anne will understand and she will be able to help you".

Elizabeth then asked Melanie what happened after that so she told her, "My mum took me back to see my GP again and she complained about my treatment by those doctors at the local hospital". Naturally, her GP was very empathetic and apologised when she heard. She wanted to refer Melanie to another consultant but that bad experience had traumatised and scarred Melanie so much that "I just refused to see anyone else after that because I couldn't bear to go through the same humiliation again, you know. I just couldn't". Her GP and mother tried to persuade her to see another consultant but she was adamant. Still they needed to know what was wrong with her so her GP told them that she was still going to refer her anyway, and that she wanted her to reconsider and to discuss further with her mother about seeing this other consultant. Melanie also told Elizabeth, "I felt bad for my mum though because she felt terrible that she didn't know how to help me so she kept trying to persuade me to change my mind about seeing this new doctor, but I still refused. I had no one to talk to or anyone who could really help me but at the same time, I was just too frightened to see anybody else. I felt completely alone and I couldn't deal with it so I just tried to blank this from my mind". Then she said that a few weeks later, a letter from this other hospital arrived with an appointment for her to see a consultant. By now, she said that "I had become so depressed and I was not coping at all so in the end, I had no choice and agreed to go with my mother to see him. This consultant did a blood test and organised an MRI scan for me and when my mother and I returned for the results, he told us that I had MRKH. He told us that he also had no experience in treating girls like me so he offered to refer me to someone else who would be able to help me". She told Elizabeth that all she remembered him saying was "I was born with no womb and no vagina. I immediately felt so terrible because I didn't know what I was anymore. I really felt like I was a freak and I then remembered that doctor saying that I was freakish".

Now, Elizabeth really felt like she was there with Melanie because this was exactly how her story went too and how she felt all along so she hugged Melanie and told her, "I know exactly how you feel. I felt like a freak too when I first found out and sometimes I still do". They were both crying together now.

They felt better afterwards and because they now had each other, it was comforting to know that at last, they were not alone with this anymore. For Elizabeth, she had always wanted to be really understood too and irrespective of what anyone had told her or reassured her, somehow it was still not quite the same as this, meeting and talking to someone like herself, someone with MRKH. With Melanie too, she found that they did not have to explain to each other how they really felt because they both felt the same and they totally understood each other. They seemed to have such a remedying effect on each other to finally meet someone with their same condition that they were so overcome by emotions and they could not help feeling happy and sad at the same time. Elizabeth thought about this but she could not even try to explain how she was feeling then, but she also felt that nobody could understand it unless they were the same.

Melanie also told Elizabeth that "I still feel really bad for my mum because she was in a worse state than I was and she would cry every time she looked at me, so we've never spoken about it since. I couldn't talk to her about how I was feeling because it would upset her even more and yet we were very close before". Elizabeth told Melanie that "my mum was the same and she sobbed when we were first told so I also found it hard to talk to her". She looked at Melanie then and she could tell that she was still in a lot of pain and Elizabeth could feel her loneliness because Melanie lowered her voice as she continued. "I feel ashamed of myself all the time and I know that my mum is embarrassed and very disappointed in me too but I can't do anything about it. I hurt too and I still had no one to talk to". After that, she said that she tried to cope by pretending that what was happening to her never really happened. Unfortunately, it did not work because she could not move on with her life. It was always with her and she could not fit in anywhere. She told Elizabeth that "I feel so abnormal and I always feel like an outcast looking in. I am always frightened of anyone finding out too so that's why I don't have any friends, none whom I can trust anyway". Elizabeth thought that this was why she never saw Melanie with anyone and why she was always on her own, poor Melanie. At least, she herself had plenty of support from her parents and friends so she really felt for Melanie because she had always wondered how other girls coped without any support, and now she knew how truly awful it really is that it made her both sad and angry again for them.

Elizabeth then asked Melanie, "So what happened after you saw the other consultant who was referring you?"

"I can't remember but I didn't want to see anybody else after that. I can't remember being sent any other appointments anyway, otherwise I'm sure my mum would have made me go but I was only sixteen then so I didn't know much only that I was very scared and lonely" Melanie said. "So how did you cope, I mean without any help?" asked Elizabeth. She told Elizabeth that "I just blocked everything out and I pretended that none of this was real because everything was just too painful, so for the last two years, I kind of just drifted along alone and always alone. It was horrible but what could I do? I didn't know who to turn to. Nobody seemed to know much about this condition and all they could say is that they would refer me here and there. I couldn't bear to go through the same thing with different people over and over again so that's why, in a way, it was better that I kept to myself. At least, this way no one will find out that I am not a normal person". Elizabeth remarked, "You must have been so lonely!" so Melanie said "I still am. I hated it and sometimes when I think about it, I still do. I hated my life and everything and at one point I even thought of jumping in front of the train, but I guess I didn't have the guts to do that so instead I did this". She rolled up her sleeves and showed Elizabeth her arm so Elizabeth gasped. "Huh! Oh my god Melanie! It must have been very painful!" Melanie's arm was just covered in cuts. She was self-harming and had been cutting herself with a razor because she explained, "At least this pain was better than the MRKH". Now Elizabeth thought she had seen it all. Of course, she knew exactly what it felt like to have MRKH and at one time she had also thought of burying herself in the ground or running away, but she had no idea that Melanie would even hurt herself like that. Then again, she felt that Melanie was probably so driven because she was so badly scarred and affected by her experience and having no support, that she suddenly wondered if she would have done the same had she been in Melanie's shoes. The thought of this possibility really frightened her, so she tried her best to advise Melanie to stop harming herself because she was now having the appropriate help. Melanie said, "I am trying and I have stopped cutting myself since I came here, and Anne is helping me with this too". Elizabeth was still shocked but relieved after Melanie told her that she had stopped her self-harm but she still said, "Please promise me you won't start hurting yourself again. I'm here for you now so if you need to talk to someone, you can ring me ok?"

"I will and I will try very hard not to do it again," said Melanie.

Melanie told Elizabeth that she was feeling better since she started attending the Centre and she was also feeling quite positive that her life would now change for the better. She said that she also got herself a job as a salesgirl in a local shop, with not much career prospects, but she was an intelligent girl and she had her plans for the future too, so she said that she used the money she earned from this job to fund her acting career. She always loved drama and her dream was to become a renowned actress. She just did not have much real opportunities although she said that she had plenty of practice. She told Elizabeth that "I must be the best actress there is because my acting was so good that I managed to convince everyone I was living my life normally, so for the last two years, no one suspected or knew that I was suffering or in pain every day. Isn't that amazing?" Elizabeth did not want to feel pity for Melanie because she hated this herself, but there and then she felt that her heart was bleeding for Melanie. It made her more appreciative of her own charmed life and at the same time she could not help feeling ashamed too because she had so much yet Melanie had nothing but pain and misery.

Melanie said that she came from a working class family and money was not always fluid, especially now that her parents were divorced. She lived with her mother and her three siblings in a small modest flat in a council estate in London, which was sometimes quite notorious so they kept to themselves to try to keep out of harm's way. Still, she remained resolute to make something of herself, and she was going to be that actress. She worked in a shop since she left school at sixteen because she was the eldest of her siblings and she did not have much option but to work soon as she was old enough. She was a good girl and she would give her mother half of her salary every month to help pay their bills, and the rest she saved to pay for her tuition fees. When she saved up enough money, she enrolled herself in a school in London to do dramatic arts. It was whilst she was researching for her drama colleges that she found the courage to google her condition one day and she found this Centre in London. She said, "I rang and spoke to Lucy and because she sounded so nice and caring, I agreed to come here. I only started coming to this clinic recently". In fact, the last time Elizabeth saw her in the clinic was her first attendance. Elizabeth thought that it explained why she had waited so long to get referred. "Poor Melanie," Elizabeth thought again even though she did not want to feel sorry for her, but she could not help feeling upset for the girl the more she heard her story. She also kept feeling that Melanie's treatment by her doctors was unforgiveable. They failed Melanie and had she not found this place herself, she would be lost amongst she did not know how many out there, and she vowed that she would never do that to her patients when she became a doctor. She thought that Melanie was so courageous and she was very touched by her story. The two of them chatted for over an hour and it was obvious that they had connected. Neither of them had met nor spoken to anyone with their condition before so they felt a sense of relief and a sense of belonging. It was also comforting and it felt good.

Elizabeth said to Melanie, "I've just completed my treatment". She was very encouraging and told Melanie that she could too and that "I'd like to help you, Melanie. I want to support you through yours or we can just be friends that is, if that's ok with you. I know that Lucy and Anne are also helping you and they're very good so I know they will help you because they have helped me a lot". Elizabeth was also being respectful, especially after Melanie had told her that she had preferred to keep to herself, although Elizabeth considered herself to be different from her past encounters. Of course, Melanie felt that Elizabeth was different from the rest because she was like her. They both have MRKH so she said "I'd like that very much, thank you. You're the first person whom I know that I can trust. Oh and by the way, please call me Mel". They gave each other a hug and they exchanged their mobile numbers and promised to stay in touch. Elizabeth then asked Melanie, "I came up with my best friend Sally and we're probably going for something to eat before we head off home so would you like to join us?"

"I'd really like that, thank you," replied Melanie. From that day onwards, they became the best of friends. Melanie found her new best friend or rather her only friend and Elizabeth gained another best friend. Elizabeth felt so self-gratified that she wished she had done this sooner but in fairness, she was not ready to talk to anyone until now.

When they got out of the Centre, Elizabeth rang her mother to tell her briefly about her appointment and to confirm their arrival time at the station because she and Sally had decided to take the later train home. They had only picked up a sandwich for lunch so they decided to go for a burger and a drink before heading home. Elizabeth introduced Sally to Melanie and then the three of them set off together. Melanie being a Londoner, she knew where to take them for a nice burger since that was what they wanted for their dinner. The three of them got on very well and it was evident that they liked each other and despite their different social backgrounds, they were young and shared common interests in music, films, clothes, shopping but most of all, they had similar values and principles. They were three good decent people. Melanie was such a lovely, easy going person and she was kind and humble so it was not difficult to like her. Of course, the main connection between Elizabeth and Melanie was their MRKH but it did not bother Sally, who was strangely the odd one out amongst them. Sally just liked them for who they were and not what they had so she treated them normally, as friends do. Before they parted company, they arranged to meet up again when Elizabeth had her next appointment, which also coincided with Melanie's appointment with both Lucy and Anne.

Paul and Jan were waiting for them when Elizabeth and Sally walked out from the station. Elizabeth was so pleased with her trip up to London this time round that she voluntarily updated her parents about her appointment and then she told them about Melanie. She was so excited that she did not realise that she had not stopped talking about Melanie all the way home. Sally also added that "Melanie's such a nice girl and I'm really glad that I got to meet her too". Jan and Paul could not be more pleased to see Elizabeth so enthusiastic and they were especially happy to know that she had finally spoken to another person with the same condition because although Sally was a very good friend, they could not help feeling that it was not quite the same as knowing someone else with MRKH. They always sensed that Elizabeth felt very isolated so they hoped that apart from Elizabeth helping Melanie, they also believed that this new contact would help Elizabeth, and she would not feel so alone anymore. No doubt Elizabeth might seem to have got on with her life now but they knew that she still felt that she was the only one. Furthermore, ever since they were informed of other girls with the same condition, Jan and Paul had been hoping that Elizabeth would have the opportunity to meet them. When they reached home, Jan was still thinking about it and she suddenly could not wait to meet Melanie. She also wanted to encourage their friendship so without much hesitation, she suggested, "El, I was just thinking that perhaps you could invite Melanie down for a weekend during your next school break since the both of you seemed to get on so well together". To Jan's surprise, Elizabeth was very quick to reply and said, "Yes I think that's a great idea mummy. I'd like that very much. I'll ring Mel later and ask her and we can arrange it".

When Elizabeth went to her room, she suddenly felt very weary and threw herself on the bed. It had been a long day and a very emotional one too but all in all, it was a good day. She could not forget Melanie though. She found her story so inspiring and moving and for the most part, she found herself identifying with Melanie's story, and wondered if it would be the same for all the girls with MRKH. Nevertheless, she also found Melanie's experience very disturbing and sad, so much so that she could still hear the pain in Melanie's voice. Elizabeth could not help wondering again how many other girls there were out there, who like Melanie, were still struggling to cope on their own. She was glad for Melanie that through her own strength and courage, she managed to find the appropriate help and Elizabeth felt reassured that she would be alright now because this London team would be able to help her. She was rather amazed and had full admiration for Melanie though, because despite her past awful experience, she was not bitter. Then again, Melanie had explained that she had already lost and spent two years of her life in total isolation and despair, so she was not going to waste another minute of her future on being bitter or angry. She told Elizabeth that whilst it still pained her, she refused to dwell on it preferring to move on with her life, as it served no purpose, especially now that she was receiving the appropriate treatment and support. Elizabeth really admired her stance in the matter. It demonstrated her maturity and strength in character and she wished that she was more like her because she doubted that she could disregard something like that this easily herself. Melanie was definitely a survivor and a tough cookie in the nicest possible way of course but for her, Elizabeth understood that it was a case of having to, coming from a humble background, so Melanie knew how to survive. Melanie said that she also surprised herself because she managed to rise above everything she had been through, which was something beyond her own expectation, so she meant to continue and to not look back. Her positive attitude and humility again made Elizabeth feel ashamed of the privileged life she had yet Melanie was not once envious but instead, she told Elizabeth that even though they both had MRKH, she realised that they came from different backgrounds, but she never minded other people's different backgrounds anyway. She said that to her the most important thing was, "No matter what life throws at me, it's what I make of my life in the end that really counts, so I intend to make something of myself and I am going to be that actress".

It was uncanny to hear such profound words from such a pretty little girl but of course, she was eighteen and she was wiser and older than her looks. Elizabeth found herself in awe of her new friend and really admired her and the more she learnt about Melanie, the more she liked and respected her. They agreed to ring each other once a week because Elizabeth really felt that she could support Melanie with her treatments but after talking to her, Elizabeth wondered exactly who would be the one who needed supporting, but, no matter, she decided that they would support one another.

What a day she'd had, Elizabeth thought, because she never expected her day would turn out as it did, but she was glad of it. At last, she got to meet someone else with her same condition. More amazing was that listening to Melanie's story was just so surreal because her own was so similar. She never imagined that it could be like this but of course, Melanie was the first and only person she had met who was the same as her. Still she felt that she could not have met a nicer person. Strangely though, now that she got to meet Melanie, for the first time, Elizabeth was not just thinking about herself anymore. In fact, she almost forgot about herself until she remembered that she had to ring Tom, so she picked up her mobile and called him. They chatted for a while and ended up arranging to see each other again before she went back to school and before he started university. Afterwards, she had a shower and then she went to bed and fell asleep straight away because she felt completely drained. She was both exhausted from her own personal experience and her emotional engagement with Melanie.

Elizabeth arranged to see Tom the following week. Her mother was going to give her a lift into town but Emma was not feeling well that day and Jan had to stay home to look after her, so Elizabeth rang Tom. "Hi Tom. My sister's sick and my mum needs to stay with her so can you come and pick me up please?" Tom who was desperate to see her said, "Of course. I'll leave now so I'll see you in a few minutes," and he left straight away. They went to their usual haunt and ordered their usual pizzas and drinks. They stayed there for a while, just chatting and catching up. Of course, Elizabeth told him about Melanie, but not excessively because she was conscious that this was their time. They had not seen each other since Barcelona although they rang each other every day. They missed one another terribly and they knew it would be worse when he was to start university because they would not see each other at all until the Christmas holidays, whereas in school they could at least meet at different school functions from time to time and their group would also meet up some weekends when they had their free passes. Tom held Elizabeth's hands across the table. He thought she looked so beautiful and he could not resist holding her in his arms again so he asked her, "El, would you like to come back with me to my place now?" My dad's working and my mum is playing golf at her local golf club and she won't be back till later this evening so the house will be empty". Elizabeth nodded and said, "Ok, why not," so he very quickly asked for the bill and paid it. Then he said excitedly, "Ok, shall we?" as he pulled her chair out for her and automatically put his arm around hers, as they walked to the car park.

Elizabeth had never been to Tom's house before but she knew it was not too far from hers. It was a big five-bed-roomed detached house with a beautifully styled wide frontage and a separate garage on one side of the house that could house four big cars. The rear garden was tastefully landscaped and maintained too, and set in a few acres of land. Elizabeth especially liked the summer house, which sat at the back of the right side of the garden, because she thought it was so lovely with its cosy garden chairs, loungers and a heater but most of all, she felt that it was somewhere private that one could escape to for some peace and serenity, as it was almost hidden, surrounded and camouflaged by sweet scented flowery bushes and fruit trees. It also over-looked a beautifully created waterfall pond, which gave a real good karma feel and she found it very soothing and relaxing, as she briefly laid down on one of the loungers. She would have quite happily stayed out there had Tom not suggested that they went back into the house.

The interior of Tom's house was just as elegantly decorated too. The kitchen and dining lounge was open-plan so it was spacious and felt very comfortable. There was also a separate dining room for formal parties, as Mr. and Mrs. McGuire entertained a lot. Their living room was bright and stylish and led to two other rooms, Mr. McGuire's study and their family entertainment room. The latter was Tom's second favourite room after his own. Elizabeth could see why too, because the room was exquisitely designed and looked inviting and warm. It had a full leather furniture suite, with a few scatter cushions on its three- and two-piece settee, which made it look homely, and the wall cabinets and cupboards also complimented and completed this end of the room. It was perfect for watching films and movies on their own television and home cinema system and listening to their wireless music, because the room had fantastic acoustics too. At the other end of the room, there was a billiard table in the middle and on the side of it, a drinks cabinet and a small bar with a couple of bar stools. Elizabeth also liked this room and thought it was completed to perfection because despite all its mod-cons, it had a warm lived in feel about it. In fact, she loved his house because it was beautifully and elegantly designed without being ostentatious.

Tom went to the kitchen to get a couple of Cokes for himself and Elizabeth and then he showed her upstairs to his room. Tom's room was nothing like Elizabeth had expected, although she would not know anyway because she had never been to any of the boys' rooms. She was just surprised that it was so neat and organised, which was quite striking because she somehow thought that it would at least be a little untidy being a boy's room, not that she would have minded anyhow, as it was not her room. She just never knew that Tom was so tidy and to be honest, she was impressed, especially since she was a neat little buff herself. She thought that it must be his training all those years at boarding school and also being the head boy and all. Nevertheless, it was a boy's room and there were some telltale signs with the blue duvet cover and a large mural of a formula one driver in his race car on the wall just above his double bed, and a variety of cricket trophies and cups on two shelves that were mounted on the wall. Tom played cricket at school and his bag of cricket bats and gloves was also evident, sitting neatly in the corner next to his reclining sofa, but this still did not seem out of place. He had a big room but it did not feel uncomfortable because of his personal effects. He also had an *en suite* bathroom which was not too dissimilar to hers, except that he had a proper shower enclosure instead of a bath and obviously he had his male toiletries in the shower and bathroom. In the bedroom itself, he had a long floor to ceiling built-in wardrobe with white finished drawers and doors and in the middle, was a soothing blue-coloured custom-made recessed box, housing his built-in television and his CD player and Playstation which were also placed there under the television.

Then, continuing on the other side of this recess, was also a full length white-coloured built-in bookcase filled with his books, CDs and model F1 racing cars completing that side of the wall. Adjacent to it were two large double-glazed windows that allowed natural light to come through so the room was bright enough, but it was also effectively darkened when the matching blue-linen roller blinds were pulled down. Under the windows, there was his built-in desk and two small cupboards with a set of drawers on both sides. There was also a chair neatly tucked in the middle recess of this and a small paper bin sitting just next to his desk. He had his laptop and printer scanner on the desk and also a couple of packets of printing paper, a desk tidy with odd pens and pencils and on the right hand side of the desk, he had a desk lamp. His room was well organised but not clinical. Elizabeth liked his room a lot, she thought it was very chic and warm and she immediately felt welcomed. She could easily picture Tom and his friends playing games on his Playstation and having fun in his room.

Elizabeth was admiring Tom's model cars because she did not know that he was such a Formula1 fan. She knew that he played cricket because when they were out with the group, the boys would sometimes talk about their own games and obviously the professional cricket matches, but she could not recall them talking about Formula1 races. She realised that she did not know very much about him but then again, it was only fairly recent that she and Tom became an item and even so, she was too engrossed with her own problem that when they were alone together, they never talked about anything else except her problem. Tom was so involved that he gave all his time into helping and supporting her so she just took it and never gave it a second thought. Now, she realised how generous he was and it made her feel ashamed at how selfish she had been because she never really considered him or tried to find out more about him or his interests apart from his involvement with her condition. That was all she had cared about. She did not like herself much then. It made her think about her parents and Emma too, then Sally and Tom again, how patient everyone had been with her and she thought that she must have been hell to be with but she was better now so she would make it up to them.

Her mind then flashed back to Melanie and she thought how lonely she must have been, and she could not help feeling sorry that she did not have any friends to support her, so she was especially keen to help her new friend. She realised how much Sally and Tom had done for her so she knew how much it meant to have good friends especially when MRKH is such an isolating condition.

Tom came from behind Elizabeth and he put his arms around her so she turned to him and kissed him and said, "Thank you Tom for everything". Tom kissed her back whispering, "Nothing to thank me for. I'm just happy that you are happy. I love you so much" so Elizabeth told him "I love you back too". They started taking each other's clothes off and then he carried her to his bed and they made passionate love. They were just a normal couple and so much in love. It was all so very normal and Elizabeth actually forgot that she even had a problem in the first place as did Tom because he managed full penetration without any difficulty. Furthermore, they both enjoyed it and their sex seemed to be getting better each time. They stayed in each other's arms without saying a word for a long time as if neither wanted to break that magical moment and they wished that the moment would last until they would be together again.

Elizabeth was so comfortable that she could have easily drifted off to sleep but instead her mind drifted off to somewhere else again. This time though, she thought that her MRKH had a positive side after all. It was so ironic, but for the first time she was actually grateful for it, because she found she did not have to concern herself about contraception. She always had a strong view on teenage pregnancies, much as she loved children, so she was determined not to be one of those teenage girls who accidentally fell pregnant when they were not ready to be mothers. To Elizabeth, she felt that they would not be able to achieve their potential and it would also not be fair to their children. She thought about the young girls who could not cope and had to give their children up for adoption. She felt that they were very brave because it must have been very hard for them to have to give their children away and she felt very sad for them. She could never do that herself but then she rationalised that it was probably the best for the children's sake, at least they will go to a home where they will be loved and well taken care of. Then she thought selfishly, "How else would someone like me be able to adopt if these women did not give their children away". She suddenly felt an immense sense of gratitude towards them. She looked up at Tom and convinced herself that she and he would make good parents one day, just like his and her parents. Then it hit her. She had been so preoccupied with her initial problem that she did not have time to really consider what it would be like to adopt. She knew that she could love and bring up any child as her own but she was not sure if she would treat the child as if it was her own or as an adopted child. Furthermore, she also did not know how Tom really felt about this either, even though he seemed very agreeable with the idea of adoption in the past. She had to know, she had to be sure but before she could open her mouth, Tom asked her, "Why are you looking at me like that?" so Elizabeth said, "I was just thinking that you'd make a great dad," to which Tom added, "And you'd be a fantastic mum too. Why would you even think otherwise? El, what's really going on in that pretty head of yours?"

"I was just thinking of adoption. I mean do we tell the child that she or he was adopted and would we then treat the child any differently from our own. We love children and I'm not saying that we would mistreat any child or anything but if we cannot treat her or him as our own flesh and blood, wouldn't it be unfair to the child?"

"Not really. Doesn't mean that we would love it less if he or she was adopted and of course, we have to bring the baby up as our own. I think I understand what you mean though but don't you see El, we would be giving this baby a chance in life otherwise it has none, that's why it was up for adoption," Tom clarified, so she said, "I know. You're right. I don't know what I was thinking. I got a bit unstuck and I needed to know how you really felt about it. I just want us to do the right thing. Do you think your parents would…"

"It has nothing to do with them but yes, they would be alright too. All grandparents love their grandchildren," he interrupted. Elizabeth contemplated briefly, so Tom asked her "what's brought all this on?" and she answered, "I don't know, I wasn't really thinking about it. It just popped into my head just now, maybe I'm better now and I can think ahead, I don't know". Tom could not agree more, he noticed the change in her too. She was definitely better and more relaxed with herself so he said, "That's ok, that's really good. I'm so pleased you're ok now too".

They lay quietly for a while, both deep in their own thoughts. Then Tom remembered Lucy mentioning something about IVF surrogacy and he thought this would be a good time to bring it up whilst they are on the subject of children. He also rather liked the idea of having their own baby and naturally preferred this if there was a possibility, because she would be beautiful like her mother. He expected Elizabeth to be more enthusiastic so he was quite surprised with her dismissive response, but she later explained that as much as she would love to have her own baby, "I don't want to pass my genes to my baby. I don't want our baby to have my MRKH. I won't let her go through what I did".

"We don't know that for a fact," said Tom but Elizabeth was emphatic, "I don't care, I won't take that risk, I can't. I'd rather not have a baby than to give our baby my MRKH". Tom realised how upset she had become so he told her, very calmly and sensibly, "Ok, it's cool. We don't have to decide now but it's another option to consider and maybe you should ask Lucy about it when you next see her. I mean, to be sure". Elizabeth knew that Tom was right of course so she nodded as she tried to contain her emotions. She thought afterwards that perhaps she should not have assumed the worst but in a strange way, she was glad she did. At least she managed to voice her trepidation and her innermost concern aloud instead of keeping it in until she reached boiling point, like she did before with her MRKH. It was also a bonus having Tom with her this time. He was what she needed because he was so understanding and objective and it helped her to maintain her rationality and mental equilibrium. Elizabeth really appreciated him and it made her love him even more so she snuggled up closer to him and kissed him. Then she told him, "Thanks Tom, I'm so glad you're in my life. I love you so much". Tom, who could not be happier to be in her life, responded naturally, "I love you more and I will love you forever".

"I'm going to miss you so much when you go to university. I wish we can just stay here like this forever and I don't want today to end because I don't know when we can be together like this again" Elizabeth said as if she was already missing him. "I know, I feel the same way but I was thinking that maybe when you come up to London for your appointments, you can stay the night with me" Tom suggested. Elizabeth got very excited and said, "That's a brilliant idea, Tom" then she thought again "but I would probably come up with either my mum or Sally, so that might be a problem". Then Tom had another suggestion and said, "Or you could always just come up for the weekend to visit me. I'm sure your parents won't mind because they seem like quite modern and open-minded parents and besides, I think your mum approves of me, ha ha". Elizabeth still looked unconvinced so he then reassured her saying "we'll work something out when the time comes. Don't worry I'll think of something".

As Time Went By…

It was nearly a year now since Elizabeth found out about her condition and it had been a very traumatic year for her and for everyone at home and for her friends. So much had happened since, but as time went by their crises also subsided and the Appleton household was back to normal. There was no more angst or tension and everyone was just getting on with their lives as usual. Elizabeth seemed to be doing well in school, at home and with her friends and as time passed she found it easier to cope with everything in her life. She no longer harped on about her condition but every now and again, she would think about IVF surrogacy, and her conversation with Tom. She really liked the idea too but was terrified of passing her defective gene onto her baby. She had also spoken with Sally about this, and together they googled but there was not much they could find on the internet. She wanted the experts to confirm this with absolute certainty to allay her concerns but when she rang to make an appointment with Lucy for the same day she had the appointment with Anne, Lucy was fully booked. Still, Lucy managed to reassure her that there was no evidence so far to suggest that her baby, if female, would inherit her condition. It was comforting to hear and it gave Elizabeth the confidence to consider this option further, but she knew that she would be more convinced if she could just meet with the women who had normal baby girls through this method. Lucy gave her the contact details of a couple of these women and she also told her that she would try to see her on the day but if not, that she would pass her some more information and the organisations offering the service. Elizabeth did not feel comfortable contacting anyone herself as yet, much as she wanted to know so she decided to wait till she had more information from Lucy.

One evening, whilst she was helping her mother prepare their dinner in the kitchen Elizabeth reminded her mother, "Mum, I have another appointment with Anne a week Tuesday but if you're busy I can go up to London by myself because I know the route so well now," because she also thought that she should perhaps try going by herself, so that when the time came for her to meet up with Tom, her mother would not think it as being unusual but, of course, Jan did not forget that she had already decided to accompany Elizabeth this time, so she told her daughter, "I know and I've already booked our train tickets darling. I want to go with you this time and we can go shopping afterwards".

"Oh ok, that'll be nice" Elizabeth told her mother, because although she thought that she would go on her own, she was not too bothered that her mother decided to go with her. Jan wanted to take Elizabeth shopping because she wanted to buy her, her birthday present for her seventeenth, which was only a few weeks away. She was going to have a small party for her at home too, before she went back to boarding school, but Elizabeth knew how busy her mother was at this time of the year with her work and with Christmas drawing near again, so she told her that she would just go out and celebrate her birthday with her friends. Jan noticed how mature and independent Elizabeth had become and she had also learnt to let go a little, but at the same time, being a mother, her motherly instinct was to protect her because no matter what, Elizabeth was still her baby.

Elizabeth was also aware that she had been spending a lot of time away with her friends recently so she was glad to be going with her mother and to have her company for a change. She appreciated her parents staying in the background to let her grow up but she was always aware of their support, because without it, she knew she could not have done what she did and got this far, and she loved them for it. She just forgot to tell them of late again so now that she remembered, she hugged her mother and told her, "I love you mum and I really appreciate what you and dad have done and given me" and her mother told her, "And we love you too, darling". Elizabeth also missed talking to her mother so she decided to ask her, "Mum, how do you feel about IVF surrogacy? I know that it would be sometime yet in the future before Tom and I would be ready to embark on something like this but I like to know what you think". Jan remained supportive and encouraging and said, "I think it's a wonderful chance for any woman who can't carry her own baby, and if you and Tom should decide that you want to go for this then I think it would be lovely, because at least this way you'll know that the baby is yours and Tom's". Then Elizabeth told her mother "I think it'll be nice too and I think that Tom quite likes the idea but I'm frightened that I'll pass my MRKH gene to my baby if it is a female baby". Her mother said something similar to Tom, "You don't know that for sure, so you should ask them at the Centre. We can ask them when we go up this time".

Elizabeth then told her mother that she had already asked Lucy and that Lucy told her there was no evidence to suggest this possibility as yet, but she said that she was still not completely convinced because it was not full proof. Jan said, "Then maybe you should also be more open to new developments. You're both young and who knows by then you might be able to consider the possibility of having a uterine transplant" and Elizabeth, who was very mature about it, said, 'I guess, we'll have to wait and see". It felt good to talk to her mother and to learn her opinion and it reminded her how clever her mother was. Jan also missed her daughter and was gratified that Elizabeth had decided to confide in her again. She had hoped that it would be like how she used to in the past, but she accepted that because Elizabeth had grown up so much and they had also both been through a lot, that even if they could not get back what was already lost, she was happy that at least this was a start. Somehow she felt that finally, she had got her daughter back and she was also grateful that she and her family had survived their past experience. Jan had learnt a lot the past year and nowadays she felt happier and was more reconciled with herself too. She thought that her husband was so right because he did say that they would get through this together as a family and they did.

It was during the final week of her summer holidays that Elizabeth and Jan made the trip up to London. This was also going to be her final appointment with Anne. They went straight to the Centre as she had a mid-morning appointment, and when she finished, she saw Lucy very briefly to collect the information as arranged. Lucy also took the opportunity to thank Elizabeth for supporting Melanie, as Melanie had sung her praises for her support and friendship. Afterwards, Elizabeth met up with Melanie. Jan had been looking forward to meeting her ever since Elizabeth mentioned their acquaintance, but probably more because it meant that her daughter would no longer be alone. When Jan first met Melanie, she thought that Melanie appeared as normal as her Elizabeth and although she was not expecting anything to be different, she almost said out aloud, "But you look so normal and so pretty". It was bizarre and she could not explain why she would even conceive of such the ridiculous notion that Melanie would look otherwise, especially when she knew full well that their condition would not be physically evident to the naked eye. No one would ever know that both Melanie and her daughter had MRKH, just to look at them. Jan knew this yet she could not stop her initial reaction or thought, perhaps it was a sheer relief to finally meet someone else with the same condition as her Elizabeth's. It was most absurd and she could not explain it but all the same, she hoped that this might have also occurred to the both of them and that maybe it would help them to reinforce their sense of normality.

Melanie came across as a delightful, humble and sincere person, and Jan liked her straight off. She was particularly pleased to see how well the two girls got on too. Jan watched them and she could not quite believe what she was witnessing because it was as if the two girls had known each other for a long time, yet they had only become friends recently. Still, Jan could see that this new relationship between them was strong because they had something in common, something that was only common to them and no one else they knew. This was their bond and only they would know in entirety, how and what it was like to have MRKH, so they understood each other fully without having to explain themselves to each other. It was a powerful connection and it was also another important aspect of their treatment, which the experts knew all too well. In fact, their condition was so complex that they acknowledged that not one single treatment could work on its own and only a holistic approach to their care and management would suffice, which was why their treatment usually needs to encompass an overall picture of all the needs of the women, in order for them to get better and to enable them to lead normal lives, Jan distinctly remembered reading this on one of the websites she found. She thought that right now Elizabeth was in a good place. Elizabeth also felt that she was very fortunate to have the appropriate help and the loving support of her family and friends so now she felt that she was ready and was in a good position to help Melanie and she was determined to do the best she could for her friend.

Melanie, unfortunately, was not doing too well with her treatment. She was having difficulty doing them due to her college and work commitments. She was also sharing her room with one of her siblings so it was not always easy to have privacy. She admitted that she was struggling to focus sometimes, especially when she was tired and when she felt that she was not making any progress, so she appreciated Elizabeth's phone calls and support immensely because they at least spurred her on to continue. Besides, she told Elizabeth that "I'm terrified because Lucy suggested that I could postpone my treatment until such time that it would be more convenient but for me it's now or never, because my situation is not going to change for some time so there is not going to be another more convenient time". Melanie felt rather sad as she thought of her own circumstances then and she added, "I know I haven't made any progress and it's my fault for not doing my treatment properly but I've only just got here so I know that if I were to give up now, I won't come back for some time yet. I know this and I know myself, because this was what I did the last couple of years, so I don't want to stop my treatment". Elizabeth could not believe that Melanie was exactly like her. She behaved and thought exactly like her, because at the time she had also told Lucy that she did not want to have to stop her treatment as she knew that if she did that, she too would not return. She was again reminded of how alike she and Melanie were and the more Melanie told her story, the more Elizabeth felt like she was seeing herself through Melanie again. She could not believe how easily she identified with Melanie in so many ways because of their MRKH irrespective of their very different backgrounds. She was becoming increasingly convinced that perhaps all the women with their condition must share their similar stories and experiences and she was learning more about her condition too.

Elizabeth could never understand before how any of the women would want to stop or give up their treatment, as she herself was always adamant that she was not going to be one of them, but now she could appreciate how this could happen, especially if they were in similar circumstances to Melanie's or if they simply did not have the right help and support, because she knew only too well how difficult it must be to do this on one's own. Yet, Melanie was like her and she was also adamant that she was not going to give up that easily, although Elizabeth would have understood if she did.

She also remembered Lucy telling her that the treatment would only work if the woman was ready and wanted to do it properly, so she could see Lucy's point in suggesting that Melanie might want to postpone her treatment since, according to her, Elizabeth knew that she was not doing it properly, if at all. It was not entirely Melanie's fault of course since her circumstances were not conducive for her doing so. She again admired her friend's strength and resolve and she could also understand her rationale because, in actual fact, Elizabeth too believed that Melanie would not return if she was to stop and defer her treatment now, as she had proven in the past, which was why it took her two years to find the courage to do something about her condition.

However, Elizabeth was slightly confused, because she thought that if Melanie said that she was desperate to do her treatment and was adamant that she did not want to stop, then she asked, "why isn't she trying harder?" The more she thought about it, the more she felt that Melanie was starting to drift again and despite her obvious difficulties, Elizabeth was not completely convinced that these were her only reasons for not doing her treatments so she decided to ask her friend. Melanie was very frank and told her, "I do want to do the treatment, honest I do, because I want to feel normal, but I really hate the dilators. I don't like sticking them inside me and I don't like the pain because it just reminds me of the time when those doctors stuck their fingers inside me and I hate it, so you see, I find it very hard to motivate myself". Elizabeth felt that this was more like it, because she suspected that her friend must have had a better reason, especially when she told her that she wanted to change her life. She really empathised with Melanie, so she asked her, "Have you spoken to Anne or Lucy about this?" and Melanie replied, "Yes I have. Anne is helping me to overcome this, although she also thinks that I should postpone my treatment and to try to work out my issues first. You see El, I told you I'm messed up so maybe they're right. Maybe, I shouldn't be doing the dilators if I feel this way but then if I don't do the treatment now, I know that I never will. I just know that I have to continue because I want to feel normal otherwise I'm just a freak just like those doctors said". Elizabeth asked her, "But how are you going to manage if you feel this way?" Melanie said "I don't know but I just know that I can't stop the treatment. I guess I'll have to try harder and blank this out from my mind and just get on with them. After all, I'm very good at pretending that things are not real so I will have to think of something else or like Lucy advised, just think of the end result if I want to continue. The funny thing is when I do the treatment with Lucy, I'm ok because she talks to me all the time but when I have to do it on my own, it's not the same because I can't help thinking too much. Maybe the next time I do my treatments, I'll have to pretend that she's with me or maybe I'll record her voice like she's talking to me".

Then Elizabeth said, "I know what you're saying Mel because I also found it easier when I did my treatment with her. She really talks to you so you don't think of anything else, and the treatment goes quickly but it's definitely harder doing it on your own. I found that I had to egg myself on to do them but after a while though, it does get easier". Then she suggested, "Mel, maybe I can ring and talk to you when you are doing your treatment, will that help?" so she said, "Yes, maybe. We can give that a try but no, you can't ring me every day because I know you're busy yourself so it's not fair on you and I also work shifts so it'll be difficult to know when I can do the treatments. No, I'll just have to do this myself. I'll just have to try harder because to be honest, I know that I haven't tried hard enough. I think I can do it if I really tried. Thanks El, you've made me want to try harder now. I'll let you know how I get on," and Elizabeth said, "Ok but I will if it'll help you. I really don't mind".

Afterwards, Elizabeth thought about what the doctors did

to Melanie and she felt very angry for her again. She blamed her first consultant and his doctors because she really felt they had traumatised and damaged an innocent young sixteen-year-old girl so badly that she was still suffering from that horrific experience. She felt that what they did to her friend was wicked and it just showed their ignorance. It also strengthened her belief that there is definitely an important place for centers for rare and unusual illnesses and conditions and hoped that these would continue to prevail so that the minority group of patients would not be left out or be forgotten or be so horrifically treated but instead that they would get the appropriate and specialist treatment that they need.

Elizabeth kept wishing that she could do more to help her friend because she really felt that life had not been kind or fair to her. It made her appreciate her own privileged life even more and she wanted to give something back. She needed to help Melanie achieve her goals, but right now all she could do was to encourage and to give her friend moral support with her treatment, although for Melanie, this was actually what she needed and more than what anyone had done for her, so she was just appreciative that Elizabeth was there for her. When Elizabeth spoke with her again, Melanie told her "I'm determined to hang on but I'm so frightened that they will force me to postpone my treatment again because I'm still not doing it properly. The trouble is then I'll be back to where I was again and I cannot bear to repeat the last two years". Elizabeth tried to reassure her that, "I'm sure they won't do that. Lucy won't do that to you. She might have suggested it but if you don't want to stop, she won't force you. I know them very well and they're not like that at the Centre but maybe you should try to do your treatments more regularly. I know it's difficult for you with your circumstances at home and with you working and going to college and I know you have your issues, but even if you can manage to do them twice a day, it will still work.

I know this because Lucy told me, it'll just take longer that's all. I know it's hard at first but once you have a routine going it usually works better. That's how I did mine".

"I know but I'm not using excuses this time," said Melanie. "It was really because I didn't have time as I had to do my assignment for college so I had to go to the library and I would get home late and then I was so tired after that. I am improving though, because I did it every morning, but I know I have to do at least two treatments. It's the one in the evening that's a problem because I find it hard to make myself do the treatment after I come home from college or work. Sometimes I feel like I want to give up because I don't seem to make any progress and it's still so painful". Elizabeth sensed that Melanie was feeling rather down and she thought that perhaps she must just be tired too, so she asked her, "Do you really want to give up, Mel?" Melanie said, "I don't know what I want anymore. I guess I'm tired and I'm fed up so although I really want to finish the treatment, a part of me is saying, just forget it and just get on with your life because you don't need it, but then I know that I can't get on with my life. That's the problem. I just wish that I didn't have this horrible condition then I won't have to do this, I won't have to do anything. It's like I'm always struggling but I don't seem to get there, and it's really getting me down to tell you the truth". Elizabeth really felt for her then because she thought that she herself might not have coped too if she had Melanie's problems so she could not fault her at all.

In fact, like Melanie, she too hated her condition and kept wishing that she did not have it and it was only recently that she started to feel better about herself. She knew that it was a process they had to go through before they would get better and feel better so she reckoned that Melanie was only at the beginning of her journey, and now, having gone through a similar journey herself, she felt sure that her friend would also get there in the end, despite having a tougher ride.

Nevertheless, she had only known Melanie to be a fighter and a survivor and she was not usually a negative person, even when she could well have been, given what she had been through so she tried to encourage her. "Mel, this is not like you. I think you're just very tired and you're having one of your bad days. I was like that too. In fact, I had a lot of bad days but I still managed to get through it and now I am in a happier place and you will be too".

"I really hope so El, that's why I tell myself every day to be positive because I believe that things will improve for me soon. I'm sorry to be such a whiny baby today, especially when you're so good to me. I must be more tired than I know. I will try to do better, I promise, because I really want to succeed. Thanks for ringing me to give me your support El, I really appreciate it and I feel slightly better already," Melanie said thankfully so Elizabeth told her, "You're very welcome Mel but there's nothing to thank me for. I told you that I'm here for you and besides, it sounded like you needed to get stuff off your chest. I get it. Anyway, I'm pleased that you feel better for it. I'll speak to you again on Friday yeah?"

"Sure thanks, speak to you then" Melanie answered.

Elizabeth could not help thinking of Melanie's situation, so she decided to ring Lucy to update her on her friend. She thought that she would need to leave a message but was surprised to catch her in the office. She highlighted Melanie's problems and fear and said that she would continue to support her friend, but was not sure how else she could otherwise help her, so Lucy told her, "Thanks for letting me know, El. You're a good friend but that's all you can do and all that we'd expect of you so don't worry too much. Anne and I will help her from our end. Anyway, how are you getting on yourself?"

"I'm fine and doing ok. Busy with my studies and school as usual but otherwise no problems. I've finished my therapy with Anne now. Thank you, guys for helping me again. Now I am just getting on with my life," Elizabeth replied, so Lucy said, "It's a pleasure. I'm so pleased that you are doing well now and thank you again for supporting Melanie but if it becomes too much, please let me know".

"No Mel's my friend now and I want to help her as much as I can".

A Mother's Love

Elizabeth invited Melanie down to her place for the weekend. She had got on so well with Melanie that she was sure that her other friends would also like her. It was her birthday soon too, although she did not tell Melanie because she did not want her to feel she had to buy her a present. Elizabeth so enjoyed her company and also thought that it would be a nice and deserved break for her. Initially, Melanie was not going to go because she could not afford it. Elizabeth really wanted her to be there and even offered to pay for her train fare but Melanie would not accept it, although she appreciated the gesture. She might not be rich but she still had her pride and she was not going to be a charity case nor take advantage of Elizabeth's generosity either. Melanie had mentioned Elizabeth and her invitation to her mother in passing but told her that she was not going. Since meeting Elizabeth, she felt less isolated and alone. She also started to talk to her mother without both of them getting too upset because her self-confidence had grown and she must have then projected some of this confidence onto her mother too. Mrs. Smith could see the positive influence Elizabeth had on her daughter so she knew how important their friendship was and it meant that Melanie was supported and was not struggling on her own. She herself was unable to help Melanie, so she was grateful to Elizabeth for helping her daughter where she had failed, something she was not proud of as a mother. She also felt guilty every single day for not supporting Melanie with her problem because she did not know how to and was struggling with it herself, and she still had to keep her household together with three other younger children to consider and take care of. It was tough on her ever since her husband left her for a younger woman. He never contributed a penny to his children's maintenance either, because he was made redundant, and Mrs. Smith also did not want to have anything to do with him after the divorce. It was a real struggle for her initially because she could not get a job and leave her young children at home, so she had no choice but to go on benefit, something she was not particularly proud of.

It was not ideal but two years later when all her children were old enough to attend school, she managed to get a part-time job at their local supermarket. She was a good mother and she lived for her children. She loved them, they were all she had, and, under the circumstances, she could only do her best. Sometimes, it was difficult to balance her books but she always made sure that her children were fed and clothed and she kept them safe as best as she could. Melanie knew how hard her mother worked so she always planned to help her when she started working. She loved her mother and felt ashamed that she had disappointed her because of her abnormal condition. She also felt bad that because of her abnormality, she was adding to her mother's problems and she could not bear to upset her mother further. She saw how affected her mother was when the doctor told them the diagnosis, so much so that she chose to keep her MRKH to herself, and they had never spoken of it again since. It was only recently that Melanie began to speak to her mother about it, although she was mindful to keep it to a minimum. She told her mother that she found a specialist Centre that was helping her with her problem and that it was also where she met Elizabeth. Her mother could not be more pleased that Melanie was getting help and that she also found a friend too. She also suspected that Melanie did not have any friends because she was frightened of anyone finding out about her abnormality and always felt bad for her. She had been praying for something good to happen for Melanie and thought that maybe now, Melanie might have a chance to change her life around.

Elizabeth planned to celebrate her birthday a week before her actual day to ensure that her friends could attend. She had already organised a party table for them at one of the Italian restaurants in the city centre, and afterwards they would proceed to the local discotheque there. That night, she rang Melanie as she usually did every week. She asked Melanie again if she would come down to spend the weekend and was very pleased that Melanie had changed her mind and agreed to come and stay. It was Mrs. Smith who encouraged her daughter to go to Elizabeth's, as she could tell that Melanie really wanted to, and she also suspected that Melanie only said she was not going because she could not afford it. She felt that her daughter was such a good girl and deserved to have some fun for herself. Unbeknown to Melanie, her mother had pawned her gold wedding ring and saved up the money for a rainy day. This was such a day and it could not have given her more pleasure than to treat her wonderful daughter for a change. She was also desperately trying to make it up to her so knowing how important her friendship and weekend with Elizabeth was to Melanie, it was worth everything she could afford, just to be able to make her daughter happy. She gave Melanie the cash for her train ticket and some spending money for her weekend away. Of course, Melanie was curious as to where her mother had got the money so her mother said it was some money she had been saving for such an occasion, and that she was not to worry about it and told her to go and enjoy herself instead. Melanie did not argue because she was so excited to be able to go. She thanked her mother and then she quickly went on her laptop to check the train times and fares.

As it so happened, she managed to get a cheaper return ticket so she went ahead and booked it there and then. She was suddenly excited not just to be going, but it also dawned on her that it would be the first time that she would be going anywhere outside of London, so it felt like she was going on a holiday. Yes, she was excited alright and so looking forward to it that she went straight to her room to start packing. She packed her clothes into her knapsack but it was too small to hold anything else other than a couple of jumpers and a pair of jeans. She still had to bring her cotton tops, t-shirts and a few bits and pieces and did not want to have to squash everything in it, so she borrowed a small hold-all bag from her mother. She made a note on a post tip to pack her dilators in last because she still had to use them for her treatments. Then she thought that she should ask Elizabeth first, because she was not sure of the sleeping arrangements and wondered if she would get the opportunity to use them whilst she was there. She rang Elizabeth to ask, "El, should I bring my dilators with me because I'm not sure if I'd be able to do them at your place?" Elizabeth of course, encouraged her and said, "Yes of course you have to bring your dilators. You'll have your own room, our guest room so you'll have your privacy to do the treatments," because she knew only too well how important it was for Melanie to continue with her treatments especially at this early stage. In a strange way too, Elizabeth was really looking forward to Melanie staying at her place because she felt that she could support and supervise her treatment better. She was taking her supporting role very seriously and felt that she could really help Melanie because she had first-hand knowledge and experience, having gone through the same process herself not so long ago. It also made her feel good to be doing something like this for someone else especially when that someone was such a nice person like Melanie. Furthermore, now that she felt normal again, she also wanted Melanie to make it and to be able to feel as good as she was feeling now.

Weekend At The Appleton's

Elizabeth was really looking forward to seeing Melanie again, and she also wanted her friend to enjoy her weekend stay with her. She could not explain how she was feeling but it was a mixture of excitement and anxiousness. It was different when she had Sally to stay but then Sally was her best friend and they had known each other for a long time. She thought that perhaps she did not really know Melanie that well but she still wanted her to have a good time with her family and for her friends to like her. Then all of a sudden, she had a worrying realisation. She realised that her friends, apart from Sally and Tom, did not know about Melanie. She was sure that they would want to know how she knew Melanie and why they had never met her before and then, "Oh no, they'd find out about my MRKH". She had tried so hard to keep it a secret but now she felt that everyone would surely find out and she did not know how to prevent it. She felt a slight panic come over her and she also felt terrible because now it would not just affect her but Melanie too. She wished that she had anticipated this sooner because she would not have invited Melanie. It was not such a good idea after all. She even thought of cancelling but then she could not disappoint Melanie and it would not be fair to her especially when she had already bought her train ticket and was looking forward to coming. She was in a quandary as to what she should do best.

In the end, she felt it was best to discuss it with Melanie first. Elizabeth thought afterwards that if it was just herself, she actually did not mind her closest group of friends knowing that she had MRKH now. She was at a comfortable stage where it did not bother her much anymore these days but she had to consider Melanie's feelings. She was certain that Melanie would mind because not so long ago, she herself was at this early stage of treatment and she was paranoid about anyone finding out. It was the strangest thing but suddenly she had assumed the role of Melanie's protector and she was trying to guard their secret but more for Melanie's sake. Besides, these were her friends but they were total strangers to Melanie so she was keen to avoid a situation where Melanie would be forced to reveal her condition to them, especially when it was something so abnormal like theirs. Elizabeth was also concerned about her friends' reactions and the effect they might have on Melanie because she could still remember what it was like when she first told Sally and Tom. Then she thought that maybe she was overthinking the whole situation. After all, Melanie had not obviously thought of this, otherwise she would have mentioned it. She also felt that Melanie was quite resilient and certainly more so than her, so she might not mind too much but then she thought again, if that was the case, why had Melanie not ever spoken or told anyone about her condition? Of course, she also remembered Melanie telling her that she had not told anyone because she had no one whom she felt comfortable confiding in but she was so afraid of any of her school friends finding out so for the most part, she had deliberately kept her private life to herself. This was too poignant to ignore. Elizabeth really felt wretched now because deep down, she knew that Melanie was exactly like her... terrified of anyone finding out. She could feel Melanie's sadness and isolation and it reminded her of her previous self. Now, even though she had moved on to a better place in her life, she still wished that she and Melanie were not so different from everyone else, so abnormal. She could not believe that her MRKH would come back to haunt her again when all she wanted was to have a normal enjoyable weekend with Melanie and her friends. Now, she was convinced that it would end up disastrously unless she did something except she did not know what that something was. She had to speak to Melanie, maybe come up with a plan but whatever, they must be prepared.

Elizabeth left a text message for Melanie to say that she would call her later for a chat. She deliberately did not mention the reason for her call because she did not want Melanie to be worrying the whole day. She knew that Melanie was doing extra hours at work during her summer holidays because it was their busy time with sales and promotions going on in the shop so her employers had asked her to work some overtime for them. It also suited her because she needed the extra cash to pay her tuition fees when college reopened and as it was coming up to that time of the year, she knew she needed money to buy her family their Christmas presents and to go out with her work colleagues for their Christmas night out. Melanie was organised with her finances in this way, but then it was a case of having to be and she was used to it. She was always thrifty but not mean or stingy and she was not a freeloader either. She always paid her own way and she would rather do without something if she could not afford it than to be indebted or to take advantage of anyone. She was brought up well because she and her family were decent honest people too and they always maintained their dignity. She also liked Elizabeth for this reason because this was also something else they had in common. She really appreciated Elizabeth's support and she was planning to get her something nice with her overtime money she was earning. No, she really did not mind working all those extra hours because she was also hoping to treat herself to something nice if she had money left over.

After all, she was only eighteen years old herself and of course like any young girl, she loved to have new clothes, shoes and maybe a new handbag, so now she was earning more money it was all good in this respect. The only problem was she was working such long hours every day that she did not have the time or motivation to do her treatments as regularly as she should, so she was again not making much progress. It was a viscous circle because the less treatments she did, the less her progress and the less progress she achieved, the less motivation she had to do her treatment properly. In fact, she was only doing her treatment once a day and on some days, she was too tired or she would forget, unless Elizabeth called her up, and only then would it remind her to do them. She knew it was her fault that she was not progressing with her treatment because she was not motivated enough, but who could really blame her? Poor Melanie, she needed the money, so she rationalised that it was more important for her to earn as much money as she could now whilst the opportunity was there. In the end, something had to give. She was just too exhausted because all she did for the past few weeks was to work, come home for dinner, maybe do her treatment, sleep and then it was back to work again. She desperately needed a break, just some time to chill out and to get away from her tiring mundane routine before she started back at college so she was really looking forward to her weekend at Elizabeth's.

Meanwhile, Elizabeth was at home alone in her room, feeling rather unsettled because she could not wait till the evening to talk to Melanie. She was feeling slightly annoyed and frustrated too, because she had fought hard the past year to forget her condition and she had started to get on with her life normally but once again, she had to be reminded of it over something as innocent and trivial as a weekend with her friends. "Not now again" she pleaded. This time though, she refused to let it affect her so. She could not go back, she could not go through what she had been through again and it made her more determined not to do so. Of course, she was now in a stronger position so she was in better control this time. She soon accepted that no matter how far she had come, she would never be rid of it. It was always going to be a part of her, this was who she was and if she was to have a chance of having a normal life, she knew she would have to learn to deal and live with it, no matter how it presented itself again. In reality she actually thought she already had. She figured that maybe, this was just another test on how well she really was doing. Then she remembered, "Lucy did say that it is normal to be still affected by certain situations directly or indirectly relating to my MRKH at different phases of my life," so this made her feel better afterwards. Then she felt quite sure that it was all part of her growing up too. She took a deep breath and told herself that she would deal with her problem objectively. She wished that she had been brave enough to tell the rest of her friends earlier and although she felt that she was not bothered if they knew about her condition now, she still had to think of Melanie. At least that was what she kept telling herself and it probably was true because she was not that angsty about herself anymore but maybe she felt also cushioned because now there was the two of them.

In any case, Elizabeth was genuinely more concerned for Melanie this time, especially when she felt that Melanie was not ready to reveal her secret yet. She was sure of this because she compared herself with Melanie and because of this she felt that Melanie would need more time... just as she herself did back then. She thought of ringing Anne but she knew that Anne would be too busy to take her call and furthermore, she felt that Anne would only tell her that it was ultimately her decision. She wished her mother was home so that she could seek her advice but she was at work so instead she decided to call her two best friends. She called Sally first but unfortunately, this time her best friend also could not help her either because the decision was not just Elizabeth's to make. Sally did suggest though that, "Maybe you should tell our closest friends about your MRKH before Melanie's visit" but Elizabeth was reluctant because she felt "it would be awkward for me to suddenly bring this up unless the situation presented itself and I also think it's too close to call don't you think Sal? Besides, I don't know how they are going to react if I was to suddenly bring this up. Do you remember when I first told you? You were so shocked and you're my best friend and we spent the whole day talking about it. No, I can't just tell them now because I'm afraid it might just make matters worse. I don't think that I can just tell them something like that now out of the blue". Sally said "Yeah, you're probably right but what are you going to do then?" Elizabeth said "I don't know yet but I'll have to think of something fast".

Afterwards, she decided that she would ring Tom to ask for his opinion but then she remembered that he was out playing cricket at his local club and besides she felt that he would only suggest what Sally just did and it might worry him unnecessarily, so she resigned herself to the fact that she was on her own this time. Then she thought of a solution. She would tell her friends that Melanie was an old family friend whom she met up with when she was in London. She was not totally comfortable about lying, so she tried to convince herself that it was better to tell a white lie than for Melanie to get hurt. She also justified it as being the truth because she truly felt that Melanie was indeed her friend and an extension of her family now albeit through this weird genetic connection they both shared. After rehearsing it several times in her head, she felt reconciled that this was the best thing to say.

When her mother came home, Elizabeth could not wait so she quickly told her about it, "Mum, I just realised that I have a problem with Mel joining us because none of my other friends know her. I'm so worried that they'll want to know about her and then they'll find out that we both have MRKH. I'm really worried for Mel so I thought that if I told them that she's a family friend from London, they might be ok with it. I know I'm kind of lying…" and as she continued to tell her mother, she became very self-conscious and uneasy because of the truthful person that she always was, and instantly felt that her mother would disapprove, but to her surprise her mother simply condoned it. Elizabeth could not believe it but then Jan explained that it was the best for everyone concerned under the circumstances as she said, "Nobody will get hurt and nobody needs to get hurt". Besides, she had also strangely come to regard Melanie as an extended part of her family. It was strange indeed but because of their unusual condition, Jan actually felt that she suddenly had two daughters, because Elizabeth and Melanie were so alike and it was as if they were genetically connected as sisters. In any case, Elizabeth felt better having her mother's support because irrespective of how grown up she had become, she still valued her mother's opinion and approval... and when all was said and done she was just sixteen going on seventeen.

Elizabeth waited till after dinner to ring Melanie that evening. She started by encouraging her with her treatment as usual and then very mindfully, she mentioned their potential problem. Melanie had not even thought of it as she was too exhausted every day anyway, but before she could properly register their conversation, Elizabeth told Melanie her plan and asked for her opinion. She was hoping that Melanie would not find her white lie objectionable unless she could come up with a better idea, but more to her surprise Melanie agreed without any hesitation. She even told Elizabeth that she was used to it. "You are, how come?" Elizabeth asked in surprise. Melanie replied, "El, my life's been a lie ever since I found out I had MRKH". Melanie was not usually a mendacious person and like Elizabeth, she did not like lying either, so she qualified that it was ok because, "I'm not hurting anybody and I haven't lied about anybody. All I've done is to lie to herself and about herself". She also told Elizabeth "I've even pretended to have periods by keeping a diary and some tampons," because she could not risk letting anyone of her school mates know that she was different. She said that there were groups of unsavoury students in the state school she attended, some were bullies and very cruel and even though she used to hang out with a group of girls in school, she could not trust any of them. They were decent enough, but she could never be sure if they would turn on her if they knew she was abnormal. She guarded her secret so well that apart from a teacher and the headmistress, whom her mother informed, no one else knew any different.

Even then, she was always weary and terrified that one day, someone would find out. She told Elizabeth, "If you knew the students in my school, you'd understand. I was always terrified of any of them finding out because they would surely ridicule me and make me the laughing-stock of the whole school. They're a very cruel and ignorant lot and this was the only way I could protect myself". Elizabeth could only say, "Oh Mel, how awful for you, you poor thing. That's really horrible," and it again made her feel more appreciative of the very cushioned and comfortable life she led, but unfortunately, this was the environment Melanie grew up in. Needless to say, she felt that she had no choice but to keep up with the pretence and lie about herself. It was the only way she knew to survive too but she still lived with the same fear every day that she went to school, so "that's why I studied hard and I could not wait to finish my GCSEs fast enough," she continued. Melanie was a smart girl and she got her five GCSEs in Performing Arts, English, ICT, French and Social Science. After that, she left school and started looking for a job because she wanted to help her mother, who was struggling to keep her family together, with mounting bills and all the needs of her young family. It also drove her to do well because she wanted better things for her mother and her siblings and to give them a better chance in life. That was why she was working so hard to put herself through college. She knew she had to get her drama degree if there was any hope of her landing an acting job and to achieve her dream as a famous actress, especially when she told Elizabeth, "I am fully aware that there are a

311

lot of unemployed actors out there so I know that it will not be easy but then nothing is ever easy for me anyway. Still I am going to try my best to be a better actor than them so that I can fulfill my dream".

After listening to Melanie, Elizabeth was so emotionally touched that she did not know whether to cry or just to root for her, so she chose the latter because she felt that Melanie was filled with determination and pride and she was not looking for sympathy. Elizabeth wished more than anything then, that her friend would one day be able to make her dream come true, saying, "I really hope that you'll make it Mel. You deserve it more than anybody else. I'll keep rooting for you". She truly believed that Melanie deserved a good break because she was such a wonderful person and Elizabeth could actually visualise her as a great actress, because of her passion and her life experiences, and what she could offer to her roles. Melanie also told Elizabeth that she had recently joined her local amateur dramatic company and had been in a couple of their local productions and she was sure that acting was what she really wanted to do with her life. Elizabeth always felt happy and sad every time after she spoke to Melanie. Perhaps, Melanie was real and despite everything she had been through, she remained positive about her future so talking with her always made Elizabeth feel humbled afterwards and she really valued their friendship.

Elizabeth waited outside the train station so she could spot Melanie quickly as she came out, because she was aware that it was Melanie's first trip out of London. She could still recall her own first trip to London and even with her father leading the way, she felt it was all rather nerve wracking and confusing, those long walks to the platforms between stations and the pace, she remembered all too well, because it was so fast and furious. Melanie was so tired that she could have easily slept on the train, but she was too excited and even more terrified of missing her stop.

She finished work early that Friday so that she could go home first to have a shower and to pick up her luggage. She kissed and hugged her mother and siblings as she said goodbye to them and then made her way to the tube station. Luckily for her, Melanie was used to the London public transport but it was still unnerving for her catching the overground train, so she asked for assistance to make sure that she boarded the correct one. The train was not full because it was not the rush hour yet which was why she managed to get a cheaper fare so she had a two-seater to herself all the way there. As the train pulled into the train station, the destination sign on the train confirmed her stop and there was also an announcement by the driver over the intercom, so she swiftly put her backpack on and picked up her little bag so that she was ready to disembark when the train stopped. She was used to this, being a Londoner but then there was no rush. In fact, there was not even a hint of that at all. The train sat at the platform for a while and Melanie noticed the slow and relaxed pace immediately. She thought, "This is different, no one is rushing". Still, she thought she could not relax yet, at least not until she had met up with Elizabeth.

When she walked out of the station, Elizabeth saw her first and called out to her. They hugged and gave each other kisses, one on each cheek, "Hiya so good to see you, Mel. How was your journey?" Elizabeth asked so Melanie replied, "Hi. Yeah, it was alright, it was very pleasant actually". Then Elizabeth said, "I'm so glad you came, Mel. Oh, this way, my mum's waiting for us over there," ushering and pointing to the direction where Jan was parked up. "Hello Mrs. Appleton" said Melanie as she got into the car. Jan smiled and responded with, "Hello Melanie, lovely to see you again. How was your train journey?" Melanie said, "It was good. All the trains were running on time and it wasn't too crowded either. Thanks for coming to fetch me, Mrs Appleton".

"It's a pleasure and you may call me Jan," and Melanie said, "Ok".

"Are we all ready to go home?" Jan asked rhetorically, as she started driving away. Melanie liked Jan and thought that she was such an attractive and elegant lady. It was obvious that she came from an affluent background from the way she dressed and spoke but she was also kind, gentle and down to earth, so Melanie never felt intimidated by her. In fact, she could see where Elizabeth inherited her traits because she was as beautiful and lovely as her mother and Melanie felt that she could not have met two nicer people. Yes, she really liked them and she would never have got to know them if not for her rare condition she shared with Elizabeth, which she felt was at least one good and positive aspect of her condition.

When they got in, Jan said, "Welcome to our home Mel and please make yourself at home. I want you to be comfortable and enjoy your weekend with us. Elizabeth will show you around while I get us a snack and something to drink. What would you like to drink?"

"I'd love a cup of tea please, thank you" replied Melanie. Elizabeth then picked up her bag and said, "Come on, I'll show you around the house and show you your room". When they got there, Elizabeth said, "This is your room so you can put your stuff in here first and then we can join mum outside". Melanie thought the house was beautiful and it was also huge compared to her little flat. The guest room was twice the size of her own bedroom at home and the living room was probably the size of her whole flat put together. She had heard that there were a lot of rich people around. This was the first time she saw how the other half lived and thought to herself that one day, when she was successful, she would buy a big house for her mother and family too. Just then she remembered her mother so she rang her as she had promised, to let her know that she had arrived safely.

Elizabeth and Melanie joined Jan in the living room afterwards. They just sat chatting and had their tea and cakes
until Paul came back with Emma. He had picked Emma up
from her friend's place on the way back from work.

"Hi dad, this is my friend, Mel," Elizabeth introduced
them. Paul stretched his hand out as he said, "Hello Mel, nice
to finally meet you. I've heard so much about you". Melanie
shook his hand and said hello back. Then Elizabeth looking
at her friend, continued as she hugged Emma, "and this is
my little sister, Ems," and they said "Hi" to one another.
They chatted for a while, getting to know each other, but
mostly they were interested to know more about Melanie,
which Melanie did not mind because she felt that they were
genuinely interested. Then Jan noticed the time and asked
Melanie what she would like to eat for dinner so Melanie
replied "I don't mind, anything that's convenient". By now,
she was actually quite hungry, having skipped her lunch
and worked through her break so that she could leave work
slightly earlier to catch her train. In the end, it was Emma
who piped up, "I fancy a Chinese, can we have Chinese,
please?" Everyone laughed because it was so childlike and
typical of Emma but no one minded so they went to their
usual local in the high street. It was a real treat and Melanie
enjoyed the meal very much. It was probably the most substantial meal she had all week too.

Afterwards, Melanie felt that she had eaten too much so
all she felt like doing when they got back was to curl up in
a corner and sleep. It had been after all, a long day for her,
as she had been up since six that morning to go to work
and she had not really stopped until now, as the shop was
very busy with shoppers doing their Christmas shopping.
Nonetheless, she did not wish to be rude so she mastered
enough strength and stayed awake until Jan very consid-
erately said, "Mel, you must be very tired having worked
all day. Perhaps you'd like to have an early night so please
don't let us keep you," so Melanie said, "I am a little tired,

thank you and thank you for dinner too". Then they all said good night to one another. Elizabeth went with Melanie to her room and reminded her about her treatment because she suspected that Melanie had not had the time to do it. She also had the impression that Melanie was not bothered either. She remembered Lucy telling her about the girls who sometimes gave up because they were not motivated to do their treatment properly and although Melanie had said that she would not give up, somehow Elizabeth could still identify Melanie as one of them. Elizabeth earnestly wanted to help her friend succeed but she was not sure how to approach the subject without upsetting her so she decided that she would talk to her after she had done her treatment and showered and freshened up. She thought that she would maybe share her own success story with Melanie again because she herself had never minded doing her treatment, because she was just determined to succeed and to finish it, although she was fortunate not to have Melanie's added problems. Still she really hoped that it would encourage and motivate her friend to be more diligent with her treatments as she so wanted Melanie to finish her treatment too.

As she came out of the shower, Sally rang to ask if Melanie arrived as planned and if everything was alright. Elizabeth knew exactly what she meant and told her that they did not get a chance to talk about "it" yet. In all honesty, since talking it over with Melanie, Elizabeth had completely forgotten about it and with the excitement of her arrival, her family were busily getting to know Melanie and making her feel at home that they had not had a moment to themselves yet. Besides, what was now more uppermost in Elizabeth's mind was Melanie's treatment. Sally was planned to come by the next day and the three of them would then go into town together for their night out so she asked "what time shall I come over, El?" and Elizabeth said "any time in the afternoon". They exchanged their goodbyes, "Ok, see you tomorrow. Bye". No sooner, she clicked her mobile off, it rang again. This time it was Tom, his usual nightly call. They spoke for a while and Elizabeth told him about Melanie and that she could not wait for him to meet her. She felt sure that he would like her too, not only because she was such a lovely girl but that she also had MRKH, just like her. She knew it was the most ridiculous reason because what would this have anything to do with liking the girl anyway, but this was how she felt. In any case, she was very keen and excited about their meeting. It was as if she wanted to 'show Melanie off' to Tom. Was it because she was trying to prove that she was not the only one so that she was not that unusual or abnormal after all, she just could not say with certainty, but she was certain of one thing though. She felt good having Melanie around and despite being surrounded by her loving family and friends, she still felt a sense of isolation sometimes but with Melanie, they belonged together. She did not wish to sound ungrateful but it was just different because whenever she spoke to Melanie or was in her company, that hint of isolation and the feeling of loneliness, always vanished. Somehow, she also felt 'safe' so maybe it had something to do with safety in numbers. She just did not know but she was past trying to reason and felt again that perhaps only someone with their condition could really truly understand what she was feeling.

Elizabeth gave a gentle knock on the door. She did not want to disturb Melanie in case she was in the midst of her treatment but she needed to speak to her before she went to bed. She was surprised when Melanie opened the door straight away. In fact, Melanie was waiting for Elizabeth too. She felt refreshed after her shower and had gone past her tired phase. They chatted for hours, first about Melanie's treatment. She admitted that she was still having difficulty with her treatment and felt she was not going anywhere with it so she told Elizabeth, "I feel like giving up sometimes but at the same time, when I think of how much time I have already lost and how helpless I was, it just makes me feel that

I have to persevere with it". Elizabeth encouraged her to continue and told her, "Mel, from my own experience I can tell you that if you do your treatments more regularly you will make progress otherwise, the treatment will not work," but Melanie said, "It's just so hard you know. I want to but then I'm always so tired when I come home from work". Elizabeth then said to her, "I understand because I also felt like it when I first started my treatments but I found it easier when I kept it to a routine," so Melanie said, "It's not that easy for me. I also share my room with my little sister and she doesn't know about me. No one knows except my mum, so I don't have any privacy to do my treatment without her finding out. I really don't know that I will ever succeed and it makes me very sad. I try not to think about it but it's always there at the back of my mind, you know what I mean".

Elizabeth knew exactly what she meant and she felt equally helpless at Melanie's situation. Then she had an idea. She knew that Melanie would never be able to do it alone so she advised her to engage her mother's help. She suggested that, "You could ask your mum to put a lock on your door or you could ask your mother to keep your brothers and sister out of your room when you are doing your treatments so either way, you'll at least have some privacy". Melanie agreed, "Yes, it's a good idea but still realistically, I will only be able to do my treatment twice a day" so Elizabeth told her that "it's better than not doing it correctly because if you only do it once a day, you won't see any progress".

"You really think so El?" she asked and Elizabeth said reassuringly, "Oh, definitely". Melanie gave her a hug and said "thanks El, you're a true mate," to which Elizabeth responded "So are you. That's why I want to help if I can. I'm here for you ok and you also have Lucy, she's lovely and she's very good. Mel, I know you can do it. It's just harder for you because of your circumstances but you just need to focus on the end result. The treatment really works, look at me, I'm the living proof". Melanie smiled and said, "I'm so happy for you. I wish I was there but I have a long way to go. Anyway, I don't have a partner so I guess there's no rush. Do you like um... have to still use your dilator if you have sex?"

"Nope, that's why it's so great. Lucy said that once the vagina is fully stretched, it's normal so we don't need to keep using our dilators," she informed Melanie, who said, "That's good otherwise, we'll never be normal. To be honest with you, I already told you that I really hate the dilators, don't you? They keep reminding me that I'm not normal, as if I don't already know".

"I know exactly how you feel but that's why you need to complete the treatment so you can then throw the dilators away for good. I never really minded doing the treatments because I just focused on the completion and it really helped," Elizabeth said very encouragingly, remembering that all too familiar feeling.

Afterwards, Elizabeth talked about her group of friends and she also told Melanie about Tom. She updated her on her plans for their night out and they went through 'their plan' again, just in case. She also told her that Sally was coming over tomorrow and that her mother would then drop them off at the restaurant in the evening. She wanted Melanie to know their plans in advance for the next day so that she could then organise her treatments accordingly. She even suggested to Melanie, "Maybe you'll be able to do your treatments three times a day while you're here because now you have your own room" and Melanie said, "Ok, I'll try". The evening had gone perfectly and when it was time to sleep, they were both ready for bed so they said goodnight and then Elizabeth went back to her room.

When Elizabeth left, Melanie thought about her friend's suggestion. She suddenly did not feel that tired anymore so she decided to do her treatment once more as she had complete privacy for a change this time. She thought that she should make the most of it and especially after she had said that she would try, following her chat with Elizabeth.

She also felt more compliant with her treatment then, so she did it. It was hard and it was painful. She was still using the small dilators and even these seem to hurt as before. She wished they did not hurt as much. Still, she tried and pushed them in as hard as she could, which nearly brought tears to her eyes. When she finished, she examined herself only to find that her vagina was still that shallow dimple and felt slightly disappointed. Then she told herself that, "Tomorrow's another day".

Supporting Melanie

Melanie woke up feeling totally refreshed. She could not remember the last time she had such a good night's sleep. She went to the window, opened the curtains and had to close her eyes immediately when the bright ray of sunshine almost blinded her as it shone straight into her face. The weather forecast for the day was good and promised a whole day of glorious sunshine. It seemed to lift her spirit. In fact, she was feeling so chirpy that she promised she would be good and do her treatment properly from now on. No more excuses and no more drifting. She must be focused on finishing her treatment, just as Elizabeth had done. She must apply the same focus and drive as she was doing with her acting career if she was to succeed. Besides, she was getting very weary of being alone and having to be secretive and feeling like the odd one out all the time. She knew that she needed to sort this out first before she could move on with her life. She did not have a boyfriend although she would not have minded and she felt then that this might help to motivate her more if she did have one. There were a few boys who were interested in her but she was too frightened and always put up a screen before anyone got too close. She knew she was no longer a child and would be nineteen soon, but she was too messed up to start a relationship. How could she when she felt so abnormal. She wished she was not abnormal and sometimes it pained her when she had time to think because she felt that she already had a lot on her plate, without having to feel like a freak too, although Elizabeth had told her that she had as well.

She hated feeling this way which was why for the most part, she chose not to think about it. She had become so good at pretending that she was someone else, a normal person that she managed to carry on with her life this far, but it was not really helping because it was not her true self and she was only wasting precious time. She wanted to be herself, only her true self was not normal and she hated that her MRKH was always there, inside her and always with her no matter how hard she tried to forget or deny it. She really felt trapped within her own body. She was desperate to move on so now she decided that things had to change and she needed to get her act together. She would now make time for what she had to do, to make herself normal.

She went into the bathroom to brush her teeth and to wash her face first. Then she took her bag of dilators and some tissue paper and put them on the bed. She laid herself on the bed ready to start but then remembered Lucy always advising her to urinate first so that she would not have to interrupt her treatment. She also knew from experience that she would be better able to withstand the pain if her bladder was empty so she made a quick dash to the toilet. When she was ready, she took a deep breath and then she started her treatment, using the smaller dilator first and then the next size up. It was the same again, the pain was excruciating but she continued to push the dilator in as hard as she could. She hated this sensation because it always felt like her inside was splitting up and she also had to try to blank her mind of her past. The pain was unbearable but she could just about tolerate it for a few more minutes. She could not wait for the pain to subside and the numbness to take over so she tried to occupy her mind by thinking of something else. She wished Lucy was with her then because she would be talking her through it and somehow the pain always felt more tolerable when she was doing the treatment with her. She started talking to herself. "How I wish I could take Lucy home then I wouldn't have to do this on my own. I'm sure that I would make progress if Lucy was with me all the time".

She liked Lucy too because she was always patient and

encouraging to her and she never gave up on her, even when she had suggested previously that she could postpone her treatment until she was ready to do it properly. She shuddered to think where she would be if Lucy was not around to help her. She could not bear going back into limbo again. She tried to focus on the outcome instead, like Elizabeth had told her, and very soon she was finished with her treatment. When she took her dilator out, she noticed there was blood on it and when she wiped herself, there was more blood. She was panic stricken, so she quickly rushed to the shower to wash herself, but the blood would not stop and kept trickling down her legs. In the end, she decided to line some tissues on her panties and then quickly got dressed. She washed her dilators in the sink but the sight of the blood was making her head swim and she suddenly felt dizzy so she rushed to the bed and plonked herself on it. Her heart was pounding hard and fast and she was shaking all over. She was petrified! She could not remember what happened next. She did not know if she had fainted or not but when she was aware again, her face and body was covered in beads of cold sweat and she suddenly felt cold... so cold. Then she remembered the blood. She felt sure that she had damaged herself. She blamed herself because she had not done her treatment the last couple of days because of her late shifts at work and now she must have pushed the dilators in too hard. "Oh no, what should I do?" she asked herself.

She decided to ring Lucy, she would know and she would tell her what to do. Then she remembered it was Saturday and Lucy would not be there so now she started to panic again. She must tell Elizabeth because maybe she will know what to do. She knocked on the door but there was no answer so she thought that Elizabeth was probably still asleep so she crept back to her room. She did not know what else to do so she sat on the bed nervously shaking both her legs and biting her nails. She was so terrified by now that she could not even think about anything anymore so her mind just went blank.

Within the next few seconds, Elizabeth was knocking at her door so Melanie quickly opened the door. Elizabeth saw the look of panic on her friend's pale face so she asked, "What's wrong Mel? Are you ok?"

"No, I'm not, I'm bleeding! I think I've damaged myself, El," Melanie replied, holding her hands over her eyes and face to hide that she was crying. Elizabeth instinctively put her arms around her to pacify her and asked, "Have you rung Lucy?" Melanie said, "She won't be there. It's the weekend".

"That's true but maybe we can ring the unit. One of the staff must be able to help us," Elizabeth suggested. She was equally frightened but she tried to stay composed for Melanie's sake, no point in the both of them panicking, she thought. She tried to think fast then she remembered the conversation she had with Lucy previously so she said, "Lucy told me once that some girls can bleed but it doesn't mean anything so don't think the worst, Mel. I actually asked her about this and she said that sometimes she would advise the girls to continue with their treatments but if there was a lot of bleeding, she would advise them to stop for a few days and restart when the bleeding stops. I'm sure you'll be fine when the bleeding stops. This doesn't mean anything and you can still finish your treatment". Melanie shook her head and said despairingly "I don't think I can do it, El. I'm a failure".

"No you're not. You don't believe that. You just hit a problem. C'mon, let's ring the Centre," insisted Elizabeth. She handed Melanie her mobile that was sitting on the bed and noticed that there was blood on the duvet cover. Melanie also saw it then and immediately felt embarrassed so she said "I'm really sorry about that" pointing to the stain. "Don't worry about it, it's not a biggie. That'll come off in the wash. You're more important!" Elizabeth brushed it off and instead she urged Melanie to call the Centre again, so Melanie did and she managed to speak to one of the staff there. She advised Melanie to stop the treatments so she felt better but not before she went to check on her bleeding again. Her bleeding seemed to have eased slightly so she relined her panties with fresh clean tissues. Afterwards, she told Elizabeth that it was probably her fault for not doing her treatment properly and that she must have forced the dilators in too hard earlier on. The bleeding really scared her and shook her confidence so she was more than happy to leave her treatment until she saw Lucy again, as she was advised. Nevertheless, she felt sad and disappointed as she told Elizabeth, "I don't know why this is happening to me, El. I'm not a bad person but it seems that I keep being punished over and over. I want to be positive but it's getting harder because the more I try, the more I fail so I should just give up". Elizabeth said "Hey, you're a fighter and you don't give up. I know you keep getting these problems but you are stronger than me and you will get through this. I know you will". Melanie responded, "El, you have such confidence in me and I also believed that I could do this but I'm not sure anymore. I mean I was so positive earlier on but just when I have finally decided to address my treatment constructively, something has to go wrong. You know that I'm not usually a bitter or negative person but now I'm beginning to wonder if anything good will ever happen to someone like me".

By now, Elizabeth was not sure what she could say anymore to Melanie because she was also beginning to feel that misfortune seem to be following her friend, so she just hugged her and said, "Mel, you're going to be fine. I'm here for you and I'll always be your friend". Just then, Melanie realised that something good did happen to her and she said, "You're right, El. I'm going to be fine. Something good did happen to me. I met you, and you might be my only friend but you are the best friend anyone could wish for. Thanks, El. Thanks for everything and thanks for being a good friend". Elizabeth was very touched by Melanie's words and she appreciated what their friendship really meant to each other. They decided to change the duvet cover and Melanie insisted that she would sort it out by herself so Elizabeth gave her a clean one. When she was sure that Melanie was ok, Elizabeth went back to her room to get changed and left Melanie to it. Melanie felt really embarrassed about the blood on the duvet cover so she tried her best to rinse it off with some hand wash and water in the bathroom. She managed to get most of the blood off, but of course there was still a slight stain which she just could not get rid of. She felt bad about it but decided that there was nothing else she could do and hoped that it will come off in the wash just as Elizabeth had told her. Then she draped it over the chair in her room for it to dry.

Elizabeth came back for her and then the two girls made their way to the living room. Paul was sitting on the settee reading his *Financial Times* and having his coffee. They exchanged their "good morning" wishes. When Jan heard them, she came out of the kitchen and also wished them a "Good morning. Hope you girls didn't stay up too late last night," and then addressing Melanie, she said "I hope you slept well, Mel".

"Good morning. Yes, I did thank you, Mrs. Appleton" Melanie replied and Elizabeth also wished her mother a good morning. "So what would you girls like for breakfast?" Jan asked them looking at Melanie "Just tea, thanks. I don't usually have breakfast," she said, to which Jan said, "No wonder you're so slim," then turning her head to look over to her daughter, she asked, "how about you darling?" Elizabeth told her mother, "I'll just have some toast with my coffee, thanks mum. Mel, please have some toasts too?" and encouraged her friend to join her, so Jan said "I'll make toast for everyone". After breakfast, Melanie and Elizabeth helped to take their used plates and cutlery and followed Jan into the kitchen. Melanie really wanted a quiet opportunity to tell Jan about the bed linen because she felt really embarrassed. Still she felt comfortable talking to Jan so she apologised for her 'accident' with the duvet. "Oh, don't worry about the duvet. Are you alright though?" enquired Jan with concern, and Melanie replied, "I am now, thank you. I was really frightened just now but luckily El was with me and she was very good". Jan then offered her some sanitary pads, but when Melanie saw them, she thought they looked too big so she declined. She also asked herself "isn't this so ironic that I never had to use a sanitary pad before because I don't have periods but I have to use them for this now?" Jan could understand from her facial expression why Melanie declined the pads too, even though she thought that they were only the normal standard size so, without much fuss, she brought out some panty-liners for her instead. She suggested that these would be more comfortable and appropriate to use than toilet tissue paper. Melanie agreed to try the liners because they looked slimmer and less scary so she thanked Jan. She felt that Jan was so kind and thoughtful and she really appreciated her compassion and understanding. She then went to the bathroom to check on her bleeding and was relieved that it was getting less. She used one of the panty-liners that Jan gave her and it was indeed more comfortable.

There was a lot of laughter coming from the living room when Melanie returned. She noticed that Emma was up and she seemed very excited. Elizabeth was in the midst of opening her presents from Emma and her parents. Melanie also noticed the two big birthday balloons floating in the room, and soon realised that it was Elizabeth's birthday. She felt really awkward that she did not know about it because she would definitely have bought Elizabeth a card and a present too but instead all she could say was "Happy birthday, El. Why didn't you tell me it was your birthday? I feel really embarrassed I didn't get you anything".

"Don't be, I didn't tell you because I didn't want you to have to buy me anything" said Elizabeth. Then Melanie remembered that she had bought Elizabeth something so she said "wait up" and promptly disappeared into her room. She came back as quickly as she went and she was holding something glittery in her hand and gave it to Elizabeth saying, "Sorry this was supposed to be your Christmas present but now it will have to be your birthday present," and she added "I'll give you your Christmas one when we meet up in London the next time, ok?" This time it was Elizabeth who was embarrassed, so she said, "Oh Mel, now you're embarrassing me. I deliberately didn't tell you because I didn't want you to get me anything," but Melanie was insistent and she said to Elizabeth, "Please take it. I really want to give you something because you have been such a good friend to me and it's also to say thank you". Elizabeth gave her a hug and a kiss on her cheek as she thanked her for the present. When Elizabeth opened her present, she was thrilled because, "Aww, this is really beautiful, thanks Mel". It was a personalised silver pearl friendship bangle, so she put it on straight away.

Elizabeth continued to open all her presents. She loved all of them and she was kissing and thanking everyone. She also tried to ring her grandparents to thank them for the card they sent her but they were not at home so she rang her grandmother's mobile next and managed to speak to her then. This reminded Melanie to ring home so she excused herself and went to her room to ring her mother. Afterwards, she went to check on her bleeding again. It was definitely under control with only a minimal blood streak on her panty-liner, but she was suddenly aware of soreness in that region. She knew it was not her imagination because she also felt it earlier when she sat down but she did not like making any further fuss so she ignored it. She already felt bad having caused enough excitement for the day and she also did not wish to further spoil Elizabeth's special day, now that she knew it was her birthday.

Sally came around three in the afternoon, in time to join them for afternoon tea. Jan had planned a small birthday surprise for Elizabeth at home even though Elizabeth had said that she would go out to celebrate her birthday with her friends later on. She felt that they could still have a small celebration with the family and close friends so unbeknown to Elizabeth, Jan had also invited Tom, who arrived soon after Sally. Then like clockwork, the doorbell went so Emma quickly went to answer it and soon after, she walked in with her grandparents. When Elizabeth saw them, she was amazed and said, "Oh my god! Grandma, granddad! No wonder you weren't at home when I called you. Mummy, when did you do all this?" Jan just shook her head and smiled and before she knew it, Elizabeth's grandparents were kissing her and wishing her a happy birthday as they gave her the present they bought her. Elizabeth was so pleasantly surprised because she had absolutely no idea. Then again, she was so engrossed with her own little problem that she did not notice anything else that was going on. She was even more surprised at her friends because she had been speaking with them all week and yet neither gave anything away so Elizabeth, now addressing Sally and Tom, exclaimed, "I can't believe that the two of you never said anything about this to me!" Sally replied "It wouldn't be a surprise then if we did, would it?" They laughed and hugged each other, as good friends do.

When everyone gathered around, Jan brought out her birthday cake. It had seventeen lit candles on it and as she walked in with the cake, everyone sang 'Happy Birthday' to Elizabeth. Of course, this was another one of the scrumptious cakes from their local patisserie. It was a pure chocolate indulgence. The whole cake was chocolate, with chocolate-ganache filling and it was beautifully decorated on the outside with white and dark chocolate flakes, truffles and other edible chocolate decorations. Jan also ordered some finger-licking snacks and bites and she herself made some salmon and cucumber sandwiches and cheese and ham sandwiches. The dining table was full with food and drinks and birthday balloons and streamers, compliments of Emma, of course. It was just right for a delightful afternoon birthday tea party. Elizabeth loved her birthday surprise! She sat back for a minute to enjoy the moment and smiled to herself. She had much to be thankful for, surrounded by all the people she loved and who loved her. She felt she could not have asked for anything better than this for her birthday.

A Great Night Out

Elizabeth was right. Tom liked Melanie too, she was such a lovely girl that there was really nothing to dislike. Elizabeth reminded Tom not to mention their MRKH to the rest of their friends because they did not know about it, as if he would forget, but she was also being cautious. Tom thought Melanie was such a pretty girl and so normal looking that he would not have known there was anything wrong with her, very much like Elizabeth. He could not get his head around the fact that they could appear so normal and yet have this rare condition, not that he ever minded but he still thought it was so strange, if he was honest. Why, only a year ago before Elizabeth told him, he was unaware and had never ever heard of MRKH and now right in front of him, were these two gorgeous beautiful girls, with this very condition. It made him feel very honoured and fortunate to know them and to have them in his life. The last year had just flown by and he did not have time to reflect on the so many things that had happened in his life, but he had no regrets. It was mind blowing. Still he was pleased with how things had turned out because he got the girl of his dreams. There were some tough times too but he thought that he would do it all over again if he had to because Elizabeth was worth it and he could not have done better if he tried. Honestly, it was all good, he felt.

They got to the restaurant early because Elizabeth wanted to be there before everyone arrived. She was also keeping a close eye on Melanie because of her scare earlier, but Melanie wanted Elizabeth to enjoy her birthday without having to worry about her, so she tried to play it down, "I'm fine now so stop worrying about me. Just enjoy yourself please. It's your birthday". In any case, her bleeding had practically stopped so Melanie had almost forgotten about it, except for the slight tenderness she felt whenever she moved or sat down. The waiter came to their table to ask if they wanted to order anything first so they ordered their Cokes and checked the menu whilst they waited for their friends to arrive. Joanne and Sasha arrived together because they met up, as they were being dropped off by their respective parents and, shortly after, John, Sean and Adam also arrived. The group was always punctual which must have been their training and grooming at boarding school, because they were taught never to be late and that it was rude to keep someone waiting. They all hugged and kissed each other as they normally did and wished Elizabeth "Happy birthday". Of course, they also gave her their individual presents and cards they had bought for her. Elizabeth thanked them and then introduced Melanie to them as a friend of the family. Everyone said, "Hi Mel, nice to meet you," and she replied, "Hi, nice to meet you too". Once the civilities were over Elizabeth was mindful not to give her friends a chance to ask any questions about Melanie, so she very quickly and subtly suggested that they looked at the menu. She even told them what she had decided to have for herself and urged them to do the same so that they could place their orders first. Everyone did as they were told and within the next few minutes, the same waiter came round to their table again so everyone gave their orders in turn.

They continued talking and then the conversation veered round to Melanie just as Elizabeth had anticipated. She knew her friends too well and although it was no surprise, she was still hoping it could be avoided but then she heard Joanne ask "El, how come you've never mentioned or invited Mel out with us before?" Elizabeth sneaked a surreptitious glance at Melanie and told everyone at the table that it was because "Mel lives in London and it's also only recently that we met up and got together again during my trip to London". She thought she should stop there because she was beginning to feel uncomfortable with what she just said and she could not bear spinning a further web of lies to her friends. Thanks to her good friend, she did not have to, as Sally, who could also feel her discomfort, turned the attention to Tom and asked him, "Tom, how are you enjoying living in London and your university?" Elizabeth quietly breathed a sigh of relief and thought Sally was ingenious to do that. Tom told them that he found "University life is very different. I'm getting used to it and I'm enjoying my course. London is very exciting because it's just urban busy so the pace is faster and there is so much to do and see. Actually, I like living in London very much". John was also in London reading law although he and Tom were not at the same universities so he said "Yeah, Tom and I keep in touch and we've met up several times". The rest of the group had never been to London before so they listened with envy and then they started to plan a trip up. They asked Melanie "you're a Londoner, Mel. What's it really like to live there?" Melanie said "I love London because I've always lived there so I guess I'm very much a city girl and I'm used to the city life. I think if you're young, London will always be exciting, and I also love that everything is there, but of course sometimes it can be very stressful too living in London, when I think of my commute to and from work, especially during the rush hour. It's like a rat race sometimes, everything is very fast moving". She then told them that, "I immediately noticed the difference in pace when I came down yesterday. Actually, it was a nice change from the shoving or rushing about or having someone trying to sell you something or trying to con you. I don't miss this ugly side of the city". The friends were amazed to hear this because until now, they had not realised how protected they had been, so Sasha said "Wow, sounds pretty scary".

Then Sean, who was up in Oxford, said that he did not find that much difference with the city life there although he felt that university life, was a different thing. The boys all agreed that university was an eye opener. They were used to having responsibilities, making decisions and taking part in different school activities in boarding school but they also had plenty of guidance and had to abide by the rules and regulations. It was very different at university. They told the girls that at university, they were free from that and instead they were encouraged to be independent and to fend for themselves and while there were the tutors, lecturers and student unions around for support and for socializing, ultimately it was up to the individual student to make something of himself or herself. There were lots of things the boys had to learn or to research themselves, and to experience for themselves, not just for their grades but for their personal development too, so that on graduation, they could stand on their own two feet and be prepared for the real world. The girls listened with interest and as the conversation went on, everyone had relaxed. Their food arrived too in the midst of their conversation so everyone started to eat their meals. They were very happy with their individual meals and they managed to enjoy the evening as they usually did when they were out together. Elizabeth thought that Tom had changed. In fact, she thought that all the boys had. They seemed all grown up, more mature and they were no longer boys but young men, and she liked what she was seeing. They proceeded to the local disco afterwards. The group really loved dancing and they had a blast of a time! Everyone had a great night, including Melanie, who completely forgot about her problem except for a slight ache she felt every now and again when she moved.

Melanie had a fantastic time and thoroughly enjoyed her weekend stay. She thanked Elizabeth and her parents for their hospitality and generosity. Then when she was getting into the car, she apologised to Jan again for the inconvenience she caused with the bed linen so Jan told her, "It's not a problem so don't even worry about it. I hope you have enjoyed your stay with us". Melanie replied "Oh yes, I enjoyed it very much and thank you so much for having me". Jan also added, "Maybe we'll see more of you so you'll have to come again". Melanie replied, "that would be very nice. I'd love to". Jan and Elizabeth dropped Melanie off at the station after brunch and Melanie promised to let Elizabeth know the outcome of her appointment with Lucy. On the way home, Jan praised Elizabeth for her bravery and competence in dealing with Melanie's incident and said she could only imagine how frightened they must have been, and that they should have told her sooner. Elizabeth admitted, "At the time, I was very frightened, mum. I could see that Mel was bleeding a lot, but then I saw that she was even more terrified than me so I tried hard to just focus on supporting her. I'm actually quite surprised at myself that I managed to hold it together". She also told her mother, "You know mum, I'm so glad that I didn't bleed whilst I was doing my treatment because I don't think that I would have been this sensible".

"I'm so proud of you, darling. You took good care of Mel and handled everything very well. It shows how confident and grown up you've become. I hope you will stay in touch with her because right now, Mel needs your help and support and I can tell that you are good for one another too," Jan advised. Elizabeth replied, "Of course we will, mummy. Mel's really nice and I like her. We've become very close. I can't explain it but we just understand each other, you know what I mean". Jan knew exactly what her daughter meant and this was another reason why she not only encouraged their friendship but she was rather grateful that Elizabeth had found a friend in Melanie. It was so obvious that much of it had to do with their MRKH so she nodded her head and just said in an understanding tone, "I know, darling".

Elizabeth was back at school, but however busy she was she did not forget about Melanie. She was very serious about supporting her and it was a way of staying in touch with her friend too. She also knew how much Melanie valued her support so they continued to talk every day and on a few occasions when she was unable to, she texted her. She was very pleased to hear that Melanie had restarted her treatment and had no further bleeding since that episode. Lucy confirmed that there was a small tear when Melanie went to see her but it healed without further complications. She was again advised to do her treatments regularly and was also informed that only then would her skin become more elastic, especially when her skin was quite taut to begin with. Lucy also advised her against intermittent treatments as this would not make her skin stretch continually and might cause further bleeding if excessive force was then used. Lucy believed that Melanie truly wanted to do this dilator treatment but, in fairness to the girl, she also felt that Melanie had too many unresolved issues going on in her life then and because she knew from her wide experience how important the timing, the readiness and the mindset to commit is to complete this dilator treatment, she could not but help feel that it would be better for her to defer her treatment for the time being. She was also concerned of the negative effect it might have on Melanie if she was to continue as she was doing because she could become disappointed and disillusioned if she made no progress later on, even though it was that she had not been doing her required treatments. She had already spoken to Melanie about this and each time, Melanie promised to do better but nothing had changed. She decided to have another chat with her about this but Melanie was still unhappy to stop and became rather tearful as she said, "I really want to do the treatment and I don't want to stop. Please don't make me stop otherwise I won't come back and then I will be back to square one. I promise I will do my treatments properly from now on but don't stop my treatment please," so Lucy reassured her, "I am not going to force you to stop so don't worry. I'm only suggesting it if this will help your situation because I can see that you feel guilty about not doing your treatments and I don't want you to feel this way. It's not right and it's not fair on you, especially when you have enough to contend with at the moment. I also don't want you to feel that the treatment hasn't worked when in fact you know that you haven't done it properly. You might not think it now but when you carry on for a while, it might get you down and I don't want this to happen to you. Do you understand what I'm saying Mel?" Melanie then said, "I know what you're saying and I promise I won't say that because I know that it's my fault so I will really do it this time. I have to. I want to feel normal and good about myself and I want my life to get better so I want to do and finish the treatment. Please don't give up on me". Lucy assured her, "No, of course, I won't. I'm here to help you, not add to your problems". Lucy did not doubt Melanie's determination for a second but she could not say the same for her mindset to follow it through. Still she felt that maybe this time Melanie might take her treatment more seriously, so she was as keen to help her because she also wanted her to succeed. Besides, Melanie was too frightened of bleeding again.

After doing the treatment under Lucy's supervision, Melanie felt more confident, but then she always found it easier when she did it with her. Furthermore, her skin had become slightly more elastic since her bleeding episode so she felt that the over-stretching had a positive outcome at least, not that she would care to repeat that terrifying experience.

Melanie started to do her treatments properly from that day on and in doing them properly she did not bleed again, and she was making some progress too, so it added to her motivation. She had also engaged her mother's help with her privacy situation at home, which helped her with her treatment and together with Elizabeth's encouragement and support, she finally felt more focused on doing and completing her treatment for the first time. Elizabeth also felt more confident about her friend this time and she was pleased that she was able to help. Somehow, it felt good to be giving something back after all the help and support she received herself. She also thought, "Who better to help and understand Melanie than myself," because she was like her and they shared similar if not the same experiences. Elizabeth felt that her personal support to Melanie was also different from that given by the experts. She did not wish to belittle the experts, whom she respected very much but she still believed that despite their expertise, only someone with MRKH could truly understand and know how it felt to have this condition so her support to Melanie was something extra and something special to them too.

Closure: Journey's End

"Yes! Yes! Mummy…" Elizabeth shouted excitedly as she ran to look for her mother to tell her the good news. She found her father sitting out on the patio with his laptop and his coffee. Her mother was by the trellis, pruning and training her clematis and wisteria climbers, so Elizabeth waved the letter in her hand as she ran outside. "Look dad, I've been accepted at Guy's Hospital too," Elizabeth told him and showed him the acceptance letter. He gave her a kiss on the head and said, "well done, darling" and started to read the letter. When her mother heard, she quickly came down the step ladder and walked fast towards them, removing her gardening gloves as she did, and then she placed them with her secateurs on the table. Then she spontaneously hugged her daughter and gave her a big kiss on her cheek and said, "Congratulations darling, so proud of you". Emma heard the noise and excitement so she ran outside to see what was happening. When she found out, she too was thrilled for Elizabeth. Elizabeth had applied to three medical schools, two in London and one locally although she always preferred the London hospitals. Now, she had been accepted by the two London hospitals so her father asked her, "Have you decided on which one you prefer yet?"

"No dad. I've been googling to see what other people have said and they are both top hospitals so I don't mind either. I'll talk to Sally first because she was also waiting to hear from Guy's and since mine came today, hers might too. I'll call her now". Elizabeth went to her room to ring her best friend but Sally had not received her letter yet, so when Elizabeth went outside again to tell her parents, they said it was early days and she had plenty of time to decide.

Her father decided that they would celebrate, so he said he would treat all of them to a nice meal out that evening. He promptly rang the restaurant and made a booking because he was aware that it was usually a busy day for the restaurant, being a Saturday. Whilst he was doing that, Elizabeth went to her room and rang Tom to let him know. "Congrats, El… it doesn't matter which you choose really because they are both good". She was excited because she thought that they would be able to see more of each other if she was studying in London, although she was aware that medical school was going to take up most of the five years of her life. Furthermore, Tom would be finishing his studies, and although he was going to do his Masters degree too, he would still finish before her and would move back home. Still, they would get to see more of each other. In any case, she was more excited to be starting medical school and she would make it work and she was prepared to work hard too. After all, she had planned and worked towards this day for so long that she felt she could not be more ready.

Elizabeth and her family had the most satisfying and enjoyable dinner. When they got home, Elizabeth went to her room to ring her other friends. She rang Melanie first because she wanted to share her news with her. The two of them remained good friends and were in constant contact even though Melanie did not need her support with her treatment anymore, as she finally completed it. Still, their common link seemed to have made their friendship stronger but they never spoke or referred to it again after Melanie's successful completion of her treatment and therapy. Perhaps, they did not need to anymore although they never really made a conscious decision not to. It was just understood. They had come to accept that it would always be a part of who they were and they had both learnt to live with it. It was a part of their journeys and having successfully gone through the process, they were ready to leave the past behind and they moved on with their lives. For now, they were both at better places. Elizabeth could also visualise everything with much clarity now and for once, everything was going to plan and everything was within her reach. She was on course to fulfilling her ambition. She completed her 'A' levels in the sciences and mathematics with distinctions and was ready to start medical school, as did her best friend, Sally. Together again, they would enter their first year in medical school in the autumn at the university of their choosing.

Melanie was also doing well. She had started seeing someone and although it was early days, she felt confident to be in a relationship. At last, she dared to take this plunge. It was better than having to force herself to be a lesbian when she actually preferred the opposite sex, but that was how she thought she had to live her life previously when she felt she had no chance of a normal relationship. Now, she had a boyfriend for a few months and they seemed happy together. However, she had not plucked up enough courage to tell him about her MRKH. Then again, she did not think that her relationship was at that serious stage yet although she had been thinking about telling him because she really liked this guy. She did discuss this with Elizabeth though and she told her that, "At the moment, we're just good friends although I can feel that he wants more. I will tell him if the relationship develops further because I feel that it will otherwise not be a good way for us to start with. I want my relationship with him to be an honest and truthful one if it has a chance to succeed. I don't want to mess things up again". She also felt, more importantly, "At least this way, I will know for sure that he truly loves me for who I am and not just for sex," although by now, it would not be a problem for her to have sexual intercourse because her vagina was normal, having completed her treatment anyway. Elizabeth, who was again being a good friend and trying to protect Melanie, told her "Just make sure that he's the right one first before you tell him. I don't want to see you get hurt, Mel" so Melanie said, "I know, that's why I haven't said anything yet". Furthermore, she said, "I'll have to find out his views on children and having a family first," because she wanted to eliminate any unnecessary tension and angst later on in their relationship. Besides, she continued, "I am even prepared for a negative outcome so if he walks when I tell him about my MRKH, then he does. I think I can handle it. I'd rather find out now sooner rather than later". Then Melanie said "You know El, we're always thinking that everything has to do with our MRKH. What if it's just a normal progression in a relation-ship and normal couples break up anyway," so Elizabeth quickly said, "Yes I suppose but if he's not the one, you don't have to tell him anything do you, unless of course you really like him a lot".

"I do because he's kind and he's a real gentleman. We enjoy each other's company and he makes me laugh and treats me like I'm someone special. Can you imagine, no one's ever made me feel normal, never mind special, so I think he will understand if I told him" said Melanie. It showed how mature and self-confident she had become and how far she had come and she said, "Another thing El, I was just thinking. We don't talk about our MRKH anymore do we?" Elizabeth answered, "No we haven't for a while but it's probably because we're both alright now so we don't have to. Tell you the truth I've been so busy with my exams and applications anyway. I sometimes talk to Tom about children and that and even then I don't get angry about my MRKH anymore. I think I've just accepted it so it doesn't even come into my life now. Lucy and Anne were right because they said that once we can accept our MRKH then we can move on and we both have". Melanie agreed and said, "Yes, thank goodness we had them to help us. I can't believe how far we've both come because at the time it was so painful, so unbearable but now I don't feel that anymore. I don't even mind my MRKH anymore. I know that I've been very busy too so I haven't thought about it until now, but even now, it's so different. I don't feel ashamed and it doesn't affect me like it used to anymore. In fact, that's why I'm not that frightened to tell Ben that I have MRKH". Elizabeth still thought that Melanie was very brave and pointed out that he might tell other people about her condition if things did not work out between them, remembering making Tom promise not to tell and to keep her secret before she told him. Melanie said, "I'm aware of this and that's why I haven't told him anything yet but I just have a good feeling about him," and added, "anyway, we're not doing anything intimate yet so we'll wait and see how things go. Wish me luck El".

"Sure lots and lots of luck. You deserve it Mel," Elizabeth wished her, but she also told Melanie to let her know when she did. Elizabeth seemed to be more nervous than Melanie was on this, but perhaps Elizabeth had become very protective over her friend and she could not bear to see her getting hurt, especially after all that she had been through, even though they were both stronger girls and they were at better places now.

Melanie was in the final year of her acting course. She went for a couple of auditions and already she managed to get an appearance for a television commercial. The other was a small talking role on a two-part television drama. She continued to work part-time in the shop too because she needed the money and it allowed her to chase her dream until she found it. She was a real believer and she was waiting for her one big break in her career so she was prepared to wait for that day to arrive. Right now, Melanie was in a very good place. Things were improving at home too. Her mother was promoted to a supervisor at the supermarket and was also working permanently and since she was earning regularly herself, she did not need Melanie's contributions anymore. She was always conscious that her daughter was very generous so she wanted Melanie to have some money to spend on herself after paying off her own college fees. She had always wished that she did not need Melanie's monthly contribution but with three other children at school ages and other bills, her contribution was much appreciated then and, Melanie also did not mind as she was only pleased that she could help her mother, whom she felt had done nothing but provide for her and her siblings. So now, it was good to have this extra bit of money because it meant that she could have a social life and to engage an agent for her acting roles. This was how she got her parts for the commercial and the drama, which she felt was a good starting point. She also made a couple of good friends, one from her workplace, and the other was Ben, an electrical engineering student from her college and whom she was seeing. She went out with them whenever she could because she was always busy balancing her college, work and acting roles. She really did not have much time to herself but it was better this way because now she did not feel too much of a loner anymore.

Melanie was finally getting on with her life normally. She was very glad that she persevered and completed her treatment, as Elizabeth and Lucy had encouraged her to because she did not realise how much this was actually weighing her down. She was not constantly reminded of her MRKH and somehow having created her vagina, like Elizabeth, she also did not feel so abnormal anymore. In fact, since finishing her treatment, she also managed to work out her complex issues with Anne and soon after, she forgot about her MRKH. She just moved on with her life. Life had improved, life was good and Melanie was not just drifting alone anymore. She felt that she was at last getting somewhere. She was happy and most of all, she was at peace with herself.

It had been an amazing two years for Elizabeth too since she was diagnosed with MRKH, at just sixteen. She went through a life changing journey where she was forced to grow up very quickly. It was a painful and emotional journey and naturally she was very frightened, confused and was unprepared to deal with it, being just an innocent sixteen-year-old adolescent. Nevertheless, it was an important journey she had to take before she could live her life normally again, and she could not have done it without the help and support from the experts, her family and close friends. It was a roller coaster ride for the most part as she went through the different phases, first trying to understand and to make sense of her condition and learning to cope with the changes affecting her. It totally shook her confidence and she lost her self-worth and it was a long fight before she could accept it all. This was the most terrifying and painful... accepting that she was not the same person she thought she was but someone very different from the norm, someone with an uncommon and unusual condition. It took everything out of her but once she reconciled with it, she was able to come to terms with herself and she could see her future. Elizabeth had finally come to the end of her journey. It was a long arduous journey to recovery and it was also an experience she would never forget but one best not to dwell on so she decided she would live in the present and look to the future.

It was not all bad though because through some of her unusually unpleasant and painful experiences, she managed to overcome both her emotional and physical challenges, which made her a stronger, more compassionate and discerning person. She also achieved a remarkable outcome having successfully completed her necessary treatment and not only that but she met some really nice people along the way, made a new good friend and most of all, she met the best boyfriend she could ever have in Tom, the love of her life. They remained together and their relationship grew stronger than ever. Life was also good for Elizabeth because she had finally found her inner peace and now she was at peace once more.

Ten Years Later

"You look so beautiful darling," Jan said to Elizabeth, as she gently adjusted the wedding veil over Elizabeth's face. She was the happiest mother in the world today and she thought Elizabeth was the most beautiful bride and she could not be more proud. She was also looking forward to welcoming Tom into the family and having him as her son-in-law. He stuck by Elizabeth all these years and even ten years on, he was still very much in love with her. Jan could not believe that the last twenty-six years had flown by so quickly and that her little girl was getting married this day. It was every parent's wish come true to see their children grow up and getting married. Elizabeth looked so radiantly happy too and Jan could not be happier for her, because all she ever wanted was for Elizabeth to be happy and be safe. She also felt that no one deserved it more and thought that after today her little girl would be leaving home and starting a family of her own. Just then, she was suddenly saddened as she remembered that Elizabeth would not be able to have her own family, not that easily and not naturally anyway. She gently wiped her tears off with a soft tissue as she felt them just beginning to well up in her eyes so that Elizabeth would not notice and she was also mindful not to smear her mascara in case it ruined her makeup too.

When it was time, Paul came to the room to collect Elizabeth. He also told her how beautiful she looked and he could not be prouder to be walking her down the aisle. Tom was waiting for them at the altar and he too looked so handsome in his tuxedo. Paul could not be happier to be giving his daughter away to Tom, for whom he had the highest regard, and he felt that Elizabeth could not have done better. It was the happiest and proudest day for him too. All that planning and organising, and finally the day arrived. His beautiful daughter's wedding — it was all worthwhile, he felt.

Elizabeth had been working right up until a few days prior to her wedding. In fact, it had not been an easy time for her even when she was in medical school. She found it especially difficult to try to balance medical school and seeing Tom as often as she could. As her course progressed, she sometimes did not see him for weeks and they would miss each other so terribly that it was unbearable. It was worse after Tom graduated because he moved back home. He started working for his father, who was grooming him so that he would take over the company when the time came, as his father did when his own father retired. Tom knew that this was always the plan and was happy to follow in his father's and grandfather's footsteps. He was an intelligent guy and a quick learner so he made junior partner of their company after a year of being there.

Elizabeth graduated as a doctor and applied to do her internship in a children's hospital in London and later successfully secured her registrar post there too. She managed to go home a few times when she was off and sometimes Tom would go up to London to spend the weekend with her, when he was not away or entertaining business associates. They planned to get married when she made registrar and that day finally arrived. Elizabeth had been working very hard and doing calls since she qualified and on one of the weekends that she was off, Tom arranged a luxury weekend away for them to Paris, staying at one of its finest hotels in the heart of the city. Tom had remembered Elizabeth telling him how much she wanted to go back to Paris with just the two of them. It was going to be a special weekend too because he wanted to make her wish come true but he also had something very special planned. They had a wonderful time in Paris. The hotel was an experience in itself because it was exquisitely decorated and luxurious and it could not be more grand or opulent. It was magnificent! They also dined at the hotel every night at its 3-star Michelin restaurant, which Elizabeth appreciated as fine dining at its best. On their last night stay, after they had finished yet another exceptional and romantic dinner, Tom suggested that they retired to their room early because he wanted to ask Elizabeth something in the privacy of their room so as not to embarrass her. When they entered their room, there was a bottle of champagne already sitting in an ice bucket on the table. He walked over to the table and poured them each a glass of the champagne whilst Elizabeth went to sit down on the chair by it. He handed her a glass and they toasted each other. Then he went down on one knee, reached inside the inner pocket of his jacket and held out a diamond solitaire ring and asked "El, will you marry me?" Elizabeth suspected that Tom had something up his sleeve that night, because the last few nights they had stayed behind to have drinks and listened to the live music at the restaurant bar after their dinner, but still she did not expect this. She had learnt to not take anything for granted so she dared not expect too much. Naturally, she was ecstatic and replied, "Yes Tom, of course I will marry you". As he slipped the ring on her finger, he told her, "You've made me the happiest man in the world. I love you so much El, and I know I said I'd wait for you forever but now I can't wait for us to be together always," and then he kissed her tenderly. Elizabeth also felt that it was time that they tied the knot and made it official. She too quite liked the idea of being his wife. She felt that Tom had been so patient with her because they had been together for such a long time now, ten years to be exact. She could never forget when and how they first got together as a couple but as she tried to recall that emotionally unsettled time of her life, it did not hurt anymore. The only thing she could remember vividly was that Tom stood by her and has continued to profess his love for her till today. The rest of it was only but a distant memory. This however was real. She was a real woman and she was getting married to Tom.

A few months before the wedding, Jan and Sally made a few trips up to London to help Elizabeth choose her wedding dress. Elizabeth had already seen a dress that she liked but she wanted their opinions and they would also help her choose the bridesmaids' dresses. Of course, Elizabeth asked Sally to be her maid of honour, and she had Emma, Melanie, Sasha and Joanne as her bridesmaids. As she did not have any young cousins or relatives of children age and neither did Tom, they decided that they would not have the usual flower girls and page boys. John was Tom's best man and together they were the wedding posse members. Elizabeth chose a white bridal gown with a sweetheart bodice in shimmering embroiled beaded tulle and a beaded sheer lace neckline with three quarter length sleeves, and the bodice continued seamlessly into a fitted and flared gown with an attached Chapel train. The back of the dress was a high sheer lace back with matching beaded embroidery in the middle, which also camouflaged the buttons and zipper. She also chose a crystal tiara and a short veil because these complimented her face and hair as she planned to wear her hair down for this special occasion. She bought a pair of open-toed bridal stiletto shoes in a white satin glittery material to match her dress and when she was all dressed up for her final fitting, she looked so beautiful that not only her mother and Sally said so but her seamstress also told her that she looked sensational.

Just then, Jan thought that Tom was such a lucky man but then she thought again, so was her daughter a lucky woman. Suddenly, the memories came flooding back as Jan started to remember the circumstances that brought both Elizabeth and Tom together in the first place. Now, ten years on, this was the first time that she had actually thought about it or had any cause to think about it. It all seemed like such a long time ago for her now because everyone had moved on with their lives. So much had happened since too that neither she nor Elizabeth nor anyone of her family and friends really thought or talked about the past anymore, and for the first time, Jan had a strange admission. She never thought that she would ever be thankful to Elizabeth's condition but she had to admit that if not for her MRKH, her daughter might not be marrying Tom today, and she too would miss out on having Tom as her son-in-law. It was strange how things turned out in the end, she thought gratefully because she could not have imagined it ever being possible at that time but now all that pain and angst had gone with time. Now, all she could see around her was happiness. Everyone was happy and smiling and most of all, her Elizabeth was the happiest she had ever seen her.

A Summer Wedding

"Do you Thomas Alexander McGuire take Elizabeth Marie Appleton to be your lawful wife, to have and to hold, from this day forward, for better or for worse, for richer or for poorer, in sickness and in health, to love and cherish until death do you part?" Father Benedict asked Tom. Tom replied "I do". Then Father Benedict asked Elizabeth the same and after she replied, "I do," he instructed both Tom and Elizabeth to repeat after him, "I take this ring as a sign of my love and faithfulness, in the name of the father, the son and the Holy Spirit. With this ring I thee wed and pledge thee my troth". The priest continued reading them the rites of marriage and then he joined their right hands together to declare their consent before God and the church. Tom and Elizabeth also read their self-written vows to each other. Tom's was obvious because he said that he always knew she was the only one for him from the moment he met her. He fell in love with her then and he had never stopped loving her so it made him the happiest man to be with Elizabeth forever. Elizabeth then read her vow to him. "Tom, you have seen me at my darkest and lowest point yet you have stuck by me and chosen to share your life with me for always. You showed me the strength of your love and you taught me how to love... I will also love forever..." Father Benedict then blessed their rings and continued with "What God has joined together, let no man put asunder". He gave them his blessings and said "I now pronounce you man and wife" then looking over to Tom, he said "you may now kiss your bride".

The wedding ceremony took just over an hour and afterwards, Elizabeth and Tom went outside to have their photographs taken. Their photographer had also taken photographs during the service and he wanted to take more outside, as the church was a rather sweet one and its grounds were very idyllic. They were then taken away for more photoshoots and afterwards they joined their guests who had gone ahead to the hotel for the cocktail reception. Sally was a brilliant maid of honour, tending to her best friend's needs and arranging Elizabeth's dress every now and then and making sure that she would not trip over her Chapel train and that her veil was in place and sitting nicely on her head. After the official wedding photography, Elizabeth and Tom had time to mingle with her friends and the other guests whilst the photographer continued taking pictures of them and all the guests for the video he was making for them later. Elizabeth looked so relaxed once the church ceremony was over that she was able to enjoy the rest of her wedding day. Soon it was time for the evening reception and Elizabeth changed out of her bridal dress so she could be more comfortable for the rest of the evening. She wore a silver-sequined gown with a strapless sweetheart neckline and the gown had a high slit at the slim skirt, which showed off her long slim legs, and made her look sexy and elegant. John invited everyone to raise their glasses as they toasted to the bride and groom. Then he gave his speech with different funny anecdotes, which had everyone laughing. Afterwards, Paul also gave his father-of-the-bride speech but his was very moving as it came from the heart. After the speeches and the meal, the dancing and disco commenced and continued till two in the morning. Elizabeth and Tom stayed till one because they were enjoying themselves so much. The following morning after breakfast, their families, close friends and guests who were staying at the hotel waved them goodbye as they were driven away to start their honeymoon in the Seychelles.

The Seychelles was a honeymoon paradise and both Elizabeth and Tom had a wonderful ten days of peace and seclusion by themselves. The hotel where they stayed also had a romantic feel and the islands and the views were picturesque and delightful. They relaxed, sunbathed and swam on the first couple of days that they were there. After that, they hired a yacht to visit the nearby islands. They spent a few days island-hopping to Mahe and also the quieter islands of La Digue and Desroches and thoroughly enjoyed the different beautiful views and experiences that each island offered. Both of them had never snorkeled or scuba-dived before but it was too inviting to resist, especially when the seas were so clear and blue. It was an experience of their lifetime as they got to see sting rays, sharks and many different and colourful reef fishes. Afterwards they felt so energised that they decided to go to Curieuse Island too and there they walked up to see the giant granite cliffs and even had time to see the green turtles and unusual wildlife birds. They had done so much and had such an interesting time on the islands that they decided to just relax when they got back to Praslin. They especially liked the beach in Anse Lazio where they were staying because of its pure white sands and clear warm turquoise seas.

When Elizabeth was lying in bed next to Tom, she thought that this was the best honeymoon she could ever dream of and one that she would never ever forget. In fact, her wedding had gone so smoothly that she also managed to enjoy her special day with all her loved ones and people that mattered to her most. She would always cherish these precious memories. She felt very fortunate right then especially when she felt she had the best husband in the world. She was getting quite used to being Mrs. McGuire, and liked it very much when the staff at the hotel addressed her as that. "I'm so blessed" Elizabeth thought. Just then she remembered her nightmare some ten years ago when she was just sixteen and how she wished for her nightmare to stop, but it was just a vague memory and it seemed like such a long time ago. Now she could only remember that she was married and in the arms of the most loving husband and it felt so good. She suddenly became slightly unsure if this was in fact real or but a dream because if it was a dream, she did not want it to end and she wanted it to be real. She quickly asked Tom to confirm that she was not dreaming so he held her tighter towards him and kissed her. Then he told her "it's not a dream, El. It's all real. We are real ".

Epilogue

I hope that this book will be well received especially by the women who have MRKH and their loved ones. I am very aware that there are many more and well deserving stories to tell and maybe they might also not be too dissimilar to the stories of my two characters with MRKH in this book. I am also happy to say that in my years of working with so many women with this condition, it is the tiny minority who had suicidal tendencies, for which I am very thankful because I wish to remind the women again that there is professional and other help and support available, so that they need not be alone nor take the journey by themselves. Therefore, I wish for them to stay strong, believe in themselves and continue to have the courage to get the appropriate help so that they can be happy and be able to lead normal lives, just like anybody else. There is no longer a need to hide and be alone, no need to be frightened and no need to be ashamed or embarrassed, but instead be proud of the person you are, because you are truly beautiful and the nicest people, I have ever known.

To the women with MRKH wherever you are, if you need help, support or further information, please try any of the following sites below.

www.mrkh.org.uk (Centre for Disorders of Reproductive Development & Adolescent Gynaecology, London, UK)

www.mrkhconnect.org (MRKH Connect, England and Wales)

livingmrkh.org.uk (Living MRKH – England)

youngwomenshealth.org (The Center for Young Women's Health – Boston, USA)

www.beautifulyoumrkh.org (Beautiful You MRKH Foundation)

www.mrkh.org (MRKH.Organization, Inc)

www.sistersforlove.org (Sisters for Love MRKH Foundation – Sydney, Australia)

youngwomenshealth.org > mrkh-parents (Boston, USA)

www.surrogacyuk.org (Surrogacy UK)